KING OF THE ISLES

"Ye shouldna have done it, Evie." His warm breath caressed her face as he touched his lips to her eyes, to her cheek, to the corner of her mouth. He swirled his tongue over the cut and her moan of pleasure joined his. Spearing his fingers through her hair, he drew her head back, exposing her neck to his hot, hungry mouth. He suckled deeply, sending a heated jolt of desire so deep inside her it was as though his lips touched every part of her.

"Ye're so sweet, so beautiful. I canna get enough of ye."

Through the erotic haze that blanketed her senses, a niggling of fear he'd forgotten his promise managed to slip through.

"Nay." He took one last lingering sip before lifting his heavy-lidded gaze to hers. "I would never hurt ye, Evie," he said, then took her mouth in a mind-numbing kiss . . .

Books by Debbie Mazzuca

LORD OF THE ISLES

WARRIOR OF THE ISLES

KING OF THE ISLES

Published by Kensington Publishing Corporation

KING
of the ISLES

DEBBIE MAZZUCA

ZEBRA BOOKS
KENSINGTON PUBLISHING CORP.
http://www.kensingtonbooks.com

ZEBRA BOOKS are published by

Kensington Publishing Corp.
119 West 40th Street
New York, NY 10018

All Kensington titles, imprints, and distributed lines are available at special quantity discounts for bulk purchases for sales
promotion, premiums, fund-raising, educational, or institu-
tional use.

Special book excerpts or customized printings can also be
created to fit specific needs. For details, write or phone the
office of the Kensington Special Sales Manager: Attn. Special
Sales Department. Kensington Publishing Corp., 119 West
40th Street, New York, NY 10018. Phone: 1-800-221-2647.

Zebra and the Z logo Reg. U.S. Pat. & TM Off.

ISBN-13: 978-1-4201-1007-4
ISBN-10: 1-4201-1007-1

First Printing: January 2012
10 9 8 7 6 5 4 3 2 1

Printed in the United States of America

To April, Jess, and Nic,
for being the most wonderful children
a mother could ask for.
I'm so proud of you guys.

Chapter 1

Fae Realm
June 1607

For the greater good.

Hidden within the shadow of ancient oaks, a safe distance from Rohan's palace, Evangeline repeated the familiar mantra, allowing the sentiment to smooth over the ripples of doubt seeking to gain a foothold in her mind.

It was her only option, she reassured herself. Fae law prohibited the magick she was about to attempt, but the law had been put in place to protect the Fae, and that was precisely what she intended on doing. She may not be a seer, but Evangeline knew danger lurked amongst them and no one could tell her otherwise.

The Faes' opinion no longer mattered to her.

If she could break through the barrier between the Fae and Mortal realms, she would have secured a viable escape route should the standing stones be disabled. The granite monoliths were portals between the two worlds. Portals Rohan, high king of the Seelie Council and overseer of the five Fae kingdoms, had closed before. She couldn't risk being trapped on either side. The thought of leaving her friend Syrena unprotected in the Mortal realm was as difficult to consider as leaving the Fae unguarded.

But more importantly, Evangeline would have proof her magick surpassed the most powerful of wizards and would serve her well when the time came to protect the Fae of the Enchanted Isles. And with Lachlan MacLeod, the half-blood highlander, as their king, she knew without a doubt that day would soon be upon them.

Concealed by the dense foliage, reasonably certain she was safe from prying eyes, Evangeline widened her stance. Flexing her fingers, she tipped her head back and inhaled the sweet, earthy fragrance of the forest to center herself. A gentle breeze riffled the leafy canopy above, caressing her face as though it was encouraging her efforts. A soft smile played on her lips and she closed her eyes, raising her arms to call upon the magick within her. A warm white glow blossomed low in her belly and she welcomed it as though it were a much-loved friend.

Snap. On a startled gasp, her eyes flew open. Heart racing, she frantically searched the woods. A bird, its iridescent blue and yellow tipped wings flapping noisily, shot from the branches overhead with an outraged shriek. Evangeline jumped, then shook her head at her nervous display.

No one knows what you attempt, she chided. *The Fae have no interest in you.*

Her bitter laugh punctured the enveloping silence. That was not entirely true. They watched and waited for the day she would show her true colors. For the day the seeds everyone said her mother Andora had sown inside her took root.

She ignored the dull ache in her chest. Their censure didn't matter. Perhaps at one time it had caused her pain, but no longer. She would prove to them all she was nothing like Andora. She would protect them as her mother had once destroyed them. They would have no choice but to acknowledge she was not evil then.

And you, Evangeline, will that be enough to make you believe you are not? a voice inside her asked.

With an impatient flick of her hand, Evangeline shooed the question from her mind and resumed her stance. A rustle of leaves drew her attention and she squinted, scanning the shadows for movement, unable to shake the sensation someone was watching her. She lifted her gaze to the leafy canopy, thinking perhaps it was another bird. When moments passed without the brightly plumed creature making an appearance, she concluded her frazzled nerves were to blame.

Hastily, shoving aside the sense of foreboding, she returned to her previous position. There was no time to waste. Rohan had called an emergency meeting of the Seelie Council, and it was a meeting Evangeline refused to miss. Not with that fool Lachlan MacLeod about to receive his comeuppance. At the thought, she called upon her magick with a self-satisfied smile.

A soft moan of pleasure escaped her parted lips as the white light flooded her with power, exciting her as nothing or no one else could. Her body crackled with heat, blue sparks shooting from the tips of her fingers. With a keening howl the wind gusted through the trees, lifting the carpet of leaves from the forest floor to swirl about her in a frenzied dance. The words of the forbidden spell she murmured joined the wind on a rising hum of power.

Captured in the whirlwind's grip, she spun with dizzying speed. Her pointed toes dug into the damp loam, flinging it in every direction. Beneath her feet the ground cracked open and, on an exultant cry, she disappeared below the surface. Within a sphere of white fire, the bright flame illuminated the cavernous depths. She carved easily through layer after layer of earth and granite until she hit the barrier with a resounding bounce.

Sprawled facedown, her frustrated groan was smothered in a thick, jellylike substance. Gritting her teeth, she peeled herself off the sticky film. She pushed and prodded the dense membrane, but it resisted her efforts. Refusing to admit defeat, she dug deeper inside herself than she ever had before. Her muscles quivered with the demands she put on her powers, the transparent fabric shivering beneath her. Then, with a loud tearing sound, she exploded through the membrane, somersaulting with stomach-wrenching speed through wispy clouds. Disoriented, fighting against panic, it took a moment before her vision cleared. Focusing on the moors far below her, she flashed to the top of a hill in the Mortal realm of the Hebrides, landing with a soft thud.

Wrapping her arms about her waist, she embraced her accomplishment, drowning out the niggling of guilt with a joyful laugh. A low whicker interrupted her celebration and she followed the sound to the base of the verdant mound. Two dark-haired men on horseback stared up at her in open-mouthed astonishment.

"An angel, Padraic, we've found ourselves an angel," the younger of the two said in an awestruck voice.

"Nay," his companion said, not taking his intent gaze from Evangeline. "Angels no' 'ave 'air as black as night."

"And 'ow many angels 'ave ye seen?"

She lingered, interested in the man's response. After all, if angels were making an appearance in the Mortal realm, it was something she needed to know.

But the one named Padraic ignored his friend's querulous question. His dark eyes locked on her chest, a salacious grin creased his rawboned face. "And 'tis sure I am they no' 'ave the curves—"

"Mortals . . . men," she muttered, rolling her eyes. They were all the same. Her mind turned to a certain mortal— half-mortal—and the talk of Lachlan MacLeod's lusty appetites. She harrumphed; if King Rohan had his way, that was all about to change.

Unwilling to miss the arrogant highlander being taken to

task before the council, she raised her hand, flicking a finger at Padraic. The words he was about to utter came to a gurgling halt in his throat. Eyes bulging, he clutched his neck with both hands, shooting a panicked look at his companion.

Since the spell would not last long, Evangeline wiped both men of their memories before she shot back through the clouds to hover beneath the tear she'd made in the barrier.

Lying prone beneath the length of membrane that flapped in the gentle breeze, she was aware of the importance attached to mending it carefully—to leave no weakness as a port of entry. With a low murmur, she called on her magick, frowning at the lukewarm heat and dull wash of white that responded to her call. Spidery threads of panic latched on to her guilt. Did breaking Fae law somehow cause her powers to diminish? As if in answer, a wisp of black smoke snaked its way through the light, wrapping its inky tendrils around her mind, dragging her deep inside herself to a dark and tortured void. With chilling certainty she recognized it for what it was—the evil within her.

What had she done? Fighting against her horrified alarm, she clawed at the shadows.

Why do you protect them when they condemn you? A voice slithered through her senses, stopping her cold. *Show them your power, treat them as they treat you,* the voice cajoled seductively. *Destroy them as they would destroy you.*

"No," Evangeline cried, digging feverishly through the muddy light for her magick. Her vision hazed. *Breathe, just breathe.* She found a finger of light and latched on to it, tugging until a glowing ball exploded inside her, eviscerating the darkness. She gasped for air, trying to banish the words from her head. But the fear she'd inadvertently unleashed the evil her father Morfessa said dwelled within her overwhelmed her. She couldn't rid herself of the thought that by using forbidden magick she'd finally become the monster he said her to be.

No! She refused to listen to his spiteful opinion of her. He'd hated her from the moment she'd drawn her first breath. Shielded by the knowledge, she searched her mind for a logical explanation.

It was an anomaly, she finally decided, clinging desperately to the explanation. Her body and her magick had simply been traumatized from coming through the barrier. The mind-numbing fear that held her in its grasp eased somewhat, but any pleasure she'd felt at her accomplishment evaporated. Knowing she could not remain suspended in midair for much longer, she raised a trembling finger to the membrane. Sparks sizzled, smoke filling the air as she repaired the fissure. She prodded the area where the tear had been to be certain the seal was as strong as it appeared.

After one last poke, her ability to remain hanging above the clouds vanished. She dropped like a stone. Her stomach lurching as she fell from the sky, she tried to shake off the panic the violent free fall induced. As a child, the idea she could fly like the angels had intrigued her. She hadn't known the ability was beyond her and had foolishly jumped from the top of a mountain. Unable to control her magick, she'd slammed into the rocks at the base of the cliff. Her broken body had repaired, but it had taken months for the bones to painfully knit together and she'd never gotten over the experience.

Forcing herself to take slow deep breaths, she focused on the circle of standing stones far below in the Mortal realm and transported there. Dwarfed by the granite slabs, she took one last uneasy look up at the barrier to assure herself the membrane was secure, then stepped through the stones to enter the Fae realm.

Flashing to Rohan's palace, she reminded herself that no one knew what she'd done, least of all witnessed the consequences of her actions. She pushed open the gilded doors. Before she crossed the marble entryway, she took a moment to compose her features into a mask of icy disdain. A mask that was as much a part of her as her magick. A mask that dared the Fae to trifle with her . . . Evangeline, the most powerful wizard in the Fae realm.

Crouched behind a tree, Morfessa spat out his silent contempt on the forest floor. *What is the she-devil's spawn up to?* He shifted his weight, leaning forward to see around the thick trunk. A branch snapped beneath his foot and she jerked her gaze in his direction. He eased back, assuring himself it was not for fear of what she would do upon discovering him there, but fear he would miss the opportunity to learn what she tried to hide.

A bird flew from the branch above him and he saw the moment she let down her guard, a look of relief upon her face. A face as hauntingly beautiful as her mother's—the woman who'd ruined him. Even now, twenty-six years later, the thought of Andora's betrayal caused his stomach to churn. As if using him to destroy the Fae of the Enchanted Isles had not been enough, the traitorous bitch had borne him a child. Evangeline, a constant reminder of his failure, his weakness. If not for Rohan—the softhearted high king of the Seelie Council, the man he served—staying his hand, Morfessa would've been rid of the she-devil's spawn long ago.

Soon, he promised himself, *soon*.

But he had to proceed with caution. If he took her life without evidence of her evil, Rohan would strip him of his position as Imperial Wizard to the Seelie Council. Morfessa would never let that happen—his position was all he had left, all that mattered to him.

He ignored the niggling of doubt that he would be able to kill her. *She is not that powerful. Not yet*, he amended. From the time she'd been a small child, she'd exhibited an aptitude for magick well beyond anything he'd ever witnessed. He'd warned his king, made his concerns known, but Rohan paid him no mind. It was Andora's fault. She'd diminished him in his king's eyes.

His knees ached from holding the cramped position. He shifted, rustling the leaves beneath his feet. She stiffened, and he cursed inwardly. He should have sent someone in his stead. Someone like his apprentice, whose agile body would not feel the strain as Morfessa's did, but he couldn't deny himself the satisfaction of being the one to condemn her.

She murmured an ancient chant, the words rising and falling on the wind. He strained to hear what spell she wove. He picked out first one word, and then another.

No, she wouldn't!

She couldn't!

Reeling from the shock of what she attempted, Morfessa staggered from his hiding place. She spun in a swirl of light and leaves, then the ground cracked open and she disappeared.

The magnitude of the power she now wielded brought him to his knees on the damp upturned earth where she'd stood. His heartbeat hammered in his head, drowning out the roaring hum of her power. The knowledge that her magick now surpassed his own was like a cesspool spewing its poison inside him. But the thought he now had proof of her evil spurred him to action. If he hurried, he'd catch her coming through the barrier.

Staggering to his feet, he transported to the stones. With the knowledge he would soon have her at his mercy, the haze of his fury dissipated, allowing him to think clearly. It was then he realized Rohan would never believe him. She'd wormed her way into his king's confidence, usurping Morfessa's rightful place at Rohan's side. One more reason she deserved to die. He slammed his palm against the granite slab. He had no choice. He had to return for a witness.

The first person who came to mind was his assistant, and he flashed to the library of spells deep in the bowels of the three-story whitewashed building beside the palace. He cursed the wards that prevented him from transporting in and out of the library and flung open the thick oak door. The wards had been placed on all buildings in the Fae realm to prevent a surprise attack from their enemies. But today, they simply served to stymie his attempt to capture the one woman he'd always known would become their greatest threat.

He hurried across the wood-planked antechamber, uttering an impatient oath when he came to the door leading down to the library and found it sealed. It was his own fault. He'd activated the binding spell earlier in the day. He hadn't trusted his assistant Tobias not to try to escape from his duties.

Minutes later, he opened the last of the seals. "Tobias," he yelled as he pounded down the spiral staircase, leaning over the oak rail to seek out the boy. Frustrated when his assistant failed to make an appearance, he slammed down the rest of the steps, bellowing as he went, "Tobias!"

"Yes . . . yes, I'm here, Your Imperialness." His assistant scurried from between the floor-to-ceiling bookcases lining the back wall. Noting his heavy-lidded gaze, the imprint of a hand on his gaunt cheek, Morfessa was certain his assistant had been sleeping. But now was not the time to berate him. Striding toward him, he grabbed Tobias by the front of his navy robes and hauled him up the stairs after him.

"I confess! I confess! I was sleeping," the boy shrieked.

"Quiet!" he shouted, in no mood to listen to his assistant's inane jabbering.

As soon as they stepped from the stones into the Mortal realm, Morfessa lifted his gaze to the clear blue skies for some sign of her. He prayed he was not too late. His vision impaired from years of using the caustic potions in his experiments, he launched from the stone circle, dragging Tobias along with him to fly toward the barrier.

In a frenzied panic the boy wrapped his gangly arms and

legs around him. "Master, we're not angels, we cannot fly. Set us down!"

"Calm yourself!" Morfessa tried to shake free of Tobias's strangling hold while searching the skies beneath the barrier. If he didn't need his assistant as a witness, he would shoot him with a bolt of his magick. When he could find no sign of her, his anger knew no bounds and he did exactly that.

Tobias, a flurry of arms and legs, rocketed toward the ground. Morfessa scowled when the boy's terrified screams ended. His broken body splayed at the base of the stones. The fool didn't even have the sense to use his magick. With a disgusted sigh, Morfessa once more scanned the skies beneath the barrier, then flashed to the stones. He took hold of the boy's arms and dragged him through the portals, leaving him on the ground in the Fae realm. Someone would find him. And when his assistant recovered, Morfessa would dismiss him. The incompetent fool had delayed him.

Consumed with rage at his inability to find evidence of her perfidy, he stalked toward his apartments in the building that housed the library of spells. He stopped short. What was he thinking? He could not let her actions go unpunished. Proof or no proof, he must confront her. There were ways to make her confess.

The two liveried guardsmen who stood in stony silence at either side of the massive gilded doors didn't bother to acknowledge Evangeline as she entered the Seelie Court.

At one time the council had met in the forest, but Rohan had moved the council to his palace for reasons of safety. Creatures of habit, the Fae demanded the ambience of the woods, and Rohan had ceded to their wishes. Evangeline had to admit the branches of white ash trees encircling the room while water spurted from iridescent blue fountains that fed the waterways lining the outer edges of the chambers had a calming effect. King Rohan, seated on his ornately carved wooden throne at the head of the table, stopped midsentence, arching a brow in her direction.

She dipped her head in acknowledgment of her tardiness. Gliding to his side in a rustle of silk, she averted her gaze from the curious glances of the four men seated with Rohan—the three kings and the wizard Uscias. She tamped down her disappointment that the full council was not in attendance to bear witness to the highlander's set-down.

"You're late, my dear. Is something amiss?" Rohan glanced over his shoulder to where she'd taken her place to stand behind him.

Heat suffused her cheeks and she damned the telltale flush. "No. I simply forgot the time, Your Highness." Pleased that unlike her face her speech did not reveal her discomfiture.

Her gaze collided with Lachlan MacLeod's, who sat sprawled in the chair to Rohan's right. She attempted a nonchalant smile, but couldn't quite pull it off under the intensity of his golden gaze. Her upper lip curled, and a lazy grin quirked his full sensual mouth. Her hands balled at her sides. How she longed to wipe that supercilious smile from his too-handsome face. When she remembered the reason the council was meeting, a genuine smile curved her lips. The inept king was about to receive his comeuppance. If she had anything to say in the matter, he would have no choice but to acquiesce to his uncle's demands.

Lachlan blinked, then narrowed his gaze on her. She suppressed the urge to stick her tongue out at him as she'd seen his cousin Rory's sons, Jamie and Alex, do.

"She's here now, Rohan, so can we get on with it?" King Broderick of the Welsh Fae demanded testily. Reminding her why she'd never been overly fond of the taciturn king.

"Certainly. I've received a missive from King Magnus," Rohan began with a pointed look in his nephew's direction.

A nephew who paid no attention to him.

Her nails dug into her palms. The fool was too busy contemplating the mead in his gold-encrusted cup to be aware of his uncle's censure. Uscias, wizard to the Enchanted Isles and Lachlan's mentor, jabbed an elbow in his king's side.

Lachlan grunted, skewering the wizard with a disgruntled glare. "Bloody hell, what was that fer?" he demanded in his deep, rumbling voice.

Uscias jerked his silver-bearded chin to Rohan. "Your uncle requires your attention."

The highlander raked his hand through his thick tawny head of hair and raised his gaze. "I was distracted. What were ye sayin'?"

"What else is new," she muttered under her breath. Obviously not as quietly as she'd thought since Gabriel, king of England's Fae, snorted a laugh and Lachlan shot her a censorious look.

"King Magnus thought I would be interested to know that you refused the offer of his sister's hand in marriage," Rohan said, drawing Lachlan's narrow-eyed attention from Evangeline.

"Why should he think ye'd be interested? The matter is no concern of yers, Uncle."

Her temper simmered. *The man truly is a fool.* Did he not realize how precarious their relationship with the Fae of the Far North was and what his outright refusal could mean to his subjects? Magnus was powerful and until recently had aligned himself with Dimtri, king of the European Fae. Dimtri no longer answered to the Seelie Council. He looked for a way to overthrow Rohan. Keeping Magnus content would ensure his loyalty to the council and go a long way toward protecting the Isle Fae.

About ready to tear her hair from her scalp at Lachlan's inability to see the danger he put his people in, she snapped, "If you didn't spend all your time womanizing, your pea-sized brain would comprehend the peril you put your loyal subjects in."

If not for the tightening of his beard-shadowed jaw, the slight twitch of a muscle there, she wouldn't have thought her remark had penetrated his thick skull. His lack of emotion grated on her nerves. If he couldn't bring himself to care about the Fae, they would never be safe.

Out of habit, she glanced at the Sword of Nuada—the magickal weapon awarded the king of the Enchanted Isles— resting against a thickly muscled thigh encased in form-fitting trews. The golden sword magnified its bearer's emotions. Not once in the two years since the highlander had been presented the weapon did it indicate the man was anything more than an empty shell. Knowing what he'd suffered in the past, a part of Evangeline understood why he'd shut down his emotions, but it only served to validate her belief that he was unfit to protect the Fae.

A faint glow of red radiated from the blade. Her eyes widened, a glimmer of hope stirring to life inside her. But that hope faded as quickly as the emotion faded from the blade when she jerked her gaze to Lachlan's ruggedly handsome face. With an arrogant smirk, he said, "Pea-sized, is it?"

Evangeline curled her fingers around the back of the throne before she gave in to the temptation to render him mute.

Rohan reached over his shoulder and patted her hand in an attempt to calm her. "I'm sure Evangeline meant no disrespect by the remark, Lachlan, but she does have a point. Your outright refusal could spark a confrontation with Magnus, encouraging him to take up with Dimtri again. Now, Evangeline and I have spent some time going over the matter." Rohan glanced back at her. "Perhaps you should give my nephew your opinion of his options."

Evangeline smiled. Nothing would give her more pleasure. She wouldn't need her magick to render him mute.

Chapter 2

Oh, aye, Lachlan was certain the bloody woman had an opinion on what he should do. When had she not? Evangeline was a pain in his royal arse. But, he thought, as he met her flashing violet eyes and temper flushed her cheeks a becoming pink, she was easy on the eyes. And if he was honest, the pointed barbs the sultry beauty aimed in his direction were a welcome change from the bowing and scraping to which he'd grown accustomed.

He leaned back in his chair, crossing his arms over his chest. Mayhap he'd tweak her temper a bit further. "Aye, Uncle, I'm quite accustomed to her makin' her opinion known where I'm concerned. Why ye'd think I'd be interested in hearin' it is what I'm wonderin'."

It was no secret his uncle set great store in what the lass had to say. Lachlan supposed it was because of her much-vaunted powers. He'd heard she was not to be trifled with. Even Uscias, as powerful a wizard as he was, seemed in awe of her abilities. But it didn't mean Lachlan was. He was a king, after all—king of the Fae.

He snorted at the idea. He'd held the title for over two years now and to this day found it difficult to believe he'd accepted the role. He'd grown up despising the Fae—the man who he'd thought was his father had seen to that—and hiding his Fae heritage. But Lachlan's secret had been discovered by a cadre of devil-worshipping aristocrats. They'd held him hostage, tortured him, draining him of his blood in hopes of using his magick to release the dark lords of the underworld.

Magick, he thought contemptuously. The only magick he possessed came from his sword. Reflexively, his hand closed over the jewel-encrusted hilt.

His uncle cleared his throat. "Evangeline, perhaps you should tell my nephew what it is you've learned."

"Lord Bana and his brother Erwn seek to overthrow you," she said in that melodious voice of hers. It was bloody annoying that her voice seemed to mesmerize him even when what came out of her mouth was meant to torment or belittle him.

Lachlan glanced at Uscias, who merely shrugged his narrow shoulders. "Nay, ye're mistaken, they . . ." He stopped, thinking better of telling her his late father's trusted advisors were his constant companions. They consumed round after round of ale together while playing cards and enjoying the bountiful charms of the willing women who abounded in his palace. She already thought him a lecherous lout who did nothing but see to his own pleasure. He wasn't about to add another arrow to her quiver.

In her typical supercilious manner, she raised a perfectly arched black brow.

"Ye're mistaken," he repeated. "Besides, how would ye ken? Ye doona come to the Enchanted Isles." He praised the Lord for small mercies. It was bad enough he had to put up with her during council meetings and at Lewes for family gatherings. No matter how often he asked her not to, Syrena, his sister-by-marriage, never failed to include Evangeline in the festivities. It was his misfortune the two women were best friends.

"I've heard rumors," she said by way of explanation, avoiding his gaze when she did so. He knew then that she lied. But before he could question her, she said, "Has Syrena not told you of the difficulties she had with them?"

His brother's wife, who at one time Lachlan had thought to be his half sister but later turned out to be his cousin, had once ruled the Enchanted Isles. "Nay, but even if she did, I doona understand what Bana and Erwn have to do with me marryin' Magnus's sister."

She sighed in a manner that suggested she thought she dealt with a slow-witted child. "They question your ability to rule without magick. You need someone with magickal abilities to stand by your side. Magnus's sister would be a good choice. Another benefit to the union is that the king of the Far North would no longer feel compelled to join Dimtri in his bid to gain access to the Seelie Hallows."

Dimtri and Magnus were jealous of the powerful Hallows the Isle Fae held—Lachlan's sword, the stone, the cauldron, and spear—asserting they had as much right to them as the Isle Fae did. Dimtri even went so far as to claim they'd been stolen from the European Fae.

"I have my sword. 'Tis all the magick I require. And I'll no' let Magnus force my hand. *If* I decide to wed, 'twill be me who chooses my bride."

Lachlan was certain he could hear Evangeline grinding her teeth before she opened her mouth to give him another of her opinions. "It's not enough. You are responsible for the safety of your subjects. You leave yourself as well as them vulnerable without magick."

Gabriel tipped his goblet in Lachlan's direction. "I've fought with him a time or two, Evangeline, and I can assure you your worries are for naught."

Lachlan smiled his thanks. He hadn't spent much time in Gabriel's company, but he was an affable sort despite his startling good looks. Gabriel had been there the night Syrena and his brother Aidan had rescued Lachlan from Glastonbury. The pity he'd glimpsed in the other man's eyes had made Lachlan uncomfortable, but over the last year they'd developed a friendship of sorts.

"I agree. As always, you overstate the danger, Evangeline," Broderick said. The dark-haired king was more reserved than Gabriel, but Lachlan had grown accustomed to his brusque manner and had come to respect his opinion. *Now more than ever*, he thought, grinning at Evangeline's baleful expression.

"I have to disagree, Broderick. I think her concerns hold merit. Lachlan, I have asked Evangeline to put together a list of prospective brides for your perusal."

"She'll be wastin' her time. I—"

Rohan held up a hand to stem his heated protest. "You are half-Fae, nephew. The best way to dissuade those who seek to overthrow you is to take a full-blooded Fae to wife. As for Magnus, I shall send a missive advising him you've had a change of heart and his sister Jorunn is among the women you are considering. That will give us time to find another way to retain his loyalty should you not choose his sister."

"Ye canna force me, Rohan," he gritted out between clenched teeth. He didn't wish to marry, and he'd be damned if he'd let any one tell him to do so. The last thing he needed was a woman demanding his attention, his affection.

"As High King, I most certainly can."

A smile played upon Evangeline's lips, her fine-boned features glowing with pleasure. Lachlan was tempted to strangle the meddlesome wench. Her gaze shifted to his sword and her smile widened. He glanced down at the blade glowing red and frowned. What the bloody hell was so interesting about his sword? Whenever he journeyed to the Mortal realm, Syrena did the same thing, then he'd catch a look of sorrow in her eyes before she turned away.

Daft, that's what the two of them are.

"Rohan, is it a requirement that the prospective bride be of royal blood?" Uscias asked. A thoughtful expression on his weathered face, he stroked his knee-length silver beard and looked from Lachlan to Evangeline.

Lachlan's blood ran cold. Marrying was bad enough. Marrying Evangeline was out of the question. The woman would never give him a moment's peace. If he ever wed, it would be a marriage of convenience. And there'd be nothing convenient about marrying Evangeline.

Before Lachlan could disabuse his mentor of the notion, the wizard Morfessa burst into the chambers. Black robes swirling about him, he stalked to the table pointing an accusatory finger at his daughter. "Guards, arrest her. Now!" he yelled when the two men who followed behind him hesitated, their uncertain gazes seeking out Rohan.

Lachlan watched in amazement as the indomitable Evangeline cowered in the face of her father's fury. Color drained from her pinched features and what appeared to be fear darkened her violet eyes. He'd heard rumors that her father despised her, but until now had doubted their veracity.

"Morfessa, what is the meaning of this?" Rohan demanded, waving the guards back to their position along the wall.

"Do not protect her, my liege! Ask what she was doing in the woods this day. Ask her!"

Rohan shifted in his throne. "Evangeline?"

"I practiced my magick, Your Highness. That is all."

Lachlan noted the white-knuckled grip her slender fingers had on the back of Rohan's throne, the slight quiver of her full bottom lip belying her pretense of calm.

"Liar! You're a lying evil bitch like your mother." Morfessa had worked himself into a frenzy, his body vibrating with rage.

A haunted look shadowed Evangeline's eyes. She seemed fragile, vulnerable, so different from the woman Lachlan had come to know. The muscles low in his belly twisted. The urge to take her in his arms and comfort her overwhelmed him. He knew all too well what it was like to have a father who hated you. Alexander MacLeod, the man Lachlan had grown up believing was his father, had hated him. Despised him for his Fae blood, despised him enough to try to kill him. If not for his brother Aidan, Lachlan would've died that rainy night on the cliffs. But instead, it was Alexander who plunged to his death. Lachlan shoved the memory away along with the emotions that went with it.

Morfessa snarled, his hands bunching into fists. Intent on protecting Evangeline, Lachlan leapt from his chair. The wizard hurled himself at her at the same time, colliding with Lachlan before he had a chance to prepare for the blow. The force of Morfessa's momentum threw Lachlan off balance. While he regained his footing, Morfessa lunged past him, grabbing a fistful of Evangeline's robes. He dragged her from behind Rohan's throne before Lachlan's uncle could stop him.

Inserting himself between the two powerful wizards—Lachlan knew a moment's gratitude that the hall was warded against magick—he wrenched Morfessa's hand from Evangeline's neck and shoved him away from her.

"Enough, Morfessa!" Rohan bellowed, stepping around his throne. But the man was beyond hearing. He charged Lachlan with his head lowered. The blow to his gut sent Lachlan into the soft body behind him. He heard Evangeline's startled gasp, the thud of her hitting the floor. Before he could turn to assist her, the wizard came at him again. Lachlan rammed his fist in the man's belly, leaving Morfessa gasping for air. Out of the corner of his eye, he noted Gabriel and Broderick calmly quaffing their ale. They'd know he didn't need their help nor did he want it. The pleasure of shutting up the lunatic was his.

Morfessa once more launched himself at Lachlan with an enraged cry. A contemptuous smile curved Lachlan's lips before he drew back his arm and smashed his fist into the wizard's jaw. Eyes rolling back in his head, Morfessa would've crashed to the floor if not for Gabriel, who leapt from his chair to catch him.

Lachlan rubbed his reddened knuckles and turned to Evangeline, who Rohan helped rise from the floor. "Are ye all right?"

She nodded, adjusting her silken robes before raising her gaze to his. "Yes. Thank you."

From where Gabriel had laid him out on the marble floor, Morfessa moaned. Lachlan glanced over his shoulder to see the wizard struggling to sit up. Rubbing his jaw, Morfessa pinned his daughter with a malevolent glare. "I saw you. I know what you did. I heard the spell you uttered."

Upon hearing Evangeline's strangled gasp, Lachlan swung his gaze back to her.

He placed his hands on her shoulders. "Sit." Overriding her murmured protest, he gently forced her into his chair. Uscias motioned for one of the servants who attended them to bring her a cup of mead, patting the hand she gripped the edge of the table with.

"Take a seat, Morfessa," Rohan ordered, jerking his chin at the guards who hovered nearby. The two men took hold of the wizard, depositing him in a chair at the far end of the table. "Now, you will tell me what possessed you to attack your . . . Evangeline."

Morfessa snarled. "She broke through the barrier between the realms."

Shocked gasps from the guards and servants greeted the wizard's indictment. Evangeline's shoulders stiffened beneath Lachlan's hands. He absently smoothed his thumbs over the taut muscles. When she looked up at him, he gave her a reassuring squeeze. He hadn't realized his hands remained there until that moment, but refused to read any significance into the gesture. He simply offered his support. She was Syrena's friend. His sister-by-marriage would expect him to protect her.

Out of the corner of his eye he caught Uscias studying

them, rubbing his beard between his thumb and forefinger. Lachlan muttered an oath and let his hands drop to his sides.

"Come now, there is not a wizard alive with magick powerful enough to perform such a feat and you expect me to believe Evangeline was able to do so?" Rohan said.

From where Lachlan positioned himself, he could see the circles of pink form on the high slant of her cheekbones, her perfect white teeth worrying her plump bottom lip.

Bloody hell. She did do it.

He caught his mentor's eye. Uscias gave an almost imperceptible lift of his shoulder. So, he'd seen her reaction as well. Lachlan decided to leave it up to his mentor as to whether they exposed her or not. The thought he could one day use the knowledge to his benefit didn't escape him. He only hoped his silence would not come back to bite him in the arse.

"Evangeline, the charge your fath . . . Morfessa levels against you is a serious one. What have you to say for yourself?"

She cleared her throat. "The only magick I performed, Your Highness, is that which protects the Fae. I would never practice magick that would put them at risk."

Lachlan considered her response. *She's good*, he thought, *no admission, yet no denial*. He wondered how far his uncle would push her.

"If you have no proof, Morfessa, this matter is to be dropped. You owe Evangeline an apology."

Surprised he did not press her further, Lachlan shifted to study his uncle. Was there more to Rohan's relationship with Evangeline than he knew? He frowned at the tension tightening his belly. Surely the reaction had nothing to do with the thought his uncle might have bedded her. He scowled when as if in answer, his tension ratcheted up a notch—relieved when Morfessa shot from his chair to distract him.

The wizard shoved back from the table, his chair clattering to the floor. "Why can you not see her for what she is, Rohan?" he implored. Then, with a defeated shake of his head, he jerked his hand through his shoulder-length black hair. "No, don't bother to answer. I know why. She's bewitched you just as her mother bewitched me."

"I protect her because you never did, Morfessa. You've let your hatred of her mother blind you to who—"

"No, you're wrong! And one day you will see I was right, only it will be too late. She will destroy us as her mother once did." With one last scathing look at his daughter, Morfessa stalked from the hall.

Gabriel and Broderick stared into their goblets, their expressions giving nothing away. The same could not be said for the guards and servants who remained in the hall. It was obvious from the surreptitious black looks they cast in her direction that they believed Morfessa's charge against her. As she was Andora's daughter, the majority of the Fae hated her. Holding her to blame for her mother's actions, they treated her abysmally. Since King Arwan, Lachlan's father, was reputed to have been a murderous bastard, it seemed unfair they judged her so harshly yet him not at all. But she didn't help her cause. She was cold, aloof, and arrogant, as though she held herself above them all. And now it would only get worse for her.

He didn't know how she withstood their contempt day in and day out and found himself softening toward her. He quickly shook off the disturbing sentiment by reminding himself she'd been a thorn in his side from the moment he met her.

"If you'll excuse me, Your Highness, I shall return to my quarters to prepare a list of suitable brides for your nephew."

At her pronouncement, whatever sympathy Lachlan had felt for her fled as quickly as she fled from the council chambers. Gaze narrowed on the sway of her curvaceous behind, he thought of the knowledge he'd filed away only moments ago. He had no doubt she'd broken through the barrier. And now there was a distinct possibility he'd be holding the information over her head sooner than he'd anticipated.

* * *

Seated at a desk in the cramped quarters of her chambers in the palace's tower, Evangeline crumpled a piece of parchment then tossed it on the floor. She blew out a frustrated breath upon seeing how high the pile beside her desk had become. With a flick of her finger, the evidence of her failure vanished. Now if she could only make her thoughts of Lachlan disappear as easily. Images of the too-handsome highlander had invaded her mind for the past two days.

Since only Rohan and his daughter Syrena had ever defended Evangeline, she found it disconcerting that the man she'd regarded with such contempt had done so. He'd turned her preconceived notions of him on their ear. Absently, she rubbed her shoulder where he'd rested his hand. At the memory of his comforting touch, the muscles low in her belly contracted.

"You're being ridiculous," she chided, "letting a simple gesture of kindness affect you so." Perhaps because so few were kind to her, she reasoned, it explained her reaction. Accustomed as she was to the Faes' contempt, was it any wonder she responded to him? And now, after Morfessa's inflammatory charge, she'd be vilified further.

As much as Rohan's support meant to her, it would do little to sway the Fae. She damned Morfessa for putting her in the unenviable position of lying to Rohan, a man who'd been more a father to her than Morfessa had ever been. But it couldn't be helped. She'd needed to test the limits of her power, to know that if the stones were tampered with, there was another means of escape. Besides, it was not as if she'd use her magick against the Fae.

Her stomach churned as she remembered the black tendrils snaking through the pure light of her magick, the voice inciting her to strike out against the Fae. She pushed the memory from her head—an aberration, that's all it had been, no matter what Morfessa would have her believe about herself—and got back to the matter at hand.

Tapping her pursed lips with the quill, she once more tried to think of a suitable bride for Rohan's nephew. *Princess Tiana of the Welsh Fae, Broderick's niece*, she wrote. Then she scratched it out, certain Lachlan would find the young woman's incessant chatter as annoying as Evangeline did. She frowned at the thought he might also find Tiana's voluptuous figure and beautiful face outweighed the teeth-grinding screech of the girl's voice and her inane prattle.

"Men," she grumbled as she once more wrote Tiana's name.

She came up with four others and added them to her list. But for each one she found a reason for their unsuitability— too young, vain, foolish, not enough magick—and, along with Tiana's, rubbed them out. Her task was proving more difficult than she'd first imagined. When she'd suggested the idea to Rohan, she'd been only too happy to saddle the high-lander with one of the women she'd just erased. But since his defense of her at the Seelie Court, she found it difficult to do so.

Disgusted with herself, she tossed the writing utensil on her desk and rubbed the dull ache throbbing in her temples. Perhaps she'd been too hasty. After all, she'd witnessed the red glow of his sword. Surely if a man who held his emotions so tightly in control could feel anger, he could eventually be made to feel something for his subjects. As for his lack of magick, well, she could always offer her services.

Evangeline groaned. What had come over her? Lachlan MacLeod represented everything she despised in a man. He was a philanderer—a man who did little but appease his lusty appetites, a man who'd spent the better part of his life hating the Fae. And worst of all, he looked like his father King Arwan. No, she wouldn't allow her mind to go there. Just as she'd done all those years ago, she firmly closed the door on the re-volting memories.

Glancing down at the ink-smudged holes where there'd once been names, she crumpled the parchment. She needed a breath of fresh air to clear her head. She'd spent the last two days in her room attempting to complete her task, although she admitted, avoiding the Faes' derision had just as much to do with her self-imposed confinement. Perhaps a visit with Uscias was in order. After all, no one knew the king of the Enchanted Isles as well as his mentor. Her spirits rose at the thought of spending time with Uscias. Assuring herself it had nothing to do with the possibility of seeing Lachlan again, she left her chambers.

Moments later, she stood deep within the forest of the Enchanted Isles. Her gaze was drawn to Lachlan's palace—sparkling in the noonday sun—perched high atop the mountain that cast the valley in shadows. Perhaps she should go there first. After all, it was most likely where Uscias would be. And if she happened to run into Lachlan, she could thank him properly for coming to her rescue. Absently she smoothed her hair, then realized what she did. For Fae sakes, she was primping! Huffing an exasperated breath, she set off with a determined stride for Uscias's cottage. As she walked through the forest, she found it oddly quiet, the leaves crackling beneath her slippers overly loud. A prickle of unease skittered along her spine and she picked up her pace.

Turning onto the cobblestoned path, she came to an abrupt halt. The door to Uscias's cottage had been ripped from its hinges and lay splintered on the forest floor.

Her heart jammed in her throat. "Uscias," she cried, tripping over the planked door. She regained her footing and rushed inside. Her horrified gaze took in the destruction. Uscias's belongings were tossed about the small room, furniture viciously smashed and strewn throughout the cottage. She shoved aside a broken chair with a growing sense of alarm.

From behind an overturned settee in the corner of the room,

she spotted a pink satin slipper. Aurora. So concerned was she for Uscias, she'd forgotten the little seer he trained. She tried to calm her staccato breath. Steeling herself against what she might find, she knelt down and peered beneath the settee. Anger intermingled with fear at the sight of the little girl lying so still and bound in irons. With a blast of her magick, Evangeline sent the blue settee flying across the room.

Careful to avoid the thick links of chain—iron drained the Fae of their magick—she placed her cheek next to Aurora's colorless lips. The child's warm breath caressed her face, and Evangeline's shoulders sagged in relief. She quickly identified the sickly sweet smell that caused her nostrils to twitch. Aurora had been drugged with a sleeping draught. Ridding the child of the chains that drained her of her powers was Evangeline's first concern. She focused on a spell to remove them.

Inches above Aurora's diminutive form, she held her hands palms down. Her magick hummed but didn't produce the desired results. Whoever had chained the little seer had placed several wards around her. She wondered if Uscias, thinking to keep the child from following him or antagonizing those who'd taken him, had created the wards. If so, that would mean he'd also created a protective barrier between Aurora and the iron, the reason Evangeline could not immediately break through the wards. Taking that into consideration, she drew on her powers once more, sending a steady stream of white light into the chains. The thick rings of iron snapped and, with a wave of her hand, vanished.

Conjuring a goblet, she filled it with a potion to counter the sleeping draught and knelt beside Aurora, pressing the rim to her lips. "Wake up," she urged, brushing the silky white-blond curls from the child's angelic face. "That's it," she said as the little girl's blue-veined lids fluttered open.

Licking her pale lips, Aurora squinted as though trying to bring her vision into focus. Evangeline carefully tilted the goblet. The child drank greedily, pushing it away once she'd drained the potion. Raising sky-blue eyes to Evangeline, her voice came out a dry croak. "Did you rescue Uscias?"

Evangeline bit her lip. Knowing how much the child cared for her mentor, she wished she could spare her the truth. But she needed whatever information Aurora could give her. She shook her head. "Can you tell me who took him?"

Aurora nodded, swallowing hard. "They were from the Far North, King Magnus and his men."

Evangeline struggled to contain her temper. She'd known all along that fool MacLeod would put the Fae in danger. He'd refused Magnus with no thought to the consequences, and now look what had happened. She wanted to strangle the big oaf, or at the very least shake some sense into him.

"Don't worry, Aurora, I'll get him back." She placed an arm behind the child's back and helped her sit up. Noting the tremors shaking her tiny frame, Evangeline said, "Rest for a moment and then we'll go to the palace."

They'd go to the palace, all right, and the inept king would learn firsthand what his reckless decision had cost them. She scrubbed her hands over her face. How could he be so incompetent as to have his wizard stolen right out from under him? Where were the guards? Why were the perimeters of the forest not warded, alarmed? Caught up in her inner ranting, she'd been unaware Aurora now knelt before her, the child's small hands coming to rest on either side of Evangeline's face. Knowing no secret was safe from the budding prophetess, panic kicked up inside her. She tried to pull away, but there was no pulling back from the mesmerizing effect of the swirling colors in the little seer's eyes.

In the ragged voice of an old woman, Aurora proclaimed, "Deep within you a battle rages. Good versus evil, light over darkness. Overcome your fears, or evil shall prevail and both Mortal and Fae shall pay the price."

A chill iced Evangeline's limbs, freezing her to the wood-planked floor. The child had seen the evil within her, giving voice to Evangeline's greatest fear. Her father had been right all along. Closing her eyes, she battled against the heavy weight of despair that threatened to paralyze her. She didn't have time for this, not now. She'd be of no use to Uscias if she succumbed to her fear.

He needed her.

The Fae needed her.

If Magnus was able to break Uscias and gain his secrets for conjuring magickal weapons as powerful as the Sword of Nuada, the Fae of the Enchanted Isles would be decimated.

Aurora's hands slid from Evangeline's face. The natural color of the child's eyes returned and she blinked up at Evangeline. Pushing the prophecy to the dark recesses of her mind, Evangeline rose unsteadily to her feet. Helping Aurora to hers, she reminded herself that never had the child remembered the words she uttered when in a trance.

For now, Evangeline's secret was safe.

Chapter 3

Certain word of Morfessa's charges against her had reached the Fae of the Enchanted Isles, Evangeline squared her shoulders as she entered the palace with Aurora. Lachlan's servants stopped what they were doing to regard her with a mixture of fear and unbridled loathing. She lifted her chin. If they thought to wound her with their contemptuous looks, they'd be sorely disappointed.

"Where is your king?" she demanded, adding a touch of disdain to her voice.

After a brief hesitation, three of the women turned their backs on her and went about their business. Two of the younger maids, who appeared ready to provide an answer to her question, snapped their mouths closed when one of the older women shot a silencing glare over her shoulder.

Evangeline bit back a frustrated oath. She had no time for their petty machinations. With a flick of her fingers, she filmed the white marble floor beneath them with a thin coat of ice. The women's outraged shrieks bounced off the glass-domed ceiling as they slid across the floor in a frenzy of pinwheeling arms and legs. Trying to regain their balance by holding on to one another, they only succeeded in pulling each other down into an ever-growing heap on the floor.

"Now, answer my question."

From the bottom of the pile, the older woman pushed her head out from beneath upturned skirts and flailing legs. "He's in the State Room."

Evangeline shuddered at the memory of what Arwan had used the State Room for when he'd ruled the Enchanted Isles. If the son was anything like the father, she would not be taking Aurora into that den of iniquity.

Evangeline felt the child's gaze upon her as she hustled her up the marble staircase. "Maybe if you didn't play tricks on them they would like you better, Evangeline."

"No, Aurora, I'm afraid no matter what I do, they shall never like me." Her answer appeared to sadden the child, and she gave her hand a reassuring squeeze. "Don't worry, I've grown accustomed to their enmity. It doesn't bother me anymore."

For the most part it was the truth. If Evangeline wanted companionship, she went to the Mortal realm and spent time with Syrena. Although, since her best friend was now the mother of a two-year-old and soon to deliver another child, they didn't spend as much time together as Evangeline would've liked. This was partially due to the fact Evangeline did not do well with small children. They didn't seem to like her, and if she was honest, she didn't like them very much either. Their incessant crying and whining got on her nerves, and more often than not they were dirty and smelt bad.

If she did on occasion feel the need for female companionship in the Fae realm, she could always seek out Fallyn and her sisters. Having fled the kingdom of the Welsh Fae on the eve of Fallyn's nuptials to King Broderick, the women had taken refuge in the Enchanted Isles when it was under Syrena and Morgana's rule. The three sisters had formed a lasting friendship with Syrena, assuming prominent roles in her army of women warriors. Since Evangeline had been forced to flee the Enchanted Isles when Morgana had accused her of killing Arwan, she'd been glad Fallyn and her sisters had been there for

Syrena when she couldn't be. But with Syrena now residing in the Mortal realm, the women looked to Evangeline to take her place. Not that Evangeline had much time for friendship; she was too busy honing her magick and dealing with matters at the Seelie Court.

"I like you, Evangeline," Aurora said, closing her small fingers around Evangeline's.

"Oh . . . thank you. I . . . I like you, too, Aurora." Evangeline was surprised to find she spoke the truth. At eight, Aurora was much easier to manage than babies; like an adult, only smaller.

She and Aurora spent a frustrating fifteen minutes traversing the maze of corridors. Due to the heightened tensions in the Fae realm, Uscias had recently warded the palace, rendering her attempts at transportation useless. By the time they reached the gleaming double doors of the State Room, Evangeline's anger at Lachlan's incompetence and her concern over Uscias's well-being had reached the boiling point. The two guards took one look at her and waved them through.

She held Aurora back. Until she'd satisfied herself the child would not be scarred by what went on in the room, she had no intention of letting her inside. As Evangeline stepped into the dimly lit interior, the heady scent of roses tickled her nostrils and she sneezed into the sleeve of her robes. Her eyes had not entirely adjusted to the subdued lighting when Aurora tugged on her sleeve.

Recalling the little girl's propensity for mischief, Evangeline decided it would be best if she took her with her. "Close your eyes."

To their right, several men and women frolicked in a pool. Noting the slick sheen of white bodies, she was grateful the water was deep. Once more she cautioned Aurora to keep her eyes closed. The tinkling of feminine laughter drew her attention to a far corner at the back of the hall. She recognized the deep chuckle that accompanied the women's high-pitched giggles and scowled. Gritting her teeth, she locked on the object of her fury lolling amongst the jeweled-toned pillows while being hand fed by a bevy of voluptuous blondes. She set off in his direction, thinking what she'd like to do with the iced cake the woman held to his lips, only to be brought to a halt by her unmoving charge.

She turned to Aurora. Groaning, she placed a hand over the child's wide-eyed gaze. "I told you to keep your eyes closed." With her free hand, Evangeline dressed the man climbing naked from the pool in a robe. She met his disgruntled look with one of her own then pointed to Aurora.

Aurora tugged at her hand, and with a sigh, Evangeline removed it. Taking the child by the shoulders, she firmly pointed her in the king's direction. The lazy grin Lachlan bestowed on the woman running her fingers through his golden mane faded the moment he spied Evangeline stalking toward him. His companion, uncaring she had an audience, ran her hands over his broad chest in a suggestive manner while another massaged his shoulders. Her barely concealed breasts pressed to his cheek.

As though realizing the image he presented, Lachlan grimaced and waved his harem away. Ignoring their simpering protests, he came to his feet with leonine grace. "To what do I owe the *pleasure* of your visit, Evangeline?"

The women shot her waspish looks as they sauntered past with an exaggerated sway to their hips. Evangeline rolled her eyes, then returned her attention to Lachlan, opening her mouth to answer. The sight of him in cream-colored robes trimmed with gold left her speechless. When he came to court, he dressed in trews and a tunic, the same as in the Mortal realm, although there he sometimes wore his highland garb.

He was a big man, bigger than most of the Fae, but it was not the outline of his wide shoulders, muscled arms and thighs that rendered her speechless; it was the resemblance to his father, King Arwan. She took an unconscious step backward and he frowned.

She fought back a wave of nausea at the memory of his father's brutal hands upon her, his cruel mouth . . .

"I ken my bonny looks can be distractin' but if ye doona mind, ye're keepin' me from my . . . duties."

His sarcastic tone snapped her back to the present. Thinking of Uscias in Magnus's hands, the disturbing images from the past burned away in the heat of her anger.

Standing beside her, Aurora giggled. Lachlan winked at the child.

Was there not a female born who was immune to his charms? Of course there was—her.

She balled her hands into fists to keep from wiping the cocky smile from his face. No doubt what she was about to tell him would serve the same purpose. "Do you know where Uscias is?"

He drew his attention from Aurora, brow furrowed. "Aye, he's at his cottage."

"No, he is not," she bit out between clenched teeth.

He rubbed his hand over the darkened stubble on his jaw, then lifted his shoulder in a nonchalant shrug. "I'm no' his keeper, but I'm sure he'll return shortly. Ye should go to his cottage and wait fer him there."

At his obvious attempt to be rid of her, Evangeline's temper spiked. She closed the distance between them, thumping his broad chest with her finger. "No, he won't be back *shortly!* While you cavorted with your . . . your . . ." She sputtered, waving her hand contemptuously at the women who kept a vigilant eye on her. "Magnus kidnapped Uscias, ransacked his cottage, and drugged Aurora, leaving her chained in irons."

His easygoing demeanor vanished. His amber eyes darkened, his expression turned fierce. As though she weighed no more than a feather, he lifted her out of his way to crouch in front of Aurora. "Are ye all right, angel?"

Aurora nodded. Her blue eyes glistened with unshed tears. "They took Uscias. I couldn't stop them. I tried, but they . . ." She sniffled, rubbing her eyes.

"It's your king's job to protect his subjects, Aurora, not yours."

Lachlan came slowly to his feet. He turned to her, standing so close she could feel the heat of his anger. "Ye blame me fer this?"

Tipping her chin, Evangeline met his narrowed gaze head-on. Danger, the fiery glint in his golden eyes seemed to warn, but she refused to be intimidated. "Of course I do. You rejected his sister's hand in marriage and instead of spending time shoring up your defenses, I find you seeing to your pleasure. I knew something like this was going to happen with you as their king. I just knew it," she said, as angry at herself as she was with him.

She'd failed in her mission to protect the Fae. A heavy weight settled over her at the thought. No, she refused to succumb to despair, and the best way to avoid doing so was to take action. She would leave now for the Far North. She pivoted on her heel. Her forward motion was brought to an abrupt halt by Lachlan, who took hold of her arm and spun her around to face him.

"Where the bloody hell do ye think ye're goin'?"

"To rescue Uscias. Now unhand me." She attempted to peel his powerful fingers from her arm.

"Of all the fool things I've heard in my life, nothin' compares to ye thinkin' ye can go off on yer own to retrieve Uscias." He raked his fingers through the golden waves of his luxurious head of hair. "Besides that, 'tis no concern of yers. I'll be goin' to the Far North and ye'll be remainin' here to see to the bairn's care."

Vexed beyond belief, her rebuttal came out in an incoherent sputter.

* * *

Lachlan was furious. He couldn't believe Magnus had gotten past his defenses. No matter Evangeline's charge, the Enchanted Isles had been well guarded. The bloody king of the Far North had simply managed to outmaneuver him. It wouldn't happen again.

He raised his gaze from the woman spouting gibberish in front of him to Erwn and Bana, who sauntered in his direction. "What is this about Uscias?" Bana asked as he and his brother approached them.

Evangeline couldn't have hurled her accusations at him in a civil tone, oh, nay, she'd practically shouted them at him in that husky voice of hers, making sure not only Bana and Erwn heard her, but the rest of the Fae gathered in the room. "It seems Magnus kidnapped him. I will be leavin' immediately."

Lachlan caught the furtive look Bana slanted his brother. They were mistaken if they thought he missed their silent exchange. Since Evangeline's accusation that the two men had conspired against him, he'd paid close attention to his father's most trusted advisors and had to admit, much to his chagrin, she was right. Bana and Erwn were up to something.

"Of course, you must go at once, Your Highness. My brother and I will see to the matters of state while you are—"

Evangeline snarled at the two men. "No. Fallyn and her sisters will oversee the business at court while his majesty deals with Magnus."

He'd never been more tempted to strangle a woman than he was at that very moment. "Evangeline, if you doona mind, I'll speak fer myself." Did she truly believe he was fool enough to leave his kingdom in Bana and Erwn's grasping hands? If the condescending look in her eyes was anything to go by, she did.

"You can't mean to—"

Seeing Evangeline open her mouth, Lachlan stopped Bana midstream. "Excuse us fer a moment." He grabbed her by the hand and dragged her out of earshot. Backing her into a corner, he forced his gaze from the heaving bounty of her breasts straining against her magenta robes. He pressed his palms to the cool white marble on either side of her head and drew in a deep breath to regain control. Then he gave his head a shake in hopes of ridding himself of the intoxicating feminine scent he'd just inhaled. She ran the tip of her pink tongue over her lips and he jerked his gaze back to her eyes before he gave in to the urge to kiss her, to ravish her berry-red mouth with his.

"What?" She flattened her palms on his chest and pushed.

Captured in her violet gaze, he lost his train of thought. In an act of self-preservation, he dropped his hands to his sides and took a step away from her. The blasted woman was driving him mad. "What . . . what? Ye accuse me of all manner of stupidity, take me to task in front of my subjects, then seek to instruct me on managing my affairs, and ye have the nerve to ask me . . . what!" He'd tried to keep his voice low but failed miserably in the attempt.

She thrust out her chin. "You know as well as I do that Fallyn and her sisters are the better choice."

"That may well be, but there are ways to handle matters that do not add fuel to the fire. But ye doona ken the first thing aboot bein' diplomatic, do ye?"

"I can be as diplomatic as the next person."

He snorted. "Ye're aboot as diplomatic as a priest in a kirk full of sinners."

"But you were going to—"

"'Tis no' yer place to tell me what to do. My uncle allows ye to, but ye're in my kingdom now, no' his."

She scowled at him. "While you are charming Erwn and Bana into ceding to your wishes, I shall retrieve Fallyn and her sisters."

Bloody hell, there was no reasoning with the woman. He

scrubbed his hand over his face. "They're no' here at the moment."

She narrowed her gaze on him. "Where are they?"

The last thing he wanted to do was tell her where they were. She already thought him incapable of ruling his kingdom. Not that her opinion of him mattered. But once she learned Fallyn and her sisters were at his home on Lewis, he'd never hear the end of it. She'd know—as it had happened on previous occasions—that the women had taken offense to something he'd said or done. He couldn't readily recall what had been the cause of their discontent this time.

Oh, aye, now he remembered, they'd gotten it into their heads to open a school to train women in warfare and he'd refused their request. Lachlan imagined the three sisters were at that very moment pleading their case to Syrena. It wouldn't do them any good. The men would revolt if he ceded to their wishes.

"You've done it again, haven't you?"

"What are ye talkin' aboot?"

"Oh, no, you don't. You're not talking your way out of this. I'm going to Lewes." With a haughty toss of her raven tresses, she stalked past him.

He scowled after her, throwing up his hands when she walked past the little seer without so much as a second look. "Ye canna leave the bairn. I have too much to do to prepare fer the journey."

She came to an abrupt halt. Head bowed, her shoulders rose as if she took a deep breath and then she turned and walked back to Aurora. "I won't be long. You stay with King Lachlan. And you," she pointed her finger at him, "keep a close eye on her. You've already managed to lose one wizard. We can't afford to lose another."

His subjects, who'd been listening to their exchange, gaped at her charge. Blood rushed to Lachlan's face. For the umpteenth time since the blasted woman had strode into his

State Room, his control over his temper snapped. Lachlan never lost his temper, and the fact she could make him do so only added to his fury. "Evangeline, come back here," he demanded to her retreating back.

He reached her in two strides and took hold of her arm. "That's it, ye go too far." He lowered his mouth to her ear, not wanting Aurora to hear what he said. "I'm no' a bloody nursemaid. Ye'll take the child to either Uscias's cottage or my uncle's palace."

She whirled on him. "Will you cease grabbing me?"

"I wouldna have to if ye would stay in one place and stop makin' a fool of me in—"

"Me? Oh, no, *Your Highness*, you do that quite well on your own."

She tried to struggle out of his grasp, but he held firm. "This matter has naught to do with ye and ye're wastin' my time."

Glaring at him, she flicked her finger.

A blast of fiery heat shot through his hand. He wrenched it from her arm, no more able to contain his anguished moan than he was to stifle the memories the searing pain evoked. At Glastonbury, Lamont had taken maniacal pleasure in holding a burning blade to Lachlan's flesh. He slowly lifted his gaze to hers. "Doona ever do that to me again." Ice-cold fury leaked into his voice. She gasped, taking a step back.

As though she realized she'd pushed him too far, she continued to walk backward. "I . . . I'm sorry. I shouldn't have . . ."

"Nay, ye shouldna have." He stalked her, his anger blinding him to his surroundings.

She held up her hands. "I said . . ." Her eyes widened and she fell into the pool.

Cool water splashed onto his face and robes, dampening his fury. Nervous giggles broke the tension in the room when Evangeline swam to the surface, and spurted water from her mouth. Fighting to contain his laughter, Lachlan leaned over and offered his hand. She slapped it away, hauling herself from the pool. Her dripping purple robes clung to her lush curves and Lachlan found himself searching for something to cover her with. From beneath her long lashes, she surveyed the now laughing men and women. With a disdainful sniff, she turned on her heel and walked stiff-backed from the room, leaving puddles behind her.

He winced, recognizing her attempt to cover her hurt and embarrassment with contempt. She truly was driving him mad. One minute he wanted to throttle her and in the next to comfort her and shield her from the Faes' derision.

"Your Highness, may I suggest—" Bana began.

Lachlan shifted his gaze from Evangeline to Bana and Erwn. Aurora stood between them, staring sympathetically after Evangeline. "I'm goin' to seek my uncle's counsel. Aurora." He held out his hand. "I willna be long."

It was only when they'd left the State Room that Lachlan realized without Uscias he had no way of transporting himself to his uncle's palace. He wasn't like the other Fae. For the most part it didn't bother him, but he didn't relish the idea of asking Erwn or Bana for assistance. To do so would further weaken his standing in their eyes, and Evangeline had undermined his authority enough for one day. He felt the same sense of powerlessness he had when Ursula and Lamont had him at their mercy.

Aurora drew him from his self-indulgent musings with a tug on his hand. "Where's Nuie?" she asked.

"Nuie?"

"Your sword."

He chuckled at the name she'd christened his lethal blade with. A sword that could take down Fae or Mortal in a single blow—a sword that imbued him with enough power and magick to quiet any of his detractors. The thought raised his spirits, although even his blade didn't imbue him with enough magick to transport himself. He cast a speculative eye on the child. "Aurora, do ye think ye'd be able to transport us to my uncle's?"

She nodded. "Uscias told me if ever he couldn't be here to assist you, I was to look after you."

Oh, aye, just what he wanted to hear, his mentor had appointed him an eight-year-old nursemaid. He was thankful Evangeline was not within earshot. He scowled at the mere thought of the woman, then caught sight of Aurora's wounded expression. He lifted her into his arms. "All right, my wee wizard, let's go and collect my sword."

She returned his smile. He noted the change in her eyes just as she brought a hand to his face. He jerked back, trapping her fingers with his. "Oh, no, ye doona. I've heard all aboot yer talents."

The last thing he needed was someone poking around in his head.

Chapter 4

A black cat—hair standing on end—screeched past Lachlan as he entered his childhood home in the Mortal realm on his return from Rohan's palace. He quirked a brow as his brother Aidan crossed the hall to greet him.

"Syrena?" Lachlan asked, referring to his sister-by-marriage's habit of terrifying the animal.

"Nay, Evangeline." Amusement crinkled his brother's silver-gray eyes. "And if I were ye, I'd be followin' his lead."

Lachlan scowled at the mention of his nemesis. "Where are they?"

"In Syrena's solar. Plottin' yer demise, if I'm no' mistaken. What have ye done this time?"

From where he stood a few feet from the base of the curved oak staircase, Lachlan could see through the banister on the upper level to the closed door of Syrena's solar. He shook his head at the thought of them in there scheming against him.

"Nothin'," he muttered. Then, with a resigned sigh, he returned his attention to his brother. "Evangeline thinks 'tis my fault Uscias was abducted." At Aidan's look of surprise, Lachlan frowned. "Did she no' tell ye?"

"Do I look daft? I wasna goin' anywhere near the five of them, worked up as they are. Do ye ken who took him?"

"Magnus."

His brother's features tightened, a muscle jumping in his clenched jaw. Aidan had fought the king of the Far North when Magnus thought to claim Syrena as his bride. "Why?"

"They've been tryin' to get a hold of our Hallows to even the playin' field, but to hear Evangeline tell it, 'tis on account of me refusin' to wed his sister Jorunn."

"He wants . . ." His brother stopped, his eyes widening as he looked beyond Lachlan. "What the hell happened to ye, Gavin?"

Lachlan glanced over his shoulder and groaned. His brother's man-at-arms and childhood companion, covered from head to toe in muck with only the whites of his eyes visible, dragged Aurora into the keep behind him. Anxious to be gone from Lewes before Evangeline became aware of his presence, Lachlan hadn't noticed the bairn wasn't with him. He should've realized when he met Gavin in the courtyard upon their arrival that Aurora would remain out of doors. Whenever the child accompanied Uscias and Lachlan to his home in the Isles, she took impish delight in tormenting his brother's friend.

"She tossed me in with the pigs. Fer all she looks like a wee angel, she's a demon."

Lachlan grabbed the hand the blond cherub raised. "Aurora," he said sternly. "Ye ken better. Ye're no' supposed to use yer magick in the Mortal realm."

"I was just playing with him." She turned an innocent smile on Lachlan.

"I'm no' a bairn's toy," Gavin bristled.

"Aurora, apologize and clean him up." Lachlan supposed he should take her to task for tormenting Gavin, but his relief at seeing a return of her playful nature after what Magnus had put her through held him in check.

"But, Your Highness, you just said I shouldn't use my magick in the Mortal realm."

He wondered if women were born knowing how to turn a man's words against him. Or mayhap the bairn had been spending too much time in Evangeline's company.

"Aurora," he said in an exasperated tone.

She waved her hand. Too late, Lachlan caught her mischievous grin on the last wiggle of her fingers. A dark cloud formed over Gavin's head, then opened up to drown him in a deluge of water.

Gavin stood sputtering in the heavy downpour, a puddle of mud forming beneath his now-soaked boots. With a furious glare at Aurora, he turned on his heel to stride from the hall, muttering about demonic faeries—the dark cloud following in his wake.

Crossing his arms over his chest, Lachlan forced a stern expression onto his face to look down at the giggling bairn standing beside him. His brother covered his amused chuckle with a cough.

Aurora sighed, flicking her fingers in Gavin's direction. The cloud disappeared, his tunic and trews now clean and dry. With a sweet smile, she looked up at his brother. "May I go and play with baby Ava, Lord Aidan?"

Lachlan noted his brother's hesitation and couldn't say he blamed him. Ava, Aidan and Syrena's two-year-old had, much to his brother's chagrin, displayed an aptitude for magick when only a few months old.

"Aye, if ye promise no' to show her any of yer wee tricks," his brother said.

"Oh, I don't need to teach her any tricks, Lord Aidan. Baby Ava's magick is almost as powerful as mine."

Aidan ran a frustrated hand through his jet-black hair. "Just what I wanted to hear," he muttered. Aurora, well acquainted with the castle, headed for Ava's chambers.

Lachlan understood his brother's worry. "Has she been transportin' herself again?"

"Nay, Lewes has been warded so she canna manage *that* anymore."

"Ah, Aidan, no' to cast aspersions on yer wife, but if 'twas Syrena who—"

His brother snorted a laugh. "Nay, if my bonny wife had cast the spell there's no tellin' what would've happened. Evangeline saw to it."

Lachlan grunted at the mention of the raven-haired beauty. "Right." He clapped a hand to his brother's shoulder in farewell. "I'll see ye when I get back from the Far North," he said as he turned to leave.

Aidan grabbed him by the arm. "'I think ye're fergettin' somethin'. Since ye're goin' after Uscias, ye'll be needin' to take Fallyn and her sisters with ye."

"And why would I be doin' that? Ye canna—"

"Yer Highness," Beth interrupted with a laugh as she made her way up the stairs carrying a silver tray piled high with iced cakes. Their longtime housekeeper thought it amusing that the lad whose trews she'd once mended was now a king. Like the servants in both his brother's and cousin's castles, only the most loyal knew of Lachlan and Syrena's Fae heritage. It would be dangerous if more than a trusted few shared their secret.

Lachlan lowered his voice to call after her, "Ah, Beth, doona be mentionin' my presence when ye deliver Syrena her sweets."

She stopped midway, leveling a speculative look at him over her shoulder. "And what would my silence be worth to ye, Yer Highness?"

"Are ye blackmailin' me again? To be sure, ye must have more jewels than Queen Anne thanks to me."

"Ah, well, if ye're no' willin' to part with a wee bauble . . ."

"Fine," he grumbled. "I'll bring yer *bauble* next time I'm home." He wasn't about to tell her he'd pay far more than a bauble to keep Evangeline from learning of his presence before he made it back to the Fae realm to meet up with Gabriel and Broderick. The two men had offered their assistance in rescuing Uscias, and Lachlan had tarried too long as it was. He'd only meant to deliver Aurora into Evangeline's safekeeping.

His uncle, assuming Evangeline would be accompanying Lachlan to the Far North, had volunteered Morfessa to watch over the little seer. After witnessing the wizard's treatment of his daughter, Lachlan had no intention of letting the man anywhere near the bairn. Rohan and his wizard could see to the Enchanted Isles in his absence, but he would trust only Evangeline to care for Aurora.

He felt a moment of trepidation at the thought of leaving Evangeline on her own, but then reminded himself it was none of his concern. Thinking on her powers, his worries seemed foolish. But he couldn't shake the image of her that day at Rohan's court—the stark pallor of her face and the fear shadowing her violet gaze. Her vulnerability had struck a chord in him and, despite his quarrel with her earlier, his need to protect her had not abated.

His brother watched him. "'Tis obvious yer mind's made up where the women are concerned, but I wish ye'd reconsider."

"Why? Ye feel the same as I do aboot women in battle."

"Aye, I do. But this is different. Ye doona have magick, Lan, and ye have no' commanded yer army long enough to ken who ye can trust and who ye canna. I'd feel better kenning the ones that had yer back."

Lachlan snorted. "Guard my back? They're just as likely to put a blade in it. Ye doona ken them, Aidan. They'll question my every command and they'll no' care who hears them do so."

"Nay, ye ken as well as I they'd protect ye. Ye're Syrena's brother-by-marriage. As to them underminin' yer authority, ye'll—"

Delighted squeals interrupted Aidan. At the top of the stairs, Ava bounced excitedly in Aurora's arms.

"Aurora." Lachlan urgently waved his arms at the little seer. "Take her back to her chambers. Now."

"Lan . . . Lan," Ava shrieked, putting out her arms to him, clapping her wee hands.

He cursed when the door to Syrena's solar opened. "Lachlan MacLeod, get your sorry self up here this instant."

Turning on his laughing brother, he said, "Ye see what I'm sayin'. Fallyn and her sisters are as bad as Syrena. She shouldna be bossin' me around anymore. I'm a bloody king, fer Chrissakes."

"Good luck with that. I'll see—"

"Nay." He hauled Aidan after him. "If I have to go, so do ye. I doona have time to spare, so ye'd best help me make my excuses to yer wife."

Evangeline couldn't believe Lachlan had taken time from his preparations to come to the Mortal realm. He truly had no sense. Without Uscias to guide him, he was obviously at a loss and she felt she had no choice but to offer her counsel. A heated flush worked its way from her chest to her cheeks at the memory of their earlier altercation. She waved a cooling hand in front of her face. She would not allow him to see her discomfiture. An image of her dragging herself from the pool to the sound of the Faes' derisive laughter taunted her until she remembered why she'd fallen into the water in the first place.

She closed her eyes at the memory of the tortured pain in Lachlan's eyes. If she hadn't allowed her temper to get the better of her, she never would've shot the bolt into his hand. She knew what had been done to him, she'd seen his scars.

She shook off her guilt. The damage had been done and, she reminded herself, she had apologized. Evangeline *never* apologized—to anyone, ever.

Lachlan entered Syrena's solar with his niece in his arms.

His brother followed behind with Aurora's hand in his. It never ceased to amaze Evangeline how comfortable Lachlan was with Ava. Fae men had little patience with children. Then again, the king of the Enchanted Isles was only half-Fae, or perhaps she admitted, her relationship with Morfessa tainted her observations.

"Syrena." He leaned down to kiss her best friend's cheek in greeting, avoiding Fallyn and her two sisters' pointed stares. "Ah, mayhap ye should sit down." He glanced uncomfortably at Syrena's swollen belly.

Her friend wrinkled her turned-up nose. "You sound just like your brother." She reached up to peel her daughter's arms from Lachlan's neck, ignoring Ava's whiny protest. "Oh, don't fuss. You'll see your uncle later."

Keeping a firm grip on Ava's hand, Syrena leaned over to retrieve several of the delicate pastries from the tray and wrap them in a napkin. "Off you go now," she said, handing Aurora the cakes. The little seer happily took Ava and the cakes and left the room.

Aidan cast an amused smile at his wife. "Are ye certain ye're well, my love? 'Tis no' often ye'll share yer sweets."

Syrena rolled her eyes, then lowered herself awkwardly onto the blue velvet settee. "Lachlan." She patted the spot beside her. "Sit, I'll wrench my neck if I continue to look up at you."

Lachlan shot his brother a sour look. With an almost imperceptible shrug of his shoulder, Aidan leaned against the dark-paneled wall, arms folded over his broad chest. No matter how aggravating the two men were, Evangeline couldn't help but admire their masculine beauty. Lachlan was as fair as his brother was dark. Both were big and powerfully built, and possibly the most arrogant men she'd ever met. And that said a lot, considering she was Fae.

When Lachlan finally deigned to join Syrena on the settee,

his sister-by-marriage said, "Evangeline tells me Magnus has taken Uscias. What are we going to do about it?"

"*We* are no' goin' to be doin' anythin' aboot it, I am. Yer father and Morfessa," his amber gaze passed briefly over Evangeline, "will be seein' to the Isles in my absence. Broderick and Gabriel have offered their assistance in retrieving Uscias."

From where she stood in front of the stone fireplace, Evangeline glanced across the room to where Fallyn sat stiffly erect between her two sisters. She wondered how her friend would feel about seeing Broderick, her ex-betrothed, again. Fallyn gave nothing away—her fine-boned features remained composed.

"Good." Syrena patted his knee. "And with Fallyn, Shayla, Riana, and Evangeline with you—"

"Nay, I'm no' takin'—" He released a long-suffering sigh when the three sisters came angrily off the settee across from him.

"I'm leaving!" Shayla said. With a toss of her long auburn locks, she stormed from the solar. Evangeline was surprised that was all she did. Shayla had a fiery temper and had little patience with men. From what she'd heard, the woman had suffered terribly at the hands of her husband, Dimtri. Broderick had rescued her from the king of the European Fae several years ago, but the abuse had left its mark. Riana, the youngest of the three, glared at Lachlan, then hurried after her sister.

"That's it! This is just what we were speaking about, Syrena. He refuses to acknowledge us as warriors. We will no longer align ourselves with you, *King Lachlan*." Fallyn angrily shoved a wayward chestnut curl from her flushed face.

Syrena held up a finger to stay Fallyn's departure. "Lachlan MacLeod, you will not find warriors equal to these women. If they were men, you would be begging them to join you. You put Uscias at risk with your—"

He exchanged a look with his brother, then put up a hand to quiet Syrena's agitated protest. "Fine. They can accompany me to the Far North."

It was obvious to Evangeline that the only reason Lachlan agreed was to pacify Syrena, in part due to her delicate condition. One did not argue with a woman who was eight months into her confinement.

Pleased he'd finally conceded, no matter what the reason, she said, "Now that that's been settled, have you a plan as to how we—"

His gaze jerked to her. "Ye're no' comin' with me. Ye're stayin' to mind Aurora."

How dare he! If not for her, he'd have no idea his wizard was even missing.

"I will not be left behind," she said. "You need me. You need my magick. And if you are too foolish to see that, I pity Uscias and the Fae."

With lethal grace he came to his feet and stalked toward her. Before she realized what she was doing, she'd backed into the sharp edge of the wooden mantel. She stifled a pained groan.

"I doona need ye. I doona need anyone. Remember that." His powerful warrior's body crowded her and she placed her palms against the straining muscles of his broad chest. She raised her gaze to his, noting his bland smile at her inability to push him away. But beneath his impassive facade, she sensed his barely restrained anger.

"Lachlan," his brother said, a warning in the low rumble of his voice. "Ye'll frighten the lass."

Lachlan's eyes roamed her face, coming to rest on her mouth. Under the intensity of his gaze, she self-consciously ran the tip of her tongue over her upper lip. Muttering an oath under his breath, he jerked away from her.

"Your brother does not frighten me in the least," she

assured Aidan, her voice deceptively cool considering the heated thrum Lachlan had aroused in her.

"Then 'tis ye who are the fool, lass," Lachlan said silkily from where he leaned on the mantel just inches from where she stood.

She refused to look at him—refused to give him the satisfaction of seeing even a smidgen of her discomposure. She needn't have worried. He swaggered to stand behind the settee without so much as a glance in her direction.

Syrena looked from Evangeline to Lachlan with interest. Oh, no, Evangeline groaned. Sickeningly in love with her husband, Syrena had developed the annoying habit of matchmaking. It wasn't the first time she'd looked at Evangeline and Lachlan with that particular gleam in her eyes. Love truly played havoc with one's mind if Syrena, knowing them as she did, could entertain such a ludicrous thought.

"Evangeline's right, Lachlan. You are not invincible. Magnus is not an enemy to be taken lightly. I should know. I've fought him before." Syrena ignored her husband, who along with Lachlan glowered at her. She patted her distended belly. "And if not for this one, I'd be going with you," she added as she attempted to heave herself off the settee.

"Nay, ye wouldna be," her husband said, pushing off the wall to help Syrena to her feet.

"Aidan, I don't think you understand how frustrating it is for me not to be able to help. Perhaps I should go to the Enchanted Isles and—"

"Syrena, doona try my patience."

"But I—"

"I need a word with my wife. If ye'll excuse us." Aidan swept a protesting Syrena into his arms and out of the room.

"Daft. Ye're all daft," Lachlan muttered, glaring at Fallyn and Evangeline.

They stared him down and he threw up his hands in disgust. "Fine. The four of ye will accompany us. And ye," he narrowed his gaze on Evangeline, stabbing a finger in her direction, "will do as I say. Ye willna argue with me. Ye willna tell me how *ye* think I should be doin' things. Ye will see to Aurora and nothin' more."

At the unrelenting look in his eyes, she swallowed the heated protest brewing inside her. Wasn't this what she'd wanted all along? For Lachlan to show some sign of emotion? A sign he cared for the Fae? She just hadn't thought that by doing so he would relegate her to such a subservient role. She lowered her gaze from his and smoothed her palms over her robes. She'd allow him his small victory—for now.

Fallyn rolled her eyes then left the room, leaving Evangeline alone with Lachlan. He raised a brow, waiting for her to acquiesce to his demands. "All right, but do you think it's a good idea to bring Aurora with us? She's only a child."

"If she doesna come, neither do ye. Ye're the only one I trust to see to her care."

"Oh, I . . ." Stunned by his admission, Evangeline couldn't think of anything to say. She eyed Lachlan's retreating back warily.

What did he mean he trusted her?

Except for Rohan and Syrena, no one trusted her, and to have Lachlan offer his was . . . disconcerting.

It had to be a ruse.

Chapter 5

At the top of the stairs, Lachlan glanced back to see Evangeline standing where he'd left her, a puzzled look upon her face. He blew out an impatient breath. "Quit yer wool-gatherin'. We havena the time to waste."

She blinked, then narrowed those bonny eyes of hers on him as she strode from Syrena's solar. "I'm wasting time? If not for your misguided attempt to leave your women warriors and me behind, you would have your rescue party and battle plans in place."

"They are." He snorted at the stunned expression upon her face. "Ye doona ken me, Evangeline."

"You have the layout of Magnus's palace?"

"Aye," he responded tightly, attempting to hold his temper in check while he took to the stairs.

"The warriors have been equipped, the horses prepared?"

Lachlan gritted his teeth and came to an abrupt halt. Following as close as she was, she bumped into him. He twisted, taking hold of her upper arms to steady her. He barely resisted the urge to shake her as he did so. "Aye, and aye. And 'tis the last question ye'll be askin' me on the matter. Aurora is yer responsibility. Nothin' more."

"Surely you jest," she said, wriggling out of his hold. "You can't expect me not to take part in the rescue."

He raised a brow. "What part of I'm the king and ye're the subject do ye no' understand?"

She pursed her lips, waving a dismissive hand. "Oh, please. I'm hardly your *subject*. I'm advisor to your uncle."

"Ye're an apprentice wizard."

"I'll show you apprentice wizard," she muttered, raising her finger, violet eyes flashing.

Lachlan grinned. "Temper, temper. No magick in the Mortal realm, Evie."

"Evie," she sputtered, trying to free her hand from his.

Ava's childish prattle drew Lachlan's attention. Knowing Syrena would not be far behind, he released Evangeline. "If I have to tell ye one more time how 'twill be, ye're no' comin'," he warned before heading the rest of the way down the stairs to where his niece was attempting to break free of her mother's hold.

Once she had, Ava tottered full speed toward him. Lachlan crouched and opened his arms to envelop the giggling bundle of pink. In the beginning, he'd tried to keep his distance from his niece, finding it too painful to be around her. The memory of the child he'd lost and why had been too fresh.

Pushing aside his regrets at what might have been, he came to his feet with Ava in his arms. "She's sure to beat Olivia next time they race," he said gruffly, avoiding Evangeline's canny gaze. He gently disengaged Ava's arms from around his neck to hand her to his brother.

"Aye, we've been practicin', havena we, my wee angel? Another month or two and she'll be able to beat the two demons," Aidan said, referring to Olivia's brothers, Rory and his wife Aileanna's sons, Jamie and Alex.

Syrena held up her arms to take her daughter. "You are not continuing this silly rivalry, Aidan. Aileanna and I will not allow it."

His brother shifted Ava out of his wife's reach. "Nay, she's too heavy fer ye to be carryin' now. Doona worry, my love, once Ava beats Olivia this one last time, 'twill be it."

Ava rubbed her eyes and yawned. Catching sight of Beth, who had been making her way back up the stairs, Syrena motioned for her. "Do you mind putting Ava down for a nap?"

"No' at all, my lady," Beth said, relieving his brother of the sleepy child.

Syrena returned her attention to Aidan once Beth started up the stairs with Ava. "You realize you've made that promise before. As I recall it was at the celebration of Iain's . . . Oh." A sob caught in her throat and she looked helplessly at Aidan.

Lachlan frowned. "What's the matter?"

His brother wrapped a comforting arm around his wife's shoulders, tucking her tiny albeit expanding frame against him. "I shoulda told ye when ye first arrived. We've had word from Dunvegan. Iain's wife Glenna took ill on the journey across the North Sea. She died before they reached Norway."

Evangeline came to stand beside Syrena, offering a commiserating pat to her shoulder.

Lachlan had been surprised when he'd learned his cousin planned to wed the Douglas lass. As the MacLeods were highlanders and the Douglases lowlanders, neither family had been overly impressed with the union—especially hers. But the headstrong beauty had defied her father and brothers, wedding his cousin in spite of their protests. "I thought once he'd wed, Iain meant to leave the seafaring to his partners and see to their business dealings ashore?"

"Aye, 'twas the plan, but I think Glenna worried he'd come to resent their marriage if he was forced to give up his adventures."

"Do ye ken how Iain fares?"

"Nay, but 'tis said they're soon to begin the journey home."

"It will do him good to be back with his family," Syrena murmured.

Not always. Lachlan shook off the thought. "We'd best be off." He frowned, scanning the hall. "Where's Aurora?"

"I don't know. She was with us a few moments ago," Syrena said, looking about her. She pulled away from his brother. "I'll check the kitchens."

"I'll come with you," Evangeline offered, following after Syrena.

Gavin's high-pitched shriek penetrated the thick entrance doors. "Syrena, Evangeline, I think we've found her," Aidan called out.

Lachlan passed a gimlet eye over Evangeline when the two women returned to the hall. "Ye're no' doin' a verra good job seein' to yer charge. How can I trust her to yer care in the Far North if ye canna even manage to keep her in yer sights here?" Lachlan savored the reaction his taunt garnered. Evangeline's cheeks pinked and her full lips pursed.

"You can not truly think to fault me in this?"

"Aye, brother, ye canna fault Evangeline when only a short time ago the bairn went missin' on yer watch."

Lachlan scowled at Aidan over Evangeline's head as she walked toward him then drilled her finger in his chest. "You are the most exasperating man I have ever had the misfortune of knowing."

He took hold of her finger. "I didna lose her. I kent she was playin' with Gavin. And I'm no' just a mon, I'm a king. Besides, seein' to the bairn's a woman's work, no' a mon's."

She growled low in her throat and Lachlan grinned. "Ye really need to work on that temper of yers, Evie."

"Ignore him, Evangeline. Let's go rescue Gavin." Syrena leveled Lachlan with a warning look, then led her friend from the castle.

"Ye seem to have lost yer touch with the lassies, brother," Aidan said, grinning at the disgruntled look he shot him.

"Careful," Lachlan said. "Or I'll tell yer wife I could use her assistance in the Fae realm."

"Nay, ye wouldna, ye worry aboot her welfare almost as much as I do."

"That may well be, but I grow tired of her sidin' with those bloody women all the time. I'm her kin. Ye think she could show me a little loyalty. Now I'm stuck bringin' the three of them, and *Evangeline*."

"Well, I fer one am glad Fallyn and her sisters will be there fer ye. As to Evangeline, I'm sure if ye set yer mind to it ye can charm her into doin' yer biddin'."

"I doona think we're talkin' aboot the same Evangeline."

Aidan snorted a laugh, clapping him companionably on the shoulder as they walked to the door. "Ye have to admit, brother, it would no' be a hardship attemptin' to charm her. She's a verra bonny woman."

Nay, he didna have to admit a thing. Especially to his brother, who would no doubt tell his wife, and of late, Syrena had developed the truly annoying habit of matchmaking.

As soon as they stepped into the sunlit courtyard, he spotted Evangeline, arms folded beneath her chest, impatiently tapping her foot.

His brother's laughter drowned out Lachlan's curse.

Out of courtesy to Syrena, Evangeline had let his royal high*nass* off easy, but now, after stepping through the standing stones into the Fae realm, she was going to tell him precisely what she thought of his dictatorial, high-handed manner. She turned to confront him.

"No' a word out of ye. Remain here with the bairn," he ordered in a deep, commanding rumble. His attention focused beyond her.

He strode toward the clearing, unsheathing his sword as he made his way to where a small party of warriors gathered. His blade glowed, and she started. It was nothing like she'd witnessed the other day at the council meeting. This time it was fiery red and showed no sign of fading. As tall and broad as he was, he dwarfed whoever had drawn his ire.

She nudged Aurora out of the way, angling her head to get a better look. Her stomach lurched—it was her father. Morfessa's tall, lean frame was inconsequential in comparison to Lachlan's. Her father, as if sensing her attention, pinned her with his dark malicious gaze, his thin lips twisting in a sneer.

She could feel the color drain from her face. She hadn't seen Morfessa since their confrontation in the Seelie Court. Had he found evidence of what she'd done? No, there was nothing to find, she'd sealed the tear.

Aurora's small hand clasped Evangeline's. The memory of the little seer's prophecy came back to taunt her. Prickly heat flooded her limbs. *Don't let her remember*, she pleaded silently, *don't let her repeat the damning prophecy now*. She steeled herself to look down at the child.

"Don't worry, King Lachlan won't let him hurt you."

Her throat too tight to speak, she squeezed Aurora's hand and attempted a smile. She couldn't make out Lachlan and her father's conversation, but neither could she bring herself to move closer. After all this time she should be immune to Morfessa's hatred, but she wasn't. She only pretended to be, hoping one day the act would become reality. She lived in fear he saw something inside her she couldn't or didn't choose to see. *But you have seen it*, she reminded herself, *and so has Aurora*.

"Don't let him frighten you, Evangeline. No one believes his spiteful allegations." Her mind tangled in a web of paranoid emotions, she hadn't noticed Fallyn approach.

Evangeline lifted her chin, struggling to project an unconcerned demeanor. She let the heat of her embarrassment that anyone should witness her fear melt the icy tendrils holding her hostage. No one—not even Syrena—knew how much her father and his damnation frightened her. But Fallyn was deluded if she thought no one believed Morfessa's accusations against her.

She drew her gaze from the two men to Fallyn, noting the concern in her friend's eyes. "I'm not frightened, only worried we waste time." Evangeline winced, her tone more acerbic than she intended.

Fallyn glanced over her shoulder to the clearing. "We await Broderick."

"Oh, I . . ." Evangeline didn't know what to say. Although she considered Fallyn a friend, she never felt comfortable discussing personal matters with anyone but Syrena.

Overhead the sky darkened. The shadows hovered, then descended in a loud swoosh. Seven black-winged steeds skimmed the treetops before landing in the clearing.

Fallyn rolled her eyes. "He always did like to make an entrance." With a shake of her head, she returned her attention to Evangeline. "I brought Bowen for you to ride." Placing two fingers between her lips, Fallyn whistled shrilly. With a soft whicker, Syrena's white steed sauntered from a grove of trees.

"Bowen!" Aurora ecstatically greeted the horse, immediately conjuring a shiny red apple to offer him.

Evangeline chewed the inside of her bottom lip. "I don't suppose I could just transport Bowen and myself to the Far North, could I?" she asked, eyeing the big steed with trepidation. She had never ridden before and preferred transportation to any other mode of travel. Depending on no one but herself afforded her a measure of security.

Aurora, overhearing her question, looked at her askance. "Oh, no, Evangeline, he'd become very ill if you did so."

For Fae sakes, the child was right. With the steeds' sensitivity to sound, the high-pitched vibrations of their magick during transportation, which had no effect on the Fae, rendered the animals insensible. It took weeks for them to recover their equilibrium. She began to think her apprehension at riding the big beast was having a similar effect on her.

"There's no need to be afraid, Evangeline. Bowen is the

most docile of mounts, and despite his deformity, he's as fine a steed as mine."

Evangeline's snort of derision was mimicked by Bowen. The steed apparently as offended by Fallyn's reference to his stunted wing as Evangeline was to her friend's assumption she was afraid. She wasn't afraid. For the love of Fae, she was the most powerful wizard in the realm. And it most certainly would not bode well for her if word got out she had fears.

Of its own accord, her gaze slid to Lachlan, who appeared to be sending her father on his way. She returned her attention to Fallyn. "You misunderstood me. I simply thought it would be a good idea for one of us to scout out the area first."

"Mm-hmm." Fallyn arched a dark brow as though she didn't believe her. "Here, perhaps this will make you more comfortable." With a flick of her finger, she dressed Evangeline in clothing similar to her own—form-fitting trews and a white tunic—then did the same for Aurora.

Unaccustomed to anything but the loose robes favored by the Fae, Evangeline plucked self-consciously at the crisp white shirt with the deep V that exposed the tops of her breasts. She heard a sharp intake of breath and glanced up to see Lachlan raking her from head to toe with a predatory look in his amber gaze. A look so like his father's that before her eyes, his features morphed into Arwan's. She stumbled backward. Lachlan's gaze locked with hers.

With a muttered oath, he pivoted abruptly on his heel and barked, "Mount up."

"Evangeline?"

At the note of worry in Fallyn's voice, Evangeline sucked in a steadying breath and plastered a confident smile on her face before turning to her friend. From Fallyn's expression, the smile must have appeared more maniacal than confident. "Thank you, Fallyn. I'm certain these clothes will help immensely. I shall just . . . just . . ." She studied the steed, trying to figure out how she was to mount him.

Aurora, fairly vibrating with excitement, placed her foot in the device hanging below Bowen's belly then took hold of the leather piece jutting from the top of the saddle to easily mount the big beast. As her legs were much longer than the little seer's, Evangeline didn't see how she would have a problem doing the same.

"You may want to mount up, Evangeline. His Royal Highness appears ready to move out," Fallyn advised, striding to where her steed waited at the edge of the clearing.

Evangeline stuck her foot in the steel triangle hanging from the leather strap, looking up when Aurora giggled. "What?" Evangeline asked crankily.

"That's the wrong foot," the child said, clapping a hand to her mouth. Aurora's narrow shoulders shook with mirth.

Muttering her opinion of know-it-all children under her breath, Evangeline flicked her finger and landed with a thud behind Aurora. She barely had a chance to make herself comfortable when Lachlan took the lead at the front of their small party of fifty or so warriors and motioned for the riders to follow him.

Evangeline clung to Aurora, ducking to avoid the branches that slapped at them as Bowen galloped through the forest. With a mighty whoosh, his powerful wing swept up and they lifted off the ground. Skimming over the treetops, Evangeline made the mistake of looking down. Her stomach gave a sickening lurch. She closed her eyes, tightening her hold on Aurora. The higher they flew, the harder she held on until she heard Aurora's squeak of protest.

Evangeline gave herself a mental slap. She was being ridiculous. She was no longer a child who did not know how to wield her magick. Cautiously, she opened her eyes and unclenched her fingers, releasing Aurora's tunic. Methodically, she smoothed the wrinkled fabric, then calmly placed her hands at the child's waist.

There, you see, you're perfectly fine, she told herself,

noting they now appeared to be riding in the middle of the pack. Fallyn and her sisters rode just ahead of them, and every so often her friend sent an encouraging look in her direction, which after the fifth time was beginning to wear on Evangeline's nerves. After all, she was doing remarkably well.

Suddenly, they veered to the right. Evangeline gasped, sliding sideways off the saddle. Anchoring herself on Bowen's stunted wing, she righted herself, only to have the wing sweep down. With all of Evangeline's weight on Bowen's weak side, the steed was thrown off balance and crashed into the horse on their right, who then slammed into the horse beside him. Jolted by the force of their contact, Evangeline lost her balance. With a panicked shriek, she fell off Bowen—dragging Aurora with her.

Evangeline tumbled from the sky at a breath-stealing speed. The wind ripped Aurora from her arms. Blinded by her hair, Evangeline clawed desperately at its strangling hold. If she couldn't see Aurora, she wouldn't be able to flash her back to Bowen. Powerful hands latched onto her and, with a thump, she landed in someone's lap.

"What the bloody hell were ye doin'?" a familiar voice asked. For once she was happy to hear Lachlan's deep brogue, even if his question was asked in a decidedly aggrieved tone.

Realizing she alone sat in the comfort of his embrace, she shoved her hair from her face then leaned backward over his arm to search for the little girl. "Where's Aurora?"

His arm tightened at her back and he gave her an exasperated look. Jerking his chin to the left of them, he pulled her upright. "No thanks to ye, she's safe. Bowen went after her, snatched her up with his teeth, then tossed her onto his back," Lachlan said with an admiring shake of his head.

"Good . . . that's good."

"Aye, 'tis. Now, do ye want to explain to me what happened,

because from what I can see the bairn has no problem retainin' her seat, whereas ye . . ."

From the way Aurora weaved the steed in and out of the other riders, it was obvious Evangeline couldn't blame the child for the mishap. She searched her mind for a plausible excuse, only to blurt out, "I'm unused to wearing attire such as this. The trews are . . . well . . . they're slippery, and I simply slid off the horse." Discomfited as she was, she tried to ignore the thickly muscled leg beneath her bottom and the powerful arms that held her.

"Unlike yer robes," he said dryly. "And here I thought ye were annoyin' the beast and he decided to toss ye."

She frowned. "How could I annoy a horse?"

"I doona ken, but ye're verra good at bein' annoyin', so it wouldna have surprised me."

"If that were the case, your steed would be trying to toss you."

"He couldna, I'm too good a rider. That's it, isna it?" He angled his head and studied her face. "Ye have no experience and ye're afraid." His tone gentled.

"I am not afraid," she protested a little too vehemently, striving for calm before continuing, "I have never had reason to ride before is all, and I'd much prefer to transport myself to the Far North."

At that moment, Aurora whizzed by, performing a series of intricate maneuvers that had Evangeline's belly lurching, and the thought of getting back on Bowen, even if she glued herself to the steed, held little appeal. She lifted her hand, determined to do as she said.

"Nay, ye doona." He took hold of her fingers. "Ye're no' goin' in on yer own."

"I'm not getting back on Bowen."

"Nay, 'twill be safer fer all of us if ye ride with me."

Evangeline was tempted to refuse but knew she had to choose her battles carefully. He was a king, after all, and she had to admit, the confident and commanding manner in which he handled his steed calmed her jangled nerves and queasy stomach. She just had to find a way to ignore the feel of his hard warrior's body pressed to hers, the comfort of his protective embrace, his . . . Evangeline groaned, uncertain which was more dangerous, remaining with Lachlan or returning to Bowen.

Aurora chose that moment to gallop alongside them. With an impish grin and a wave of her hand, she guided Bowen into a stomach-turning dive. A panicked cry escaped Evangeline before she could contain it.

Lachlan's warm breath caressed her cheek. "Doona worry, she's just showin' off."

A heated shiver of awareness raced through her. For the love of Fae, it would be less dangerous facing down Magnus and a hundred of his warriors.

Chapter 6

Safe. He thought it safe to hold the raven-haired temptress in his arms? Of all the fool things that had ever come out of Lachlan's mouth, that had to have been the most absurd. After the way his body had responded to seeing her in trews hugging her curvaceous hips, the tunic caressing the lush ripeness of her breasts, you'd think he would've thought twice about his offer. But no, his need to protect her overrode his need for self-preservation. Her father had seen to that.

The madness in the vindictive bastard's eyes as he spoke of his daughter had reminded Lachlan of the look he'd seen in Alexander's the night he'd tried to kill him. Morfessa's barely contained bloodlust when he pleaded with Lachlan to do what must be done to rid the Fae realm of her evil had ignited in Lachlan a rage of such blinding force, he was surprised he hadn't killed the bastard right then and there. It had taken a moment for him to regain enough control to be able to speak. Once he had, he'd warned Morfessa his daughter was under his protection. Warned him if any further threats were made against her, Lachlan would see them as a threat against his Crown.

Considering how Evangeline felt about him, Lachlan was certain she'd resent his interference. She might think her magick alone would protect her, but he knew better. Too many of the Fae hated and feared her, and too few would offer their support and protection if the need arose. Not that she would thank him for it, but she now had his.

It was why he now held the woman, who'd done nothing but frustrate and torment him, in his arms.

She shifted in his lap and he blew out a frustrated breath. Her palm pressed to his chest, her full breasts jiggled beneath her tunic as she attempted to swing her long legs over to straddle his horse.

"What are ye doin'?" he ground out when, as she wriggled into position, her firm arse rubbed his cock.

"I need to be able to keep an eye on Aurora," she informed him with a quick glance over her shoulder, as if she didn't understand the reason for the surly manner in which he questioned her.

He scrubbed a hand over his face, trying to ignore the ache in his loins. It was his own bloody fault. Of late he'd grown tired of the avaricious women who clamored for a place in his bed. He was now paying the price for not taking them up on their offers.

He'd kept a careful watch on the little seer in part to keep his roving eyes off Evangeline and her bountiful charms, which threatened to spill out of her tunic. "She's fine. Now fer Chrissakes, would ye stay still!"

"What is the matter with you? I'm just . . ."

"Ye're no' an innocent, Evangeline. Ye bloody well ken what ye're doin'." He pressed his straining erection against her to make his point, calling himself an idiot when the feel of his cock nestled against her arse only served to inflame him further. "Unless 'twas what ye intended all along."

With an outraged gasp, she wriggled farther up the saddle to put some distance between them. Lachlan curved an arm around her waist. Flattening his palm on her belly, he tugged her against him. "Ye'll fall off if ye're no' careful."

He could feel the warmth of her skin through the thin fabric of her tunic, the muscles tensing beneath his fingers. Thinking with nothing more than his cock, he bent his head and inhaled her seductive scent. She stiffened in his arms. "'Twill take some time to reach the Far North, and I can think of a most pleasurable way in which to pass it." He nipped the tip of her earlobe, swirling his tongue in the delicate whorls.

She jerked back, her skull connecting with his forehead in a jarring thwack. "Sweet Christ," he said, rubbing his throbbing brow. "Ye've got a hard head."

Shifting in the saddle, she attempted to slay him with her violet eyes. "Have you been drinking?" She sniffed his breath. "No, perhaps a spell then."

"What the bloody hell are ye goin' on aboot?"

She gripped his chin between her fingers, searching his eyes. "Someone must have drugged you or put a love spell on you. It's the only explanation."

He jerked his chin from her hold. "No one's given me potions or put a spell on me, and it had naught to do with love. 'Twas nothin' but lust. Ye're no' a maid, Evangeline. Ye should ken the difference."

She sucked in a shocked breath, her cheeks flushed. "How dare you!"

"Ye can stop with yer pretense of outrage. I've lived at the palace fer over two years now and I'm well acquainted with the Faes' lascivious nature. Ye canna expect me to believe ye're an innocent. Ye're older than Syrena. Ye're older than me, fer Chrissakes."

"Do not presume to judge me on the basis of the company you keep, Lachlan MacLeod. And what for the love of Fae does my age have to do with anything, or for that matter my innocence or lack thereof?"

"If ye've never experienced lust, never been with a man, Evie, I'm beginnin' to understand why ye're so bad tempered. I canna say I blame ye."

She elbowed him in the belly. Recovering from the blow, he almost missed her finger coming up. He encircled her wrist with his hand. "Oh, no, ye doona. Ye're no turnin' me into a toad."

"Hah, a toad is too good for the likes of you. I was going to turn you into a pig—a big fat pig ripe for slaughter."

Lachlan grinned, enjoying the furious sparkle in her eyes. Being with Evangeline was never boring. "And how were you plannin' on explainin' that to Syrena and Aidan, not to mention Aurora, who's lookin' our way?"

"Let me go," she gritted out, trying to pull her hand from his.

"Do ye promise to behave?"

"Only if you promise not to—"

"No' to what? No' to do this." He angled his head, trailing his lips along the delicate line of her jaw, down the elegant column of her neck. He only meant to tease her, but at the taste of her, his cock hardened further. He groaned. Bloody hell, what was wrong with him?

"I . . . I despise you, Lachlan MacLeod," she choked out, but the tremor shuddering through her body when his lips touched her soft skin belied her words.

"Ye say one thing, but yer body tells me another." *Just like mine*, he thought. His gaze drawn to the fractured rise and fall of her breasts, the hard points of her nipples straining against the fabric of her tunic, he couldn't resist pressing a kiss to the fluttering pulse at the base of her throat.

"Stop. You must stop."

He jerked back at the underlying panic in her voice. Sweet Christ, mayhap she was right. Mayhap someone had drugged him, bewitched him. He forced a teasing lightness to his tone, responding in the manner she'd expect him to. "My offer still stands, Evie. If ever ye wish to assuage yer lustful urgings, ye have only to ask."

She wrapped her arms around herself, glancing at him through the cover of her long lashes. "I realize you are accustomed to women falling at your feet, surrendering to your flirtations, but I'm not one of them."

Aye, and he was certain 'twas the reason for his attraction to her. Sweet Christ, he hoped it was.

"And stop calling me Evie."

"As soon as ye start callin' me King Lachlan and showin' me the respect I deserve, I'll stop callin' ye Evie."

"*Respect.* Respect for what? You spend all of your time wenching, drinking, and gambling."

"Doona ferget trainin' fer battle. I'm verra good with my *sword*." He grinned.

"You are the most frustrating man I've ever met."

"See, I kent ye were frustrated and I'm only too willin' to help ye with that. I've never had an older woman before, so 'twould be an interestin' experience." No matter that their wee chat was playing havoc on his restraint; the urge to tease her was too enjoyable to resist. "Just how old are ye?"

"I don't know."

He snorted a laugh. "Everyone kens their day of birth, Evie. Tell me and I promise no' to tease ye again this day."

"I told you, I don't know. Besides, it's only a silly sentiment practiced by the Mortals."

Something inside him stilled. "Ye truly doona ken yer day of birth, do ye?"

She shook her head. "No, but since my mother destroyed the Fae of the Enchanted Isles twenty-six years ago, I must be somewhere around that age," she said flatly.

All he could think to say was, "I'm sorry, Evangeline."

She shrugged. "It doesn't matter."

"Aye, it does," he said quietly, gently rubbing her arm. He knew how much it mattered. For the first eight years of his life, Lachlan's day of birth had been a day he feared. Alexander would get deep in his cups trying to drown out the circumstance of Lachlan's birth. Arwan, king of the Isle Fae, had seduced his mother. Only recently had Lachlan learned it had not been a love affair, Arwan had enchanted his mother. He'd been born of rape, not love. Alexander had taken out his bitterness on the child he'd once been. On his eighth birthday, a drunken Alexander had dragged Lachlan into the cold rainy night with the intention of throwing him off a cliff.

He drew Evangeline against him, resting his chin on the top of her head. They were more alike than he'd realized, and the knowledge unsettled him.

Evangeline resisted the urge to seek comfort in Lachlan's embrace. Even now her body responded to his, to the memory of his warm lips upon her flesh. He'd asked if she'd experienced lust before. She had—the lust of his father. It had been a brutal, terrifying experience, but she'd had no choice. For the greater good she'd sacrificed her innocence to a man she abhorred. She'd made a promise to herself then that no man would ever have her at his mercy again. Before this day, before now, she had never experienced desire . . . lust. How was it possible Lachlan could awaken those feelings in her? She scoffed at the question. She knew the answer. He was a practiced seducer.

She shivered at the memory of his firm lips emblazoning a trail down her neck, his warm breath, his tongue teasing . . . *Stop!* She commanded her brain. She had to stop this, it was madness. She didn't want a man in her life, especially this man.

"Are ye cold?"

The deep rumble of his voice jolted her from her heated musings. She jerked, hitting the back of her head on his chin. "Ouch," she cried, rubbing the tender spot.

"I'm the one who should be complainin'. 'Tis the second time ye've bumped me with yer head."

Drawing away from him, she was surprised to find how much cooler it had become. "We're getting closer," she mused.

"Aye." A puff of frosted air accompanied his response.

"I've never been this far north, but I was no' expectin' the weather to be any different than 'tis in the Enchanted Isles."

"At one time it wasn't, but Gabriel's wife changed that."

"I didna ken Gabriel had a wife."

"She died a very long time ago. Her name was Gwendolyn. She was mortal. It is said he would do anything for her. He loved her very much." Her gaze was drawn to Gabriel, who was deep in conversation with Broderick. "He gave her the moon and the stars."

"What do ye mean?"

"When Gabriel brought his wife to the Fae realm, it was not like it is now. Unlike the Mortal realm we did not have night, only day. It is said Gwendolyn missed looking up at the stars at night. Gabriel pleaded his case before the Seelie Council, who petitioned the angels to remove the shield. Permission was eventually granted and Gwendolyn got her wish, only to die the next day. Not long afterward, the entire Fae realm requested they, too, be granted night and day. It led Magnus to petition for the secondary shield to be lifted over the Fae North, so now his weather reflects that of the Mortal realm beneath him."

"Why did Arwan and Rohan no' do the same?"

"The Fae of the Far North like their cold weather and snow. We, on the other hand, are not particularly fond of the weather in Scotland and Ireland. It rains too much."

"So, if I petitioned the council 'tis possible to have the shield lifted?"

"Yes, but I wouldn't advise it." Not relishing the thought of a change in their temperate weather, Evangeline turned to give him her opinion on the matter. Her eyes widened. Tiny icicles clung to his hair and the tip of his aristocratic nose. His full sensuous lips were tinged a deathly shade of blue. "Why didn't you say something?" she grumbled. With a flick of her fingers, she dressed him in a long cloak of brown fur.

"'Twas no' necessary."

"Oh, it was necessary all right, you just couldn't stand the thought of asking for my help." Realizing she could use a cloak as well, she raised her hand.

"Nay." He clasped her fingers with his. "We'll no' be able to fit on the horse if ye're bundled up as well." He held out the edge of his cloak. "I'll wrap the furs around us both."

He was right, but for some reason it felt more intimate than having only his arm wrapped around her. Reluctantly, she did as he suggested. If she didn't, she'd only draw his attention to her discomfiture, and she didn't want him to know he had an effect on her.

Clutching the edge of the cloak, she looked back at the party they led, searching for Aurora.

"She's ridin' with Shayla and Riana. They're keepin' watch over her."

Finding the women amongst the pack, Evangeline noted they, too, were cloaked in furs. She frowned at the fur piece some of the others wore on their heads. Narrowing her gaze, she studied it carefully, then with a flick of her fingers, put one on Lachlan.

He brought his hand to his head and patted it. Scowling, he took it off and plunked it on hers. "I'm no' wearin' *that*." His mouth quirked when he looked down at her.

She added a hood to his cloak and, reaching over, stretched up to tug it on his head. "Don't argue. Your nose looks as if it's about to fall off." Thinking his hands and feet must be cold, she changed his boots to fur and added fur coverings to his hands.

Lachlan rolled his eyes. "I canna feel the reins through these," he said. Pulling them off one at a time, he pressed them into her hands. "I can think of a better way to keep them warm. Ye wear the mittens." Gripping the reins with one hand, he brought her closer, then wrapped her tight in the warm thick furs. He slid his hand underneath, curving it around her waist.

His big palm splayed her belly and she gasped. Not because

of the cold radiating from his hand through the thin fabric of her tunic, but because of the heat it caused to unfurl in her belly.

Tipping her head back to look up at him, she said, "You cannot help yourself, can you?"

A wicked smile spread over his face, a teasing glint in his eyes. "Nay, I canna."

His long, powerful fingers kneaded her belly. There was something oddly comforting and gentle in the way he touched her. Like a man attempting to calm a skittish animal. No one had ever touched her in that manner, and Evangeline found herself responding despite herself. When a soft moan of pleasure threatened to escape her lips, she desperately sought a way to break the connection. "Do you think Magnus will try to intercept us before we reach the Far North?"

"Nay, 'tis to his advantage to force us into his territory."

"Perhaps you should have assembled a larger contingent of warriors."

"I handpicked the warriors who ride with me, Evangeline. They're the best, equal to at least twice their number."

"I suppose I must take your word on that." Four days ago, Evangeline would not have accepted Lachlan's word on anything. But from what she'd seen of late, she thought perhaps her opinion of him needed to be revised. His command of his warriors, his decisive and confident response to Uscias's kidnapping, drew her admiration. If she could be certain he truly cared for the Fae, her worries over his leadership would be much diminished. But his lack of magickal abilities remained an issue. Syrena had not fared any better with her magick, but at least she'd been pureblood. There was no escaping it, whether he liked it or not, Lachlan must marry, and soon.

"And how's that goin' fer ye, lass? I imagine 'tis difficult fer ye, seein' as how ye havena trusted me since the first day we met," he said in an amused tone.

"How was I to trust you? You went out of your way to hurt Syrena. You threatened the two of us."

"I didna threaten ye. I kissed ye," he scoffed.

She was unlikely to forget his kiss. In the dimly lit stable, his face had been barely distinguishable from his father's, and she'd panicked.

"If ye recall, 'twas ye who attacked me. Ye strung me up from the rafters, letting me drop to the floor when Syrena demanded ye release me."

She shifted in her discomfiture and his hand tightened at her waist, ending her squirming. "I was sworn to protect Syrena. You threatened her."

"Nay, ye didna ken who I was, so ye wouldna have kenned that then. Ye strung me up on account of the kiss. I doona recall my kisses havin' that affect on a woman before. Mind ye, a few have suggested they tie me up, but no' in the same manner or with the same intention as ye did."

"Why must you do that? You cannot carry on a conversation without making it about your lustful thoughts, as though you think of nothing else. I don't believe—"

"Ye take life too seriously, Evie. Mayhap if ye had some experience with passion, ye'd no' be so quick to judge others who enjoy it." He brought his hand from her waist, cupping her jaw firmly with his calloused fingers.

Heat simmered in the heavy-lidded gaze he fixed on her mouth. The objection formulating in her mind fled the moment he skimmed his thumb over her bottom lip. When he dipped his head, the hand she should have used to push him away curled in the coarse fabric of his tunic, drawing him closer. He covered her lips with his in a kiss so warm and tender it melted her resistance as quickly as the snowflake melted on her cheek. A light wind cooled her flushed cheeks and she snuggled into his hard, muscular heat. He took advantage of her low moan of pleasure, sweeping his tongue past her parted lips. The kiss was no longer gentle but firm, no longer warm but hot, demanding, wet, and openmouthed. Panic howled inside her as loudly as the wind that now pelted them with snow. Fear iced her insides as quickly as the snow iced her face. Frantic, she struggled against him.

She had to make him stop.

Chapter 7

Lachlan toppled face first into his horse's mane. One minute Evangeline was warm and willing in his arms, the next she was gone. He shoved himself upright, straining to see through the blinding snowstorm. His pulse spiked at the thought she'd somehow fallen off his horse. No matter her magickal abilities, he couldn't shake the image of her earlier gut-wrenching tumble. His gaze whipped to the ghostly apparitions winging their way through the curtain of snow toward him. The rhythmic swoosh of their wings grew louder and his apprehension eased when he made out Evangeline astride Bowen.

The blasted woman was going to be the death of him. Her stubborn refusal to meet his gaze grated on his nerves. It wasn't as if he'd forced his attentions upon her. To hell with it; he didn't have the time or inclination to ponder the reason for her hasty retreat. Not with the raging blizzard they were now caught up in. He didn't need the distraction and, he reasoned, Aurora needed an adult with her. An adult who could retain her seat would've been preferable, but Lachlan imagined whatever had caused Evangeline to flee would be incentive enough for her to tie herself to the horse if need be.

What the hell had he been thinking?

He hadn't been. That was the problem. Mayhap at first, he'd thought to tease her. To show her what she was missing. But the jest had ended up on him. He didn't know how or why, but she'd awakened something inside him. Something he'd buried so deep he thought it long dead. Not one of the women he'd bedded in the last two years—and there'd been plenty—had made him feel the way she did.

Aye, she was beautiful. And when he went to kiss her, the sight of her long lashes resting against the sculpted curve of her porcelain cheeks, the snowflake on the tip of her elegant nose, the bow of her full lips, had enflamed his desire like no one else. But it was more than that. She challenged and entertained him with her sharp wit. Her passionate zeal, strength, and confidence were a welcome change from the insipid beauties overrunning his court. In hopes of changing the direction his lust-addled brain had taken, he added arrogant, quick-tempered, and opinionated to his list.

He should've ended it before it had begun. Before he felt the small crack in his armor, a fissure so minute as to be infinitesimal, but enough for him to vow that no matter how intoxicating that small taste of her had been, it was not worth the price he'd pay.

"Evangeline," he shouted over the plaintive howl of the wind. "Can ye abate the storm?"

She studied the sky, her long hair tangling behind her. Returning her gaze to his, she gave him a curt nod.

Good. They were back to normal, he thought with a relieved sigh.

Broderick and Gabriel drew their mounts to his side. "Don't get your hopes up. The only wizard I've ever seen manipulate the weather is Uscias. No matter how powerful Evangeline thinks she is, she's no Uscias," Broderick said as they watched her lift her arms, her head tipped back, her lips moving.

A soft glow surrounded her and she smiled. A smile so dazzling it lit her beautiful face and stole Lachlan's breath away.

As though welcoming a lover, her arms spread wide. The white fur cape she now wore parted, revealing the snow-dampened tunic molded to her breasts. Fighting an urge to hold the heavy weight of those firm globes in his hands, he tightened his grip on his steed's reins and dragged his gaze back to her face.

The air crackled around her. Shayla, who'd been riding alongside Evangeline, motioned for Aurora to jump into her outstretched arms. A husky rapturous laugh escaped Evangeline's parted lips and his jaw dropped. Bloody hell, no wonder she didn't need a lover. It was as clear as the enthralled look upon her face; no mere man could compete with how her magick made her feel.

A shower of blue, yellow, and red sparks shot from the tips of her fingers. She brought her arms over her head and the vibrant colors leapt up to illuminate the sky. When her hands came together, a teeth-rattling boom blasted the air with the force of twenty cannons fired at once. He swayed upon his mount as the sky undulated around them, shaking his head to clear the ear-rending vibration.

Lachlan lifted his palm to catch a snowflake that fell from the sky on the now-gentle breeze, then looked at the woman who'd rendered him speechless with her power.

"She did it." The awe in Gabriel's voice echoed his own.

Shayla, Riana, and Aurora, offered her their enthusiastic admiration. But the rest of the warriors stared at her in a combination of fascination and horror. Dark murmurs of condemnation worked their way through the ranks. The words *mother* and *evil* were easily discernible. Lachlan stiffened, scanning the clutch of warriors who brought up the rear where the remarks seemed to have come from. Shayla and Riana twisted in their saddles as though daring the men to repeat their charges. He returned his attention to Evangeline, who leaned across to speak to Aurora, pretending he was certain that she hadn't heard what the men said. Or was she so accustomed to the Faes' hatred that she was immune to it?

Nay, he thought, noting her tight smile—the bastards had wounded her. For their benefit, he drew his sword. The blade glowed as brightly as the sky had prior to the deafening blast. Riana moved her steed, making room for him as he brought his mount alongside Evangeline. She glanced to where his sword rested across his lap, her startled gaze leaping to his. He shifted uncomfortably on his horse, a heated flush warming his face. Mayhap he should've waited until the evidence of the desire she'd stirred in him had abated before approaching.

Surreptitiously, he glanced at his lap, relieved to find the cape and his glowing sword concealed the bulge in his trews. It struck him then that his blade had been doing that more of late, turning colors as it once had for Syrena. He wasn't sure what it meant, but he'd always assumed the sword had ceased to show its colors because it had been displeased Lachlan now held its ownership. It pleased him to think his sword no longer found him lacking.

"I thought you wanted me to get rid of the storm?"

He frowned. What had he done to make her feel otherwise? "Aye, I did. I wanted to thank ye fer doin' as I asked. I kent all along 'twas a good idea to bring ye with us." He grinned when she rolled her eyes, pleased he could take her mind off the warrior's disparaging remarks.

"Oh, yes, we are so glad you deigned to include Evangeline in Uscias's rescue," Shayla mocked him, tossing her long, auburn tresses over her shoulder as she returned Aurora to Evangeline.

"Yes, for once one of your decisions proved worthy of admiration. Oh, wait, Syrena forced you to do so," Riana said with a sneer.

Lachlan scowled at the two sisters, who eyed him with caustic derision, thankful Fallyn brought up the rear so she didn't have an opportunity to spew her contempt along with theirs. She was worse than the two of them put together.

Remembering the charged sparks that had emanated from

Evangeline's fingers, he found himself searching them for some sign of injury. "Ye have no aftereffects from yer magick?"

His concern appeared to take her by surprise. Understandably, since it had done the same to him.

"No, I'm fine," she said after a moment's hesitation, then wiggled her fingers at him.

"Good." Unable to rid himself of the misguided urge to comfort her, Lachlan took his leave before he did or said something foolish.

"I see the women are as enamored with you as ever." Gabriel chuckled, then angled his head to study Lachlan. "Although I couldn't help but notice you and Evangeline seemed to be on *friendlier* terms."

"I thought my eyes were deceiving me, but obviously not." Broderick shifted his moody gaze to Lachlan. "I'd be careful with that one if I were you. I've never paid much attention to Morfessa's allegations before, but after witnessing her power today . . . I don't know, perhaps her father—"

"Is a madmon," Lachlan snarled. "'Tis only his jealousy of her magick and her relationship with my uncle that cause him to cast his malevolent aspersions against her." He noted the two men's silent exchange and thought he should temper his defense of Evangeline before they drew conclusions that were neither warranted nor wanted. Deciding it was best to change the subject, he said to Broderick, "I'm surprised ye noticed anythin', since ye've only had eyes fer Fallyn from the moment ye arrived in the Isles."

"I noticed that as well. How goes the wooing, Broderick?" Gabriel asked.

Jaw clenched, Broderick said, "I am not wooing. I do not woo. I have never needed to woo a woman before and I don't intend to start now."

"Aye, ye were wooin' her. It just wasna workin'. Mayhap I should give ye some pointers," Lachlan suggested hopefully. If he could help Broderick win back his ex-betrothed, the three sisters would no longer be a pain in his arse. They'd be a pain in Broderick's.

"What could you tell him about wooing, MacLeod? The women practically throw themselves at your feet, begging you to take them to your bed."

'Twas true, but he was sure he could think of something if it meant getting rid of Fallyn and her sisters. He ignored Gabriel. "First off, do ye want the lass, or no'?"

Broderick stared straight ahead, then gave a curt nod.

Lachlan released the breath he'd been holding. Sweet Christ, he was saved. "All right then. Ye have to take advantage of the opportunity presented to ye. I figure 'twill take us two days at most to retrieve Uscias, so ye doona have a moment to spare. Get back there and ride with her."

Broderick shook his head. "I can't. She said I was causing her head to ache and it would be best if I rode with you since you'd need all the help you can get."

Lachlan glared over his shoulder at Fallyn, who was chatting gregariously with two of his men. He bit back an oath when she laughed at something the good-looking warrior on her left said. "I'm more than capable on the battlefield and well she kens it. She's a . . ." He stopped before he said something that would make Broderick rethink his plan to win her back. "What were ye sayin' to cause her head to ache?"

"I told her what I expected of her when we met Magnus, instructing her on the intricacies of warfare."

"Fer Chrissakes, the woman is a warrior, Broderick. And though I ken our sentiments of havin' them on the battlefield are the same, I'd no' be fool enough to instruct Fallyn on battle tactics. Besides the three of us, she could put down most of the men here."

"Lachlan's right, Broderick. You should go back and apologize to her for your earlier remarks. Explain to her you made them out of concern for her welfare."

"Aye, do what Gabriel says. Mayhap share the battle

plan with her as well and pretend ye seek her opinion on its merits."

"We do not need her opinion. The plan is sound," Broderick said with a belligerent thrust of his chin.

Lifting his eyes to the heavens, Lachlan prayed for patience. "I said *pretend*, Broderick. Now get yer arse back there. She's enjoyin' the warriors' attentions too much fer my likin'."

The Welsh king shot a look over his shoulder and with a curse brought his mount around, racing to the back of the contingent.

Gabriel guffawed. "I take it you believe if he succeeds in winning Fallyn back you'll be rid of the three of them." When Lachlan didn't deny his observation, he continued, "If I were you, I wouldn't get my hopes up just yet. Broderick isn't known for his charming ways."

Lachlan scowled at his friend. Fallyn and her sisters had been a thorn in his side since the day he'd assumed his Crown. But they'd become more aggravating than ever with their incessant badgering about opening their school. And once Uscias was back safe and sound in the Isles, he knew they'd be pestering him again. Only this time, with Syrena's support, it would be worse than ever.

"'Tis obvious he loves her. He—" Lachlan whipped around at the sound of Broderick's angry shout in time to see the Welsh king launch himself at one of the warriors who'd been paying court to Fallyn. "Bloody hell, he's goin' to ruin everythin'."

Evangeline halted mid-conversation with Shayla when a furious Lachlan charged to the back of their small party, a laughing King Gabriel following after him.

Shayla sighed. "Men. I swear we should've gathered up the women and gone after Uscias on our own."

"I don't know, Lachlan seems quite confident in his ability to free Uscias. I think perhaps we have misjudged him," Evangeline ventured, brushing the light dusting of snow from her hair.

A slack-jawed Shayla turned to her. "Are you ill? Perhaps using so much of your powers has scrambled your brain."

"No, I—"

"She's fallen under that seductive spell he casts over all women. I swear the big oaf wields more magick than we think. I have yet to meet a woman in the Enchanted Isles who's not in love with him. Besides us, of course," Riana hastily added.

"I'm not in love with him," Evangeline blustered. Lachlan, who was berating a chastened Broderick as they rode back to the head of the formation, glanced over at her, brow raised.

"I should hope not," Shayla muttered.

Evangeline scowled at him. It was his fault the two women thought she was in love with him. Perhaps he *had* cast a spell over her. Although in the back of her mind she scoffed at her own foolishness, how else could she explain why she'd allowed him to kiss her? Or how that kiss, how his powerful body pressed against hers, had ignited a desire for intimacy she'd never experienced before. But even more disturbing than the desire for his touch was how he'd made her feel protected and cared for.

This could not be happening to her. She was above this sort of behavior. She didn't need or want anyone in her life, least of all Lachlan MacLeod. He would only serve as a distraction from her one purpose in life—protecting the Fae.

Once Uscias was rescued, she'd return to Rohan's court and monitor Lachlan from a safe distance. She'd spoken the truth when she said she'd underestimated him, but she would withhold judgment until she saw how he handled himself in the Far North. And once she found the proper candidate for his bride, well, he would no longer require her attention.

Instinctively her gaze was drawn to his commanding

presence. Snow lightly fell from the sky to rest on his broad shoulders and dampen his hair to a rich, honey gold. Remembering the feel of his rippling muscles beneath her hands, the silky texture of his thick hair between her fingers, a wistful sigh escaped unbidden from her lips. She groaned. Forget rescuing Uscias in a day, they must rescue him in an hour.

"Hold fast, Evangeline," Aurora instructed as she followed Shayla's lead and plummeted from the sky in a stomach-turning maneuver. Clinging to the child's tiny frame, Evangeline couldn't help but long for the feel of Lachlan's arms around her, holding her securely in place on his steed.

As though the mere thought of Lachlan drew him to her, he brought his steed alongside Bowen. At the sight of his battle-hardened warrior's body beneath his parted cloak, she knew she wouldn't be able to resist the urge to scramble onto his lap. But knowing how dangerous a place that could be, she cast a spell instead, gluing herself to Bowen's back. If only she'd thought to do so earlier she never would've known what she was missing. Never would have experienced the comfort of his touch or the desire for his kiss.

The wind whistled in her ears and she strained to hear what he tried to tell her. He leaned into her. "Doona fash yerself, Evie. I wouldna let ye fall."

She nodded, grimacing as they swooped past the snow-covered mountains with their jagged peaks knifing through the moisture-laden clouds. Buffeted by the winds as they traversed the pass, she was grateful for his offer and the spell that held her in place. If she fell from Bowen now, she would not die, but it would take several long, pain-racked months to heal, just as it had when she was a child.

Her gaze shot to Lachlan. He was only half-Fae. When he'd been tortured in the Mortal realm, he'd taken forever to heal. The memory of his savaged body too difficult to bear, she banished the image from her mind, but she couldn't banish her fear at the thought of him plummeting to the razor-sharp rocks below.

Furtively, she wiggled her finger in his direction, casting a spell that would bind him to his mount. The pass too narrow for them to ride side by side, Lachlan motioned for them to go ahead of him and follow behind Shayla. Shrouded in a suffocating blanket of dusky gray light, they rode in the dark depths of the cavern, past the sheer rock face. Mountains soared above them, and below, it looked as though a monster opened the never-ending hole of its mouth, ready to devour them should they fall.

Only the sound of their steeds' wings broke the weighted silence. No one spoke for fear the timbre of their voices would unleash the torrent of snow and ice that hung precariously above them. Very little truly frightened Evangeline, but she admitted, if only to herself, she would be much relieved when they came out the other side.

She glanced back to see how Lachlan fared and took some comfort in the manner in which he scanned the peaks. He bore no resemblance to the man she'd always thought him to be. Gone was the lazy carefree manner in which he'd always conducted himself. His bearing confident, almost to the point of arrogance, controlled, he was . . . majestic. Her cheeks heated when she realized he'd caught her staring at him.

Hmph, he hasn't changed that much, she thought when he rewarded her perusal with a smug grin. He attempted to shift his position on his mount, then frowned. Evangeline quickly averted her gaze. His low growl clearly audible, her relief at seeing the glimmer of light just ahead of them diminished.

As they winged their way out of the cavern, Lachlan came up beside them. "Undo yer spell," he demanded in a tightly controlled voice.

Aurora cast an uneasy glance from Lachlan to Evangeline.

Evangeline was taken aback. The icy rage that glittered in his eyes seemed out of proportion for what she'd done.

She attempted to explain. "I only meant to protect you. I didn't—"

"Take it off me now. And doona ever cast a spell on me again."

"But you could have—"

"Remove it. Now," he gritted between clenched teeth.

She much preferred his typical display of temper to this cold fury emanating from him. With a flick of her wrist, she removed the spell.

"King Lachlan's very angry with you, Evangeline. I don't think you should use your magick on him anymore," Aurora said when he rode away.

"I won't," Evangeline muttered. The ingrate could fall to his death for all she cared.

Aurora gasped.

Evangeline frowned. She didn't think she'd made the comment out loud. She followed the little girl's wide-eyed gaze to the snow-frosted valley. Magnus's crystal palace glistened in the distance, and there to greet them was an army twice their size. The men on their winged steeds below them raised their swords, bellowing a challenge. A thunderous clamor so loud it ricocheted off the granite walls. The mountains trembled as if frightened by the sound, triggering a wall of snow to barrel down from the ice-capped ledges. Bowen lurched forward, taking them out of reach of the vacuum of air that threatened to suck them back into the cavern.

"Fallyn!" Shayla screamed.

Evangeline's gaze shot back to the pass and the trapped warriors on their terrified steeds. "Bring Bowen around," she yelled to make herself heard above the deafening roar.

She drew on her magick as Aurora urged the steed into position. Her body warmed, growing hotter until the heat exploded inside her. She sent shafts of vibrating light at the cascading snow and ice. Instantly, the avalanche halted, suspended in midair. Digging deeper, Evangeline raised her arms in the direction she wanted the frosted cloud to flow. It followed her command to perch once more on top of the mountains. As the warriors cleared the pass, interred in snow, it took a moment for her to recognize Fallyn.

Once she did, she sagged against Aurora, exhausted. Controlling the weather earlier had depleted much of her strength, and now with this latest effort it felt as though she'd drained the last of her powers. Her stomach churned at the thought. Overwhelmed by a sense of impotence, she didn't dare test her magick. The confirmation of her helplessness would be too much to bear. She comforted herself with the knowledge that she'd be back to full strength within a few hours. But in truth, she couldn't be certain, as she'd never used this amount of magick in one day.

Shaking off the snow from her cloak, Fallyn brought her steed alongside Bowen and leaned over to embrace Evangeline. "Thank you." Fallyn pulled back and winced. "You've depleted your magick. You should have asked for help."

"No, I haven't. I'm perfectly fine." Evangeline would admit her weakness to no one, and Fallyn should know she'd never ask for help. It was too dangerous to depend on anyone but herself.

She didn't need anything or anyone, just her magick.

A magick she was sadly lacking at the moment.

Chapter 8

Lachlan took stock of the enemy as they gathered in the valley. He'd known they'd wait, forcing him to come to them. After his warriors had a chance to recover, he'd gathered them on the extended ledge below the mountain's peak to set out the plan of attack, all the while keeping an eye on Evangeline, who sat on the frozen ground with her back to the rock face. He noted the slight tremor in her hand as she pushed her glossy black mane over her shoulder. Exhaustion pinched her delicate features. She could barely keep her eyes open. In passing, Fallyn had mentioned Evangeline's magick was depleted, but he knew she'd be too stubborn to admit it.

He hadn't spoken to her since she'd cast her spell on him, not even to thank her for rescuing half of his warriors from certain injury. It didn't speak well of him, but he didn't care. He hadn't been that incensed since his captivity at Glastonbury. She'd made him feel powerless—stripped him of his freedom, his control. Instinctively he'd known she'd done it to protect him, but he couldn't thank her for it, nor would he apologize for his anger. No one wanted their weaknesses exposed, even if only to oneself.

His plan laid out, he made his way through the throng of warriors to go to her. She watched his approach through the cover of her lashes. He crouched at her side. "We'll be leavin' momentarily. I want ye to remain here with Aurora."

With a stubborn jut of her chin, she shook her head. "No. You cannot expect me to sit idly by while you and the others risk your lives. You need my protection."

"Ye're exhausted and yer magick is depleted." He held up his hand to stop her protest. "Doona try and deny it."

She snorted in disgust. "Even if that were true, I'd still have more magick in my baby finger than all of them put together." She waved a dismissive hand at the warriors crowded around the campfire.

He quirked a brow, unable to keep from smiling. "Humility is no' yer strong suit, is it, Evie?" He admired her pride, respected it even, but not when it put her at risk. Syrena would never forgive him if anything happened to her.

"And it's yours?"

"I'm a mon, and a king, we're no' meant to be humble. And ye, my loyal subject, will do as I command. Nay, I'll no' waste time arguin' with ye." He placed two fingers to her parted lips, instantly regretting it when the urge to replace them with his mouth overcame him. Bringing his hand to his thigh, he said, "Do as I ask, Evie. I canna fight and worry over ye and Aurora at the same time."

"You don't have to worry about me. I don't want you to," she said, a mulish expression on her beautiful face.

He wished he didn't, but it appeared his need to protect her was not about to vanish as easily as she could. "I need ye well rested so that when the time comes ye can go in and retrieve Uscias." After witnessing the magnitude of her power earlier, he'd known she was their best hope of freeing Uscias without incident.

"Oh, I . . . I thought you only brought me to protect Aurora."

"Aye, until we've created the opportunity fer ye to get

inside Magnus's palace. Once we have, Fallyn and her sisters will guard the bairn."

"Or Broderick and Gabriel could do so."

He rolled his eyes. "Doona push it."

She searched his face. "You really do trust me, don't you?"

At the bewildered look in her bonny eyes, his chest tightened. He brought his hand to her face, stroking her satiny smooth cheek with his thumb. "Aye. And anyone who doesna is a fool."

Her skin warmed beneath his fingers and a slight smile touched her lips. "Then the Fae realm is overrun with fools."

"Aye, 'tis." He let his hand drop before the urge to banish every cursed word the Fae ever said to her overrode his vow to keep his distance. He came to his feet. "I'll send Fallyn fer ye when 'tis time fer ye to play yer part."

"Be careful," she said in that husky voice of hers. A voice that made a man think of sin and seduction.

"Aye." He shook off the thought then turned to walk away. At the sudden heaviness in his legs and the uncomfortable weight bearing down on his shoulders and chest, he frowned. He took a step, heard the clink of metal against metal. Looking down, he opened his ankle-length cape—thick plates of hinged steel shielded his body. Bloody hell, she'd coated him in armor!

He pivoted on his heel, glaring down at her. "Evangeline." A helmet clunked onto his head. "What part of doona use magick on me did ye no' understand?"

"You said do not put a spell on you, and I didn't."

At the aggrieved look he shot her, her defiance faded. "I'm just trying to keep you safe. You can't fault me in that."

Seeing her disheartened expression, he cleared the frustration from his. If he was truthful, he'd admit her need to protect him, although annoying, was well-intentioned. And . . . and it . . . Nay, he was not about to acknowledge the emotion her solicitude garnered in him. "I appreciate your concern,

Evie, but I canna move in the armor. 'Tis more a hindrance than a help."

With a resigned sigh, she removed the metal plates.

"Ye doona need to worry aboot me. My blade and prowess on the battlefield more than make up fer my lack of magick." As he walked away from where she was sheltered amongst the boulders, he noted the air had cooled substantially and turned back to her. "Mayhap ye should add an extra layer of clothin'. Ye doona want to catch a chill."

Lachlan bore down on the warrior he faced, frustrated when for the second time the man vanished before he could touch him with his blade. The warrior reappeared, a broad grin splitting his face. Lachlan cursed. The last five men he'd fought had done the same. In the end, he'd bested them, but not without depleting his strength. If anyone had told him that one day he'd desire the magickal abilities of the Fae, he would've quickly disabused them of the notion. But at that moment, there was nothing he desired more.

"Ye're no' much of a warrior if ye have to depend on yer magick to fight me," Lachlan taunted.

"I'd heard rumors the mighty king of the Enchanted Isles was a half-blood, now I see it's true. If not for your sword, you'd be dead." With a scornful laugh, his opponent lunged.

"Bloody Faery," Lachlan spat out contemptuously. He'd show him just how little magick he required to take him down. His blade vibrated. Roaring his clan's battle cry, he fought with renewed vigor. Their swords clashed again and again and he knew he had to go in for the kill before the warrior once again used his magick to disappear.

Aware it took little more than a nick of his blade to steal their immortality, his enemy stayed well beyond the reach of his sword. Lachlan was surprised there were those willing to fight him considering the cost, but he imagined the thought of getting hold of his sword offset the danger and the odds. He had no choice but to drop his guard to lure the warrior closer. He did. As soon as his opponent struck, Lachlan shifted, then brought his blade up to slash the man's sword arm. Blood spurted from the deep gash, splattering over the snow-covered ground.

The warrior dropped to his knees, clutching his crimson-soaked arm to his chest. Raising his malevolent gaze to Lachlan, he growled, "Savor your victory, half-blood. Your wizard won't hold out much longer. Soon the Fae of the Far North will hold the secret of your mighty sword and we'll destroy you all." His eyes spit fury even as the death gurgle rattled in his throat. On the warrior's last breath, his body turned to ashes. The wind picked up, burying the bone-gray remains beneath the snow.

Glaring at Magnus's crystal palace in the distance, Lachlan battled his fear that Uscias faced certain death if they didn't reach him soon. Nay, he promised himself, they'd retrieve his mentor, and Magnus would rue the day he went up against Lachlan. He threw himself into the heart of the battle—heedless of his vulnerability, heedless of anything but the need to reach Uscias.

The cluster of boulders straddling the mountain's ledge hid Evangeline from the enemy's sight. But from where she lay atop the granite slab, she had a clear view of the battlefield, and her temper grew.

Hiding. She, the most powerful wizard of the Fae realm, was hiding because that fool of a highlander, who was fighting with a complete disregard for his own safety, demanded she do so. And since when did she heed another's advice or command when she knew better?

"Aurora." She waved the little girl to her side. "I must go to the king's aid. If I don't, I'm certain he shall be killed."

Aurora climbed up the rock to lie at Evangeline's side, peering down over the battlefield. "He doesn't look like he's in danger." Nose wrinkled, she glanced at Evangeline. "I don't think he'll be happy if you disobey him."

Evangeline waved a dismissive hand. "It matters not. I have vowed to protect him, and so I shall. You must promise me you'll remain here."

She felt a small pang of guilt at leaving the child on her own, but it couldn't be helped. Lachlan had no magick and the little seer did. She noticed the tremble in Aurora's bottom lip. Awkwardly patting the child's shoulder, Evangeline helped her down from the boulder then crouched beside her. "Don't worry. I'll leave Bowen and place you in a protective shield," she said, tucking the furs around Aurora. Rising to her feet, Evangeline wove her spell.

From within the filmy bubble, the little girl warbled, "What about Bowen?"

"He wouldn't like being confined. He might hurt you without meaning to do so. I promise, he'll be fine," she reassured her with a smile.

Confident in her decision, Evangeline flashed to Lachlan's side. Recalling how Fallyn and her sisters carried a sword into battle, she conjured one for herself. The weight of the weapon felt awkward in her hand and she conjured another, and then another. Giving up with a frustrated sigh, she adjusted her grip on the hilt then looked to Lachlan's stance for guidance.

Concentrating on his opponent, he'd yet to note her presence, but his enemy did. "So, you need a woman to fight your battles, half-blood? I can't say I'm surprised."

The instant Lachlan's gaze shot to her, Magnus's man took advantage of his inattention. The warrior's blade ripped through the fabric of Lachlan's tunic, slicing his sun-bronzed skin from shoulder to elbow. "I swear, if ye doona get me killed, Evangeline, ye'll rue yer decision to disobey me," he growled, parrying the man's next blow to regain control of the fight.

She reluctantly curled her fingers into her palm, knowing he'd be even angrier if she brought his opponent down using magick. The muscles rippled across his broad back as he fought with lethal grace. She had to admit he did indeed know how to use his sword. But seeing the blood staining the sleeve of his white tunic, she couldn't bring herself to leave, afraid he would soon weaken and require her assistance.

"Only a half-blood couldn't control his bitch. But rest assured, when I'm done with you, I'll control her," his opponent chortled, lunging at Lachlan. The warrior's laugh ended on a gasp. Lachlan's blade protruding from his belly, he turned to ashes before he hit the ground.

Lachlan, his chiseled profile as cold as the Far North, wiped the blood from his blade in the snow. His manner carefully controlled, he slowly turned to level her with a furious glare. She took a wary step back, her eyes darting from his bleeding arm to the hard set of his features. "I was just trying to help."

"Aye, and that worked out well, didna it? I was doin' fine until ye showed up." He prowled toward her. Slapping her blade with his, he almost knocked it from her hand. "Ye're no' even holdin' it properly. Ye'll get yerself killed. Ye're in more danger than me."

"No, I'm not, I'm pureblood. Don't you see that's—"

"I doona want yer *help*." With a disgusted shake of his head, he scanned the battlefield. Small pockets of warriors remained fighting and it appeared the battle was almost over. Victory would soon be theirs, Uscias's release secured.

At the thought her time to play her part had come, she said, "I shall go—" She stopped abruptly, the ground was trembling beneath her feet. In the distance she heard what sounded like the steady beat of a drum, hundreds of drums.

Lachlan jerked his gaze to where Magnus's palace had

stood earlier. The castle and its towers were now shrouded in a frosted mist. The vaporous cloud crept toward them and the rhythmic pounding grew louder. "Go, Evangeline, go back to Aurora!" he shouted as he ran to his steed.

"What is it? I don't . . ." Her mouth fell open as hulking, white beasts ripped through the curtain of fog.

Torn between doing as Lachlan asked and protecting him, she hesitated. Lachlan bellowed her name just as a polar bear lunged for her, taking her down before she had a chance to react. She landed on her back, hitting her head on the hard, snow-packed ground, trapped beneath hundreds of pounds of sinewy muscle. The beast's thick, white fur filled her mouth. She couldn't move, couldn't breathe. Pinpricks of light flashed before her eyes and panic overwhelmed her. Suddenly the weight lifted, the bear rolled off her. She dragged in harsh gulps of frosted air.

Lachlan knelt beside her, his worried gaze raking her from head to toe. He brought his palm to her cheek, searching her eyes. "Are ye all right?"

"Fine . . . I'm fine," she managed to say, trying to ignore the pain arcing through her as he helped her to her feet.

Behind him a beast rose on its hind legs. Standing at least twelve feet tall, it towered above him. "Lachlan," she cried out. The animal's powerful jaw opened. Its ear-splitting roar blew the hair from her face. Anchoring her to his side, Lachlan twisted then lunged, burying his blade in the bear's massive chest.

All along the battlefield the high-pitched shrieks of the horses rent the air as the white bears viciously attacked both animals and warriors. "Go now, Evangeline!" he yelled, shoving her behind him as another of the bears padded toward him, tossing its huge head. "Go to Aurora," he bellowed when she didn't move.

At his mention of the little seer, Evangeline's gaze shot to the mountain. Two warriors mounted on the great beasts clambered their way over rock and ice toward Aurora and Bowen. Shooting a bolt of magick at the lumbering beast approaching Lachlan, Evangeline took one last uncertain look at him before flashing to where she'd left Aurora in the protective bubble.

She wasn't there.

"Evangeline!"

She jerked her gaze in the direction of the child's cry. From behind a pile of rocks, Aurora sat astride Bowen, her face a frozen mask of terror as she watched the beasts come over the rocky ledge. Evangeline shot a bolt in their direction, then flashed to mount behind the frightened child. "Fly, Bowen, fly," she urged the steed.

"I'm sorry, Evangeline. Bowen was scared and I couldn't leave him on his own."

She tucked Aurora's trembling body against hers as the winged steed took to the sky. "It's all right. Everything's going to be all right," she murmured.

"Evangeline, look!" Aurora cried, pointing to the battle-field.

From the scattered snow-covered mounds surrounding Lachlan, it appeared he'd managed to kill several of the bears, but the one he now fought looked more like a monster than an animal. The beast swiped its massive clawed paw at his blade as though it were a child's toy while a second creature lumbered toward him. "Lachlan, behind you!" Evangeline's panicked scream ripped from her throat.

She sent a bolt at the bear closing in on him. It missed. Too far, she was too far away, but she couldn't risk leaving Aurora on her own or taking her into the battle. "Closer, a little closer," Evangeline urged Bowen.

Hovering a safe distance away, she shot another bolt. The thin arrow of light landed several inches from the second bear, doing little more than sending up a fine spray of snow to coat the hind legs the beast rose up on. Her heart pounded frantically against her ribs. There was something wrong. Again, she had to try again. Her magick couldn't fail her now. He couldn't fight both animals at the same time.

Your magick is depleted. You're wasting time. Your pride will get him killed.

"Help me, Aurora, add your magick to mine." With their hands joined, they shot a bolt at the bear approaching from behind Lachlan. Hitting the beast in the back, they brought it down. But the enraged animal wouldn't be stopped. It dragged itself across the snow toward Lachlan. Clamping down on his leg, it gave a furious shake of its head.

With a pained bellow, Lachlan twisted and slashed his blade through the bear's neck. Trying to free his leg from the dead animal's locked jaw, Lachlan turned enough that Evangeline could see the blood dripping from his face and arms.

Barely had she choked back a desperate cry when she saw the other bear about to take advantage of Lachlan's inability to defend himself. The animal batted at him as if he was a plaything.

"Again, Aurora! Again!"

They shot another bolt, so powerful the air crackled around them. It slammed into the bear's chest just as it charged Lachlan. Both man and beast crashed to the ground. The animal roared, revealing sharp, bloodied teeth. Lachlan raised his sword.

"Again!" Evangeline cried, praying she retained enough magick. Lachlan's sword came down on the animal at the same time as their heated stroke met its mark.

Terrified she didn't have enough power left to lift the beast off Lachlan, afraid the animal would smother him, she scanned the battlefield and spotted Gabriel pulling his blade from the bear he'd just killed. "Gabriel," she cried, pointing to where Lachlan lay crushed beneath the beast.

With a quick glance at Evangeline, then to where she pointed, Gabriel bellowed. "Retreat . . . retreat!"

Evangeline tried once again to throw the bear off Lachlan, but her limited power only managed to lift the animal a few inches in the air. "Aurora, get it off him." She could barely get the words past her emotion-clogged throat.

Before Aurora had a chance to do so, Gabriel had flashed to Lachlan's side, hurling the bear off his blood-soaked body. Gabriel lifted Lachlan carefully into his arms, then disappeared.

A violent tremor shuddered through Evangeline sitting frozen behind Aurora. She wrapped her arms around herself to try to contain the uncontrollable shaking that took hold of her.

"King Lachlan will be all right, won't he, Evangeline? He'll heal like we do."

"Yes . . . I'm certain . . . of course he will." But she wasn't certain. She wasn't certain of anything. From where they hovered above the battlefield, she'd seen the look of horror on Gabriel's face when he'd lifted Lachlan into his arms.

Beneath them the warriors who were not injured retrieved the bodies of those who were. They fled on their steeds or transported when no animal was available for them to ride. The white beasts rose on their hind legs and roared in triumph. The heat of her fury at what they'd done to Lachlan loosened her frozen limbs. No matter her diminished powers, the bears would pay.

She searched the ice-covered landscape for an opportunity to seek her revenge. Noting the frozen fjord the bears must cross to reach Magnus's palace, she drew on her magick and watched and waited while the beasts lumbered across the glacier. Tracing the body of water that snaked through the valley with her finger, she snapped her hands at the point the animals now crossed. A mournful groan vibrated through the air. A wide crack raced along the middle of the fjord. The bears roared as the ice floe heaved and tossed them into the frigid waters, smashing them against the rocks.

"To the mountain, Bowen." Her voice cracked from the strain of keeping her emotions in check. They followed the silent procession of horses and riders to the low plateau where their army would make camp. The wind whistled through the brooding ice-capped peaks. Beneath them the blood- and ash-covered snow swirled until there was no evidence of the battle that had taken place. Her cheeks stung and she wiped away the moisture that clung to her face. Although she could only remember crying once in her life, somewhere within her turbulent emotions she registered she did so now.

She didn't realize Bowen had landed on the rocky precipice until Aurora shakily dismounted from the horse. Evangeline flashed from the steed, turning to find Fallyn and her sisters watching her. All three bore signs of a hard-fought battle, but none were seriously injured. She worked the saliva to moisten her mouth. "How is he?"

"Not good. Gabriel doesn't—"

A fury unlike she'd ever felt before rose up inside her. "Don't!" She shoved her way past the women. "Where is he?" she demanded, searching the clusters of men who cared for the injured within the shelter of white tents.

"Broderick thought it best to get him out of the—"

"I didn't ask why, I asked where," Evangeline snapped.

"There, in the cave," Fallyn said, pointing to the carved-out opening.

Feeling as though she was about to be sick, Evangeline swallowed hard, clenching her teeth. She tried to keep the memories at bay, but her mind granted her no quarter, flooding her with images of Lachlan—kissing her, teasing her, touching her, infuriating her. She pressed her lips together so hard it hurt.

"Evangeline?" Fallyn placed a comforting hand on her shoulder, and Riana and Shayla stepped closer. Evangeline shook her head, holding a finger up to warn the sisters off. If she allowed them to comfort her, she would be unable to keep the choking emotions from overtaking her. Drawing in a calming breath, she strode to the entrance of the cave and ducked inside.

Upon her entry, Gabriel and Broderick looked up from where they knelt at Lachlan's side. A fire blazed in the hearth they'd conjured a few feet from where they'd laid him on a pallet of furs. More pelts covered him from the waist down. She wished they'd covered all of him. His skin, what little was not bandaged in white linens or badly bruised, had a bluish gray cast to it.

Struggling to keep her fear in check, she unsteadily sank to her knees. Tentatively, she touched his cheek, reeling at the chilled dampness. He looked as though he was a statue carved in marble—the statue of a beautiful, lifeless angel.

"Evangeline, if we don't act quickly, I fear we shall lose him."

She latched on to the small shred of hope Gabriel's words offered. "What? What can we do?"

"He needs blood."

"Yes, of course. I'll go to the Mortal realm. I'll get Aidan." Even as she made the offer, she realized the level of magick required to transport them was beyond her. She bowed her head, fighting tears of despair. How could her magick fail her when she needed it most?

"No, his injuries are too severe. He needs Fae blood. The blood of a Fae with very strong magick. He needs *your* blood, Evangeline."

Chapter 9

You're just like your mother. Evil is in your blood.

Morfessa's indictment echoed in her head as loudly as the hammering of her heart. "No! I can't. I can't do that to him."

Gabriel's startled gaze shot to hers.

"If you don't, the blame for his death lies at your feet," Broderick snarled, then stormed from the cave.

Broderick's accusation left her fighting for breath. They didn't know what they asked of her. Her chest felt so tight she struggled to get the words out. "He doesn't understand, Your Highness. Lachlan is not like us. He denied his Fae heritage until it was forced upon him. He hated that part of himself. I tell you, he will not thank us for this."

"I've come to know Lachlan over the last two years, Evangeline. He will understand," Gabriel gently assured her.

No, she wanted to yell at him, *he won't*. How could he? She stared at the shadows undulating across the cave's ceiling, blinking back the moisture in her eyes before facing Gabriel. "Perhaps he would accept your blood more readily. You are his friend."

"I would gladly do so, but other than Uscias, your magick is the most powerful I've ever seen. He needs you to do this."

"My magick is weakened." The admission left a bitter taste in her mouth.

"*You* are weakened, not your magick. You alone can heal him. I know you don't want him to die. Please, Evangeline, give him your blood."

Her throat ached from trying to contain her fear, her sorrow. She swallowed hard before answering, "No . . . no, I don't want him to die."

She didn't, and not only because of the heartbreak his death would cause his family. Lachlan had proven to her he could become the king the Fae needed. He was nothing like his father. She wanted to see him live up to the promise of his potential. And . . . and she wanted him to smile at her again. To tease her in his thick seductive brogue, to comfort her with his touch and warm her with his kiss.

Stroking his beard-roughened cheek with the back of her fingers, she realized then how much he'd come to mean to her. She choked back a hollow laugh. She could be nothing more to him than what she was. He was of royal blood. Destined to marry one of the princesses whose names she'd scratched on the parchment that littered her desk.

"I'll do it." She owed Lachlan that much. She'd failed to protect him. She only hoped by giving him her blood she did not condemn him to share her fate. No, not fate. Fear, she corrected, reminding herself that since the day she'd broken through the barrier there'd been no sign of the malevolent shadows weaving their way through her magick—no voice urging her to seek revenge.

"I'll leave you alone with him. Call if you need me." Gabriel placed a dagger in her hand. "If it eases your mind, although I'm not an expert in these matters, I don't think he will retain your magick for long."

Concerned with what her blood would do to Lachlan, she had given no thought to what sharing her blood would do to her. A depressing weight settled low in her belly, as heavy as the sense of powerlessness she'd felt earlier. Desperately she searched Lachlan's deathly pale countenance for some sign of recovery. Some sign they were wrong and he would heal on his own.

They weren't wrong; for every moment she wasted, his life slowly ebbed away. She clung to Gabriel's assurance, pushing aside her conflicting emotions. It was a small sacrifice to make. What were a few hours without her powers at full strength to ensure Lachlan lived?

"Evangeline." Gabriel drew her attention to where he now stood at the mouth of the cave. "He may fight you, you know, on account of Glastonbury." Their eyes met as the memory of his torture passed between them.

An icy chill emanated from Lachlan's long, well-made body. It was difficult to reconcile the man lying so still on the pallet with the one who'd fought with such effortless strength only a short time ago. Evangeline flicked her fingers to the hearth in the futile hope the blaze would somehow take the cold from his body, the pallor from his skin.

Her magick sputtered. Taking into consideration what Gabriel said, she thought perhaps not only her exhaustion played a part in her inability to draw on her magick. The fear and despair that had overtaken her couldn't have helped. Closing her eyes, she breathed deeply, letting the tension ease from her shoulders, and tried again. Relieved to see a weak stream of white light, she built up the fire, then added another blanket of furs to Lachlan.

Tugging up her sleeve, she drew the blade across her wrist, then held it over his mouth. His breath so faint it merely whispered across her skin, she fought back a sense of panic.

He couldn't die.

She wouldn't let him.

Stretching out beside him, she carefully slipped her arm beneath his head to cradle him in the crook of her arm. Droplets of crimson pooled on his blue-tinged mouth. He stirred, licking the blood staining his lips with a barely audible murmur of pleasure. Shifting beneath the furs, he winced.

She stroked a lock of hair from his forehead. "Stay still," she pleaded.

A grunt emitted from low in his throat. She searched his face, disappointed his sun-bronzed complexion had yet to return. His beautiful face was still as frighteningly pale as when she'd entered the cave.

"Take more," she begged, pressing her wrist to his chilled lips.

His tongue rasped the wound and he suckled weakly. A sliver of heat coiled low in her belly causing Evangeline to steel herself against a moan of pleasure. It was only because he accepted her blood, nothing more. But as he drank more deeply, the heat spiraled lower, belying her attempt to explain away her reaction.

"So sweet," he murmured, lapping hungrily at her wrist. Within the thick column of his neck his Adam's apple bobbed with each swallow. She raised her gaze to his face. His long, gold-tipped lashes fluttered, a hint of color tinting his skin and giddy relief bubbled up inside her at the sight.

He would live.

"More. I want more of ye." His hands grasped her wrist and forearm. Warm hands. Powerful hands. He arched under the coverings, moaning. "I need more of ye. Give me more."

Hungrily feasting on her wrist, he snaked an arm around her waist, holding her tight against him. He drank deeply, noisily, tugging her closer still, her breasts molded to his heated skin. It was all Evangeline could do to stop herself from rubbing against his hard, muscled thigh.

She was shocked by her response. He was at death's door and she wanted to . . . She wanted him to . . . No. *She* didn't. It had to be the blood, sharing blood in this manner must . . . well, it must . . . For Fae sakes, she didn't know what it must do, but it was doing something.

He rolled toward her with a wince. "Aye," he growled, rubbing his rock-hard erection to where she throbbed, moisture pooling between her thighs. She burned with lustful fever, growing more light-headed and dizzy by the moment. Through the thick haze of desire she recognized the signs.

He was taking too much of her blood.

She had to stop him.

A panicked cry escaped her. "Please, Lachlan, please, you must stop."

Lachlan's eyes flew open as Evangeline's desperate plea penetrated his lust-addled brain, her glazed violet eyes wide in her pale face. He tried to speak. Her wrist was pressed to his lips. Like a vise, his hand held it in place.

He flung her hand from him. "Sweet Christ, what have I done?" As he twisted away from her to roll onto his back, a searing spasm stole his breath away.

"No, you didn't do anything. Stay still," she said in a reedy, thin voice.

The gnawing ache eased as he returned to his side. Without the pain dulling his senses, he became aware of his hand on her rounded behind, of her soft, full breasts molded to his chest. His throbbing cock pressed to her belly.

He licked his parched lips in an attempt to offer an apology, some form of explanation, and froze at the coppery taste. Blood. His gaze shot to hers. He brought his hand to her face. "Tell me. Tell me what I have done." His belly lurched at the only explanation he could think of. He'd done to her what had been done to him.

The fog lifted from his brain. He remembered being attacked by the two white beasts—badly wounded, certain of his death. In his pain-filled stupor had he relived his nightmare at Glastonbury, dragging Evangeline into it with him?

Covering his hand with hers, she raised her unwavering

gaze to his. "You did nothing wrong. I'm sorry, Lachlan. I didn't have a choice. You would've died."

She winced. He frowned down at his hand. He'd barely firmed his grip. How could that almost imperceptible tightening hurt her? He'd been so relieved to hear her banish his fear that he'd taken her blood, only now did he begin to process what she said. "How, Evangeline? How did ye save me?"

She glanced at her hand, worrying her bottom lip between her teeth. He lifted his palm from her face, sliding his fingers to her wrist, turning it to the light. Blood dried on the mottled skin surrounding the deep slash slicing her wrist. He lifted his horrified gaze to hers. "Ye gave me yer blood?"

"We didn't know what else to do. I . . . we couldn't let you die."

At the thought he put her through even a fraction of what he'd endured in the dungeons, he said, "It would've been better if ye had."

She lowered her gaze from his, but not before he saw the shimmer of tears in her eyes. "I'm truly sorry. Gabriel said you'd understand. Because of my magick, they thought you'd recover faster if it was my blood you were given." Her body trembled as she tried to pull herself upright. Swaying with the effort, her pallor intensified.

Lachlan reached for her, wrapping his hand around her upper arm. She winced. "Why do ye keep doin' that? Are ye hurt?"

She rubbed her arms when he released her. "You're strong. My magick has made you stronger."

He prided himself on his strength. To think he'd possess even more didn't displease him, but the thought of what it had cost Evangeline did. "Lie down. Ye're as weak as a kitten." His mouth quirked when she cast him a perturbed look, relieved to see some small sign of her spirit.

Once she'd settled in beside him, he carefully placed his

fingers beneath her chin, gently forcing her gaze to his. "Be honest with me, did I hurt ye?"

"No."

"Did I frighten ye?"

A faint tinge of pink colored her cheeks. "No. I know you are worried it was my blood you were forced to accept, but they didn't give me a choice."

"Are ye sayin' ye didna wish to give me yer blood? That—"

"No, I just thought you would've preferred Gabriel or Broderick's to mine, considering my . . ."

Was she daft? When he thought of his reaction to her blood at the same time he thought of Broderick and Gabriel giving him theirs, he shuddered. He'd been consumed with lust for her. If he had to accept anyone's blood, it would be hers. Why would she think otherwise? Remembering her reaction when he said she should've let him die, he narrowed his gaze on her, certain something more was at play.

"Considerin' yer what?"

"My blood is tainted."

Something inside him stilled when he realized she thought he would have preferred death to being given *her* blood. He had a fairly good idea what her answer to his next question would be. With the tips of his fingers, he stroked her cheek. "How is yer blood tainted, Evie?"

"I carry my mother's blood."

"Ye're no' evil. Overly confident, opinionated, and cranky." He ticked off his fingers, refraining from adding verra bonny and sweet. *So verra sweet*, he thought, recalling the taste of her. "I'm sure I'm forgetttin' somethin', but if ye'll give me a moment 'twill come to me."

The beginnings of a small smile wavered on her lips. "I'm serious."

"Aye, so am I. Ye're no' evil, and doona ever let anyone tell ye ye are. And so we're clear on this, I ken ye had no choice but to give me yer blood just as ye must ken if I wasna dyin' 'tis the last thing I would want. But since 'twas necessary, ye must also ken there's no one else's blood I'd want but yers."

"Why?" she asked in a confused tone.

"First off, ye have more magick in yer baby finger than all the Fae put together," he repeated her own words back to her. "And second, considerin' the state I awoke in, I'd rather be suckin' on yer wrist than on Broderick's, Gabriel's, or the three witches'."

Her brow furrowed. "Three witches?"

"Aye, Fallyn, Shayla, and Riana."

She pursed her lips. "Is life just one big jest to you?"

Oh, no, he wasn't going to let her start poking around in his head. "Ye're too serious, Evie. Ye've got to start enjoyin' life fer a change."

"I know what you're attempting to do. I should, since I've seen you apply the strategy often."

"I doona ken what ye're talkin' aboot." He reached for her hand, stroking the delicate skin at the edges of her wound. He lifted her wrist to his lips, pressing a kiss to the bruised and swollen skin. She gave a startled jerk. "Does it hurt, Evie?" he murmured, gently sliding his lips back and forth over her abraded flesh.

"No . . . it's . . . it's much better."

The delectable scent of her, the faint whiff of her drying blood intoxicated him, and he swirled his tongue along the raised welt as the heat swirled higher inside him. Sweet Christ, he burned for her.

"I . . . I have to check on Aurora," she said. Pulling her hand from his, she struggled to her feet then stumbled head-long from the cave.

Lachlan groaned, and it had naught to do with the pain from his injuries. He'd only meant to distract her with his teasing, but instead, all he'd served to do was make himself more aware of the feelings she'd aroused in him.

A fine time to realize the jest was on him.

Chapter 10

Lachlan MacLeod wielded magick more powerful than any Evangeline had ever faced. He'd turned her into an unthinking, quivering mass of desire with his touch. But it wasn't the desire he'd ignited in her body but the desire he'd ignited in her heart that terrified her. He'd made her want things she had no business wanting. Her limbs weak and trembling, she leaned against the frozen wall of the mountain for support, pressing snow-coated hands to her overheated cheeks.

The crunch of snow heralded someone's approach. "What's wrong? Is he . . . is he dead?" Fallyn asked, clutching Evangeline's arm.

"No." *Far from it*, she thought with an aggrieved glance at the cave.

"But will he survive?"

"He is no longer in any danger." And nor would Evangeline be if she stayed far from the cave and the master seducer within. Oh, yes, he was a master seducer all right. No woman was safe from him, least of all her.

He knew the words to touch a heart bereft of kindness and compassion. He'd had many years of practice. He'd probably been doing so since he'd been able to utter his first words. "Perhaps you can ask Gabriel and Broderick to look in on him while I see to Aurora."

"I've been keeping an eye on her. I think she was most distressed by the king's injuries. She seems somewhat subdued." Fallyn pointed beyond the men hunched over the campfires. "Just follow the path. She's about a hundred yards from where the last of the tents have been pitched."

Evangeline nodded. A brisk wind buffeted her against the rock. No longer overheated, she shivered, but there was no way she would return for the cape she'd left in the cave. She flicked her finger to conjure another. Nothing. Not a low-level heat, not a faint spark. Nothing but a tortured sense of loss flared to life inside her.

Fallyn studied her. "What's the matter?"

"I'm tired, and . . . perhaps I depleted my . . . I'll be fine." She swallowed the admission, seeking refuge in the warmth of the long white fur cape Fallyn cloaked her in, hoping it would somehow ease the cold weight of her despair.

"How much blood did you give him?"

When she didn't answer, Fallyn grimaced. "Too much, I see. No wonder your magick is weakened. You should be resting. Why don't you let me get Aurora for you?"

Desperate for reassurance, she chose to believe Fallyn was right. She had to be. It was only natural her magick would be depleted. Some of the tension eased from her shoulders. "I think it would be best if I speak with her." After all, it was Evangeline's fault Aurora had witnessed the attack on her king.

"When you have retrieved her, come back and I'll prepare a meal to help replenish your blood." Fallyn tipped her chin to a larger opening cut out of the bedrock several feet from where they now stood. "You'd best hurry," Fallyn advised, lifting her gaze to the turbulent sky. "It appears we're to have another snowstorm."

Weaving her way past the white tents dotting the mountainside, Evangeline hesitated before striding past a cluster of warriors as their conversation reached her ears.

"I hear she gave him her blood," said one of the men who stood with his back to her. His companions tried to warn him of her presence with waggling brows, but he paid them no mind. "I'd rather fade than have her cursed blood in me." The man shuddered dramatically.

His companions lowered their eyes as she walked past them with her head held high. Lachlan's acceptance of her and her blood took some of the sting from the warrior's censure. Whatever small hurt remained, she cast aside to pick her way carefully down the narrow path to where the fur-wrapped child lay on the frozen pool at the base of the ice-encased waterfall.

"Aurora, come . . . Oh," she gasped. Evangeline's foot slid out from under her, sending her flying down the small incline on her back. She scraped the side of her face on the rocks protruding from the snow, then landed with a hard thud on her bottom to spin like a top before coming to a halt inches from the little seer.

Groaning, a hand pressed to her stinging cheek, she frowned when Aurora uttered not a word at her inauspicious arrival. Hands cupped to her face, the little girl peered at something beneath the ice. A chill that had nothing to do with the cold skittered along Evangeline's spine. "Aurora," she said, cautiously bracing herself.

Aurora raised her gaze. Evangeline released a relieved breath that the child's eyes retained their natural color. Her relief was replaced by guilt that she'd been the one responsible for the sorrow shadowing those vivid blue eyes. She sought to reassure her. "King Lachlan's going to be—"

Aurora shook her head. "No. It's Iain."

"Iain?" Evangeline's chest tightened, hoping against hope it wasn't who she thought it was.

"The king's cousin, Iain MacLeod. His ship foundered then broke apart somewhere in the Mortal realm beneath us. I saw him clinging to the debris. He was all alone."

Trying to keep the images Aurora's words conjured at bay, she stretched out beside the little girl. Using her cape to rub the light film of snow from the ice, Evangeline peered into its frozen depths. "I don't see anything."

"I can't see him anymore either. I keep trying, but I can't." Aurora latched on to Evangeline's hand. "Please, we must go to him. He's badly injured. I don't think he will—"

"Don't. Don't say that!" Evangeline cried, her heart aching at the thought of the handsome highlander. She'd met Iain a number of times at the MacLeods' family gatherings and had a soft spot for the charming seafarer. He'd often come to her defense when Lachlan was being his typical arrogant self and tormenting her at the occasions.

"But I can't help it. That's what I saw."

No, there had to be some mistake. Iain had recently lost his wife; perhaps somehow Aurora had tapped into his pain. "Maybe you have seen his wife's death. She recently—"

"No. She watches over him, she's an angel now, but she can't help him. We have to, Evangeline. We must go to his aid."

How could they go to his aid when they'd yet to rescue Uscias? She rubbed her temples, desperate for some way to help Iain without putting Uscias's rescue at risk. She could take Aurora with her to look for him, but the seas beneath them were vast. It could take days, and Lachlan might have need of her. And in her heart, Evangeline knew Uscias didn't have days. No, she couldn't be the one to go, but what of Fallyn and her sisters, or another group of warriors? The carnage she'd witnessed on the battlefield came back to haunt her—the carnage and the great white beasts. They were outnumbered. Her belly churned at the realization there was no one to spare. She reminded herself that there was a distinct possibility Aurora had misinterpreted her vision. She'd never had visions without being in a trance. Evangeline desperately clung to the hope the child was simply distraught after witnessing the attack on Lachlan.

"We can't help him, Aurora." She wouldn't hurt the child's feelings by saying she didn't believe her. "If I thought we could save both Iain and Uscias I would, but we can't."

"Bu . . . but he's hurt and all by himself." A tear slid down Aurora's wind-kissed cheeks. "I heard him crying out. He called for his wife."

Tortured by an image of Iain injured, calling for Glenna, Evangeline pressed a hand to her mouth, afraid she'd be ill. Even if Aurora had seen Iain, they couldn't save him—the Faes' safety depended on retrieving Uscias. No matter how much it pained her, she could not let anyone, especially Lachlan, learn what Aurora had told her. Knowing she was possibly sacrificing Iain made it one of the most heartrending decisions she ever had to make. But there was no other option available to her. "We must pray, then, that his wife will save him."

"But . . . but I think it was her who gave me the vision."

"Oh, please, Aurora, don't make this any more difficult than it already is." Raising her eyes to the heavens, Evangeline prayed the child was wrong. But she doubted the angels would listen to her pleas. They never had before. Snow pelted her upturned face and she reached for the little girl. "Come. We must seek shelter."

With Aurora's hand in hers, Evangeline sought a less treacherous path to the encampment. She refused to ask the child to transport them to the caves. Aurora had witnessed her diminished powers once today, and Evangeline couldn't stand for her to see her helpless again.

As they drew closer to the tents, she pulled Aurora aside. "You must make me a promise." She waited until she held the child's attention. "No one must know what you've seen today, especially King Lachlan. It must remain our secret."

"But—"

Her conscience balked at what she was about to say, but it couldn't be helped. Aware of Aurora's adoration of her king, she had no choice but to use it to ensure the child's silence. Lachlan must never learn of Aurora's vision. In her own way, Evangeline was protecting him from having to make a horrible choice, to save his cousin or to save Uscias.

"King Lachlan is only just beginning to recover from his injuries. To hear such news would set him back. You don't wish that to happen, do you?"

"No. I would never cause him pain. I won't tell him, I promise."

"No one must know."

"No one."

The plaintive cry of the wind captured the little girl's solemn promise, the words echoing through the deep caverns. Together they battled the blinding snow to stagger toward the opening in the bedrock Fallyn had pointed out earlier. Evangeline's gaze went to the mouth of the cave that housed Lachlan, the flames dancing within on a gust of wind. A part of her wanted to go to him and tell him of Aurora's vision, but it was hopeless. Even if it was true, they would never find Iain in time.

For the greater good.

She took comfort in the mantra's truth. What was the sacrifice of one life when so many were at stake?

The three sisters looked up as Evangeline entered the cavern with Aurora. The women had made themselves comfortable in a cave twice the size of Lachlan's. They sat on a long red velvet settee, balancing gold-rimmed plates piled high with food on their knees. Noting the floor was covered in furs and overstuffed pillows, Evangeline said, "I see you're lacking none of the creature comforts."

"Just because we're warriors doesn't mean we have to live like the half-wits. I don't know who they think to impress by surviving the elements."

She understood Fallyn's sentiments. It was like the Fae

men needed to test their endurance. As though they competed with the Mortal warriors they so often derided, but who Evangeline thought they grudgingly admired.

Fallyn flicked her wrist and another settee appeared. Two plates piled high with food appeared on top of the crimson velvet. Spying the slab of uncooked beef, obviously meant for her, Evangeline wrinkled her nose.

"Don't turn up your nose. You need the meat to replenish your blood. Sit and eat." Fallyn motioned them over to the settee with her gold-tined fork.

Evangeline tentatively nudged Aurora, who stood staring out into the blizzard, and prayed the child kept her promise. "Aurora." She tipped her chin toward their dinner, relieved when the little girl walked over to the settee, sat down, and took up her plate without a word.

Shayla gasped. "Evangeline, what did you do?"

Her breath caught. "What are you talking—"

"The side of your face, it is scraped and bruised."

"Oh, that." She released the breath she'd been holding. "I slipped on the ice."

The three sisters sat tight-lipped, staring beyond her. Evangeline glanced over her shoulder to see Gabriel and Broderick enter the cave, shaking snow from their cloaks. "I hope you ladies don't mind sharing your quarters for the night. There's no room left for us to set up our tents," Gabriel said as the two men made themselves comfortable beside the blazing hearth.

Absently stabbing the meat on her plate, Evangeline said, "I thought you would be staying with Lachlan."

Gabriel frowned. "No. Although he seems much improved, he may require more of your blood, Evangeline. It is you who should be with him in case he has a setback."

"As he means to lead the charge against Magnus at first light, I suspect there is no question he will require more of your blood," Broderick said around a mouthful of chicken, waving the leg at her.

She shoved a piece of meat into her mouth before she said something she'd regret. How could she refuse without drawing attention to her apprehension at returning to the cave?

"The two of you have made yourselves overly comfortable, considering we've yet to agree to your request," Fallyn informed the men in an imperious tone.

Broderick licked his fingers, arching a black brow. "Gabriel was just being polite. You cannot deny hospitality to your betters."

"Broderick," Gabriel said in an exasperated sigh.

A shard of rock broke free from the ceiling to land on the Welsh king's head. Gingerly rubbing the spot, Broderick scowled at Fallyn, who merely shrugged. "It happens all the time. Perhaps you should reconsider your decision to remain with us."

While Broderick and Fallyn glared at one another, Gabriel angled his head to regard Evangeline. "Do you not think it best for you to return to Lachlan? I had assumed you would be with him, or we wouldn't have left."

Considering the probing look in Gabriel's eyes, Evangeline couldn't think of anything to say without revealing her true reasons for not returning to the cave. Forcing a smile, she stood and offered a hand to Aurora. "Come. You can bring your dinner with you." At least with Aurora's presence she wouldn't have to worry she'd fall prey to Lachlan's practiced seduction.

"Oh, no, she's staying with us," Fallyn said, leaping from the settee to take hold of the child's other hand, shooting a triumphant look in Broderick's direction.

"No." Evangeline tugged Aurora back to her side. "She's coming with me." She wasn't about to let Fallyn steal away her chaperone. Fallyn might think she needed more incentive to keep Broderick at bay. But it wasn't fair; she had her sisters and Evangeline had no one.

"No, she's not." With a firm jerk, Fallyn pulled Aurora closer to her.

The little girl looked helplessly from Evangeline to Fallyn.

Scowling at Fallyn, Evangeline tugged harder. "I said, she's coming with me."

"Here, Aurora, look what I have for you." With a victorious smirk, Fallyn conjured a white ball of fur. The little girl tugged her hand free from Evangeline's with a delighted squeal. A dog! Fallyn had conjured a dog just like the one Aurora played with in the Mortal realm. Considering the state of her magick, Evangeline would be lucky if she could conjure a furball. She glared at her friend—ex-friend—and stormed from the cave.

Lachlan raised his gaze from the piece of steel he twisted in his hands to Evangeline, who ducked into the cave, an angry flash in her violet eyes, a contemptuous sneer on her lips. Muttering something about Fallyn under her breath, she closed the wooden door Broderick had affixed to the mouth of the cave before they had left. The two men hadn't wanted to leave him, but he'd insisted they do so. He didn't want them wasting what little time Broderick had left to woo Fallyn.

Evangeline shook the snow from her tousled mane as she stomped to the hearth. He grinned at her familiar demeanor. Now this was the Evangeline he was comfortable dealing with—unlike the one who'd lain vulnerable in his arms with the shimmer of tears in her luminous eyes.

"Who are ye fashed with now?"

Tossing her cape to the floor, she turned toward him.

"What the bloody hell happened to ye?" The muscles in his belly knotted at the sight of her bruised and swollen face.

"I fell," she grumbled, wincing as she lowered herself to her cape.

"Did ye hurt anythin' besides yer face?" Considering the look she shot him and the manner in which she'd lowered herself to the ground, he gathered her backside had taken the brunt of her fall. His tension eased at the knowledge she'd not been badly hurt and the injuries she'd sustained were the result of an accident. "Lucky ye have extra paddin'."

With an affronted gasp, she said, "I cannot believe you said such a thing to me."

He chuckled. "I meant the thickness of yer cape." He dropped his gaze to concentrate on the piece of steel in his hands. If he didn't, he'd be tempted to think on the delectable feel of her firm, rounded behind filling his hands.

"Oh. What are you doing?"

"Ye mean this?" He held up the piece of metal he'd twisted into a knot. She nodded. "I've been testin' my strength. Ye were right. I canna believe how much stronger I am." His smile of wonder faded at her disgruntled expression. "What's the matter? I thought you'd be pleased with the speed of my recovery. At this rate I can lead the charge against Magnus on the morrow. And this time, we'll no' fail."

"I am pleased."

"Ye coulda fooled me." He noted the tremor that shook her slender frame, relieved her arms were crossed over her chest. "Ye're cold." He'd been too preoccupied to notice the fire had burned down to glowing embers. Now that he thought about it, he was surprised he didn't feel the chill. "Why doona ye relight the fire?"

She nibbled on her bottom lip then lifted her hand to flick her finger at the hearth. Nothing happened. "It's no use," she said wearily.

Slowly, he lowered the metal to the ground beside him. "'Tis because I took too much of yer blood, isna it?"

"I'd already depleted much of my mag—strength before I gave you my blood. I should be fine by morning." From the troubled look in her eyes, he didn't think she believed that and felt a twinge of guilt at the pleasure he'd been taking in his increased strength.

"Ye need yer rest. Come here." He lifted the covers, shoving aside the thought he was a fool to let her close to him. He offered her comfort, nothing more. In all good conscience, how could he not? He was the reason for her suffering, and it was not as though he couldn't control himself. It was Evangeline, for Chrissakes, his sister-by-marriage's best friend, the woman who'd been nothin' but a pain in his arse for as long as he'd known her.

She hesitated as though she, too, questioned his intentions.

"I offer ye warmth and a place to lay yer head, nothin' more. I was no' myself earlier. 'Twas only on account of sharin' yer blood that I . . ." He clamped his mouth shut, not about to tell her how much he'd wanted her. How she'd inflamed a desire in him more fierce than any he'd ever known. Nay, he spoke the truth, 'twas her magick that had fired his blood.

Obviously her need for warmth won out. Avoiding his gaze, she came to his side. "Sweet Christ, ye're freezin'," he said when she joined him beneath the covers. He drew the furs to her chin then wrapped his arms around her.

She made a halfhearted attempt to wriggle from his hold.

"Doona be daft, ye're shakin' like a leaf in a windstorm." He rested his chin on top of her silky hair, trying to ignore the voluptuous curves pressed against him. "So, how do ye think Broderick's farin' in his attempt to woo Fallyn?" he asked, hoping to distract himself. If he didn't, he was afraid he'd soon give her reason to question his intentions.

She tipped her head back, brow arched. "You can't mean to tell me he actually thinks he's courting her?"

He scowled at the wry glint of amusement in her eyes. "What's he done now?"

"He told her she had to cede to his request for shelter as he was a king. She made a rock fall on his head."

"'Twas no' the smartest thing fer him to say, but did she agree?"

"Yes, although she's not pleased, hence the falling rock, but why are you so interested in what goes on between them?" He raised his brows and held her gaze. She rolled her eyes. "I should have known. Well, I don't mean to disappoint you, but I doubt very much Broderick will win her back. You'll just have to accept the fact you're stuck with them. If you'd just agree to their proposal you'd save yourself a lot of aggravation. What exactly is your objection to them starting a school?"

"The men havena entirely forgotten or forgiven what happened when Morgana ruled the Enchanted Isles. A school to train women to be warriors would not be well received. How could it be when the men had been treated little better than slaves by the lot of them? I have enough to deal with without addin' . . ." He frowned at her stunned expression. "What?"

"I . . . well I thought you objected to the school simply because you didn't believe women could or should be warriors."

"I told ye, ye didna ken me."

"I'm beginning to see that perhaps I misjudged you."

He laughed. "Doona look so disappointed. Ye're no' entirely wrong. I doona think women should be warriors. It just wasna the reason I objected to the school."

With a derisive snort, she shook her head. "Fallyn and her sister's fighting skills are superior to some of your own warriors'. So are Syrena's. Perhaps you have forgotten she, too, was once a warrior."

"She still is." He grinned before adding, "And I doona dispute their prowess on the battlefield, Evangeline. I just don't believe they belong there." He didn't think she'd appreciate it if he told her where he thought they did belong.

"You are . . ."

He placed a finger on her lips before he gave in to the urge to quiet her with a kiss. For all his good intentions, he was too aware of her body molded to his. And the direction their conversation was headed didn't help matters. "Doona waste yer breath. I ken well enough what ye think of me. Why doona ye get some sleep now? We'll have need of yer magick on the morrow."

A flicker of emotion shadowed her eyes.

"Doona worry, Evie, we'll get Uscias back."

"We have to. Nothing matters more than stopping Magnus from gaining access to weapons with the power your sword contains. Nothing!" Her gaze fell to his blade lying within easy reach at his side.

He frowned. Not sure he liked what she appeared to be saying. "Evangeline, I doona give a bloody hell aboot Magnus. All I care aboot is makin' sure Uscias is safe and unharmed. If he has to reveal his secrets to keep him that way, then so be it. We'll deal with the consequences later."

She pulled away from him, then twisted to skewer him with a furious glare. "No! No matter what the cost, we have to prevent Magnus from arming his warriors with weapons such as yours. He will be unstoppable. He will destroy the Fae of the Enchanted Isles. You have to understand!" She broke off on a choked cry.

Shocked as much by what she said as the desperation in her voice, Lachlan stared at her.

"What has gotten into ye? Ye canna truly mean to say ye would sacrifice Uscias to stop Magnus?" He didn't even try to keep the contempt from his voice.

Her shoulders sagged as she lifted sorrow-filled eyes to his. "I will do whatever I must to protect the Fae of the Enchanted Isles. Whatever it takes, I will do."

"I thought I kent ye, Evangeline. But I see I was mistaken."

Chapter 11

Evangeline wriggled beneath the blankets, trying to absorb warmth from the hard wall emitting heat at her back.

"Careful, lass," the heat-producing mountain of muscle murmured close to her ear in his thick brogue, his big hand splayed across her belly. Her eyes flew open and her sleep-befuddled brain cleared in an instant. She jolted upright, hitting her head on his chin.

"Bloody hell, would ye quit doin' that. I swear ye broke my jaw this time," Lachlan grumbled.

"Sorry." Her apology came out on a crystallized cloud. No longer sheltered by his embrace, she shivered in the frigid air of the dank cave.

"I'll forgive ye if ye light the fire and give me back the covers."

Without thinking, she flicked her fingers at the hearth. It wasn't until the flames danced on the walls that she realized what she'd done. She pressed her hands to her chest, practically giddy with relief. Her magick had returned. Not that she'd doubted it would, not really, but it was not an experience she wished to repeat. She didn't know how Lachlan stood it, being dependent on others, feeling helpless and out of control. There could be nothing worse.

"If ye doona mind, Evangeline, 'tis still freezin' in here."
He yanked the covers back.

She conjured more blankets and dumped them on his head.

"I see ye're back to yer charmin' self this mornin'."

Last eve he'd thought her overwrought and exhausted—
distressed over her lack of magick. He'd said as much before
she'd drifted off into a restless sleep. He was wrong. Her distress had been caused by her inability to make him understand that there was no price too high to pay to stop Magnus.
It was the futility of her attempt to convince him that had
frustrated and disheartened her. She supposed the knowledge
she'd possibly sacrificed his cousin for the cause added to the
turbulence of her emotions. He'd never forgive her if he learned
about Iain.

The thought didn't trouble her as much as it had the night
before. Her magick had returned, and with it her confidence
and conviction. She believed without a doubt she was right, although that didn't assuage her conscience completely. Lachlan appeared to be well healed with no chance of a setback,
and she wondered if she should inform him about Aurora's
vision. She quickly pushed the thought from her head. He'd
have the unenviable task of choosing between saving his
cousin or his mentor. No, it was up to her to relieve him of the
burden. Besides, she was not certain what Aurora had seen.

He nudged her with his knee. "If ye're fallin' asleep, ye
might wish to do so lyin' down."

She glanced over her shoulder. With his arm crooked
behind his head, he watched her. The firelight bronzed the
sculpted muscles of his bare chest, the dark highlights of his
golden hair. She tore her gaze from his masculine beauty,
swallowing hard before answering, "I'm wide awake and I'm
quite certain it's morning." With a low murmur, she removed
the door. At least a foot of snow tumbled across the threshold;
a swath of dull gray sky barely visible through the whirling
white torrent beyond. The wind howled through the opening.

"Fer Chrissakes, put it back."

With a disappointed wave of her hand, she set the door in place. "We'll have to wait out the storm."

He sat up beside her, scrubbing his hands over his face. "No' necessarily. It may be just what we need to give us the advantage. They'll be expectin' us to stay holed up here until it abates."

His broad shoulder brushed against her, and her gaze drifted to the dressings covering his wounds. Despite the obvious strength of his battle-hardened body, she couldn't completely shut out the memory of how close he'd been to death. "Are you certain your wounds are sufficiently healed?"

He cocked his head as though surprised by her question. "Aye."

Afraid his desire to lead would override his common sense and put him at risk, she quirked a finger. "Let me see."

He shrugged and presented his back. She moved behind him then carefully removed the linen bindings. Tentatively, she traced the tips of her fingers over the raised pink welts crisscrossing his broad back. The corded muscles flexed beneath his bronzed skin, and the urge to press her lips to his healing wounds overwhelmed her. She leaned closer, inhaling his warm, masculine scent.

"Yer fingers are cold." His husky voice jolted her heat-fuzzed brain.

Hastily, she withdrew her hand. "You've healed remarkably well." Her voice revealed nothing of her flustered state. The desire that had flared to life inside her.

"Aye, thanks to yer blood."

She twisted her hands in the blankets to keep from touching him. "Gabriel and Broderick thought you might require more. If you think you . . . well, hmm . . ." What was wrong with her? She swallowed a pitiful groan. She knew exactly what was wrong with her. She craved the feel of his body enveloping hers, the feel of his mouth on her skin, her lips.

"Are ye offerin' me yer blood, Evie?" He reached for her hand. Holding her gaze, he traced the tips of his calloused fingers over the sensitive skin of her palm in the same manner she'd smoothed hers over his back. The look in his amber eyes caused the muscles low in her belly to clench and her yes came out on a breathy sigh.

She closed her eyes, certain he knew how he made her feel. Somehow she managed to say, in a more controlled voice, "If you think it will aid you in defeating Magnus." She had no choice but to make the offer. Wasn't it her duty to do everything she could to guarantee their mission's success? Her arm felt heavy as she lifted it toward him.

"Oh, aye, I'll take what ye offer," he murmured. Lying back amongst the pillows, he gave her arm a tug. "Come here, Evie."

"But I thought . . ."

He pulled her into his arms. His heated whisper warmed her cheek. "Ye think too much."

If that were true, what was she doing snuggled up against a man she'd vowed to keep her distance from? Worse still, she'd only just regained her magick and now she risked him going too far, taking too much and leaving her powerless once again. She placed her palm on his chest to lever herself up.

As though he read her thoughts, he covered her hand with his. "Nay, ye doona have to worry. I willna take too much. Just a sip, a small taste of ye is all I need." He brought his hand to her face, trailing his fingers along the curve of her cheek, along her jaw, and down her neck. Replacing his fingers with his lips, he murmured into her neck, "Here."

"Yes," she breathed. Unable to resist him, she smoothed her hands over his shoulders and down his arms. Her lust-addled brain cleared enough that she managed to conjure a dagger. She pressed it into his hand.

He stiffened. Rising up on his elbow, he searched her face, then bowed his head with a groan. "Nay, I canna do it."

She took the blade from his clenched fist. He released a shuddered breath then touched his forehead to hers, reaching for her hand. "Nay, I willna let ye do it."

She managed to make a small nick in the hollow of her neck before he wrenched the blade from her. He jerked his shocked gaze to her throat. "Christ, I told ye, I canna do this."

Ridding herself of the dagger, she placed her palm on his beard-shadowed jaw. "Yes, you can. I want you to." *I need you to.*

"Ye shouldna have done it, Evie." His warm breath caressed her face as he touched his lips to her eyes, to her cheek, to the corner of her mouth then feathered kisses along her jaw and down her neck. As he swirled his tongue over the cut, her moan of pleasure joined his. Spearing his fingers through her hair, he drew her head back, exposing her neck to his hot, hungry mouth. He suckled deeply, sending a heated jolt of desire so deep inside her it was as though his lips touched every part of her—her breasts, her belly, her womanhood. She writhed beneath him, her nails digging into his broad shoulders.

"Ye're so sweet, so beautiful. I canna get enough of ye."

Through the erotic haze that blanketed her senses, a niggling of fear that he'd forgotten his promise managed to slip through.

"Nay." With one last lingering sip, he lifted his heavy-lidded gaze to hers. "I would never hurt ye, Evie," he said, then took her mouth in a mind-numbing kiss.

She tunneled her fingers through the thick waves of his hair, holding him in place. Parting her lips on a moan, she allowed his practiced tongue entry. His lips were firm, demanding, possessive. She squirmed, trying to get closer—her body on fire for him. He skimmed his hand along the curve of her waist to her hip, then cupped her behind to mold her to him. Moving in rhythm with his tongue, he rocked his straining erection where she was hot and needy . . . and it . . . terrified her.

Not like his father had once done. No, this had nothing to do with Arwan. Lachlan was nothing like his father. This was about her. She was nearly frantic with desire for him and it scared her half to death. He swallowed her desperate whimper, rolling to his side with her in his arms. His kiss gentled and he drew his hand from her behind to rub her back, his fingers kneading the tension from her neck.

From beyond the thick walls of the cave, men called out to one another, penetrating the rough rasp of their breathing. Lachlan broke their kiss, pulling back to look into her eyes. "I think 'tis a good thing I am healed, Evie. Because if we did this again, I'm no' sure I could stop. I'm no' sure I would want to, and we both ken 'twould never work out between us."

She did. And what was wrong with her that at that moment she didn't care?

Standing on the snow-covered ledge, Lachlan was like a stag in heat; he couldn't keep his eyes off Evangeline. Frustrated, he dragged his hand through his hair. What the bloody hell was wrong with him? He hadn't let things go too far, so why did he feel like he had? Why did he feel like he'd already taken that last step to fall spiraling out of control over the mountaintop?

He shot a furious glare to where she stood talking to Fallyn. Evangeline's glorious mane of raven-black hair tumbled down the back of her white fur cape. Her exquisite face was animated, her lips delectably kiss-swollen, her . . . bloody hell, there was something in her blood that was making him feel this way. It was the only explanation. The only reason all the emotions—emotions that had nearly driven him mad after his rescue from Glastonbury—he'd worked so hard to shut down, vowed never to feel again, were bubbling up inside him. It was bloody annoying is what it was, and he was not about to let one woman tear down the walls he'd painstakingly raised. Destroy the comforting peace he'd finally found in the emptiness.

From the moment he'd assumed his title, she'd nagged him to care—care for those he ruled. Now she'd gone and succeeded. She'd made him care all right, made him care about *her*. And it had nothing to do with him admiring her, respecting her and her passionate zeal to protect the Fae, no matter how misguided. No, it all came down to her blood. He was intoxicated by it, craved it.

Well, no more.

As though she felt the intensity of his perusal, she met his gaze through the falling snow. It was as though only the two of them existed. The raucous chatter of the warriors preparing for battle faded to a low hum on the wind. He scowled at her, but he no longer held her attention—his sword did. A winsome smile curved her lips and he promised that once this was over, he'd learn what she found so bloody interestin' aboot his blade changin' colors. Nay, he wouldna. Once this was over, he'd avoid her like the plague. He'd ban her from the Enchanted Isles. Aye, that's what he would do.

Feeling someone's gaze upon him, he looked back to see Broderick and Gabriel regarding him oddly. "What?"

"We've been trying to gain your attention for several moments now. Are you certain you are well enough to lead the assault?" Gabriel asked, concern furrowing his brow.

"Aye, never better." It was the truth. Never had he felt so strong and powerful. And now, with his course of action in dealing with Evangeline decided, no one could defeat him. "Let's put an end to this, shall we? I mean to be in the Enchanted Isles before nightfall."

As they prepared to mount their steeds, Lachlan thought to ask Broderick, "How did ye fare with Fallyn last eve?"

Gabriel snorted a laugh. "He spent half of it unconscious. The rocks had a most interesting way of falling on his head. If it wasn't so hard, I'm sure he'd still be out cold."

"Perhaps if you would've been more helpful I would have made some progress, but you were too busy wooing Shayla," Broderick retorted testily.

"I was not wooing the woman. I conversed with her was all. It speaks much to your failure with Fallyn that you think having a simple conversation constitutes *wooing*, Broderick."

The Welsh king grunted and stalked off to speak to his men.

"No," Gabriel said firmly when he noted Lachlan's considering perusal. "I have no intention of taking Shayla and her sisters off your hands."

Lachlan turned to regard the subject of their conversation. "She's verra bonny and . . ." He tried to think of another attribute to entice the king of England's Fae when Evangeline came into his line of sight, obviously giving the sisters last-minute instruction. He rolled his eyes. He'd never met anyone as opinionated or controlling as the blasted woman. If she knew what was good for her, she'd best heed his command to stay far from the battlefield until someone came to retrieve her.

"Yes, as beautiful as Evangeline, who you seem to be undeniably aware of, of late, yet I don't see you offering for her."

"Are ye daft? Why the bloody hell would I do that? I have nothin' to gain from weddin' the lass but a pain in my arse."

"Precisely my point." Gabriel grinned. "Although you must admit you have gained much from Evangeline, as your recent display of strength has proven."

Mayhap he shouldn't have been showing off his newfound powers earlier. "Hardly worth the aggravation, nor did I have to wed her to obtain it."

"Again, you've proven my point."

Lachlan grunted. "So, ye willna wed Shayla?"

"No, my friend, I do not see that happening even to save your sanity. It seems you're stuck with them."

"I've been thinkin' my uncle needs a wife. Mayhap he'd stop meddlin' in my affairs if he was otherwise occupied."

"Good luck with that." Gabriel laughed as they took to the sky.

"They havena noted our presence as yet," Lachlan said, making himself heard over the rhythmic swoosh of the horses' wings and the blowing snow. Through a curtain of heavy flakes, he discerned Magnus's scouts astride the bears patrolling the perimeter. To his left, one of the beasts roared the alert. "It seems I spoke too soon." He motioned for his army to follow him then swooped down on their enemy.

Less than an hour later, Lachlan surveyed the ash-coated snow with satisfaction. Power and pride surged within him. No matter the number of warriors he'd faced, not once had his strength flagged. Even now the blood surged through his veins, his body humming in readiness for the next battle.

With the first line of Magnus's defenses close to surrender, the king of the Far North would have no choice but to face him. Knowing it would not be long before Evangeline would play her role, he sought out Fallyn. His gaze landed on Broderick instead. So intent was his friend on the warrior and beast he battled, he was unaware the enemy approached from behind.

"Broderick, watch yer back!" Lachlan shouted, but the Welsh king displayed no evidence he'd heard him. Cursing, Lachlan started out at a run. He waved his sword, trying to gain the attention of one of his warriors who fought not far from Broderick. No luck. Just this once Lachlan wished he was full-blooded and could transport to his friend's side. No sooner had the thought entered his head then a fuzzy sensation came over him.

He shook off the feeling only to realize he now stood beside a dumbfounded Broderick. With no time to think on what happened, Lachlan pivoted, thrusting his blade in the belly of the warrior whose sword was raised to smash into the back of Broderick's head. Yanking his blade free, Lachlan turned his attention to the warrior and beast his friend had been fighting, but they'd fled.

Shaking off his disbelief, Broderick asked, "How did you do that?"

"I doona ken, but 'tis lucky fer ye that I did." A triumphant laugh burst from Lachlan. He couldn't bloody believe it, he had *magick*. Everything would be different now. Never again would the bastards call him a half-blood. Nor would his right to lead be questioned, not with both the Sword of Nuada and his newfound powers. He could not be defeated. No one would ever have him at their mercy again.

"It must be her blood. Evangeline's."

"Aye, I kent that." Deep down he had known his powers were on account of her blood. He just hadn't wanted to think about it.

Broderick clapped him on the shoulder. "Lucky for us it hasn't faded yet." He jerked his chin to the line of warrior's flooding from Magnus's palace. "Here they come. I—"

Lachlan grabbed his arm. "What do ye mean, hasn't faded yet?"

"It won't last, Lachlan. The essence of her power will soon fade."

"Then we have no' a moment to lose. Let's show these bastards what a half-blood can do," Lachlan jested in an attempt to cover his bitter disappointment, disheartened that he would soon lose the addictive freedom her power granted him.

Fallyn and her steed winged onto the battlefield. Catching Lachlan's eye, she nodded. Evangeline was ready to transport into the palace. He frowned, halting midstride. "Are ye tellin' me the power I'm imbued with is what Evangeline possesses?"

"Yes, but only a portion of it."

"No wonder the woman's so bloody arrogant."

Broderick chuckled. "Frightening, isn't it?"

"Bloody terrifyin'."

Bellowing his clan's battle cry, Lachlan with Broderick at

his side charged into the melee outside the palace gates. Fighting back to back, they took on four warriors at a time. In the midst of battle, Lachlan searched for some sign Evangeline had retrieved Uscias. He caught Fallyn's eye and she shook her head. Concerned too much time had passed, he was about to signal for Fallyn to go in when Magnus appeared in an explosion of light on the castle wall. The king of the Far North scanned the crowd beneath him.

When Magnus's gaze landed on Lachlan, a triumphant smile creased his handsome visage. "I now hold *two* hostages, MacLeod. I think it's time we negotiate, don't you?"

Chapter 12

The ice-covered peaks warbled, fading in and out as Evangeline attempted to transport from the mountain's ledge to Magnus's palace. Something was wrong. She ignored the panicked gallop of her heart and dug deeper, only to find herself slammed against the thick, glittering white exterior wall of Magnus's palace. Disoriented, she staggered to her feet, trying to understand what had gone wrong. She was certain it was not due to wards. Magnus did not have magick powerful enough to weave the spell, nor did he have a wizard to do so. And she was certain Uscias, knowing they would need to enter unnoticed, would not have aided his captor.

She groaned as the only viable explanation came to mind. Lachlan had stolen her magick. Perhaps not intentionally, but the result was the same. A sickening sense of dread welled inside her. He'd left her vulnerable. Uscias's rescue was now at risk because she couldn't resist the power of his seduction, the heat of his kiss, his tenderness. She'd lost the only thing that truly mattered to her—her magick, her ability to protect the Fae. Battling against despair, Evangeline pressed her fingers to her temples. *Think.*

"All right, better," she murmured as she thought through her options. All she had to do was get to Uscias without being found out. Lachlan had not drained her completely of her powers as he had the last time. Other than transportation, minor spells should not be a problem. Once she released Uscias, he could flash them both from the palace. She only hoped his injuries, if he'd sustained any, would not impact his powers.

From the front of the palace, Magnus's warriors bellowed their battle cry and she put her worry over Uscias out of her mind, determined to take advantage of the opportunity. Pressing her back against the wall, she eased toward the edge of the building. Warriors flooded from the opened doors, charging the front gate. With a flick of her wrist, she outfitted herself in the same attire Magnus's warriors wore—a long coat of matted brown fur with matching hat and boots.

Thankful that at least the low levels of her magick still worked, she stuffed her hair under the hat, feeling somewhat more confident. Tugging the cap lower to conceal her features, she bowed her head then swaggered around the corner to approach the front door.

Losing herself amongst the crowd, she managed to slip past the burly guard at the door.

Entering the palace, Evangeline tried to make herself as inconspicuous as possible, which was not difficult since those scurrying about the gleaming hall were too busy preparing for battle to notice her. A battle she tried not to think about as much as she tried not to worry about Lachlan. The thought brought her up short. She didn't need to worry about him. He had her magick.

Certain they would hold Uscias in one of the four towers, she took the white marble staircase to the upper floor. Sprinting along the deserted corridors, she searched for stairs leading to the towers. As no guard stood before the first set she came to, she tried to find one which was fortified. With Lachlan and his army now past his first line of defense, she was confident Magnus would take no chances in guarding Uscias.

By the time she reached the fourth and last tower, she began to doubt herself. It was not a pleasant feeling. Therefore she was more than a little relieved when two warriors descended from the narrow enclosed stairwell.

She strode toward them. "The king requires your presence on the battlefield. I'm to replace you," she said, almost choking with the effort to lower her voice.

The two men didn't move. The taller of the pair narrowed his gaze on her. "He wouldn't send a lad to replace us. Who—"

Knowing she had to act fast before their suspicions increased, she said, "Not worried about losing your heads, I see." With a negligent shrug, she pivoted on her heel. "I'll inform him of your—"

"No, we'll go," the taller man's companion conceded, obviously not happy he had to leave the relative safety of the palace to face their enemies.

Evangeline took their place. Her stance was cocky as she leaned against the wall, crossing her arms over her chest and legs at her ankles for added effect. As soon as they were out of sight, she sprinted up the narrow staircase. At the landing, she faced a rough-hewn door, surprised to find it unlocked. She squared her shoulders, preparing to remain stoic no matter the condition she found Uscias in. Pushing the door open, she strode into the room.

Two guards sat to her left playing cards at a wooden table. The one closest to her twisted in his chair to regard her from beneath bushy auburn brows. "What are you doing up here? Where are Ivor and Eirik?"

She kept her gaze turned away from where Uscias— chained in irons—sat slumped in a chair to her right. "The king ordered them to the battlefield. You're to replace them down below. Only one man is needed to guard the wizard," she said, adding a swagger to her deepened voice.

Eyeing her suspiciously, the guard came to his feet. He

loomed over her. "You're unfamiliar to me." He held a dagger and nudged her chin up with the blade. "Who—"

Jerking her head back, she brought her hand between them then aimed a shaft of magick at his chest. He staggered backward, collapsing on the floor. His companion shot to his feet and fired a bolt at her. She jumped aside, aiming another in his direction. He heaved the solid oak table on its end, deflecting her magick and then threw the table at her. Her cumbersome disguise hampered her movement and the table clipped her shoulder before she could get out of the way as it sailed past to hit the stone wall at her back. She rid herself of the heavy furs with a wave of her hand.

"They sent a woman, Olaf." He laughed contemptuously, directing his comment to his companion who remained on the floor shaking off the effects of her magick.

"Imagine that, a helpless female," she jeered, sidestepping the jagged bolt he fired at her. Pulling on her powers for all she was worth, she raised both hands, leveling the two of them with a steady stream of white light. The warrior, who'd been struggling to sit up, fell back. His companion joined him on the wood-planked floor. Wisps of smoke rose from the charred remains of their brown leather jerkins.

Tracing circles in the air, she attempted to bind them in irons. The chains rattled a few inches above the warriors, then fell with a ringing clatter on top of them. A frustrated growl vibrated in her throat. Her power was fading and she'd yet to free Uscias. She'd have to be content that the iron would drain them of their power while they remained unconscious.

She turned to Uscias, relieved to see his clear blue gaze upon her.

"What's wrong with your magick, Evangeline?" His voice was weak but he showed no visible sign of injury.

"I'll explain later. We don't have much time before someone notices no one guards the stairs." She flexed her fingers, preparing to remove his chains. "Once you're free, will you be strong enough to transport us from here?"

"Not immediately. I'll need time to recover."

She'd been afraid of that. "Don't worry. I'll find a way to get you out of here." Focusing on the ropes of iron, she fired her magick directly at the links in an attempt to weaken them. They rattled and clinked, but nothing more. Drawing on the faint ball of white low in her belly, she pulled harder. This time there were faint pops. The chain loosened, hanging about Uscias's diminutive form. One more time, she assured herself, that's all it would take. She closed her eyes, refocusing her energy.

"Well, well, well, what do we have here?"

The bastard had Evangeline. Lachlan fought to contain a surge of panic. Magnus had to be bluffing. There was no way in hell he could've got a hold of her. She was too powerful. Lachlan should know, since what little magick he'd retained from sharing her blood had left him feeling all but invincible.

As though Magnus read his thoughts, he looked over his shoulder. With a jerk of his chin, he motioned for someone behind him. Two warriors held a struggling Evangeline—hands behind her back—at a point where Lachlan could see her just beyond the closed golden gates.

"Your choice, MacLeod. Leave or negotiate." Without awaiting his answer, Magnus vanished in a swirl of light, as did Evangeline.

Broderick, Gabriel, Shayla, and Fallyn pushed their way past the crush of warriors to come to his side. Lachlan motioned for Orin, a warrior of superior skills and one he trusted. "Take the men to the other side of the fjord and await us there. If anything untoward happens, I shall send you a signal."

Orin nodded grimly, then set about doing as Lachlan commanded.

Lachlan looked to the gates as they squeaked open. "We're coming with you," Fallyn said, her expression daring him to argue.

"As are we," Broderick said, edging past the two women.

Lachlan didn't bother answering. He needed to get inside to see how Evangeline fared.

Her fury slammed into him the moment he entered Magnus's grand hall. She sat to the left of the Fae king—a thin chain of iron at her neck, her hands obviously secured behind her back—at a long banquet table in the opulent hall. Her gaze met Lachlan's, her lips twisting in a sneer. Her look of condemnation was directed at him. *Him?* Not the man who'd kidnapped both her and Uscias? Christ, 'twas no' his fault she'd failed in her mission.

Magnus motioned congenially for Lachlan and his party to take a seat. "So glad you could join us. I might have taken offense had I not had the beauteous Evangeline to keep me company." He drew a finger along her cheek, chuckling when she flinched.

Lachlan's fingers tightened around the hilt of his sword, wishing it was Magnus's neck. If the bastard touched her again, it would be. To hell with the Faes' rules of engagement.

He pulled out a chair and took a seat, catching Uscias's attention from where his mentor sat on the other side of Evangeline. Uscias answered the silent question in Lachlan's gaze with a shake of his head.

Good. He was unharmed.

Lachlan leaned back in the chair. "What do ye want, Magnus?"

"What I have wanted all along—ties to the Fae of the Enchanted Isles."

"Why?"

"If I am allied with you, Dimtri will think twice before declaring all-out war on me in an attempt to steal my lands."

"Ye expect me to believe that?" Lachlan scoffed. "Was

it no' ye and Dimtri who joined forces to attack us three years past?"

"Much has changed." The golden-haired king studied his hands, then raised his gaze, "Dimtri can no longer be trusted. The time will come when all of us will have to take a stand against him."

Lachlan raised a laconic brow. "So ye felt the best way to go aboot strengthenin' our bonds was to kidnap Uscias and now Evangeline?"

"No, you forced my hand when you refused my sister in marriage."

Evangeline hurled a contemptuous glare at Lachlan from across the table. *Wonderful.* Magnus had just confirmed her opinion of him. "I willna have my hand forced by ye or anyone else, Magnus."

"Andras, bring Jorunn to the hall," Magnus ordered one of his warriors. The muscle-bound man bore a striking resemblance to the king of the Far North. Lachlan deduced him to be Magnus's brother.

"I have heard you are a connoisseur of women, MacLeod. I can assure you upon meeting my sister, the idea of marriage to her will not be a hardship."

"I told ye . . ." At the sight of the ethereal beauty who all but floated into their midst, Lachlan's refusal stuttered to a halt in his throat. Andras guided her to Magnus's side. With a furtive glance at Lachlan, Andras whispered something in her ear before retreating to the far wall.

The lass was nothing like Lachlan had expected. He'd assumed she'd be similar in stature and manner to her overbearing brother, but it was not the case. Diminutive in height and build, she looked as though a gust of wind would blow her over. Out of the corner of his eye, he could see Broderick and Gabriel were as mesmerized by her beauty as he was.

Magnus patted the hand she clutched his shoulder with. "Don't be shy, Jorunn. Greet our guests."

Her knuckles whitened. She lifted startling blue eyes rounded with fear, her rosebud mouth quivering in her perfect heart-shaped face. "Hel . . . lo," she stammered.

Despite the evidence of womanly curves beneath the shimmering silver robes that matched the color of her long, unbound hair, Lachlan thought her to be more child than woman.

Not wishing to cause the lass further distress, he directed his question to her brother, "How old is yer sister?"

Magnus greeted his question with a self-satisfied smile, as though he believed Lachlan's curiosity and the fact he did not reject the proposal outright after seeing Jorunn meant their betrothal was as good as done. Lachlan's gaze slid to Evangeline. The tension bracketing the tight purse of her full lips confused him. He'd expected to see a smile as smug as Magnus's. Wasn't this what she'd wanted all along?

She raised her eyes to his and in that instant took him back to the cave and the fierce desire he'd felt for her—nothing like the tepid stirring in his loins when he looked upon Jorunn. No, Evangeline's sultry beauty stirred in him a hot, hungry passion like no one else could. It consumed him, destroyed his carefully conceived defenses. He was bewitched by her, by her blood.

Evangeline was dangerous; Jorunn safe. Magnus's sister would expect nothing from him and he would expect nothing from her. It would not be a hardship to look upon her beauty, and both his uncle and Evangeline's demands would be satisfied.

"She's eighteen, old enough to wed. So, MacLeod, now that you have met my sister, will you agree to my terms—Uscias in exchange for you wedding Jorunn?"

"Of course he will," Evangeline snapped, the high slash of her cheekbones flushed pink.

Fer Chrissakes, did she no' think he could speak fer himself? He glowered at her, then realized Magnus had said nothing of her release. The way Lachlan was feeling right now, she could bloody well stay in the Far North.

"Ye fergot to mention Evangeline, obviously—"

"Forget Evangeline, no, how could anyone forget her? Her release is not up for discussion. I've been meaning to take a wife, but none other than Syrena has ever captured my interest. Until now." His gaze traveled rapidly over Evangeline, who sat stiffly at his side, her face drained of color.

An uncontrollable rage ripped through Lachlan and he shot to his feet. His blood-red sword vibrated in his hand. "Nay."

Magnus frowned. "It is not for you to deny me. She is, as I understand, Rohan's subject. As she's not of royal blood, I'm certain he will see it as the honor it so clearly is."

At the mention of his uncle, Lachlan regained a measure of control. Rohan would never force Evangeline into a union with Magnus. No matter the congenial manner the man now displayed, both he and his uncle knew well the brutal bastard Magnus could be. Rohan wouldn't sacrifice Evangeline. Then, knowing her as he did, Lachlan cursed under his breath. Nay, his uncle wouldn't, but she bloody well would.

"He can't. She's already been promised to me. Evangeline is my betrothed."

Chapter 13

If Evangeline was prone to swooning, she would have. She couldn't believe Lachlan had just claimed her to be his betrothed. From the look upon his face, neither could he. Shaking off the light-headedness his remark had engendered, she barely managed to contain her frustrated shriek. Uscias's release had all but been secured. If Evangeline hadn't taken matters into her own hands and proclaimed Lachlan's willingness to wed Magnus's sister, she knew, given time, he would have. He'd obviously been as enamored with the young girl's beauty as Broderick and Gabriel.

If she was honest, she'd admit his reaction to Jorunn had so infuriated her, she'd answered for him so as not to hear him agree to the betrothal. So as not to hear him say he wanted another woman in that deep seductive brogue of his. Which was absolutely ridiculous and only served to prove how severely her lack of powers had befuddled her brain, and was obviously the explanation for the almost palpable sense of excitement rising inside her at his declaration.

No, it would not do. For the greater good, she must accept Magnus's proposal to ensure Uscias's release. No matter that the thought of doing so filled her with dread.

Magnus turned to her. "Is this true?"

Across the table she met Lachlan's gaze. The denial she meant to utter stuck in her throat at the heated intensity in his amber eyes. Her traitorous mind and body filled with the memories of the desire he'd ignited in her, of the warmth and tenderness she'd experienced in his embrace, and she found herself reconsidering her response.

The childlike Jorunn, no matter her beauty, would not be the true partner Lachlan required. He needed someone like . . . her. Who else but Evangeline could keep him from taking foolish risks that endangered the Fae? No one's magick was as powerful as hers, well, once it had returned. And Evangeline had no intention of allowing Lachlan to take it from her again.

After careful consideration, she came to the conclusion it was indeed the perfect solution. What better way to fulfill her vow to protect the Fae of the Enchanted Isles than to marry their king? She just had to figure out another way to secure Uscias's release. Considering Magnus wished to strengthen his ties with the Isle Fae, the solution was simpler than she'd imagined. Either Gabriel or Broderick would serve as a suitable replacement for Lachlan.

"Evangeline," Lachlan grated out.

"What?" She jerked her gaze to his.

"Ye have yet to answer Magnus." Lachlan appeared ready to throttle her.

"Yes, it is true. I am betrothed to King Lachlan." She narrowed her gaze on her supposed betrothed when he muttered a curse. Amid their guffaws, Broderick and Gabriel offered their condolences. No, her head still spinning with thoughts of being wed to Lachlan, she must have misunderstood them.

Fallyn and Shayla stared at her openmouthed while Uscias stroked his silver beard, an amused smile playing on his lips. At least until Lachlan slanted a highly annoyed look in his direction. Whatever was the matter with Lachlan? He had been the one to blurt out the untruth. But the more Evangeline thought about it, the more she warmed to the idea. Her mind already buzzed with plans for the added security she would put in place, the . . .

"Then we are back where we started." Magnus startled her from her strategizing with his testy remark.

"No, no we are not. I have the perfect solution."

Magnus looked from Evangeline to Lachlan, who slumped in his chair. "It seems your betrothed thinks as your soon-to-be-queen she's entitled to make decisions that by rights should be made by *you*. Perhaps I should thank you for circumventing my plans to wed her."

Lachlan snorted rudely. "Aye, ye should." Crossing his arms over his chest, he said, "Let's hear this brilliant plan of yers."

She refused to let him bait her. She was much too pleased with how everything had worked out to let his sulky mood deter her. "It's simple. King Magnus wishes a marriage to ensure his ties to the Isle Fae and our Hallows. Both King Broderick and King Gabriel are unwed. One of them shall marry Jorunn." She lifted a questioning brow in Magnus's direction.

He shrugged. "She's right. Either will do."

Fallyn shot her a murderous glare from across the table.

Evangeline frowned. "I don't see what the problem is, Fallyn. You don't want him."

"Evangeline," Shayla muttered, giving her the evil eye as she patted her sister's arm.

The taciturn Welsh king grinned, leaning into his ex-betrothed, who sat beside him. "And I thought you didn't care," he purred.

"I don't. Go ahead and marry the *child*," Fallyn said through clenched teeth.

Broderick brought his palm to her cheek, forcing her gaze to his. "Yes, you do. You're just too stubborn to admit it."

Evangeline hazarded a glance at Lachlan, anxious to see what he thought of her plan. For the first time that day, he grinned at her. Pleasure blossomed in her chest and she smiled at him. At least someone appreciated the rightness of her solution. But when he waggled those golden brows of his at Broderick and his grin widened, Evangeline realized she had provided the perfect opportunity for the Welsh king to gauge Fallyn's feelings for him, and to push his suit. The means for Lachlan to be rid of the woman warrior and her sisters. Deflated, she returned her attention to Broderick and Fallyn.

"I'm not stubborn. I—"

Broderick smothered Fallyn's protest with a kiss before pulling back to say, "You are, and it's one of the reasons I love you."

Fallyn blinked. "You love me?"

Broderick's brow furrowed. "I've always loved you. You know that."

Fallyn's lips pressed in an uncompromising line. "No, Broderick, I don't. And perhaps the fact you were kissing another woman on the eve of our marriage has something to do with it."

The Welsh king waved his hand as though his indiscretion was of no consequence. "What does that have to do with anything?"

Fallyn shoved her chair from the table. "Settle this amongst yourselves. I don't care what you do," she said before she stormed from the hall.

With one last damning look in Evangeline's direction, Shayla hurried after her sister.

Evangeline sighed, certain the two women would soon realize her solution was a sound one. Realizing the object of their discussion remained frozen behind her brother, Evangeline slanted a look at Jorunn. Because of Lachlan's obvious interest in the girl earlier, she hadn't been kindly disposed to Magnus's sister. In fact, she didn't think she'd ever despised anyone more. Given the current situation, she felt somewhat more magnanimous and offered the younger woman a comforting smile.

Jorunn leveled her with a malicious glare, a glare she

quickly turned into a look of misty-eyed innocence when she garnered her brother's attention. Magnus gave his sister's hand a reassuring squeeze.

"Well, which one of you is it going to be?" he asked, returning his attention to the men.

Lachlan and Broderick turned to Gabriel, who sat stiffly between them. Gabriel scowled at the two men. He appeared poised to give them a piece of his mind until Jorunn's choked sob reached his ears. He sighed, his gaze softening at the sight of her tears. Evangeline didn't blame him—even though she felt certain the tears were an act, the girl cried very prettily indeed.

Coming smoothly to his feet, Gabriel said, "I'd be honored to take Jorunn as my wife."

Magnus's sister rewarded Gabriel with a smile so dazzling it appeared to render the three kings speechless. Evangeline rolled her eyes, thinking the young woman adept at manipulation. Evangeline didn't worry about Gabriel, though. He was an intelligent man, and for all his chivalrous ways, she knew the king of England's Fae could be firm-minded when warranted.

Evangeline turned to Magnus. "Is this agreeable to you?"

"Yes, most agreeable. Although I must admit despite your somewhat overbearing manner, I am disappointed I cannot make you my wife. Your beauty alone makes up for the fault, and your magick from what I've been told, is impressive. Are you certain you don't wish to reconsider?"

He stroked her arm and her skin crawled. Arwan's touch had elicited a similar response. She took a deep breath in an effort to calm the nervous churning in her belly. Perhaps because she'd witnessed Magnus's brutal attack on Syrena, he reminded Evangeline of Arwan. The reason Magnus's hands upon her, like Arwan's, made her feel as though she'd be ill. She couldn't help but wonder why Lachlan, the image of his father, had never made her feel that way.

"Nay, she won't. And before I take offense to both yer suggestion and yer pawing my betrothed, I'd advise ye to release both Uscias and Evangeline and we'll take our leave."

Evangeline blinked. Lachlan's earlier good humor had disappeared, leaving in its place a hardened warrior who expected his commands to be obeyed.

Magnus arched a brow. "Not so fast. I will see my sister wed before she leaves my protection and," he slanted a look at Evangeline, "as I am not an altogether trusting man, I begin to question your alleged betrothal. After all, you simply could leave here and no more would come of it, and I would have given up my chance to wed her on account of a lie. To assuage my suspicions, I shall see you wed along with Gabriel and Jorunn."

The muscle in Lachlan's jaw jumped. Evangeline realized then that that was precisely what he had intended. And if not for her diminished faculties, she would have recognized his deception for what it was. Now that she did, she could only imagine the weight of disappointment lying heavy in her stomach was because all her plans for the Isles were now for naught.

Lachlan frowned at the look of disappointment in Evangeline's eyes. Was it because she only now realized Magnus had called his bluff? Surely she couldn't have thought he'd meant to marry her? Nay, he was the last person she'd wish to wed, just as she was the last person he'd wish to wed. Although, if he allowed the images of her in his arms, of her passionate response, his heated desire for her to take hold in his mind, he might not find the idea of marriage to her so disagreeable.

And having experienced the intoxicating rush of her power, he didn't relish the thought of losing her magick even while a part of him rebelled against the idea of taking her blood again. But he hadn't caused her pain. From her response, she'd taken as much pleasure from the exchange as he had. The power he'd gained from her blood undermined his need to keep her at a distance. He was adept at keeping his emotions locked away. With Evangeline, he'd just have to work harder at it.

If he had to wed, and his uncle seemed determined he would, why not Evangeline? Neither of them desired a true marriage, not like Aidan and his cousin Rory. They were adults. Surely they could come to an agreeable arrangement. A grin quirked the corner of his mouth at the thought that once Evangeline was his wife, she'd have no choice but to obey him. That alone made the prospect of wedding her more palatable.

"Get on with it, then. I wish to be back in the Isles by nightfall."

Magnus rose, putting an arm around his sister's shoulders. "Jorunn deserves a proper wedding. Return with your people this eve and together we shall celebrate. As a show of good faith, you may take the wizard with you, but Evangeline shall remain here."

"I would speak with my betrothed before I leave—alone."

"Certainly." With a flick of his wrist, both Evangeline and Uscias were released from the chains binding them to their chairs. Magnus waved off the guards who stood at attention around the perimeter of the hall.

Both his mentor and Evangeline, in their weakened state, had trouble rising. Lachlan offered her his hand while Broderick and Gabriel assisted Uscias to his feet. "Lachlan, Evangeline," Uscias's lips twitched beneath his mustache, "I wish you much happiness in your marriage. If you have no objections, though, I think it best I return posthaste to the Isles. I shall take Aurora with me."

Lachlan nodded, tightening his hold on Evangeline, who to his mind seemed less than steady on her feet. Almost as debilitated as Uscias, which didn't make sense as she'd been chained for an hour at most. He didn't bother asking after her well-being as he knew she'd not admit to weakness of any kind.

Gabriel, about to follow Uscias and Broderick from the

hall, hesitated beside them. "Evangeline, I'd ask a favor of you." She waited expectantly and he continued, "Would you please reassure Jorunn that she is in no danger from me. I don't expect . . ." He jerked his hand through his hair. "She is little more than a child," he said with a frustrated bark. "What the hell can Magnus be thinking?"

"Don't worry, King Gabriel, Jorunn seemed quite happy at the prospect of marriage to you. I think perhaps she is . . . stronger than she appears."

Gabriel sighed. "We shall see. But I would still appreciate it if you offered her my reassurances."

After Evangeline promised to do so, Gabriel took his leave. Lachlan angled his head to look at her. "And what aboot ye, Evangeline, does the prospect of marriage to me upset ye or please ye?"

She arched a brow. "Neither. It is but a means to an end. You will appease your uncle, and because of my powers, Bana and Erwn will be less likely to challenge your right to rule. At the very least, I shall be aware of it if they do so."

Hands on his hips, he scowled down at her. "Are ye tryin' to tell me ye think I'm the only one who gains from this union?"

"For the most part, yes, but I can't deny the opportunity to see to the Faes' safety overrules any misgivings I might have."

"Ye think ye have misgivin's. Hah. They are naught compared to mine. Mayhap I should've agreed to marry the bairn in the first place. At least she appears to be a biddable lass. One who kens her place."

Her violet eyes flashed with anger and a glimmer of emotion he couldn't name. "Fine," she said, pushing past him with a haughty toss of lustrous black mane. "I will inform Magnus of your decision."

At the thought of Magnus's fingers entwined in that shiny fall of hair, of anyone other than Lachlan claiming her soft lips, he reached for her, spinning her around to face him.

"Oh, you are . . ." She sputtered, trying to break free of his hold.

He hauled her against him. "Yer betrothed," he growled. Stopping her midsputter, he tangled his fingers in her hair. "Ye're mine, no' Magnus's." He cupped the back of her head with both hands then claimed her mouth, erasing the image of Magnus's hands upon her. She trembled, and the possessive madness that had him in its grip loosened its hold. But he couldn't let her go, not yet. Intoxicated by her tentative response, the breathy moan against his lips, he deepened the kiss until the desire to take her right then and there in the middle of Magnus's grand hall all but overrode his fragile hold on his self-restraint.

He eased away, breaking the kiss. At the flustered expression on her beautiful flushed face, he said, "I shall have to remember how well a kiss works to quiet that mouth of yers," he teased her in hopes she wouldn't see how deeply she affected him. *Her blood.* How deeply her blood affected him.

Emitting a low growl, she flounced from the hall. His forced laughter followed after her. What the hell had he gotten himself into?

Flickering candles illuminated the glistening snow-covered path from Magnus's palace to where Lachlan and Gabriel stood awaiting their brides in the frosted night air. Warriors from both armies were in attendance, muttering impatiently, anxious for the ceremony to be over and the celebration to begin.

"Fer Chrissakes, what's takin' them so long? 'Tis bloody freezin' out here."

Broderick raised a laconic brow. "If you'd worn something besides your highland garb, the cold would not bother you."

Lachlan glanced down at his plaid. Aye, his friend was right, but since his family could not be here to see him marry, he'd felt a need to have that part of him represented. In his heart he was a highlander, and that would never change. A long-ago memory tried to gain a foothold in his mind, the memory of Janet and the wedding that never took place, both child and mother lost to him in a fiery blaze. Nay, he'd not go there, not today, not ever if he had his way. "I doona ken why they have to make such a production of it," he said gruffly.

Gabriel studied him for a moment then shrugged. "We're royalty. It is how it has always been done."

To the left of them, beneath the tinkling ice-coated branches of an oak tree, three men took up their woodwinds, while two women sat at their harps. The haunting melody they played wove its way through the crowd, drawing their attention to Magnus, who guided his sister down the path toward them. Even the diamond tiara Jorunn wore atop her silvery blond mane could not outshine her luminescent beauty, her appearance as delicate as the layers of gossamer silk that peeked from beneath her white fur cape. She was the very image of what Lachlan as a lad had thought a Faery princess would look like.

Magnus placed Jorunn's hand in Gabriel's with a pointed look. Gabriel gave him a curt nod in return. Lachlan couldn't help but wonder how his friend felt about the position he now found himself in—easier to ponder Gabriel's feelings than his own, he admitted. At the ominous murmurs filtering through the gathered assembly, Lachlan lifted his gaze and his jaw dropped.

Evangeline stood alone in a velvet gown the color of her eyes. A gown which served to heighten the allure of her womanly curves, the snowy white mounds cradled in the low-cut décolletage. The Faery princess faded in comparison to her. Evangeline was a woman, lush and ripe. A sultry, bold beauty, who caused a reaction so hot and fierce in Lachlan he felt certain that the snow beneath his feet would melt.

He clenched his teeth, shifting in discomfort, all too aware if he didn't master his feverish response, those gathered would soon know where his thoughts had headed. Fallyn stepped from the throng, shooting a damning look at the men who'd uttered the disparaging remarks against Evangeline. Seemingly willing to overlook her previous anger with her friend, Fallyn took Evangeline's arm and led her to Lachlan's side.

He blinked when the white fur cape he'd wished Evangeline wore appeared in his hand. Mouthing a prayer of thanks that his magick had yet to fade, he wrapped it around her slender shoulders. She gaped at him as he firmly tugged the edges together. He shrugged. "Ye're cold."

"No, I'm not and how—"

"Aye, ye are. Hush." He jerked his chin in Broderick's direction as the man began the ceremony.

Enraptured by the starlike snowflakes falling onto Evangeline's glossy black mane, the words of the Faes' marriage ceremony were little more than a dull hum in Lachlan's ears. He stood so close her shoulder brushed his arm, her warm, floral scent flooding his senses, rendering him oblivious to the cold and anything else but her.

He barely heard the snort of amusement, but the loud clearing of someone's throat managed to penetrate his enthralled brain. He cursed under his breath when he realized he held the knowing attention of those gathered around him—Evangeline's included.

"Did ye put a spell on me?" he growled down at her.

Her elegantly arched brows drew together. "What are you talking about?"

"Nothin'," he muttered, certain despite her denial there was magick afoot this night. If she hadn't put a spell on him, then the only explanation he could think of was that her blood heightened his awareness of her. "Get on with it," he ordered Broderick. The sooner he put some distance between them, the better. At least until her magick had ceased to pulsate through his veins.

Broderick glanced down at the parchment he held in his hand, the words of the marriage vows Lachlan had written from his memory of Rory and Aileanna's ceremony. His cousin's wife had insisted they have a proper wedding once the kirk had come around and granted them a dispensation.

"We will now bear witness to the union of King Lachlan and Evangeline," Broderick informed the gathered assemblage.

Out of the corner of his eye, Lachlan noted movement, heard the murmurs of discontent from his men. He swept the crowd with a silencing glare before he returned his gaze to Evangeline, who stood with her head held high, back ramrod straight. She didn't fool him. He could see past her defiant pose. He took her slender hand in his—the need to keep his distance overridden by the desire to comfort her.

When Broderick asked if either of them knew of any reason their union should not take place, Lachlan barely registered Evangeline's momentary hesitation as several perfectly good reasons came to his mind.

Knowing it was too late to turn back, he said no at the same time she did.

Lachlan repeated the next of the vows easily enough. He would protect her willingly, see she came to no harm. Cleave only unto her, well, he might have stumbled a wee bit on that one. Not that he wanted anyone else in his bed but her; he just thought it might take some convincing to get her there. He would have stumbled more than a bit on the next vow if he hadn't thought to remove it. Love was no longer an emotion he felt capable of, and he was glad of it. Nay, neither he nor Evangeline had any illusions as to what their marriage would be.

Lost in his reflections, he'd missed the question Broderick asked of Evangeline. Considering the scowl on her beautiful face, he was confident he knew what it was and grinned.

"He didn't have to say *that*."

Broderick rolled his eyes. "He's a king, Evangeline. He's a law onto himself."

Lachlan stifled a laugh at her expression. "Come, 'tis no'

difficult, Evangeline. Repeat after me: I will obey my husband, my king, lord of all he sees."

She snarled, then muttered the words quickly beneath her breath. Lachlan was quite certain with one word missing. The only one he wanted to hear her say. He bent his head toward her. "I couldna hear ye. Mayhap ye should speak up."

"I will obey you." She practically shouted, her hands balled into fists.

He winced then rubbed his ear. "That's good to ken."

The ceremony concluded, they stood together to accept the good wishes of those gathered around them. Lachlan noted the dark smudges beneath Evangeline's eyes, a hint of weariness threading through her melodious voice as she spoke to Riana. When the king of the Far North approached, Lachlan said, "I hope ye willna take offense, Magnus, but Evangeline and I will no' be takin' part in the celebrations."

Magnus's salacious gaze roved over Evangeline. "I can't say I blame you. I'd be as anxious to bed her as you are," he said in a voice loud enough for Evangeline to hear.

At her outraged gasp, Lachlan slid his arm around her shoulders and squeezed a warning. He couldn't afford for her to take her fury out on the man no matter how much it was deserved. Muttering under her breath, she flung off his arm and stomped to where Fallyn and her sisters now stood.

Tracking Evangeline's progress, Magnus said, "I wish you luck in breaking that one. You have your work cut out for you."

The man was a fool if he thought Evangeline's spirit could be broken. "I wouldna waste the effort tryin' to do so." Nor would he want to. Her self-assurance and strength were just two of the things he admired about her. His relief he'd saved her from Magnus evaporated at the knowledge that much more than her beauty and body drew him to her. *Forewarned is forearmed*, he assured himself before addressing Gabriel. "Will ye remain fer the festivities?"

"It seems we shall. We will return to the Isles with you on

the morrow, though," he said before following after Magnus and his sister.

"Broderick?"

The Welsh king drew his narrowed gaze from where Fallyn entertained several warriors, to Lachlan. "Don't worry, I'd assumed I'd be the one to remain behind. I wouldn't expect you newlyweds to do so. Besides, I don't foresee there being any trouble amongst the men. Although there's a couple I intend on having a word with," he said, shooting a hard look at the warriors laughing at something Fallyn said.

Lachlan grimaced. It was his responsibility to see to the men, but he didn't want Magnus anywhere near Evangeline. Considering the lass his friend took to wife, he doubted Gabriel would be enjoying himself this night as Broderick had intimated. As for Lachlan, a part of him hoped he would be. He looked over at the woman he found himself married to. Her back to him, she stood alone, watching the mystical green and blue lights undulating across the sky.

He bid his friend good eve before the thought of bedding Evangeline did more than fire his imagination. Snow crunched underfoot as he walked toward her, but she appeared oblivious to his approach. At least he thought she'd been until he placed his hands on her shoulders and she said, "I would prefer not to attend the celebration, if you don't mind."

Her awareness of him shouldn't have been surprising. Nothing seemed to escape her notice. Nor should he be surprised by her reluctance to attend the festivities. He couldn't remember ever seeing her take part in the Faes' celebrations and felt a pang of sympathy for this woman who was now his wife. He wrapped his arms around her, bringing her back to his chest. She stiffened, then just as he thought she meant to bolt, she leaned against him. "I've already made our excuses," he informed her, inhaling her seductive fragrance.

She tipped her head back, the silky strands of her hair tickling his chin. "Are we going back to the caves?"

"Aye, unless ye would prefer we stay in one of the rooms here. I'm sure it can be arranged."

"No, the cave will be fine."

His cock hardened in response to her answer. All he could think about was getting her back to their hideaway in the mountain where he'd lay her down on the fur pallet and slowly, inch by inch, strip her of her amethyst gown, mold his hands to the heavy weight of her breasts, and bury his face in the soft pillow they'd be sure to make, to . . .

"Where are Bowen and the other steeds?" she asked, interrupting the heated direction of his thoughts.

"We left them at the camp. I didn't trust the bears. As for Bowen, Aurora didn't want to leave without him."

The pleased smile she rewarded him with faded. "I'm afraid I can't transport us. We'll have to ask someone else to do so." She didn't look particularly happy with the idea.

"'Tis no' a problem. I can transport us."

She jerked from his arms and rounded on him, "You? You can transport us? I knew it! I knew you had stolen my magick!"

His gaze went to the stars twinkling in a sky as dark as Evangeline's hair, and he blew out a defeated breath. His grand hopes for a passion-filled night faded as fast as the falling star that streaked across the night sky.

Chapter 14

Evangeline couldn't wait to put the land of ice and snow behind her. If she added one more layer of fur to her shivering frame, it would be impossible to remain upright. Without the comfort of Lachlan's warmth last eve—no matter the blazing fire or mountain of blankets—she was chilled to the very marrow of her being. She had expected the ball of fury that burned inside her—at the knowledge he could transport himself while she could not, the evidence he'd indeed been responsible for her failure to rescue Uscias, the reason she now found herself wed to the man prowling toward her—to keep her warm. It had not.

Sometime in the middle of the night her anger had dissipated, leaving her cold and . . . lonely. In both instances, she had been the one who offered her blood—willingly. More than willingly the second time, she grimly acknowledged, remembering how she'd ached to feel his hard warrior's body pressed to hers. To feel his warm lips demanding and possessive on hers, his powerful hands . . . The heated flush accompanying the memories was as welcome as much as the evidence of her stupidity was not. She should've known better. Now that she did, there would be no more sharing of her blood.

As for sharing the comfort and warmth of his body, well . . .

She started . . . stunned. Did she truly think to give herself to him completely? Sharing a kiss and the warmth of his embrace was one thing, but to surrender to him fully? No, surely the icy fingers of the cold had wrapped themselves around her mind to squeeze out her good sense. Their marriage would not be like that of Syrena and Aidan, or Aileanna and Rory. Evangeline's and Lachlan's served a higher purpose.

Lachlan crouched in front of her to peer up at her. "Ah, so it is ye under there. Cold, are ye?" He grinned when she chattered her reply. Coming to his feet, he tipped her chin with his gloved hand, forcing her gaze to his. "Mayhap 'twill make ye think twice next time ye decide to deny yer husband his rightful place beside ye." He stroked his knuckles along the curve of her cheek. "I ken ye were fashed I had yer magick, Evie, but ye ken well enough 'twas no' apurpose."

She did, but the vivid memory of her helplessness kept her from uttering an apology. "It might not have been intentional, but the consequences were the same. I failed to rescue Uscias and—"

"But thanks to yer magick I was invincible on the battlefield, and in the end it all worked out."

Evangeline didn't like the prideful gleam in his eyes when he spoke of the prowess her powers had awarded him in battle. But for a man with only the magick of his sword to depend on, she could well imagine how intoxicating her power must have been. "Have you forgotten it only worked out because Gabriel agreed to marry Jorunn and—"

"And I agreed to marry ye. Nay, I havena forgotten," he interrupted her.

"You did not agree to marry me! I agreed to marry you!" Truly, he was the most arrogant man she'd ever had the misfortune to meet.

He waved his hand as if it was of no consequence. "Come, Gabriel and Jorunn have arrived."

She glanced over her shoulder to see a weary-looking Gabriel helping his weeping wife onto her horse.

"Better him than me," Lachlan muttered under his breath with a grimace before tugging none too gently on her hand.

Evangeline dug in her heels, but was no match for his strength. Snow sprayed up her legs at her futile attempt to halt her forward motion. "I think I shall transport myself to the Isles," she said in a fit of pique.

Coming to an abrupt halt, he turned to look at her. "Yer magick is back, then?"

She couldn't help but note his disappointment. "Yes. I practiced earlier, and everything has returned to normal."

With an abrupt nod, he said, "Good. But ye'll be ridin' with me. We have much to discuss."

He strode toward his steed, dragging her behind him. Tired of his overbearing manner, she once more dug in her heels. Without looking at her, he released her hand. "Are ye breakin' yer vows already?"

She stalked after him. He was right. They had much to talk about, and the first item on the agenda was the vow he'd just made mention of. She'd only agreed during the ceremony so as not to embarrass him in front of his subjects. The last thing she wished to do was to diminish his standing in their eyes. That would not aid in her plan to keep the Fae safe.

He lifted her easily onto the horse. Then eyeing her bulky layers, he flicked his finger. With a disgruntled sigh, he said, "Ye'd best remove a cloak or two or there will no' be enough room fer me."

Evangeline blinked. "Did you just try to use magick on me?"

"Nay," he said in a querulous tone, mounting behind her once she'd done as he asked.

She knew very well he had and cast a sympathetic gaze at the hard set of his mouth. "I'm sorry, Lachlan. Perhaps it would have been best for you not to know what you were missing." She gave a reassuring pat to the arm he wrapped around her.

"Don't worry. I'll take care of you," she said with a smile. And she would. Not only because of her vow to protect the Fae, but as his wife it was her duty. Releasing a contented sigh, she snuggled against him for warmth. It felt wonderful to have her powers back, to be in control once again.

"As my wife, there's a few things we need to get straight. First . . . I doona need yer protection, I'm no' a bairn. Second—"

She stiffened, looking back at his unsmiling face. "But I—"

He placed a finger to her lips. "Nay, ye will listen to me, Evangeline. I willna have ye undermin' me before the Fae. Nor tellin' me how to govern the Isles. No disagreein' with my edicts, and I doona wish to hear yer opinion unless I ask fer it."

She gasped. "You can't be serious. If you didn't wish for my assistance, why did you tell Magnus we were betrothed?"

He snorted. "Ye ken as well as I do why I did. I didna want to see ye wed to Magnus. Mayhap I spoke out of turn and ye woulda preferred him to me."

Her stomach roiled at his suggestion and she shook her head.

"I didna think so," he said in a supercilious tone. "Now, mayhap I should tell ye what I do want from ye."

She jolted when he bent his head, his heated breath warming her ear. "To begin with, I want ye in my bed." His palm splayed her belly beneath the furs, and she was certain he would feel the wild fluttering his words elicited. "Slow, Evie, I'll take it slow. I ken ye're innocent," he murmured, trailing his lips down her neck.

Innocent? Thank the Fae he thought so. He would not demand more than she was willing to give, at least not yet. Relieved by the reprieve, she took a moment to realize he was continuing to speak. To rattle off a long list of her wifely duties.

". . . see to the servants and the runnin' of the palace. To the meals and the plannin' of the celebrations . . ."

"I don't have time for that sort of thing," she scoffed.

"Your security has to be reevaluated and I have to continue to study and hone my magickal skills, not to mention attend the Seelie Court."

He guffawed. "I have firsthand knowledge of yer magickal skills and I can tell ye, ye doona need anymore. As to the Seelie Court, my attendance is required, no' yers."

"Now listen here. I . . ." Her words disappeared in a dismayed shriek as, in her need to confront him, she sent herself tumbling from the steed.

She gave a grunt of pain when he caught hold of her arm and jerked her up and over the horse and onto his lap. "Ye have to get hold of that temper of yers, lass. Like obeyin' me, 'tis just one more thing ye must learn."

She struggled to break free of him while clutching his rock-hard thigh for fear of falling off again. Managing to situate herself more comfortably, she said. "You can't seriously believe I—"

As if she was nothing more than a child, he yanked her up and into his arms. "Ye're wrong, Evie. I seriously do believe ye'll obey me. In fact, I demand that ye do."

"Demand? You think—" He silenced her sputtered protest with a possessive, mind-numbing kiss.

Lachlan wanted nothing more than to show his bonny wife exactly what he wanted from her. Reluctantly, he broke the kiss, smoothing her tangled mane from her face. The back of a steed with an attentive audience was not the place to initiate a maiden in the joys of lovemaking. If she had allowed him within ten feet of her after he'd transported them to the caves last eve, he had no doubt she would now be his wife in more than name only. Instead, she'd consigned them both to a sleepless night in a cold, damp cave. He had full confidence in his powers of seduction, knew if he could have but gotten her into his arms he would have soothed her pique, but her threat to turn him into a toad had won out over his lust.

He didn't blame her for being upset, for hurling her virulent accusations at him. He knew her anger came from fear. She was terrified without her magick—terrified at her inability to control everything and everyone around her. A pang of guilt twigged his conscience at what he planned, but in the end it was for her own good, and theirs. If they were to make their marriage work, she had to learn to trust and depend on him. The only way he could think to make that happen was to limit her ability to control everything, most especially him.

"Doona worry, Evie," he said as he curved his arm around her. "It willna be so bad."

"Yes, it will, if you continue to treat me as if I'm little more than your chattel," she groused.

"Is that how ye see us? I was thinkin' more like king and minion." He laughed when she turned to glare at him. "Nay, I think we can manage to be friends at the very least." He was surprised to find he meant what he said. Other than Broderick, Gabriel, and his uncle, all of whom he didn't see often, there was only Uscias who he was close to in the Fae realm. He grew tired of the petty machinations of court life. It would be good to have an ally, someone he could trust.

"Friend?" She searched his face, then nodded. "Yes, I would like that."

His chest tightened at the shy vulnerability in her expression. She would be mortified if she knew she'd revealed it to him. Aye, his wife, for all her magickal powers, needed an ally amongst the Fae. Someone who would not judge her on account of her mother, someone she could let down her guard with.

"Lachlan?"

"Aye, Evangeline." Certain he knew what she was about to ask, he couldn't keep the amusement from his voice.

"Are you laughing at me?"

"Nay, tell me what it is ye want to ask."

"While I agree friendship is conducive to a good marriage, and a good marriage is what we shall aspire to . . ."

"Mm-hmm."

She narrowed her gaze on him.

"I was just agreein' with you. Continue."

"I think we should look at our marriage as a . . . partnership. A full partnership—an *equal* partnership."

He rubbed his hand over his mouth to hide his grin. "'Tis an interestin' notion. I shall give—" He grunted when she elbowed him in the belly. "What was that fer?"

"You were laughing at me."

"Nay. I was laughin' at how predictable ye are. We are newly wed, Evangeline, give it some time."

"You do trust me, though, don't you?"

He knew his answer was important to her. Her father and the Fae had scarred her as deeply as Alexander, Ursula, and Lamont had scarred him. "Aye, I do." It was true. To his knowledge she had never deliberately hurt anyone, although she'd been a pain in his arse on a regular basis.

"Thank you." She smiled up at him. "I promise I will make you a good wife and the Fae of the Enchanted Isles a good queen."

He tapped her nose. "Aye, I ken ye will. A good and obedient wife," he teased in hopes of getting a rise out of her. He needed a diversion to relieve the pressure building in his chest, a pressure brought on by her sweet smile and fervent promise.

"Just as I know you'll make a good and obedient husband, Lachlan."

Damn, her attempt at a lighthearted response would have eased the gnawing ache if not for the dewy softness in her eyes. In desperate need of a distraction, he searched the clutch of warriors riding ahead of them. "So, do ye think Broderick is any closer to gettin' Fallyn to wed him?"

She followed his gaze to where the Welsh king attempted to insert himself between Fallyn and her sisters. She sighed. "No. He's hopeless."

"Aye, Gabriel and I have been tryin' to instruct him on the art of wooin', but he's no' listenin' verra well. Although I thought he might have a chance yesterday."

"Perhaps that is the problem. I highly doubt you or King Gabriel have ever had to court a woman."

"Wooin' a woman to bed her and wooin' a woman to wed her are no' so verra different."

She gave him a pointed look.

"'Tis no' like we wouldna ken how, if we had to, but we didna."

"Obviously."

He rubbed his chest where the dull ache had returned. "Are ye sayin' ye wish me to woo ye?"

"It's a little late for that, don't you think, seeing as we're already wed?"

Aye, he did, and he wasn't about to bring up the fact he'd yet to take her to his bed. For all she said she didn't expect to be wooed, he wasna completely daft when it came to women. She wanted to be wooed. Were ye no' supposed to be in love to woo a woman? They were no' in love, they were . . . friends. Why in the bloody hell did he think to distract her with Broderick and Fallyn?

"Are you not listening to me?"

"What? Nay, what did ye say?"

She huffed an irritated breath. "I said, I've decided to help Broderick court Fallyn."

He snorted. "Ye doona ken how to woo. And besides that, why would ye want to help them?"

"Since I am a woman, I think I know better than you what a woman wants. And as for helping them, I can now see they're in love. They just need a little push in the right direction."

"No' like any woman I've ever met," he muttered under his

breath. "Ye'd best be careful, Evangeline. When it comes to pushin', ye have a tendency to shove."

"What do you mean by that?"

"I mean ye're no' verra subtle."

"Not *that*. You said I'm not like any woman you've ever met."

Oh, nay, he wasna goin' there with her. She'd twist his words, and who knew where that would land him? He breathed a sigh of relief when Gabriel brought his steed alongside them.

"I've decided I'd best head for home instead of accompanying you to the Isles. I'm not certain Jorunn can handle the extra time it would add, nor for that matter if I can."

He followed his friend's gaze to Jorunn, who was being comforted by her lady's maid. "Has she no' stopped cryin' since we left the Far North?"

"She has not stopped crying since after the ceremony ended." Gabriel ran a frustrated hand through his hair. "I've tried my best to comfort and reassure her, but I'm about at my wits' end."

Lachlan barely managed to suppress a shudder at the thought it could have been him married to the weeping lass.

Evangeline shot him a smug smile, obviously knowing exactly the direction his thoughts had taken. "King Gabriel, as your wife has been raised by King Magnus and his brothers, perhaps you're being too gentle with her. A more forceful approach might be in order."

"I suppose it can't hurt. Nothing else has worked. Thank you, Evangeline, I shall give it a try."

"Do ye have enough men to accompany ye?" Lachlan asked as Gabriel brought his steed around.

"Yes, we'll be fine. I'll see you at the next meeting of the Seelie Council. Hopefully it will be soon," he added before he flew to his wife's side. Gabriel's deep voice rumbled over the swoosh of wings. Jorunn's head snapped up as though she'd been slapped. She straightened upon her horse, then wiped her eyes and nodded. Gabriel sent a relieved smile in Lachlan and Evangeline's direction.

"I'm waiting," Evangeline said in a singsong voice.

"All right, lass, I bow to yer superior knowledge of females."

"More." She wiggled her fingers.

"I fear yer head will get bigger than it already is, but aye, I'm relieved to be wed to ye instead of the wee lass." He spoke the truth, but couldn't help but wonder if in the end Jorunn would've been the safer choice. But he was honest enough to admit he wanted no man, especially not Magnus, to have Evangeline.

She patted his hand. "Of course you are. For all your efforts to portray yourself as a fool, you really are an intelligent man."

Mayhap he should've let Magnus wed her after all. "I hope I can live up to your high opinion of me, Evangeline," he said dryly.

"I'm certain you will. Now . . . what to do about Broderick and Fallyn?" Arms crossed, she tapped a finger to her lips, oblivious to his sarcasm.

He shook his head. "Since we approach the Isles, whatever scheme ye're concoctin' will have to wait. Broderick will be headin' home, leavin' me to deal with the three sisters."

"You're right, I suppose, but you don't have to worry about Fallyn and her sisters. I will take care of them for you."

His relief at not having to deal with the three women was tempered by the knowledge of who would be. "Ah, Evangeline, how exactly do ye propose to *deal* with them?" he asked as they skimmed over the treetops and glided over the sparkling azure waters to circle the palace before landing.

"You need not concern yourself with such trivial matters any longer. I am more than capable of seeing to this."

Noting her happy and relaxed manner, a side of Evangeline he couldn't recall seeing before, he didn't wish to take away her pleasure, but he was confident the course of action he'd decided upon earlier was warranted if they were to have a good marriage. "That may be so, but you will inform me of yer plan of action before proceedin'."

"But I . . ." She stiffened in his arms, her voice trailing off.

Before he could question her, the reason for her reaction became apparent. Morfessa charged across the courtyard toward them, his black robes flapping with his long, angry strides.

"Doona fash yerself, Evie, I'll take care of him," he said, rubbing her arm.

Lachlan leapt from the steed, raising his arms to her. She met his gaze, worrying her bottom lip. He cursed the man who could make a woman of Evangeline's strength cower. "What do ye want, Morfessa?" he asked, tucking her against his side while he stared down her father.

Morfessa's long, angular face darkened with outrage. His black eyes raked his daughter before he brought his gaze back to Lachlan. "I needed to reassure myself that the rumors were false, Your Highness. Please tell me you weren't so foolish as to wed . . . her."

Lachlan tightened his arm around Evangeline while his fingers gripped the hilt of his sword. Against his thigh, heat emitted from the blade. "Foolish, Morfessa? Nay, I'm far from foolish."

The man practically sagged with relief, placing a trembling hand on his narrow chest. "I'm much—"

"I'd like to present ye to my wife, Morfessa. As queen of the Enchanted Isles, I expect ye to award her the respect she is due."

"No." He howled like a wounded animal, clasping his head

between his hands. "What have you done? You have damned the Fae. You—"

Lachlan drew his sword.

"Lachlan, please. It doesn't matter." Evangeline placed her hand firmly on his chest.

He kissed the top of her head. "Aye, it does." Pressing the point of his crimson blade to the wizard's chest, he said, "Go back to Rohan before I have ye locked up fer castin' aspersions against my wife." Morfessa had done enough damage to Evangeline's reputation. Lachlan didn't wish to give him further opportunity to taint the opinion of the small crowd who gathered in the courtyard.

Her father stumbled back. "You don't understand the power she wields. She uses her beauty to blind you to her evil. She will—"

"No' another word out of ye. Guards!" he bellowed to four of his men who stood gaping with the rest of their audience.

Shooting one last desperate look in the direction of the approaching guards, Morfessa yelled, "You will regret this." Then he disappeared.

Lachlan motioned for the bystanders—who gawked at Evangeline, whispering Lord knew what behind their hands—to disperse. Certain their censure was not lost on her, he said, "Doona worry, 'twill take time fer them to realize your father is a madmon and that they have nothin' to fear from ye."

With a brittle laugh, she raised her resigned gaze to his. "You're wrong, Lachlan. They have hated and feared me for as long as I can remember. I should have realized . . ."

He sheathed his sword then cupped her face in his hands. "We're wed now. Ye're no longer alone. Together we'll find a way to change the Faes' opinion of ye."

The hands she placed over his trembled, and that as much as the look of gratitude in her glistening eyes snuck past his hard-won defenses. She stretched up on the tips of her toes, placing an achingly sweet kiss upon his mouth. "Thank you," she whispered.

He eased away from her, managing a lazy wink. "I can think of a much more enjoyable way fer ye to thank me," he teased in an attempt to regain control over his emotions. "Though 'twill have to wait until I've seen to matters which I'm certain have come up in my absence."

Her cheeks becomingly flushed, she slowly drew her hands from his, studying him as she did so.

Striding from the palace, Uscias hailed them. "Lachlan, Evangeline, I'm glad to see you have returned safely." Not as glad as Lachlan was of his mentor's interruption. He released a slow sigh of relief, flushing under Evangeline's intent perusal. He tugged at his tunic, certain it was responsible for the tightness in his throat.

"Although it was quiet in your absence, there are a number of items Rohan left that require your attention. He sends his best wishes, by the way, and expects an invitation when you have organized your wedding celebration."

"Aye, Evangeline will be gettin' on that right away."

She arched a brow, lips pursed. Lachlan laughed, the tension easing in his chest.

"You will have much to attend to then. I shall speak with you later. Aurora awaits her lessons." Uscias stopped midstride, lifting a gnarled finger. "That reminds me, I returned Iain to Dunvegan. I'm hopeful he will make a full recovery. I'm certain that eases your mind."

Lachlan grabbed hold of his mentor's arm. "What are ye talkin' aboot? What's this aboot Iain?"

"I assumed you were aware of your cousin's accident." He frowned, angling his head to look past Lachlan. "I thought . . ."

Lachlan shot a look over his shoulder in time to see Evangeline giving a furious shake of her head. She became aware of his scrutiny, and stopped abruptly. With a curse, he turned on her. "Ye kent Iain was injured and ye didna tell me?"

Evangeline held up her hands. "Lachlan, you don't understand."

"I think perhaps I should leave you to discuss this between yourselves." Uscias cast a sympathetic look in Evangeline's direction, then disappeared in a shower of light.

Chapter 15

Ignoring Evangeline's desperate plea to listen to her, Lachlan dragged her into the stables. "Out!" he ordered the two lads, who gaped at him before fleeing through the open doors. "Now, explain to me what it is I doona understand."

"I had no choice, Lachlan. You weren't fully recovered and . . . and I couldn't risk leaving Uscias in Magnus's hands any longer than—"

"Are ye tellin' me ye kent Iain had been injured and didna lift a bloody finger to help him?" Nay, even as he asked the question he knew she couldn't have done such a thing. She'd have to be heartless, devoid of all feeling to commit such a heinous act. Evangeline was neither.

"You're not listening. I wasn't even certain Aurora's vision could be trusted. It was the first time she had one when she wasn't in a trance."

She took his stunned silence as permission to continue. "Even if I thought it could be, there was no way to know where he was and I couldn't leave you."

His heart thudded painfully in his chest, his clenched jaw ached. "And when ye kent I had recovered, why not then? Why did ye no' tell me then?"

She bowed her head then raised her eyes to his. "I had to

make a choice. We could not spare the men or the time. It was either save Iain or save the Fae from certain death if Magnus uncovered Uscias's secrets. No matter my feelings for Iain, I couldn't—"

"Feelin's? Ye have no feelin's. Ye're a heartless bitch. I was a fool to trust ye. Yer father was right."

She gasped as though he'd plunged a knife in her heart. He clenched his hands into fists lest the fragile reins he held on his temper snapped and he shook her within an inch of her life. As though she sensed his intention, she backed into the stall behind her.

"I'm goin' to Dunvegan. When I return, I want ye gone from here." He took a menacing step toward her. "I'm warnin' ye, doona let me see ye again or I willna be accountable fer what I do. Do ye *understand* me?"

"Yes . . . yes, I do." She made no effort to wipe away the tears tracking down her colorless cheeks.

"Ye're good, Evangeline, one might actually believe ye cared." Lachlan ignored the dull ache in his chest at her devastated demeanor. He strode from the stables past Fallyn and her sisters, who were headed toward them. Not bothering to acknowledge them, he kept walking. If they thought he was a surly bastard before, it would be nothing to what they would think of him if he actually stopped to speak to them as they appeared to want him to.

Broderick, who'd been trailing behind the women, smirked. "I see you're being your charming self with the ladies."

Lachlan held up his hand. "I'm no' in the mood."

Broderick's brow furrowed. "I can see that." His friend took hold of Lachlan's arm as he proceeded to walk by him. "What's happened?"

Shrugging off Broderick's hand, he said, "I doona have time to waste. I must get to Dunvegan."

"Unless you retain Evangeline's magick, you will require—"

He whipped his head to glare at the man. "Doona mention her name in my presence again."

"Hold up, MacLeod. I'll transport you to the stones."

Lachlan chafed at the idea, however, he had no choice but to accept Broderick's offer. He was bloody powerless without her magick. As powerless as he'd been to rescue his cousin, and it was all because of her.

Broderick studied him, then laid a hand on his shoulder. They reappeared at the standing stones just beyond Uscias's cottage. His friend held him back before he entered the stones that would take him to the Mortal realm. "What did she do?" he asked quietly.

"I told ye, I doona have time fer this."

"Yes, you do. I'll go through the stones with you then transport you to Dunvegan."

Noting the stubborn set of Broderick's jaw, Lachlan relented. The journey to his cousin Rory's home on Skye would take him the better part of the day without Broderick's aid. "My cousin Iain was injured. Christ, fer all I ken he lay dying, and that heartless bitch did nothin' to help him. She sacrificed him without a thought to what my family would suffer. All because she couldn't bear fer Magnus to gain weapons such as my sword." He scrubbed his hands over his face, sickened once more by what she'd done.

"As you're aware, I have never completely trusted Evangeline, but I also know how important Syrena and your family are to her. I can't believe she would let your cousin die if she thought she could save him."

"Well, believe it. She admitted as much to me." He shoved the image of her stricken eyes, her pale, tear-stained face from his mind and stepped through the stones.

As Lachlan breathed in the clean, heather-scented air on the Isle of Lewis, the memories of his youth crowded in on him. They weren't all bad. Sweet Christ, how he missed the land and his family; if not for Arwan seducing his mother, his life would have been perfect. The Fae had screwed him over from the moment of his conception. He could no longer call the Mortal realm home, but nor was the Fae realm his home. He might be a king, but he'd always be a half-blood in their eyes—never fitting in, in either realm. Evangeline's blood had changed that; for the short time he'd held her powers he'd felt as if he was one of them. But now the thought of her blood pumping through his veins filled him with disgust. He felt like an idiot. He'd begun to think with her at his side he had a chance to make the Fae realm his home.

"Have you decided how you will handle your marriage?"

"I'm no' married. I have banished her from the Enchanted Isles."

Broderick grimaced. "That may not have been the wisest move on your part, Lachlan."

Gritting his teeth, Lachlan said, "How can ye think I'd want her near me after what she's done?"

"I'm just saying a woman with Evangeline's powers is a dangerous one to cross. Do you think your family will shun her as you do?"

Lachlan gave a disgusted shake of his head. "Ye canna be serious? Of course they will. She will be as unwelcome here as she is in the Enchanted Isles."

"That's my point. Besides Fallyn and your uncle, your family are the only ones who do not shun her. I'm concerned the pain she will surely feel at the loss will put her over the edge, and she will not care who her magick hurts. If she retaliates, neither Mortal nor Fae shall be safe."

Fingers of unease crawled up Lachlan's spine. "Are ye sayin' ye believe she's evil?"

He shrugged. "She is her mother's daughter, but more than that, from what I've seen of her power, she'd be a formidable foe. I only hope for all our sakes I'm wrong."

Broderick left Lachlan on the steps of Dunvegan. As he pushed open the oak doors, his shoulders sagged in relief at the sound of the bairn's high-pitched laughter. Surely that boded well for Iain.

Alex and Jamie, his cousin Rory's sons, came shrieking out of the grand hall as if the hounds of hell were after them and ran headlong into Lachlan.

"Uncle Lachlan, save us!"

Rory and his wife had named both Lachlan and Aidan honorary uncles as they only had the one—Iain. Lachlan's heart twisted at the thought of his cousin. He scrubbed his face then looked down to where the lads clung to his legs. "From what?"

"Oh, nay, Lachlan will no' be protectin' ye. No' this time. Get out from behind him, demons," Aidan said fiercely, striding toward them.

Lachlan rolled his eyes. He should've known his brother was behind the boys' hasty exit from the hall. There was no love lost between the three of them. "What did ye do this time, lads?"

"I'll tell ye what they did." His brother turned to show him his arse. "They slathered my chair with honey. I nearly tore the seat out of my trews when I got up."

Stifling a laugh, Lachlan said, "Yer Auntie Syrena will no' be happy if ye used up all the honey."

"Nay, we didna, we saved her a pot." Alex smiled innocently from beneath a tousled mop of ebony curls.

"Aye, we wouldn't do that to Auntie Syrena. We love her," Jamie added. As fair as his brother was dark, he shot Aidan a look that said they didn't feel the same about him.

His brother took a threatening step toward them. Lachlan raised his hands. "Now, Aidan, I'm sure—"

"Aidan, whatever is the matter with you? Ava and Olivia have just gone down for their naps. You'll be the one looking after them if they awaken." Syrena waddled crossly toward them.

"Me? 'Tis the wee demons makin' all the racket."

The lads hurled themselves at Aidan's wife. "Auntie

Syrena, he said he was goin' to wring our bloody necks if he—"

"Jamie MacLeod, what have I told you about cursing?" Aileanna, the twins' beautiful mother, her belly almost as rounded as Syrena's, came down the last of the steps with a hand to her lower back.

Arms crossed, Syrena shook her head at her husband. "It's not their fault, Aileanna, Aidan has been threatening them again."

"I see nothin' has changed," Lachlan remarked dryly.

"Lachlan," both women cried as if they'd just noticed his presence then embraced him awkwardly, their rounded bellies getting in the way.

His cousin Rory, drawn from the hall by the commotion, joined Aidan to regard their wives with an amused grin. The two men with their dark hair and brawny good looks were often mistaken for twins themselves.

Syrena looked past Lachlan, then frowned up at him. "Where's Evangeline? Uscias told us of your marriage. I thought she'd be with you."

Everyone looked at him expectantly. "She's no' here, and if I have anythin' to say aboot it, she'll never set foot near my family again."

"Lachlan, how can you say such a thing? She's your wife, and more importantly, she's my best friend."

"Syrena," his brother warned. Coming up behind his wife, he laid a hand on her shoulder. "What's this aboot, Lan?"

He held his brother's gaze. "She kent Iain had been injured and did nothin' to help him."

Aidan and his cousin cursed.

Aileanna leveled the two men with a pointed look before she said, "Jamie and Alex, off you go. Your dog has dug up Mrs. Mac's garden again. You'd best find him before she does." The bairns, who'd been about to protest their dismissal, tore from the keep without a backward glance.

"I don't believe you. Evangeline would never do such a thing."

"Syrena is right. She's like family to—"

"Enough." Lachlan held up his hand to stem the women's defense of Evangeline. "Would someone please tell me how Iain fares?"

"Aye." Rory came to stand behind his wife, smoothing his big hands rhythmically up and down her arms. "If no' fer Aileanna, I doona think he would've survived."

Aileanna reached back to caress her husband's clenched jaw. "By the time Uscias brought him to us, he was suffering from severe hypothermia. And his leg . . ." She sighed and lifted her shoulders. "I managed to save the limb, but we won't know for some time if he will regain full use of it."

Lachlan thanked God for Aileanna's prowess as a healer. She'd been taken from her time in the twenty-first century, where she'd been a physician, by the magick of the fairy flag. If anyone could save his cousin, it would be her.

"I'd like to see him."

"Aye, go on up. But, Lan, he's no' himself. Between his injuries and the loss of Glenna, well, he's . . ." Rory's voice trailed off.

"Lachlan, wait," Syrena called to him as he headed up the stairs. He bowed his head, blowing out a ragged breath before looking back at her. "I'm sorry, Syrena, I ken she's yer friend, but even ye canna condone what she did."

"But—"

"Nay, I willna speak of her again."

The stable doors creaked open, flooding the barn with sunlight. Evangeline rose stiffly from the cold stone floor. She turned her back lest whoever had entered witnessed her sorry state, discomposed she'd allowed Lachlan to reduce her to tears—shocked he'd been able to do so.

"Evangeline, what's happened? I've seen Lachlan angry before, but never like this," Fallyn said, as she came toward her.

Angry was such a pitiful word to describe the vindictive rage Lachlan had lacerated her with. Her stomach churned at the memory of what he'd said to her, at the icy contempt in his voice. She wrapped her arms around herself to ward off the chill the memory of his condemnation evoked. Never before had she felt so miserable and alone.

She closed her eyes, flicking her fingers at her side to call on a small portion of her magick. Grateful for its comforting warmth, the confidence it instilled in her that allowed her to face Fallyn.

Her friend's eyes widened as she drew near. "What in the name of Fae did he do to you?"

He hated her. He'd rejected her, making her feel more evil than her father ever had. He'd demolished the small fluttering of hope that she could be happy, that she'd found someone who truly cared for her. She choked back a bitter laugh. How could she, the daughter of Andora, ever believe she had a right to happiness?

"He was angry I did not inform him of his cousin's accident and that I did not go to Iain's aid." Despite the pain of losing Lachlan's friendship and trust, in her heart Evangeline knew she would not change what she had done. She only wished he'd given her the chance to explain her actions so he would understand.

"I'm confused. Start from the beginning. When did this happen?" Fallyn asked, leading her to the white marble bench against the back wall.

Evangeline sat beside Fallyn and told her everything that had happened. Her voice dropped to a strained whisper when she repeated what Lachlan had said to her.

"No wonder he was furious with you. Surely we could have spared the men to search for Iain?"

Evangeline jerked her hand from Fallyn's, then leapt to her

feet. At the very least she would have expected Fallyn, a warrior sworn to protect the Fae, to understand the necessity of what she'd done.

Fallyn slowly came to her feet, intently studying Evangeline. "You truly believe you had no choice but to do what you did, don't you?"

"If I thought otherwise, do you not believe I would have helped Iain? I would've done everything in my power to go to his aid. He's Syrena's family. I consider him my family . . ." She averted her gaze from Fallyn's. Evangeline had spoken the words without thought, hadn't recognized the truth until she'd said them aloud. The MacLeods had always gone out of their way to make her welcome, to include her in their family's celebrations. They probably had no idea how important they were to her. Syrena would, though. And surely if anyone would understand why she'd had no choice but to sacrifice Iain, it would be her best friend. The band lashed across her chest eased somewhat at the knowledge. She turned on her heel.

"Where are you going?"

"To Dunvegan."

"Are you certain that's wise, Evangeline? From the sounds of it, Lachlan doesn't want you anywhere near his family."

"I don't care what he wants." Her stomach clutched at the lie. She wished she spoke the truth. "I am no longer his wife, nor am I his subject. I can do as I please. He has no say in the matter."

"You may be powerful, but you are not invincible. Although Lachlan has no magick, he does carry the Sword of Nuada. One nick from his blade and you'd be dead. Believe me, Evangeline, the man does not need magick the way he wields his sword." Fallyn held her gaze then sighed. "You appear determined, so all I can do is wish you luck. Perhaps you're right and an apology will go a ways in gaining their forgiveness."

Evangeline frowned. "I'm sorry Iain suffered as a result of the decision I was forced to make, but I go to seek their understanding, not their forgiveness. I have nothing to apologize for. And once I make them see I—"

"Oh, Evangeline, honestly, you are . . ." Fallyn's gaze focused on a point beyond Evangeline, and her lip curled. "I thought you would be gone by now."

"Not without bidding you farewell, my darling."

Evangeline turned at the sound of Broderick's voice only to meet the condemnation in his dark gaze head-on.

He scowled at her but directed his remark to Fallyn. "You should be careful in the choice of company you keep. You have no—"

"Mind your tongue, Broderick. Evangeline is my friend."

"Like I was about to say, you have no idea what she's done."

"Yes I do, and while I might not condone her actions, she believes she had no other choice."

"Since neither of you appears to require my presence, I shall be off." The certainty Syrena would understand, and the comfort of her magick, helped Evangeline to feel more like herself. She would make everything right. Eyeing Fallyn and Broderick, a slow smile curved her lips. *Indeed, that would be most helpful*, she thought. Being queen of the Enchanted Isles was the best opportunity she had to protect the Fae. With Syrena's help, she was certain she could convince Lachlan she had taken the only course of action available to her. By bringing Fallyn and Broderick together as she'd promised him, she'd prove her worth.

The couple—caught up in their heated exchange—were oblivious to Evangeline. Tiptoeing toward the stable's entry, she drew on more of her magick. "Better, much better," she murmured as the warm white light further filled the hollow emptiness left by her confrontation with Lachlan.

Backing out the stable doors, she flicked her fingers and, out of the couple's line of sight—not that they would have noticed, engrossed as they were in each other—she conjured a table. After adding a white linen cloth and some wine, she hesitated. As food was not important to her, she was not entirely certain what Fallyn and Broderick would like to eat. She thought of Lachlan, lying amongst the satin pillows being fed sweets by the empty-headed beauties who doted on him.

She tried to ignore the disturbing thought that at that very moment he could be appeasing his anger at her with those very same women. Relieved when she remembered his intention to head straight to Dunvegan—which was exactly where she needed to be. After loading the table with fruit and sweets, she shifted her gaze to the hard bench along the far wall.

Not at all conducive to the couple's comfort. She gave one flick of her finger and an oversized settee appeared; two flicks . . . pillows, and on the third, blankets. She smiled at the romantic atmosphere she'd created while drawing deeper on her magick to ward the interior. Confident they wouldn't be going anywhere until she decided to let them out, Evangeline was about to close the stable doors when Fallyn's gaze jerked to her.

"Evangeline, what are you—" Her eyes widened as she took in Evangeline's handiwork. "No . . . no," she cried, running toward the stable doors. Evangeline had them locked and warded before Fallyn hurled herself against them. At least that's what Evangeline assumed the loud thunk implied.

"You let me out of here right now, Evangeline! Evangeline!"

Evangeline gave herself a mental pat on the back, inordinately pleased with her solution. With no way to escape each other's company, Broderick and Fallyn would have no choice but to work out their differences, then Lachlan would realize just how useful having Evangeline as his wife could be. She rolled her eyes at the threats Fallyn yelled from within the stable, certain her friend would come to realize Evangeline had been right to take matters into her own hands and would soon be thanking her.

When she came through the standing stones on the Isle of Lewis in the Mortal realm, some of her confidence faded. Her heart beat a little too fast, her palms were a tad damp. She drew on more of her magick to ease the discomfort. "Better, much better," she murmured, then transported to Dunvegan.

Jamie and Alex sat on the steps outside the castle doors, elbows on their knees, chins resting on their hands. At their forlorn expressions, she stood frozen to the cobblestones. "Jamie . . . Alex, what . . . what's wrong?"

They glanced up at her and she steeled herself for their answer. "We lost our dog. And if Mrs. Mac finds him, she'll give him to Cook."

She exhaled a grateful breath. "Oh, that's good to hear." Meeting their horrified expressions, she quickly amended, "No . . . no, that's not what I meant. What I meant is that's good because it's something I can help you with."

They bounded to her side, expectant faces looking up at her.

"Did you try calling him?"

Jamie rolled his eyes. "Of course we did, Evie."

The smile his comment drew from her faded when she recalled the only other person who called her Evie. And how when Lachlan said it, it felt like an endearment.

"And you've looked in all his favorite hiding places?"

With a shake of his head, Jamie looked at his brother. "She's no' goin' to help us, Alex."

"Of course I am. You just have to trust me. I know what I'm doing. Now, what does he like best to eat?"

"Little cakes. The kind Auntie Syrena likes," Alex offered.

She smiled. Her friend would live on sweets alone if she had her druthers.

Jamie scoffed. "Nay, he likes meat on a big bone."

"We'll try both and place them near his hiding spots."

"'Tis a good plan, but Cook willna give us any food."

"We don't need Cook, Jamie," Evangeline said, conjuring

up a plate of cakes and then another plate with a chunk of meat still attached to the bone. "All right, now—"

"What the hell do ye think ye're doin' here?" Lachlan stormed from the castle, his face twisted in rage.

Evangeline opened her mouth to speak, but he cut her off. "Doona answer, just leave!"

"Nay, Uncle Lachlan, she's helpin' us find our dog."

His attention was so intent on her, she didn't think he heard Jamie. Lachlan drew his sword from its sheath.

She stepped back. Drawing the boys with her, she pushed the plates of food on them. "Go . . . go and set them out for your dog." She kept her tone even despite the frantic pounding of her heart.

Alex, looking wide-eyed at his uncle's furious face, tugged on his brother's arm. "We'd best go, Jamie."

Eyes blazing, Lachlan's long, menacing strides ate up the ground between them. He pointed the tip of his glowing blade at her chest.

"Nay!" Jamie threw himself in front of Evangeline at the same time Lachlan lifted his sword. She jerked back then ducked. Grabbing Jamie around the waist, she flung herself to the ground, rolling away with the little boy cradled protectively in her arms.

Lachlan's jaw dropped. He looked from the blade to Evangeline. Uncertain if his momentary madness had passed and needing to protect the children, she raised her hand, shooting a charged bolt at his chest. The current lifted him in the air. He landed in a heap at the opposite side of the courtyard.

She followed a horrified gasp to the castle doors. The MacLeod family stood there, staring at her as if she was evil incarnate.

Breaking free from her hold, Jamie's giggle rippled through their condemning silence. "Did ye see that, Alex? Uncle Lachlan can fly!"

Chapter 16

Pointing to the tawny long-haired dog that sniffed Lachlan's prone body through the smoke spiraling from his chest, Alex squealed, "Look, Jamie, she did it!"

Aileanna hurried to Lachlan's side, shooing off the boys and their pet while Syrena rushed to Evangeline's defense, standing protectively in front of her. "Stop it, both of you. Help Aileanna with Lachlan," she ordered the two men who towered threateningly above her, matching muscles jumping in their steely jaws. Evangeline felt certain that if not for Lachlan's pained moan, the men would have set Syrena aside and happily torn Evangeline limb from limb.

Aidan glared at her then, turning on his heel, tromped to his brother's side.

"Lachlan's fine. Now do as Syrena asked and help him to his feet," Aileanna said, positioning herself in front of her husband. "When you have composed yourselves, we will discuss this matter in my solar," she said, nudging Evangeline toward the castle.

"Fer Chrissakes, Aileanna, ye're no' bringin' her into my home."

With a stubborn jut of her chin, Aileanna tapped her finger

on her husband's broad chest. "Oh, it's your home, is it, now? Well, excuse me if I thought it was mine, too."

"You're twistin' my words. You ken exactly what I mean, and I expect you to obey me in this."

"Obey . . . obey, why—"

Rory rested his hands on his wife's shoulders. "*Mo chridhe*, doona get fashed. 'Tis no' good fer you or the bairn."

Taking advantage of the couple's discord, Syrena hustled Evangeline into the keep. "What, by all that is Fae, were you thinking?" she asked as she dragged Evangeline across the entryway.

"I was thinking he was going to kill me and the children."

"Evangeline, he would never . . ." As the men's voices filtered through the open door, Syrena pushed her up the stairs. Breathless by the time they reached the upper level, Syrena pointed in the direction of Aileanna's solar.

"You will take some time to calm yourselves before joining us," Aileanna ordered the men from the bottom of the stairs.

At the disappointed look on Syrena's face as she closed the solar's door, Evangeline protested, "You didn't see him, he had his sword pointed at my chest. What was I—" She stopped as the door opened, relieved when only Aileanna walked in. She needed to get her friends on her side before dealing with the MacLeod men.

Closing the door behind her, Aileanna leaned heavily against it. A loud knocking came from the other side and she huffed an exasperated breath, opening it a crack. Jamie and Alex pushed their way inside, brandishing wooden swords.

"Boys, what do you think you're doing?"

"We've come to protect Evie," they told their mother, then crossed to where Evangeline hovered by the stone fireplace.

Before Aileanna could protest, Rory, Aidan, and a pale and disheveled Lachlan stormed into the room.

"I told you not to come up here until you'd—"

"Ferget it," Lachlan growled.

"You may be a king in the Fae realm, Lachlan MacLeod, but you're not one here. Now sit down before you fall down," Aileanna ordered. "All of you."

Lachlan shoved a hand through his tousled hair and shot an indignant look at his cousin.

Rory shrugged. "Might as well do as she says. The bairn makes her cranky."

Jamie and Alex raised their swords when Lachlan pinned Evangeline with a vengeful glare and took a threatening step toward her.

"Lachlan, sit down before the demons take ye out at the knees."

Grunting, he did as his brother asked. The three men's hulking frames sat smushed together on the settee.

"Evangeline, I want you to tell your side of the story. And you three," Syrena swept her finger over the glowering MacLeods, "will not say a word until she's finished."

Focusing her attention on the two women, Evangeline started her tale at the very beginning—from when she'd first given her blood to Lachlan to save his life. Her voice dropped as she relayed what the state of her magick had been at the time. And she made sure they understood how very real the danger to the Enchanted Isles was if Magnus got hold of Uscias's secret. Several times she had to raise her voice to be heard over Lachlan's derisive mutterings. But in the end, she was certain at least Syrena and Aileanna understood why she'd had no choice but to sacrifice Iain.

"As for using my magick against Lachlan in the courtyard, you know as well as I do, Syrena, if I'd wanted to kill him instead of simply stopping him from harming the children or myself, I could have . . . easily. Just like that," she said, snapping her fingers in Lachlan's direction. She grew tired of defending herself and listening to him malign her character.

Jamie exchanged a glance with Alex, then nodded. Lowering their swords, they walked to the door.

Lachlan snorted. "Ye see, even the bairns will no' stand in yer defense after hearin' what ye did."

Evangeline's heart pinched. Although it wasn't as if the boys could protect her, their support had been comforting.

Jamie looked at his uncle, furrowing his brow. "Nay, we're hungry is all. We fergot Evie doesna need us to look after her. She can just go like this," he flicked his finger at Lachlan, "and turn ye into a bug," he giggled, "or make ye fly. Ye should have seen yerself, Uncle Lachlan."

Alex laughed appreciatively at his brother's impersonation of Lachlan flying through the air. Evangeline dropped her gaze to the wood floor and bit the inside of her lip.

"'Tis no' somethin' to tease yer uncle aboot. Be off with ye now," Aidan ordered.

The boys glowered at Aidan, beating a hasty retreat when he made to rise from the settee. Before he closed the door behind him, Jamie said, "Evie, if Uncle Aidan yells at ye again, turn him into a toad."

"Out!" Aidan bellowed.

The door cracked open an inch. "But if ye do, doona ferget to come and get us. We can use him for bait when we go fishin'."

Aidan jumped to his feet and Jamie squealed, slamming the door. "'Tis no' funny, Syrena," he muttered.

"No, of course it's not," Syrena said, dabbing at her eyes. Her expression grew serious when she looked at Evangeline. Blowing out a frustrated breath as she tried to lever herself off the settee, she thanked Aileanna for her helpful push.

"Evangeline," Syrena said as she came to stand before her, "no one could ask for a better friend than you. You have always been there for me. You've protected me without any regard to your own safety. I know you better than anyone in this room." She directed a quelling look at Lachlan, then took Evangeline's hand in hers. "And that's why I know in your heart you truly believe you did the right thing. But even you must admit you went too far this time."

"What are you saying, Syrena? I—" A hurtful ache built in Evangeline's chest. The one person she thought would support her now appeared to condemn her.

"No, let me finish. It's important for you to see that in your need to prove your father and everyone else wrong, you've overreacted. You see danger where none exists, and put others at risk."

Evangeline swallowed past the lump in her throat. The room blurred in a misty haze and she blinked her eyes. "I'm not evil, Syrena. I truly believe . . . believed I had no other choice."

"No . . . no, Evangeline, we do not think you're evil," Syrena said emphatically, squeezing her hand

"Lachlan does." Her throat ached, but she pushed the words out, sweeping her gaze over his family. "I'm sorry for the pain I caused Iain. I would like to tell him so if you'll let me."

At a nod from Rory, Syrena said, "Yes, of course."

"Thank you." Evangeline walked toward the door, tugging absently on her magick, but even the warm glow no longer comforted her.

Lachlan flinched as Syrena stalked toward him. She drilled her sharp-tipped finger into his chest. "You told her she was evil?"

"Nay." He pushed deeper into the couch. "Fer Chrissakes, Syrena, she left Iain to die." His heated defense of his actions no longer felt justified. Not after listening to Evangeline tell her side of the tale. She truly believed she had no other choice. Despite his anger at what she'd done, he shouldn't have let his fear for his cousin cloud his judgment. And never should he have lashed out at her the way he had.

"You made her cry. Evangeline never cries!"

"I didna make her cry." But he had. And even whilst caught up in his embittered fury, he'd felt a twinge of guilt for attacking her as he did. Now it was much more than just a twinge, and neither Syrena nor Aileanna were helping with their condemning looks.

"You will make this right, Lachlan. You will apologize to your *wife*, and we will have a celebration to welcome her into this family. Surely even you must recognize how important the MacLeods are to her and that she would never willingly do anything to harm us. If you think otherwise, then you're a fool."

Lachlan snorted, ignoring the dull ache in his chest. "Ye can say that because she's never hung ye from the rafters, taunted ye and goaded ye until she aboot drives ye mad. And I'm bloody well growin' tired of everyone callin' me a fool!"

"She was protecting me! And if she goads you, it is only because she needs to know you care enough to protect the Fae." Syrena seemed to lose steam, tears welling in her topaz eyes. "Don't you see, Lachlan? She lives in the shadow of her mother's evil and tries so hard to make amends. She just doesn't know she can't. They won't let her."

Aye, he knew that, probably knew it better than anyone in this room, and yet in his fear for Iain, he'd lashed out at her. Christ, he was no better than Morfessa and the rest of the Fae. He scrubbed his hand over his face. Nay, he was far worse. After what they'd shared in the Far North, he could only imagine how much he'd hurt her. He knew he couldn't take the words back, but somehow he had to make Evangeline understand he didn't mean them.

"Ah, angel, come here." Aidan tugged his wife onto his lap, wiping at her tears with his thumbs. "Doona—"

The couch broke and the four of them toppled to the floor in a heap.

"I'm so fat I broke the settee!" Syrena wailed, burying her face in her hands.

"Sweetheart, ye're no' fat." Her husband struggled to contain his mirth, his shoulders shaking.

Lachlan attempted to do the same, but one look at Rory and the two of them ended up howling like a pair of fools. When Aidan joined in, Aileanna, who was attempting to help Syrena up, leaned over and clouted him. "Honestly, Alex and Jamie are more mature than the three of you put together."

Wiping his eyes, Lachlan was suddenly struck by the realization he'd never seen Evangeline laugh. Nay, that was not true. He'd seen her laugh once before, a joyous, exultant laugh when she'd called upon her magick. For some inexplicable reason it became important to him that she did so again. Not in response to her magick; he wanted her to share her laughter with him. He wanted to make her laugh instead of cry.

Chapter 17

Evangeline crept into the candlelit room. She needed to see for herself that Iain would recover then she'd return to the Seelie Court. But if Rohan had found out what she'd done, perhaps he, too, would condemn her. Was Syrena right, did she see danger where none existed? Would she protect the Fae at any cost?

She looked down at Iain, sucking in a horrified breath at the scar that ravaged the left side of his handsome face. His leg, thickly bandaged, was rigged in a contraption that raised it several inches above the bed he lay so still upon. The once ruggedly virile man was pale and emaciated—a mere shadow of his former self.

With the evidence of the pain her decision had caused staring her in the face, she lowered herself weakly into the chair beside the heavy oak four-poster bed. Somehow she would make it up to him. She tried to think of what she could do to ease his pain and began compiling a list in her head. A movement beneath the white counterpane drew her attention. She tilted her head, watching as the lump at Iain's side wriggled and squirmed. She reached over to lift the covers, only to realize Iain had awakened. A weak smile curved his lips when she drew back the covers to reveal a silky blond head of curls nestled against him. Ava, Syrena's daughter. Evangeline hesitated, not relishing the prospect of waking the little hellion.

"Nay, leave her be. She's better than heated stones fer keepin' me warm." His voice was rough and scratchy.

Evangeline sat on the edge of her chair. "How did she get in here?"

He shrugged, then winced. "Syrena warded Dunvegan."

Evangeline cast a worried glance around the dark-paneled room. Syrena's spells never turned out quite as one expected. "I'll take care of it before I leave." Considering his remark regarding the little girl's warmth, she conjured several blankets, then stood to carefully tuck them around him.

He angled his head, a question in his eyes. She lifted a shoulder. "I thought perhaps you were cold."

"Thank you."

She smiled, relieved she had done at least one thing right. "I noticed your throat sounded dry. Would you like some water?"

"Nay, but I wouldna mind some ale."

"Of course." She conjured a tankard of ale and a mug. Setting them on the bedside table, she took several minutes to prop the pillows at his back to her satisfaction. Once she had, she held the mug to his lips. Nodding when he'd had enough, she set it aside.

"Evan . . ."

She dabbed at his mouth and chin with a cloth. "There. Would you like something to eat? I—"

He frowned, the movement puckering his stitched wound. "Evangeline, what's goin' on?"

Plucking at her robes, she said, "I don't know what you mean."

"Aye, I think you do."

Averting her gaze, she swallowed past the lump in her throat. "I . . . want. I need . . . to apologize to you. I'm very sorry, Iain. It's my fault you were injured."

He narrowed his gaze on her. "You caused the storm?"

"No, I . . ." She sighed, and for the third time that day she repeated what she had done. And after explaining to the one person her decision had most affected, she realized what everyone had been trying to tell her. For the first time in her life Evangeline conceded, if only to herself, maybe she'd been wrong after all. Her shoulders bowed under the weight of her heavy heart. She prepared herself for Iain's condemnation, his anger. She deserved it.

"Evangeline. Look at me, lass."

She raised her gaze to his. Instead of seeing censure, she saw understanding.

"'Tis all right. In truth, I wish Uscias had left me there." He drew his gaze from hers, staring vacantly at the opposite wall.

Instinctively she knew it was not his injury but his sorrow at losing his wife that made him say such a thing. She hesitated for a moment, then reached for his hand. "She was with you, you know. Glenna. Aurora saw her. She believes it was your wife who gave her the vision in hopes we would help you."

Her heart ached at the look of sorrow etched on his face, the shimmer in his amber eyes. He withdrew his hand from hers. "If you doona mind, I will try to get some rest."

"Yes, of course. Would you like me to take Ava?"

"Nay, but mayhap you can do that wardin' thing you do so she canna just pop in and out whenever she pleases."

"I will . . . and," she conjured a bell, placing it within easy reach, "if you need me, just ring and I shall come." She'd decided she would stay and see to Iain's care. At least until she assured herself he was out of danger.

He held her gaze. "I understand why you did what you did. You doona have to make amends, Evangeline."

"Thank you. I think you're the only one who does. If you don't mind, though, I'd like to stay and help for a while."

"Suit yourself. And you can tell my family I doona hold you responsible and that I will take offense if they continue to do so."

She nodded, unable to get her thanks past her painfully tight throat. Closing the door softly behind her, she leaned against it and swiped at the moisture gathering on her lashes.

"Evangeline."

She groaned and turned her back. The last thing she wanted was another confrontation with Lachlan.

His hand came down heavily upon her shoulder. "Doona worry, Evie. I'll speak to Iain. I'll make him understand ye didna mean him harm."

The gentleness in his tone as much as what he said took her by surprise. She snuck a peek over her shoulder. He didn't look as though he'd taken leave of his senses, nor did anyone hold a sword at his back, at least not from what she could see. "Thank you, but that will not be necessary. Your cousin does not hold me accountable for his injuries, not like the rest of you."

"Aboot that, Evangeline, I—"

At the sound of the bell clanging loudly from within Iain's chamber, she said, "Excuse me, I must see to your cousin." Anxiously, she pushed past him. Ava, an impish grin on her angelic face, lay across Iain with the bell gripped tightly in her hands, swinging it for all she was worth.

Evangeline rushed to the bed, scooping Ava into her arms. "I'm sorry. Did she hurt you?" Balancing the child on her hip, Evangeline held the bell while she straightened his covers.

"Nay, I'm sure my ears will stop ringin' momentarily."

Tightening her grip on the squirming child, Evangeline stumbled when there was nothing left to hold on to. Ava had disappeared.

"Let me guess. Syrena warded Dunvegan," Lachlan said dryly from behind her.

Evangeline's heart tripped at the sight of Ava in her uncle's arms, staring up at him adoringly. The little girl was as beautiful as Lachlan. "I'll ward the castle," she murmured, setting the bell back on the table.

"Ah, Evangeline, ye fergot somethin'." Lachlan held Ava out to her expectantly.

"She seems content with you." Much more so, Evangeline knew, than she would be with her. "Iain, is there anything I can get for you?"

"Nay, I'm good."

"Just let me fix . . ." Leaning over him, she adjusted the pillows, then smoothed and retucked the blankets. Hands on her hips, she looked over the bed with a critical eye. "I think you could use . . ." She conjured two more feather pillows, carefully stuffing them beneath his elevated leg. Noting the dampness of his chambers, she glanced to the hearth across the room. The fire little more than a few dying embers, she wiggled her fingers and reignited it.

"Evangeline," Lachlan said, a thread of panic in his voice.

She spun on her heel and her jaw dropped. Ava, mimicking Evangeline, wiggled her fingers and ignited a fire at the foot of Iain's bed. With a quick wave of her hand, Evangeline extinguished the flame—reaching Ava just in time to catch her fingers before she raised them again. "Oh, no, you don't."

"Ye'd best take her," Lachlan said, pushing the little girl into her arms. Ava kept a hold on her uncle causing Lachlan to bump into Evangeline. She stumbled and he wrapped an arm around her waist. Held tight against him, a tingle of awareness rippled through her. "I think she wishes to remain with . . ." Ava disappeared.

Evangeline steadied herself with a palm pressed to Lachlan's chest.

"Syrena!" Aidan bellowed from below them in the castle.

"Mayhap it would be a good idea fer ye to get those wards up." Lachlan grinned. He held her close, his gaze roaming her face.

"Yes, I think you're right." She couldn't seem to make herself move away from him and he made no attempt to release her. If anything, he held her closer.

"After ye do, Syrena wants to celebrate our union."

"I didn't think . . . You said—"

He pressed a finger to her lips. "I ken what I said, and I wish I could take it back. I'm sorry, Evie."

She shook her head, lifting her eyes to his. "No, you were right. All of you were. I—"

"Shh, we'll talk of it no more," he said, smoothing the hair from her face.

"If you doona mind takin' yer discussion elsewhere, I'd appreciate it."

Lachlan searched his cousin's face. "Sorry, Iain," he said quietly.

Iain sighed. "Nay, 'tis me who should apologize. I hope you'll both be verra happy."

Evangeline's heart went out to Iain. How difficult it must be for him to see them together. Newly wed, with their future before them, reminding him of all that he had lost. She started at the thought. No, her and Lachlan's union was nothing like Iain and Glenna's. They were . . . friends.

Seated in the grand hall drinking ale with his brother and cousin, Lachlan gritted his teeth at the ringing of the bell. He was sorely tempted to go upstairs and tell his cousin what he could do with the bloody thing. For the last two days, Evangeline had no time to spare him. She was too busy waiting on Iain.

"Ye canna be jealous of yer own cousin, a grievously wounded cousin at that." His brother eyed him speculatively over his mug.

"What are ye talkin' aboot? I'm no' jealous."

"I doona ken aboot that. What do ye think Rory, jealous or no'?"

"Jealous." The two grinning fools sitting across from Lachlan clinked their mugs together, sloshing ale on the scarred wood.

"The two of ye are in yer cups."

"Aye, and our wives are drivin' us to it. Ye wait until Evangeline is heavy with yer child and ye'll see what 'tis all aboot."

Lachlan choked, spewing his ale. Wiping at his tunic, he cursed his brother. The last thing he wanted to envision was Evangeline carryin' his bairn. "Our marriage is no' like yers. We'll no' be havin' bairns."

His brother and cousin gaped at him. "What do ye mean, yer marriage is no' like ours?" Aidan asked, his brow furrowed.

Lachlan hadn't intended to blurt it out in that manner, but mayhap it would be best if the two men knew so they wouldn't expect more of his and Evangeline's union. "We were forced to wed. If I didna marry Evangeline, Magnus would have petitioned Rohan fer her hand."

Aidan's gaze hardened. "Ye did the right thing. I wouldna have wanted to see her tangled up with the likes of him."

Rory chuckled. "I doona ken. I think our Evangeline can take care of herself."

"Well, that is no' all of it. Rohan has made it clear he would no' stop until he saw me wed. Evangeline was as good a choice as any."

"So ye're sayin' ye doona love the lass and yer marriage, fer all intents and purposes, is a sham?"

His brother and his questions were beginning to grate on Lachlan's nerves. "Nay, 'tis no' a sham. It serves us both well. Most marriages are no' like the two of yers. We like each other, fer the most part."

Lachlan shifted uneasily under his brother's intent gray gaze. "I wanted more fer ye than a marriage of convenience, Lan. I wanted ye to have what I have with Syrena. What Rory has with Aileanna."

"I doona. This I can handle, Aidan. I doona want bairns. I . . . I'm content."

"And Evangeline, are ye sure she will no' expect to be loved, to have children?"

"Nay, she lives only to protect the Fae and is as satisfied with the arrangement as I am."

"She may be now but I wonder how long 'twill last. Women are notorious fer changin' their minds."

His grip tightened on his mug, uneasy at the thought his brother could be right. He chastised himself. What did a pair of drunken fools know? Evangeline accepted they would be companions and nothing more.

His cousin's brow furrowed. "You mean to hold true to yer vows, doona you? You'll be faithful to the lass?"

Gritting his teeth, Lachlan grated out, "Aye."

Aidan angled his head to study him. "Do ye plan on becomin' a monk, then?"

"Fer Chrissakes, I may no' be in love with my wife but it doesna mean I doona want to . . ." He scowled at the pair of them, crossing his arms over his chest. "I'm no' talkin' aboot this with the two of ye."

"I'll no' ask ye anythin' more if ye answer me this one question." His brother arched a brow expectantly.

Lachlan nodded, raising a finger. "One more and then we're done with this."

"So, are ye sayin' ye no' want to bed yer wife?"

"Are ye daft? Have ye taken a good look at my wife? Of course I want to bed . . ." He looked at the two men, a dull flush working its way up their faces. "She's standin' right behind me, isna she?"

Aidan grimaced and Rory nodded.

"Ah . . ." He cursed. "I'm goin' to kill the two of ye." He shoved back his chair, turning in time to see his wife stride from the hall. Her glossy black mane swaying in time with her backside, a lushly curvaceous backside that thanks to his brother Lachlan couldn't bloody well take his eyes off. "Evangeline," he called out to her. "Hold up. Let me explain." And how the hell was he supposed to do that?

As he left the hall, his brother's and his cousin's voices stopped him cold. "I'll wager you they're in love in a month and expectin' a bairn in two."

"I'll wager ye they're in love already and are too foolish to ken it and they'll be expectin' a bairn in a month."

Chapter 18

Men. Mortal or Fae—half-Fae—they thought of one thing and one thing only, especially when imbibing spirits. Evangeline stomped up the curved staircase half expecting to hear Lachlan fast on her heels. He wasn't.

She frowned.

Hadn't he said he wanted to explain his remarks to her? Not that they were difficult to understand. He wanted her in his bed. He found her . . . desirable. And why in the name of Fae should that make her smile? She knew why. Knowing he desired her instead of despised her was reason enough for her to do so.

Aileanna met her on the stairs, brow arched. "You're making enough noise to wake the dead, or at the very least the children."

Evangeline grimaced. The last thing she wanted to do was wake Ava and Olivia. She didn't know how Syrena and Aileanna managed. If they didn't need the extra hands to care for Iain, Evangeline would happily return to the Enchanted Isles for some much-needed peace and quiet.

Looking past her with a frown, Aileanna asked, "Is Lachlan ill?"

"Not that I'm aware of." Evangeline glanced over her shoulder. Now that Aileanna mentioned it, he did appear unwell. His typically sun-bronzed complexion had turned a sickly gray and he was rubbing his chest as though it pained him.

She shrugged, returning her attention to Aileanna. "The three of them are drinking in the hall, perhaps he overindulged." Which was highly likely, Evangeline thought, given his earlier remark.

A curse followed by a low moan came from one of the chambers on the second floor. Aileanna grimaced. "I can guarantee they'll be well into their cups before the night is out. Syrena's in labor."

There were times when Evangeline found Aileanna's choice of words bewildering, and this was one of them. "Labor?"

Aileanna patted her shoulder. "Sorry. She's having her baby. Would you mind sitting with her for a while? I have to let Aidan know, and there are a few things I need to prepare for the delivery."

"Um. Can't Mrs. Mac sit with her?" Evangeline asked, knowing Dunvegan's housekeeper was much better suited for the duty.

"Evangeline, what's the matter? You've gone very pale all of a sudden."

"I'm not good with babies. I wouldn't want to—"

Aileanna laughed, waving off Evangeline's excuse. "Don't be silly, it will be hours before the baby arrives. Go on up. I won't be long."

"I won't be long. It will be *hours* before she has the baby," Evangeline mimicked Aileanna's trilling voice as she stomped down the stairs. She stumbled and grabbed hold of the balustrade, thinking perhaps she'd had a little too much of the wine Mrs. Mac had used to revive her. She'd warned them. But had they listened? No, of course not. As Evangeline had never attended a birth before and she was now newly wed, they thought it important she do so.

Why in the name of Fae they thought it important she bear witness to her friend's excruciating pain, her cursing and moaning, she'd never know. The memory of the blood and guck, followed by the arrival of first one slimy, squalling red-faced infant and then another made her shudder. And what was wrong with Syrena and Aileanna that they had to have two babies at a time? One was bad enough. And afterward, she'd had to listen to Aileanna, Mrs. Mac, and Syrena, oohing and ahhing over the babies and saying, *they're so beautiful*.

She shuddered again. They weren't. They looked like gnomes, wrinkly, bald, ugly gnomes.

Aidan, Rory, and Lachlan looked up when she tripped into the hall. She grabbed hold of Lachlan's broad shoulder to steady herself. In an effort to rid herself of the images etched in her mind, she reached over and took his mug of ale. Taking a deep restorative swallow, she wiped a hand across her mouth. The three men gaped at her. "What?"she asked.

"Syrena? The baby? Sweet Christ, Evangeline, has somethin' gone wrong?" Aidan asked, rising from his chair.

She grimaced. "Sorry." The color left Aidan's handsome face. She realized then he'd misunderstood her apology and held up her hand. "No. Syrena's fine and the babies are . . . fine. Healthy . . . they're healthy. You can go up now." Her brain a little fuzzy, she'd forgotten offering to inform Aidan was how she'd made her escape.

About to sprint from the room, Aidan came to an abrupt halt by the chair Evangeline had slumped into. "Did ye say babies—as in two?"

She winced. She didn't blame him for being upset. "Yes, I'm sorry, there are two of them. And they're both girls." She cringed, thinking of the little hellions Olivia and Ava.

Aidan whooped his delight while Rory clapped a congratulatory slap to his shoulder. The two men strode from the hall, announcing the good news to a handful of servants who'd gathered by the doors.

A deep rumble of laughter came from Lachlan. She scowled at him. "It's not funny. That was one of the most horrific experiences of my life." She chugged back the ale in an effort to wipe the memory from her mind. He laughed all the harder.

"You wouldn't think it so amusing had you been there." She went to take another drink and realized she'd drained the mug. "I'll have some more. Please." Covering a hiccup behind her hand, she held out the mug with the other.

Chuckling still, he wiped his eyes. "I doona think 'tis a good idea, Evie. Ye doona drink and ye just drained a mug of ale faster than most men."

She leaned toward him, feeling a little woozy when she did so. "I think we should go home." She tried to hold up two fingers, then gave up. "There's two more. That's six of them now—six screaming, crying children. Well, no, Jamie and Alex are fine, but the other ones . . ." She shuddered.

Two Lachlans leaned toward her. She closed one eye to bring him into focus. He grinned at her, his eyes all warm and crinkly, then took her hand and pressed his lips to her palm. A wave of heat washed over her and she tugged at her robe, fanning herself. "Do you find it warm in the hall?"

"Aye, verra warm," he murmured as he trailed kisses from her palm to her wrist. "I wish we could go home, Evie, but I doona trust ye to transport us. I'm no' sure where we'd end up."

The muscles low in her belly clenched with the feel of his warm mouth on her sensitive skin. She squirmed in the chair. Her gaze drawn to his bent head, his golden hair gleaming in the torchlight, she reached out and stroked her fingers through the thick, silken waves. "Your hair is so pretty," she murmured.

He chuckled into her palm, then nipped it. "Remind me to bring a jug of ale home with us."

"Lachlan, bring a jug of ale home with us."

He groaned. "Did ye eat today?"

She furrowed her brow, trying to search her befuddled brain for an answer. It took a moment to find it. "No. I was going to, and then I came to the hall and heard you say you wanted to take me to your bed. Then I met Aileanna on the stairs and she made me go and sit with Syrena. And she promised, she promised me Syrena wouldn't have the baby and she did. Lachlan . . . Lachlan, are you asleep?" she asked her husband, who rested his forehead on the table.

He shook his head then raised his gaze to her. "Nay, I—"

"Evangeline, Lachlan. Syrena wants to introduce you to your nieces," Aileanna called down the stairs to them.

"Would you tell her to stop yelling in that manner, she's going to awaken Ava and Olivia," Evangeline said, shooting a disgruntled look in the direction of Aileanna's voice. Noticing another mug, she reached for it.

"Oh, no, ye doona." He grinned, closing his hand over hers. "Up ye come."

"You go. I've seen them already. Once was enough, thank you."

"If I have to go, so do ye." He hauled her from the chair, wrapping a supportive arm around her waist.

"I must warn you, Lachlan," she whispered, stumbling up the stairs. "They think . . . they think the babies are beautiful, but they are not. You mustn't hurt Syrena's feelings, though, so just smile and nod as I did."

"I will," he said, the corner of his mouth twitching.

She studied his chiseled profile. "Are you laughing at me?"

"Nay."

She stopped him halfway up the stairs, squinting to see if he told the truth. As she did, a horrible thought came to her and she clutched the front of his tunic with both hands. "Lachlan, you must promise me that we will never have babies, ever," she said desperately.

He cupped her face with his big hands. "I promise ye. No babies fer us. Ye ken, Evie, I think I love ye."

Relieved, she patted his broad chest. "I love you, too."

Evangeline gasped and they stared wide-eyed at each other. "Like," they croaked in unison.

They made their way up several more steps to find Aidan and Rory leaning over the baluster, watching their clumsy approach. "I told ye," Aidan elbowed his cousin with a laugh. "I win."

"Nay, they have to be expectin' in a month fer you to win," Rory argued.

Evangeline frowned and nudged Lachlan. "What are they talking about?"

"Ignore them, Evie. They're a pair of drunken fools," he said. Scowling at the two men, he rubbed his chest.

"Lachlan, you look unwell. Are you in pain?" she asked, noting the color drain from his face.

"Too much ale is all. Come on."

He tugged her after him. Her stomach lurched, the floor rising up to meet her. "Me, too. I think I'm going to be ill."

"Aye, I ken how ye feel."

A warm lush weight filled Lachlan's hand. Silky strands tickled his chin, invading his senses with their soft feminine fragrance. His cock stirred to life, nudging the luxurious globes it nestled against. He wondered if Evangeline would welcome his attention. His throbbing erection certainly hoped so. It was the first time he'd slept beside her since they'd been wed. Her nights at Dunvegan had been spent curled in a chair by his cousin's bed. And last eve, when she'd said she felt ill, it had not been in jest. He smiled when in reaction to his hand at her breast, her nipple furled into a tight bud beneath the sheer chemise Mrs. Mac had dressed her in after cleaning her up.

Evangeline had been out cold before her head hit the pillow. Lachlan hadn't fared much better considering he was stretched out beside her fully clothed. It wasn't like him to imbibe as he had done. He could blame it on his desire to keep his brother company while awaiting the birth of the bairns, but he knew it was his unrequited lust for the woman now in his bed that had done him in. Unable to resist the temptation of her body curved against his, he nudged the strap of her chemise off the delicate slope of her shoulder. Pressing his lips to the hollow at the base of her elegant neck, he nuzzled the satiny-smooth skin there.

She moaned then squirmed, trying his thinly stretched restraint. Her eyes fluttered and she released a pained groan, bringing her hand to her brow. Not exactly the reaction he'd been hoping for.

From beneath her long lashes, she slanted him a questioning look. "We're not in the Enchanted Isles, are we?"

"Nay." He dropped a kiss on her shoulder. "But we can leave as soon as you're ready. Uscias has been lookin' after things long enough and I'm sure my family can manage to care fer Iain without ye." At one time his desire to return to the Enchanted Isles would've surprised him. But not now; he wanted his wife to himself.

She raised her head to look down at herself and winced. Lachlan reluctantly slid his hand from her breast. "Thank you for seeing to me. I must apologize for my behavior. I don't know what possessed me to indulge as I did."

He chuckled. "There's no need to apologize. Ye were verra entertainin'. As fer me seein' to yer care, 'twould be Mrs. Mac who did so." He skimmed his hand along the curve of her waist to her hip. "Although I would have, but I wasna in much better condition than ye were."

She rolled to her back, eyes closed. "My head is pounding. Do you think it will stop soon?"

Lachlan couldn't keep his gaze from her full breasts straining against the sheer white fabric of her chemise, the tantalizing shadow of her nipples. "Aye." He hoped it would.

Placing his palm on her flat belly, he asked, "Ye're no longer feelin' ill, are ye?"

She shifted, her hip bumping his straining erection. "No, it's just my head."

"Mine aches, too." And no' the one she referred to. Fingers splayed, he moved his thumb back and forth over her taut belly, so close to her womanhood he could feel the silken curls beneath the thin fabric. The muscles in her belly quivered and ever so slightly she raised her hips.

"I ken what would make us both feel better, Evie." He brought his hand to where the chemise bunched at her thighs, revealing long, shapely legs he wanted to feel wrapped around his waist.

"You do?"

"Aye, I do," he rasped, his voice thick with desire. "Let me take care of ye, like I couldna last eve," he murmured against her lips, caressing the inside of her velvety smooth thigh.

Her heavy-lidded gaze met his, her cheeks flushed. "You want to . . ."

"Oh, aye, I want to verra much." He teased her lips apart with his tongue, delving inside her warm mouth. The tentative touch of her tongue in return severed the last of his control.

"Uncle Lachlan, Auntie Syrena's da wishes to speak to you and Auntie Evie," Jamie yelled through the door.

Groaning, Lachlan buried his face in her breasts. Breasts he'd hoped to be touching, sucking, and licking in the next few moments. He lifted his head. Noting the look of concern upon her face, he sighed. "Evangeline, ye're my wife. Rohan willna be fashed we're sharin' our chambers, he'll expect it of us."

She nibbled her bottom lip as he'd noted her do so often when she was worried. Her gaze flicked to his. "No, it's not that which concerns me. I'm certain he now knows what happened to Iain and the part I played. As well, I have been using my magick here at Dunvegan, which as you know is frowned upon." She rose awkwardly from the bed. With a flick of her fingers, the sheer chemise he'd grown fond of vanished to be replaced by resplendent amethyst robes.

That's what he got fer marryin' a wizard. She could dress without him gettin' even a glimpse of her perfect naked body. He promised himself that would soon change. "Ye're my wife, therefore under my protection and my control. Whatever Rohan has to say, he can say to me." He stood, combing his fingers through his hair and straightening his tunic. With a surreptitious glance at the front of his trews, he deemed himself presentable.

He offered her his arm, frowning at the stubborn set of her chin and the indignant press of her lips. "What now?"

"I hardly need your protection, and as queen of the Enchanted Isles, I am most certainly not under your . . . your control."

She was the most exasperating woman he'd ever met. Here he was trying to soothe her worries and she acted as though he'd done her a disservice. He'd never used his height to intimidate anyone before but he did so now, towering over her. Somehow he had to put her in her place. "Aye, ye are, and the sooner ye realize it the better."

"You said we were partners." She crossed her arms over her chest.

He'd said a lot of things, including that he loved her, which went to show how completely in his cups he'd been. They'd both been, he reminded himself since she'd said the same. "Nay, I said there are some responsibilities I'd give over to ye and then we'd take it from there."

She tossed her glossy black mane over her shoulder and glared up at him. "You . . ." She grimaced at the sound of Ava and Olivia calling for their mothers, barely discernible above the insistent wails of the newborns. "We will continue this at home."

Aye, they would. Not the argument she seemed to be

gearing up for, but as soon as the opportunity to get her alone and into his bed presented itself, he would do so. In his experience, making love made a woman more malleable. He grinned at the thought; in his wife's case, they would have to spend an inordinate amount of time in bed to achieve the desired outcome.

Chapter 19

Anxious to witness the downfall of the she-devil's spawn, Morfessa hid within the shadows of ancient oaks beside the palace's stables. Rumor had it King Lachlan had come to his senses and denounced her as his wife. If he had not, surely when Rohan informed him of what she'd done to the Welsh king he would cast her aside. Perhaps banish her from the Fae realm altogether. Or, if the angels had answered Morfessa's prayers, in a fit of anger her husband would smite her with his mighty sword. His heartbeat quickened at the thought.

Craning his neck, he tried to peer through the crowd gathered beyond the whitewashed building to watch Uscias and the warrior woman's sister's latest attempt to break the wards. He hoped they would not be successful. The simple retelling of the tale would not be as powerful an indictment as the king seeing for himself what she'd done. It was one of the reasons Morfessa had refrained from offering his help, although in some dark corner of his mind, he acknowledged her power had grown beyond anything he'd ever seen. More reason King Lachlan, for the Faes' protection, must kill the bitch.

The conversational hum of the gathered nobility and servants rose. King Lachlan and his evil consort had arrived.

With an impatient wave of his hand, Morfessa caused those who blocked his view to stumble out of the way.

Uscias's arms dropped to his sides while Fallyn's two sisters threw up theirs when they faced the queen. "How could you, Evangeline? Fallyn is your friend!" the woman named Shayla raged.

"I didn't expect to be at Dunvegan as long as we were." The queen crossed her arms. "Really, Shayla, you don't have to look at me like that. I provided well for them. Someone had to intervene. It's obvious they love each other. I simply ensured they had the opportunity to spend some time together to work out their differences."

Shayla stamped her foot, her hands balled at her sides. "That is not for you to decide! You can't go around locking—"

"Yes, I can," the queen said mulishly.

Standing beside her with the noonday sun glinting off his golden hair, King Lachlan with his great height and the wide expanse of his shoulders was far more intimidating than even his father King Arwan had been. Morfessa rubbed his hands in eager anticipation, certain any moment now the king would strike her down. But instead, he threw back his head and laughed. Morfessa twitched with fury. A member of the ruling class had been imprisoned for days and the besotted fool laughed. He should've known better than to pin his hopes on a half-blood who was more highlander than Fae.

Morfessa shuddered when she smiled up at the king. Like her mother, she'd managed to enthrall the man with her beauty. The responsibility to rid the Fae realm of her evil now rested solely on Morfessa's shoulders.

"Evangeline." The king jerked his shadowed chin at the stables.

She shrugged then with hardly any effort at all lifted the wards—wards one of the most powerful wizards in the Fae realm had been trying to remove for the last two days. Morfessa wondered what his one-time friend would make of her magick. Surely it would cause Uscias as much concern as it did him. He shook his head in bewilderment at the look of admiration upon his old friend's weathered face, a look reminiscent of a proud father. Morfessa's hope that he could turn to Uscias with his concerns evaporated. Although he admitted it had been a faint hope. Their longtime friendship had ended the night he'd attempted to end Evangeline's life. Another reason the she-devil's spawn deserved to die.

Fallyn burst from the barn. Catching sight of the queen, she broke away from her sisters. "You . . . you . . ." She stood there sputtering.

He held his breath. Perhaps someone *would* make her pay. The Sword of Nuada's precious stones winked in the sun. "Take the sword. Strike her down," he muttered under his breath.

The Welsh king sauntered toward the woman warrior, rolling his eyes at the derisive remarks her sisters directed at him. "Now, darling, Evangeline only wished to give us time to work out our differences." He bent to nuzzle her neck. "And you must admit, for at least a few hours we were able to do so. And most enjoyably, I might add."

"Oh . . . oh, you." With a disgusted shake of her auburn tresses, the woman stomped away with her sisters at her heels.

King Broderick winked at the highlander, then chased after his ex-betrothed. "Don't be like that, darling. Come back."

Obviously the Welsh king would not press charges and the menace was free to do as she pleased. King Lachlan wrapped an arm around his wife's shoulders and together they entered the palace. She'd managed to ensnare the highlander quicker than Morfessa had thought possible. He'd dismissed the tales the warriors had brought with them from the Far North, certain she would never give up any of her powers to anyone—not even for a short time. But considering what he'd witnessed, he'd say the rumors rang true. It went a long way in explaining the king's unnatural bond with her.

As the crowd dispersed, Morfessa's gaze settled on Lords Erwn and Bana. The brothers looked as disgusted by the turn of events as he was. He'd heard something about the two men recently. He rubbed his temple, keeping an eye on the brothers as he attempted to remember what it was that had been said. Ah, yes, it was rumored they plotted the highlander's downfall. He wasn't surprised. They'd always believed Arwan's throne belonged to them—first cousins of the late king and full-blood—and not his half-blood son.

Perhaps the day had not been a total waste after all. Of the two, Bana, with his arrogance, would be most vulnerable to Morfessa's manipulation. The brothers parted ways at the far side of the courtyard. Staying within the shadows, Morfessa kept Lord Bana in his sights until he was certain of his destination. They must not be seen together for his plan to work. No suspicion cast in his direction.

He flashed to Bana's home at the base of the mountain. With the mansion warded against intruders, Morfessa had no choice but to hunker out of sight behind a rosebush, waiting impatiently for Bana to make the long journey down the steps carved into the granite cliff. Bana's vanity, like that of so many of the Fae men, would work in his favor.

The sun beat down upon him and he wiped the beads of sweat from his forehead. At the sound of approaching footfalls, he pushed the shrubbery aside. Bana had finally arrived. With a quick look down the cobblestone street to be certain no one else was about, Morfessa called out, "Lord Bana, a moment of your time if you will."

Bana, hand on the gold-plated door, frowned as Morfessa stepped from the side of the house. "Wizard? What do you want?"

With one last look down the deserted road, Morfessa shook his head. "What I have to say to you cannot be overheard."

Bana quirked a golden brow. "Inside, then."

Morfessa hesitated before he crossed the threshold. "Servants?" he hissed.

"No. I don't wish my personal affairs to be bandied about at court."

Though Morfessa paid little attention to the goings on in the Fae courts, unless it pertained to the she-devil's spawn, Bana's exploits over the years had reached his ears. *Yes*, he thought, *I've chosen well indeed.*

Bana waved him into a room decorated with a decadence Morfessa had never seen before. He averted his disgusted gaze from a painting depicting couplings of every imaginable and unimaginable position.

A knowing grin slashed Bana's aristocratic features. "My taste in art offends you?"

"It is of little import, Lord Bana, especially considering the urgent matter I must speak to you about."

Pouring green Faery juice into a golden chalice, Bana glanced at him, lifting a second goblet. Morfessa shook his head at the invitation. "Out with it, then," Bana said.

"I thought you should be aware, my lord, that your plan to overthrow King Lachlan has become common knowledge."

A shadow darkened Bana's amber eyes. "Who makes such a charge?"

"The woman who currently reigns as queen of the Isles."

Bana set the chalice on the ornately carved side table and raised his gaze to Morfessa. "Why, then, have I not been brought before the king, if, as you say, the charge has been publically made?"

"From what I can gather, he didn't believe it at first."

"And now?"

"As you must have witnessed, the queen has enthralled him. I believe within a matter of days she will manage to convince him to lay charges of sedition against you. At the very least your property will be seized and you will be banished from the Enchanted Isles."

The man sunk into the high-backed brocaded chair. "Why do you tell me this?"

"You are Arwan's cousin and a full-blood with magick. I believe you should hold the throne. Not some fool of a highlander who allows himself to be bewitched. You must stop her, Bana. She has too much power as queen, she must be . . . eliminated."

Bana's stunned gaze shot to him. "You do it."

Morfessa could not tell Bana he feared reprisal from Rohan if he did the deed himself. He bowed his head, so as not to reveal his disgust at the lie he must tell. "No matter that she is evil, I cannot kill my own child." His stomach roiled. "But you can legitimately challenge the king for the throne. Without her to go to his aid, you can bring him down."

Scrubbing his hands over his face, Bana shook his head. "We all witnessed her magick today. I have no hope of defeating her."

A self-satisfied smile twisted Morfessa's lips. "I will provide you with a weapon to match the Sword of Nuada, and I can guarantee her powers will be little more than those of a newborn servant."

Bana's brow furrowed. "You are prohibited from creating such a weapon. But more importantly, how can you mute her powers?"

"As to the sword, sometimes the end justifies the means. You can claim you found it at the ruins of Mesa." Every so often the earth around the cliffs of Mesa regurgitated relics from the battle between the dark lords. "As to her power, it is simple. Once you challenge the highlander, he will seek her blood to aid him in the fight. She will not deny him."

"You're mad! She would never give him her blood."

"She has already done so. When they were in the Far North

the king was gravely wounded and would've died without her blood. I'm surprised you were not aware of this."

"I was . . . I have been otherwise occupied of late." The way Bana's gaze lifted to the paintings, the reason for his absence from court was not difficult to deduce. "How can you be certain he'll ask for her blood?"

"What half-mortal could resist the addictive properties of Fae blood, especially when it contains the power hers does?" And the evil. "He will use any excuse he can to get her magick. He will find it in your challenge. She won't deny him."

"It's my life on the line. I need guarantees."

"I will use a compulsion on him. Addicted to her magick as I'm certain he already is, and without magick of his own, he will be susceptible to the spell. He will not be able to resist the pull. I've heard he is a very persuasive man with the women. Seeing the way she looked at him, she will not refuse him. Despite those precautions, if I see no sign of her weakness, we'll call it off."

"When do we do this?"

"As soon as possible. I have heard they celebrate their union this eve. Issue your challenge then. Set the time for the next day, midmorn."

Morfessa rose from the chair opposite Bana. "I will leave you now. On the morrow, after I ascertain she is powerless, I will leave the weapon in the shrubbery at the side of your house. That will be the sign that the plan is in motion." Morfessa started for the door, then turned back to the man sitting stone-faced and pale. "Remember, tell no one of this, not even your brother."

Staring at his painting, Bana nodded.

Inching the door open, Morfessa checked the street before he left the house then flashed to his apartments. But not to create the weapon as Bana believed. Uscias shared his formula with no one, and it was nowhere to be found in the ancient texts. Even if it was, Morfessa would not have used it. Bana wouldn't need a magickal weapon to kill Evangeline, not with her powers drained. And once she was dead, Bana's usefulness to him would be over. Morfessa could not afford to let Bana live.

For the greater good, sacrifices had to be made.

Chapter 20

Over the heads of the gathered assemblage, Lachlan spied his wife, standing alone in a corner at the back of the grand hall. With a murmured excuse to the lords and ladies who attempted to ingratiate themselves into his good graces, he wove his way through the heated crush to her side.

Propping a shoulder against the marble wall, he frowned down at her. "Why are ye no' with Fallyn and her sisters?" It bothered him to see her on her own. He berated himself for not keeping a closer eye on her. Unaccustomed to looking out for anyone, and with so many of his subjects vying for his attention, it hadn't taken much for him to lose track of her. He should have realized it would take more than her new position as his queen to endear her to the Fae.

She arched a brow in answer to his question.

"Ah, still fashed with ye, are they?"

She shrugged as though it didn't bother her, but Lachlan had spent enough time with his wife of late to recognize the strain on her beautiful face. He brought his hand to rest on the shoulder she'd raised, his fingers sliding over the gossamer silk of her exquisite gown. "Ye look verra bonny this night, Evie." To say she was bonny didn't do her justice. During the evening meal he'd had a difficult time concentrating on the elaborate feast set out before them. The golden candelabras lining the center of the banquet table had cast Evangeline in an ethereal glow, the candlelight reflecting off her waist-length hair and the crimson gown cut low to reveal the tantalizing swell of her breasts. She'd overshadowed the simpering women of his court with her vivacious, sultry beauty.

A rosy flush swept up her elegant neck to color the high arch of her cheekbones, her fingers plucking self-consciously at the revealing neckline of her gown. Drawing his attention once more to the ripe mounds his fingers itched to caress.

"Thank you. I was not certain what to wear," she murmured. Her gaze flicked to the elegantly clad couples who twirled by.

Lachlan ignored a woman who cast him an overtly provocative glance as she whirled by with her husband, and focused on Evangeline. His wife's obvious effort to fit in set off a visceral response in him. He shot a contemptuous look to where Fallyn and her sisters stood at the edge of the dance floor, fending off their ardent admirers. Could they not have put aside their anger at her for one night?

Or mayhap it was only he who could see beneath the haughty facade she presented to the Fae, her mask as carefully crafted as his own. Unwilling to stand by and watch her being hurt time and time again, he silently vowed if it was the last thing he did, he'd change the Faes' opinion of her.

He took her hand. "Shall we join the others in a dance?"

She attempted to free her fingers. "I would rather not, but by all means go ahead. There are several of your subjects eager to partner with you," she said with a pointed look at another woman who attempted to gain his attention. Until that moment, Lachlan hadn't realized how bored he'd grown with their blatant invitations. At least now he had a legitimate excuse to deny them. "Nay, I'd prefer to dance with my wife."

Her look of surprise contained a hint of pleasure, but she shook her head. "I can't dance."

"I doona believe ye. The Fae love to dance." He could've

kicked himself when her expression shuttered. Considering how the Fae felt about her, he doubted she'd ever been invited to take part in their festivities. He should've kept his bloody mouth shut. "It doesna matter. I will teach ye."

"But I—"

He pulled her into his arms and her protest died on her lips. The tension eased from her willowy frame and he savored the feel of her warm womanly curves pressed against him. With her innate elegance and grace, Evangeline fell effortlessly into step with him. "I was right. Ye can dance," he said when they took a second turn around the dance floor.

He spun her away from him, then pulled her back into his arms. Her eyes sparkled as a breathless laugh escaped her parted lips. She looked young and carefree, her luminous skin flushed with pleasure. He couldn't help but think it was what she'd look like when he had her in his bed. He decided then that they'd continue their dance in the privacy of his chambers.

He stumbled, tripping over her feet. "Evangeline, the mon is to lead, no' the woman."

She looked down at their feet. "I thought you were."

"Aye, so did I," he grumbled, certain it was a sign of things to come.

The strains of the melody stopped abruptly. Lachlan frowned at the musicians. He'd not called a halt to the festivities. Half-turned to gain their attention, he followed the direction of their gazes. A charged silence fell over the room as the dancers parted.

Lord Bana, nostrils flaring, his aristocratic features pinched, strode toward Lachlan with his sword drawn.

Lachlan kept his gaze on Bana while he set Evangeline away from him. Her fingers tightened on his arm and he gave them a reassuring squeeze. He waved off the four guards who were about to rush Bana. "What is the meanin' of this?"

"I'm challenging you for the throne," Bana grated out, a muscle twitching in his jaw.

A low growl was all the warning Lachlan had before Evangeline launched herself at Bana. Lachlan managed to grab hold of her arm before she reached the man and shoved her behind him. Bana took a wary step back, a bead of sweat trickling down his face. Erwn, obviously unaware of his brother's intention, gaped at him. "Brother, what are you doing?"

Bana ignored him.

"And the reason fer yer challenge?" Confident in his ability to best the man, Lachlan thought he deserved at least one chance to withdraw.

"Because he—"

"Evangeline," Lachlan muttered, attempting to quiet her with a look over his shoulder, but she was too busy glaring at Bana to take notice. He relaxed somewhat when Broderick slipped into place behind her. Fallyn and her sisters, warrior faces pinned into place, positioned themselves on either side of her. The last thing he needed was for Evangeline to use her magick on Bana. No matter the provocation, it would do more harm to her reputation than good.

"You're a half-blood. You have no magick. By allowing Uscias to be kidnapped, you have proven you are unworthy of the throne. But even more damning is your decision to take *her* as your queen."

He would allow the slur against his reputation, but the bastard would pay for the one he made against Evangeline. "It will be my pleasure to kill ye, Bana." He allowed a slow menacing smile to curve his lips. "I'll meet ye at first light."

"No!" Bana shot a panicked look through the crowd. "Mid—midday at the lists."

"Ye need yer beauty sleep, do ye? I'll meet ye at midday and I'd suggest ye get yer affairs in order. Guards." He motioned for his men. "Get him out of here."

Lachlan turned his back on Bana to show how little a threat he perceived him to be, then signaled for the musicians to resume playing. "Shall we finish our dance, Evie?"

"No." Her face pale, she bit her bottom lip and he noticed the telltale sheen in her eyes before she blinked it away. Lachlan cursed under his breath. She blamed herself for Bana's challenge. "Evie, look at me." When she didn't do as he asked, he tipped her chin with his fingers. "It has naught to do with ye."

"It's true, Evangeline. The two of them have been looking for an opportunity to gain the throne since Arwan's death."

No matter that Fallyn had been as big a pain in his arse as Evangeline had once been, Lachlan appreciated her attempt to reassure his wife. Not that it appeared to have worked. He took Evangeline's hand in his and stroked his thumb over her knuckles. "My wife seems to doubt my ability to thrust and parry. I think mayhap a private demonstration is in order."

The women groaned their disgust at his remark while Broderick laughed. "I'd thought to return home on the morrow, but perhaps I shall remain in case you have need of me."

"If ye're sure yer brother can handle another day of yer absence, I'd appreciate it, Broderick." Once Lachlan had taken care of Bana, he would have to deal with Erwn, and he was not entirely sure if Bana's charge would spur others to take up his challenge as well. A friend at his back would be welcome.

"Rand will be fine, and Fallyn and I have yet to complete our negotiations."

"I told you I am—" Fallyn started to protest before Broderick cut her off by sweeping her into his arms to join those who had returned to the dance floor.

Lachlan led Evangeline, who muttered something about highlanders with no sense under her breath, through the subdued throng. He acknowledged their offers of support but did not break his stride. If his wife was gearing up to give him a piece of her mind, she would have no qualms saying her piece in public. He found himself looking forward to her tirade. He'd much prefer her to vent her temper and fears at him than direct them at herself.

As she followed him from the overheated hall, she said, "This is a serious matter, Lachlan. I don't understand how you can make light of it."

"I . . ." A movement from behind one of the marble pillars in the entry hall caught his attention. He scanned the torchlit room then decided Evangeline was rubbing off on him. He was sensing danger where none existed.

"What is it?"

"Nothin'," he said, nudging her up the marble staircase, overcome by an odd sensation. The fine hair on the back of his neck stood on end. He glanced over his shoulder. A warm tingling raced through his limbs and he frowned, rubbing the back of his neck, wondering if he was just now feeling the affects of the ale he'd consumed the night before.

"You can pretend to ignore my concerns if you wish, but you know I'm right."

Reaching the second floor, he scanned the empty entry hall beneath them. "What are ye goin' on aboot now?"

She huffed out an exasperated breath. "Magick, Lachlan. Bana has magick and you don't."

He followed behind her as she strode to their chambers, eyeing the sway of her hips and the view of her lushly rounded behind. As she opened the door to their rooms, he came up behind her, nuzzling the crook of her neck. "I would if ye gave me yers." He frowned into the soft fragrant hollow. Where the hell had that come from? He'd made himself a promise not to take her blood again. The emotions it stirred in him were as powerful as they were dangerous. But the memory of the intoxicating rush of her blood, of the power and magick it gifted him with was difficult to fight.

"You want my blood?" she asked in a strained whisper as she stepped into his chambers.

Christ, he wanted to deny it, afraid of the consequences if he didn't. He wrapped his arms around her, pressing the evidence of his desire to the soft cushion of her behind. Intoxicated by her feminine scent, an insatiable craving came over him, gnawing at the denial he thought to make.

"Aye." He nipped her earlobe. "I want yer blood, Evie. I need it to make sure I defeat Bana. Leave no doubt in the Faes' mind of my right to lead." Sweet Christ, what had come over him? He was manipulating her, using her fears against her. It was her blood. It was making him mad with desire. He tried to fight it, tried to take back the words he'd uttered, but when she turned in his arms and lifted her violet eyes to his, he gave up the fight.

A battle warred within Evangeline—the urge to protect her magick as strong as the urge to protect Lachlan. When he crushed her mouth with his and enveloped her in his powerful embrace, any thought of resisting him evaporated. No matter what Lachlan and Fallyn would have her believe, it was her fault Bana challenged Lachlan for the throne. If his passionate kiss was not turning her legs and her brain to mush, she'd question why the urge to protect him was as strong as the one to protect her magick.

Never before had she put anyone or anything before her magick—until now. He tunneled his fingers through her hair, devouring her mouth, grinding his erection against her stomach. Uncomfortably aware of his size, his potent masculinity, the memory of Arwan's brutal assault assailed her.

As though he sensed her fear, Lachlan pulled back, his breathing ragged. He rested his forehead against hers. "I'm sorry, I didna mean to frighten ye."

The gentleness of his big hands stroking her back calmed the panicked racing of her heart and she relaxed in his embrace. He was nothing like his father. She had never wanted a man to touch her as she wanted Lachlan to. Never felt the heat of passion, the flare of desire he made her feel. For all that he drove her mad with his arrogance and teasing wit, his unerring need to defend and protect her left her feeling as though he accepted her as no one else could or would.

Her heart pinched at the memory of their shared smile outside of the stables that morning. She'd expected his anger and instead he had laughed. His reaction had managed to tear down one more of the barriers she'd erected to protect her heart. She knew if she wasn't careful she would soon be defenseless against him—if she wasn't already. Bringing her palm to his beard-roughened jaw, she said, "You don't frighten me." He did, but not in the way he meant.

"Nay? Good, because the hunger I have fer ye is bloody terrifyin' me." His heated amber gaze consumed her as he walked her backward to the bed. The edge of the overstuffed feather mattress hit the back of her knees and they fell in a heap of tangled limbs. Her breath left her on a whoosh when the heavy weight of his body fell on top of her. He shifted and something sharp scraped across her chest. She released a pain-filled gasp.

Lachlan rolled off her. "What's wrong? Wh . . ." His gaze followed the curve of her breast to the raised welt oozing blood.

"Your badge, it must have . . ." As she touched the ornate pin with a sun at its center, her explanation died on her lips, his attention riveted on the wound. He bent his head, his hair tickling her oversensitive skin as his tongue rasped the open cut, then lapped at her peaked nipples. She squirmed, the rocking motion of his erection stroking where she grew moist and hot. He suckled deeply of her blood, lowering her gown to her waist, baring her breasts to his hungry gaze. His appreciative groan caused a ribbon of heat to unfurl in her belly.

Cupping her breasts with his powerful hands, warm and a little rough, he kneaded them. His gaze locked on hers as he drew a nipple into his mouth, watching as he sucked her deeper into the moist heat. Desire pulled low in her belly. The gnawing ache between her legs intensifying, begging for release, she rubbed against him. As though his need matched her own, he wrenched the silken fabric over her hips then with an impatient growl stripped her completely, tossing the gown to the floor. His words of pleasure were smothered by her flesh, his mouth buried in her breast, licking her, taunting her, torturing her. His hand skimmed over her belly to her thighs then he nudged her legs apart with his knee, opening her to his teasing fingers. She bucked against the flat of his palm as he explored her slick folds, creating an explosion of sensation inside her.

On the brink of release, pinpricks of light danced across her vision, alerting her to the danger. Panic swamped her desire. She struggled helplessly beneath his heavy weight. "Lachlan, no more." Her voice a thin whisper, she tried to stop him before he drained her completely of her magick.

She tried to lift her hand, to utter a spell, but her magick was little more than a flicker of light, barely discernible within her ever-darkening vision. "No," she cried as the inky void swallowed her and her protest.

Chapter 21

Evangeline groaned as she managed to pry open the heavy weight of her eyelids. Early morning sunlight flooded the room, casting her too-handsome, bare-chested husband in a golden glow. The rays danced over his rippling muscles and she scowled up at him.

He winced, then came to sit by her side, the bed creaking beneath his weight. "I'm sorry, Evie, I didna mean to take so much," he said, gently brushing her hair from her cheek. His eyes filled with concern as he searched her face.

"Well, you did," she grumbled in frustration as she struggled to sit up. The room spun, causing her stomach to heave. She fell back against the pillows.

He scrubbed his hand over his face. "Bloody hell, Evie, ye have to believe me, I doona ken what came over me. 'Tis yer blood, it . . . intoxicates me." He frowned as though the thought disturbed him.

"More likely my magick," she harrumphed, troubled by the realization she wished it was her and not simply her power that intoxicated him. She pushed the thought aside.

A rueful grin curved his lips. "Aye, that, too," he admitted as he came to his feet. His muscles bunched as he pulled his tunic over his head, then reached for his sword that was propped against the end of the bed. He wrapped his big hand around the jeweled hilt and Evangeline's eyes widened at the faint yellow glow emitting from the blade.

She growled. The blasted man was happy—her stolen magick the reason. In all the years he'd carried the Sword of Nuada, not once had the blade glowed yellow. Only recently had the sword reflected any emotion at all, and it had been anger. A small part of her was relieved that the emotions Lachlan had fought so hard to control, to deny, had managed to escape his bondage. But another part of her wished it was not her magick that was responsible for his happiness.

Magick she had no intention of sharing with him again.

"Why are ye growlin' at my sword?"

"I didn't growl," she said, swallowing another angry rumble before it escaped. "Where are you going this early in the morn?" She grimaced at her petulant tone. It sounded as though she wanted him to remain with her in the oversized bed with the too-comfortable mattress. A bed in which last eve she'd thought to become his wife in more than name only, something that obviously hadn't happened. And why that should cause the heavy weight of disappointment to settle low in her belly, she didn't want to think about.

With a smug smile, he sheathed his sword and bent over her. He brushed her lips in a whisper-soft kiss, stroking the roughened pads of his fingers over the raised wound on her breast. A heated tremor rippled through her. He raised his knowing gaze to hers. "I would rather remain in bed with ye, but Broderick is to meet me on the trainin' field momentarily."

At the thought of Bana's challenge, her anger that Lachlan had once again stolen her magick faded. One day without her powers—considering her weakness, she hoped that was all it would be—was a small sacrifice to make given the circumstances. Lachlan had to defeat Bana. It was important the Fae of the Enchanted Isles trusted him to protect them, respected his right to rule. In the beginning she, too, had doubted his abilities, but no longer.

She ignored the first part of his comment just as she attempted to ignore the tightening of her nipples beneath the sheer lacy fabric of her chemise in response to his warm fingers caressing her breast. Meeting his slumberous gaze, she shifted self-consciously. "You are confident you can defeat him, aren't you?" His practiced fingers skimmed beneath the scooped neckline of her nightwear, and she barely managed to stifle a moan.

"Aye, verra confident." His heated breath caressed her cheek. "And I ken exactly how I wish to celebrate my victory," he murmured. His light, teasing kisses were driving her mad with desire and she fisted her hands in his tunic.

"I should come with you to make certain—"

"Nay . . . Nay," he repeated then claimed her mouth in the kiss she'd been waiting for. A hot, wet, openmouthed kiss that left her trembling, moaning with frustration when he pulled away. "Ye'll wait fer me here. I doona want to be worryin' aboot ye. Ye need yer rest." He framed her face with his hands, resting his forehead against hers.

It took a moment for her to be able to respond, for her breathing to return to normal. "You do not have to worry about me. I will be fine. It's important for me to stand by . . ." she began as she attempted to rise from the bed.

He caged her in with his body. "Ye'll obey me in this, Evie. I'll have yer word ye'll remain here or I will have ye placed under guard."

Noting the hard set of his jaw and the determined glint in his eyes, she knew to argue with him would be pointless. Considering her lack of strength and the sick feeling that overcame her when she tried to get up, she reluctantly admitted she would be of little use to him. "I will cede to your wishes this one time, Lachlan, but I suggest you refrain from further use of the word *obey*. I don't like it," she informed him, crossing her arms over her chest.

He laughed, kissing the tip of her nose before he straightened up to tower over her, looking every inch the battle-hardened warrior. "I didna expect ye to like it, but I do expect ye to cede to my wishes."

Watching as he strode to the door, she couldn't shake the unsettling feeling that something could go wrong and Lachlan would be injured despite his prowess on the battlefield. "Be careful. Have Broderick watch your back. I don't trust Erwn not to—"

He cut her off with an exasperated sigh. "I ken what I'm doin'. Ye doona have to worry aboot me."

"I'm not worried about you. I'm simply suggesting . . ." She threw up her hands at his pointed look. "Fine. I'll wish you luck and leave it at that."

He winked. "I doona need luck, Evie. I have your magick."

At least an hour had passed since Lachlan had taken his leave and still, from where she lay on the bed, Evangeline contemplated the high-handed manner of men—highlanders in particular. A hesitant knock on the door to their chambers interrupted her petulant musings.

"Enter," she called out. The slight quickening of her pulse at the thought Lachlan had returned faded with the realization he wouldn't knock. How in the name of Fae was a man she once abhorred able to ignite the wild fluttering in her belly at the mere thought of seeing him?

"Your Highness." A young maid entered, staggering under the weight of a gold tray piled high with domed dishes.

Without thinking, Evangeline flicked her finger to relieve the girl of her burden. A blue spark sputtered, then faded. At that moment, Evangeline didn't have to wonder at her feelings for Lachlan. She gritted her teeth and swung her legs over the side of the bed, waiting until the room stopped spinning to come to her feet. Thankful her legs did not collapse beneath her.

Retrieving the tray from the maid, Evangeline staggered under its weight and the dishes slid precariously to the raised handle. She managed to lower both herself and her breakfast to the bed without incident.

"Thank you. You may go now."

Head bowed, the young girl remained at the foot of the bed, shifting from one brown-slippered foot to the other. "His Highness left strict instructions that whoever delivered your tray must remain to see that you eat everything he ordered for you."

Evangeline rolled her eyes. "I gather you drew the short straw. There's no need for you to remain. Off with you, now."

The maid fled without a backward glance.

Lifting one of the domed lids, Evangeline wrinkled her nose at the slab of beef sitting in a puddle of blood. Despite her distaste for the menu, a warm feeling welled within her at Lachlan's concern for her well-being. Although it was tempered by the knowledge she wouldn't require his concern if he had but controlled himself.

When she reached for the gold-plated knife that slid beneath the white china plate, her fingers brushed the edge of a piece of parchment. She tugged the paper free, scanning the missive with a frown. What could be so urgent and secretive that Uscias wished her to meet with him in the woods? Her pulse quickened. What if he had discovered that Bana's challenge was a ruse and Lachlan would face more than just Bana? The thought had already crossed her mind. And if that were the case, how in her current helpless state could she go to his aid?

Knowing Lachlan could be at risk, she couldn't waste time bemoaning her lack of magick. She would meet with Uscias, and together they would do what needed to be done. Rising from the bed, she once more attempted to use her magick to dress herself. Blowing out a frustrated breath when the effort failed, she reached for the gown Lachlan had stripped from her the night before and dragged it over her head. At the rate she was going, she'd be lucky to reach the woods by nightfall.

On the chance Lachlan had followed through with his threat to place her under guard, she cracked the door open an inch and scanned the deserted corridor. With her back flattened against the wall, as much for support as stealth, she cautiously made her way to the stairs. She managed to make it to the stables without being seen. The effort had sapped her strength and she leaned heavily against the stable door before entering. An uneasy feeling prickled along her spine. It felt as though someone watched her and she scanned the nearby stand of trees. Unable to make out anyone in the shadows, she shook off the sensation and headed into the stables.

Bowen raised a baleful eye as she approached his stall. "I feel the same way, but there is no help for it," she told the steed. It had been difficult enough to contain her fear—no, not fear but trepidation—when she rode the big beast to the Far North. But this was worse, she didn't have her magick to protect her.

Using the slatted stall as a ladder, she climbed to the last rung. Her limbs were boneless and she weaved precariously. Grabbing hold of the post, she flung herself onto Bowen's back.

The steed tossed his white mane with a disgruntled whinny.

"Oh, be quiet and take me to Syrena's hiding place in the woods," she said, clinging to his neck while trying to ignore the violent trembling of her limbs, determined to conquer her . . . nervousness. Nothing mattered now but ensuring Lachlan's safety.

Evangeline swallowed a panicked shriek as Bowen galloped through the open stable doors, crossing the courtyard at a bone-jarring pace. As he leapt off the edge of the mountain, she buried her face in his mane. The whoosh of his wings rising, the feel of them beneath her slippered feet, did little to reassure her. She repeated the words of a protective spell over and over in her mind. It mattered not that the words were useless without her powers: she took comfort in the familiar litany.

With her eyes closed, the cool musky air of the forest was her first sign they'd reached their destination. But she didn't lift her gaze or release her breath until she felt the comforting thud of Bowen's hooves hitting the moss-covered ground. Sliding from the horse's back, she steadied herself then searched for some sign of Uscias. Out of the corner of her eye, she saw a flicker of movement. At the rustle of leaves and the snap of a branch, she moved away from Bowen. "Uscias?"

Lord Bana stepped from behind a tree, his thin upper lip curled. "I'm afraid not, Your Highness. No one here but you and me." His words took on an ominous threat with the way he caressed the golden blade he carried.

She hid her shock, her unease, and dug deep inside her. Pulling on what little magick she retained, Evangeline lifted her hand. Fear skittered across Bana's sharp features. His step faltered. When nothing but a tendril of smoke curled from her finger, the look of malicious triumph in his eyes turned her blood cold.

Pivoting on her heel, she took off in the direction of Uscias's cottage, gaining little momentum on the slick carpet of vegetation beneath her feet. As she ran, she lifted one foot then the other, removing her slippers. Without looking back, she hurled them in the direction of Bana's heavy footfalls. At his pained grunt, she knew she'd hit her target. But the harsh rasp of his breath behind her warned she'd done little to deter him. He closed in on her.

She tried to run faster, but she was too weak, her legs like jelly. Then he was there, right behind her, grabbing her by the hair, he wrenched her backward. She refused to give him the satisfaction of hearing her cry out and swallowed the pained moan. Despite his excruciating grip on her hair, she twisted in his hold. Her eyes watering from the agony the movement caused, she sunk her teeth in his forearm.

He released her with an outraged shriek. "You'll pay for that," he snarled. Shoving her away from him, he lifted his sword.

Bowen charged. With a wild whinny the steed rose up on his powerful hind legs, pawing the air, forcing Bana to stumble backward. Bowen swung his head as though urging Evangeline to take cover behind him. Bana struggled to his feet, thrusting his blade at the winged steed.

"No," Evangeline cried, launching herself at Bana.

Broderick skewered his blade in the ground, scowling at Lachlan. "If you continue to show off, I refuse to practice with you."

"Nay, admit it, ye doona want to practice with me because ye havena been able to get past my blade once this morn." Lachlan laughed at his friend's aggrieved expression.

"You wouldn't be so cocky if your wife hadn't given you her blood. Considering your prowess with the ladies, I suppose I shouldn't be surprised you managed to convince her to once again share her magick with you. But truly, you must be even more persuasive than I gave you credit for," Broderick said with a bemused shake of his head.

Lachlan's pleasure at the power surging through him faded somewhat at the memory of the insatiable hunger that had all but consumed him at the sight and taste of Evangeline's blood. The paralyzing fear he'd felt when she lay limp in his arms came back to torment him along with the guilt that had overtaken him when he'd witnessed her pallor, her weakness of this morn.

Both emotions fought a losing battle. The knowledge no one could defeat him nor have him at their mercy when imbued with Evangeline's magick was too seductive to overcome. Until it faded once more, he reminded himself. There was a part of him that hoped that this time would be different and he'd retain at least a portion of her magick. He shook off the thought, disgusted he'd even allowed himself to think it.

"Persuasion had little to do with it," he admitted, recalling how he'd manipulated her and played on her fears. He wasn't proud of what he'd done. It left a bitter taste in his mouth. Only the knowledge the magick he now held would alleviate some of the Faes' fears served to allay his guilt.

Broderick cocked a brow, eyeing him with interest. "Here I was hoping you'd enlighten me and I'd use the technique on Fallyn."

"Ye looked like ye were makin' progress when I left the hall last eve."

"Perhaps because you left before she dumped her wine on my head."

Lachlan sighed. "What did ye do now?"

"I—"

Aurora's appearance in a burst of twinkling light halted Broderick's protest.

Lachlan stiffened at the terrified look in the child's blue eyes as she stumbled toward him. He reached for her. "What is it, lass?"

"Evangeline . . . woods . . . Bana is going to kill her."

"Nay, stay with Broderick," he ordered when she attempted to follow him. He could barely hear his own command over the pounding of his heart. Shaking free of her hold, he raced to the edge of the meadow before he remembered he could transport himself. He focused his thoughts on Evangeline, not allowing himself to think of the danger she was in. The red and white flowers dotting the long grasses melded into a pink wash of color and he reappeared in the musky shadows of the woods.

His gaze jerked to the forest floor. Evangeline lay there with

Bowen beside her on the ground. The steed's head rested on his wife's belly, a spreading stain darkening her crimson gown.

The sight nearly took him to his knees. Nothing he'd suffered in the past prepared him for the onslaught of emotions that ravaged him now. A glint of light caught his eye. Bana, sword raised over his head was set to deliver the killing blow.

Lachlan's anguish, his fear that he'd lost Evangeline, reverberated in the battle cry of his clan. He descended on Bana with all the fury of a berserker.

Chapter 22

Bana's eyes rounded in horror, his mouth opening and closing around the gurgle rising in his throat before he collapsed at Lachlan's feet. Lachlan wrenched his blade from the dead man's chest. Bana's sword clattered to the ground, settling amongst the pile of ashes—all that was left of the bastard.

Lachlan dropped to his knees beside Evangeline, desperately searching for the wound that stained her gown. Carefully, he raised Bowen's head while he eased an arm around Evangeline's slender shoulders to draw her from beneath the steed. The gentle rise and fall of her chest awarded him a small measure of comfort, but she was too still, too pale for his fear to be alleviated.

"Christ, Evie, why could ye no' obey me?"

Her long lashes fluttered and she opened her eyes. Though her violet stare was glazed, she managed to level him with an all too familiar look. "You didn't save me only to kill me with your sword, did you?" She winced, attempting to raise her hip.

He looked down with a grimace, then gently lifted her while drawing the tip of his blade from beneath her. At the sight of her blood coating his palm, a mind-numbing anguish overtook him. "Where . . . where are ye hurt, Evie?"

"No." With a weak shake of her head, she limply pointed to the horse. "Not me, Bowen. Help him."

A heady sense of relief washed over him at the knowledge it wasn't her blood but the steed's. He wasn't going to lose her.

"Lachlan," she said in an exasperated, albeit weak, tone. "Bowen."

"Aye," he said, grinning like a half-wit while he leaned over to examine the steed. No wonder she'd been covered in blood—a deep laceration slit open the animal's chest. Lachlan ripped off his tunic, pressing it to the wound. Evangeline struggled to sit up in an effort to help him.

He shot her a frustrated look. "Bloody hell, would ye lie still."

Three bursts of light crackled behind him and he heaved a sigh of relief. Broderick, Uscias, and Aurora appeared at his side. He noted his mentor's concern when he took in Evangeline's condition. Uscias's brow furrowed as he bent to retrieve Bana's sword. "It appears Bana thought his blade contained magick. Lucky for you and Bowen it did not, Evangeline."

Broderick nudged him out of the way to take his place, and Lachlan came to his feet. Aurora held the steed's head in her lap, whispering words of comfort to the animal, which began to stir.

Lachlan reached for the sword, then hefted the blade in his hand. "What makes ye say that?"

"Besides the fact he intended to kill Evangeline, which he could only do with a magickal weapon like the Sword of Nuada, he used gold in an attempt to encapsulate the magick."

Evangeline pushed herself upright, the effort costing her as her pallor intensified. "Bana couldn't actually believe he had the capability to craft such a weapon?"

Studying the blade, Uscias said, "He was arrogant enough to think so, but I believe—"

"We can continue this in my chambers," Lachlan said,

cutting his mentor off. He found it difficult to listen to them nonchalantly discussing Bana's attempt to murder his wife.

Edging Uscias out of the way, he crouched down and scooped her into his arms, quieting her feeble protests with another exasperated look. "Broderick, do ye think ye can manage Bowen on yer own?"

His friend glanced at him over his shoulder and nodded. "Aurora seems to have the matter well in hand."

Lachlan's gaze shifted to the little seer. Her small hand glowed as she placed it above the animal's wound. The torn flesh melded before his eyes. Uscias shrugged in response to the question in Lachlan, Broderick, and Evangeline's eyes. "Her abilities continue to surprise even me. After our return from the Far North she was most anxious to learn the art of healing. It seems she has," his mentor said with a knowing twinkle in his eyes.

Since Lachlan knew none of the other Fae had the ability to heal anyone other than themselves, he wondered what it was that made this child so special. But the many mysteries surrounding his mentor's young student would have to wait. He needed to get his wife to the safety of the palace. If Bana hadn't acted alone, she could still be in danger. Without further delay, he transported them to his palace.

Moments later, Uscias appeared at his side, his gaze shifting from Lachlan to Evangeline. A silver brow raised, his mouth turned down in a disapproving frown. "Since you have the ability to transport yourself, Your Highness, I can only assume you have once more taken your wife's blood."

Lachlan winced at the charge as he pushed open the palace doors. "'Tis no' how ye make it sound. I—"

"I offered him my magick, Uscias, as a means to protect him. It was my decision to make."

Lachlan held her gaze. His hunger for her magick and power had nearly cost her her life, yet still she sought to protect him. No one, not even his brother stood up for him as she did. Somehow he had to show her how much it meant to him. How much *she* meant to him. The thought caused him to stumble as he strode to the stairs leading to his chambers. "Sorry," he murmured at her startled gasp, then tightened his hold on her.

The image of Evangeline lying on the forest floor haunted him. He reluctantly admitted, if only to himself, his response to her was far more than a hunger for her power and magick. She had managed to work her way into his heart, and the knowledge was almost as terrifying as the thought of how close he'd come to losing her.

In a flurry of sapphire robes, Uscias bustled after him. "It may be your decision, Evangeline, but I am not entirely certain you are fully aware of the consequences," he said as he followed them into Lachlan's chambers. "Given the state of your magick, even without a magickal blade, Bana could have killed you."

"Since I could not protect myself, I think I'm well aware of the consequences," she informed Uscias as Lachlan laid her on the bed. "But I survived and will be myself on the morrow."

With a resigned sigh, Uscias stepped to the side of the bed. "I hope for your sake that is the case, but there is a distinct possibility you will not regain your powers."

What little color had returned to Evangeline's face drained away. "No, that can't be true. I've given Lachlan my blood before, and my power returned."

"I don't mean to frighten you, but you have to be aware of the possibility your magick will not return. And if it does, I suggest you think long and hard before you give your blood again. Because the next time, I guarantee, it won't." With a sympathetic pat to the hand Evangeline twisted in the gold satin coverlet, Uscias said, "Rest now."

Lachlan followed his mentor to the door. "There must be

somethin' I can do," he said quietly, looking over his shoulder at his wife who stared vacantly out the window.

His hand on the latch, Uscias hesitated before saying, "You could return her blood to her."

Lachlan blanched at the suggestion, his mind returning to the dungeons of Glastonbury and the torture he'd endured at Ursula and Lamont's hands. The old scars came to life. Every inch of his body where they'd ripped apart his flesh, cutting him open to drain him of his blood, burned—the pain as intense as if they did so now. His stomach roiled. A torrent of heat rushed through him as though the blood drained from his body. He gritted his teeth, fighting back the familiar reaction to his nightmare. He'd thought he'd conquered it, but it seemed he was wrong.

The pity in his mentor's eyes shamed him. Uscias knew he couldn't do it.

"Her magick will return as it did before. I'm sure of it," he said as much to reassure himself as Uscias.

"For both your sakes, I hope it does."

As the door closed quietly behind his mentor, Lachlan turned to his wife. The sight of her surreptitiously wiping the tears from her cheeks caused the blade of guilt to twist deep in his belly. He walked to the bed then stretched out beside her, folding her in his arms. "It'll be all right, Evie, yer magick will return," he murmured the words into her hair.

Her willowy frame trembled in his arms. He shuddered at the thought he'd almost lost her and all because the bloody Fae feared her powers. Christ, mayhap it was better if he retained her magick. Mayhap she was safer without it. Mayhap they both were. If he held her powers, no one would ever challenge him again and the Fae would be protected just as she wanted.

Sniffling, she nodded into his chest. He leaned back to look down at her, nudging her chin up with his fingers. Her violet eyes glistened behind a watery film and he groaned.

"Nay, doona cry." He wished she would rage at him, flay him with her temper. That he could handle. He could withstand anything but her tears. They would be his downfall.

Seeing her heartache at the thought she'd lose her magick for good, he didn't dare suggest it was for the best. He put the idea from his head. She'd never agree to it. He ignored the weight of disappointment lying heavy in his belly, not sure what bothered him more—the thought she'd never be truly safe in the Fae realm or the thought he couldn't claim her magick as his own.

"I promise ye, I'll make sure ye get yer magick back." He would, but he prayed to God he wouldn't have to, afraid the cutting of his flesh, the sight of Evangeline drinking his blood would hurl him into the black pit he'd fought so hard to claw his way out of. And this time, he didn't know if he'd be able to find his way back.

Uscias's pronouncement shook Evangeline to the very center of her being. Without her magick she would be powerless, she would be . . . nothing. Never before had she felt so lost, so empty. When Lachlan lay down beside her, she'd wanted to rail at him for stealing her magick. For making her care so deeply for him that leaving herself vulnerable and helpless had mattered less to her than his safety did. She hadn't realized how much he'd come to mean to her until that very moment. And it was as terrifying as the thought of losing her magick.

Gathered in his embrace, she clung to his murmured assurance her magick would return. When he forced her gaze to his, she'd tried to pull away. She didn't want him to see her weakness, afraid he would turn away from her if he did. But he didn't. Instead he made her a promise that she knew was the most difficult promise he'd ever had to make. She knew him well enough to realize he wouldn't go back on his word.

She admired him for that, and despite the price he'd pay by returning her powers to her, she knew in her heart she would insist he do so. She couldn't live without her magick, no matter what it cost him to give it back to her.

"Do ye trust me, Evie?"

"Yes." She did, more than she trusted anyone.

"Good. Then ye can trust me when I tell ye everythin' will be all right. Ye doona have to cry anymore."

"I'm not crying," she protested, wiping her face against his tunic.

"Nay, of course ye're no'." He smiled gently, then eased her from his arms. "Come, ye'll feel better once ye've bathed."

She was about to protest, then noticed the bits of twigs and leaves sticking out of her hair, the uncomfortable dampness of her blood-soaked gown clinging to her skin. Out of habit, she lifted her hand to conjure a bath. Catching the look of pity in Lachlan's eyes, she let it fall to her side. "You'll have to do it."

"I have a better idea." He lifted her into his arms and strode across the room to a set of double doors on the opposite side.

As soon as Lachlan opened them, they were enveloped in a wall of steam. The heady scent of roses clinging to the warm, moist air. Sunshine spilled through the glass dome ceiling and danced on the sparkling waters. With its wood-planked walls and the rock-rimmed pool, it was as though they'd been transported to the forest.

He set her down on the smooth oak floor, inches from the granite steps leading into the azure water.

"I didn't know this room existed."

He shrugged, crouching to skim his hand over the water. "When I first arrived, Uscias created the pool. He thought it would be helpful with my healin'."

Evangeline wasn't surprised to see his expression shutter at the mention of his injuries. When they'd found him chained to the altar in the chapel at Glastonbury, she'd had to turn away from the sight of his tortured body lest she be ill. But the silvery scars he now bore as testament to his suffering did little to mar the perfection of his body.

"I come here often, especially at night."

"I'm sure you do," she said, unable to keep the censure from her tone. With the stars twinkling down from the heavens, the heated pool would provide the perfect setting for seduction.

He grinned as though he read her thoughts. "Nay, I keep this for my own private use. Until now."

"Hmm, well, I . . ." The water looked inviting, but she wasn't certain if he meant for her to get in the pool naked. Her cheeks heated at the thought. Even though he'd seen her body last eve, this was different. Her passion had overcome her self-consciousness, as did the knowledge only the subtle glow of candles had lit their chambers.

He stood up, cupping her face with his big hands, he stroked her cheek with his thumb. "We're wed, Evie, ye doona have to be shy."

"I'm not shy," she scoffed then latched on to the only excuse she could think of to avoid disrobing in front of him. "But I would rather not have anyone flying overhead see me." She took a step back, pointing to the glass ceiling.

Lachlan gave her a knowing smile, then waved his hand toward the dome, throwing them into complete darkness. She stumbled and he wrapped an arm around her waist. With a lift of his hand, the heavy air rippled. Pillared candles appeared along the edges of the pool, casting the room in a soft glow.

"If 'twill make ye feel better, I'll close my eyes until ye're in the water. As long as ye're sure ye're no' too weak to do so on yer own."

"I can manage," she said, waiting for him to close his eyes. She raised a brow when he failed to do so. He sighed, then closed them.

Removing her gown while keeping a watchful eye on Lachlan, she let it puddle at her feet then stepped carefully onto the smooth steps. The waters lapped gently against her legs. A moan of pleasure escaped her as the farther she stepped into the pool, the farther the delicious warmth enveloped her. As she neared the center of the pool, she could no longer touch the bottom and dipped beneath the water to swim to the far side. A ledge jutted out midway down the granite wall, forming a bench, and she sat down, immersed to her neck. Her hair swirled in ropy tendrils around her. Confident she was well concealed, she called to Lachlan, "You can . . ." She released an exasperated groan when she looked up and saw the heat in his eyes, the sensual curve of his lips. "You said you would keep your eyes closed."

"I did, but ye moaned and I was worried aboot ye."

"I did no such thing," she protested, lowering her eyes from the intensity in his.

"Aye, ye did. Evie." He waited until she lifted her gaze back to his. "Ye have nothin' to be ashamed of, lass. Ye're the most beautiful woman I have ever seen."

Considering the number of women Lachlan had undoubtedly seen naked, Evangeline supposed she should be flattered, but the thought of the days he'd spent womanizing tempered her pleasure.

"Ye doona have to close yer eyes, Evie. I'm no' shy," he said, then flicked his finger.

He stood naked on the top step and her jaw dropped. His masculine beauty stole her breath away. Framed in ambient light, his magnificent warrior's body appeared cast in gold, the thick length of his manhood jutting proudly from a thatch of golden curls between his muscular thighs. She quickly jerked her gaze back to his face, rolling her eyes when he flashed his perfect white teeth in a conceited smile.

With a low chuckle, he dove beneath the water. She drew in a startled gasp when he broke through the surface inches from where she sat. Water dripped from his hair, rolling down the broad expanse of his chest to his hard-ridged belly. As though he could see beneath the water, his gaze raked her body and she shivered. He smoothed his palms over the water and tiny bubbles formed on the surface, the temperature of the pool rising.

"Better?" he asked, the muscles in his arms rippling as he raised his hands to slick his hair from his face.

"Yes. Thank you," she murmured, finding it difficult to speak at the close proximity of his naked body. He reached for something behind her, his arm brushing her shoulder. The contact of their naked flesh sent a heated charge through her and she jumped.

"Doona be nervous, Evie. No matter how much I want ye, and I do, ye're no' yet recovered." He held up a bar of soap. "I'm goin' to wash yer hair fer ye."

She touched the tangled mess on her head. "It's all right, I can . . ."

"Nay, let me do this fer ye." He sat beside her, tugging her onto his lap.

Her eyes widened at the evidence of his desire, hot and hard beneath her bottom.

Grinning, he shrugged. "Ye'll have to ignore him. Now lie back and relax," he said, wrapping his arm around her shoulder.

She did as he suggested. The warm water lapped at her face and her breasts bobbed above the water, the cool air causing her nipples to tighten. Self-consciously she brought her arm over her chest, squirming beneath the intensity of his gaze.

"I'm havin' a difficult enough time without ye movin' aboot like that. Stay still."

His hard length jerked beneath her and her belly clenched, a liquid heat building between her thighs. A muscle twitched in his clenched jaw as he lathered her hair with soap. She

inhaled the floral scent, closing her eyes as she tried to ignore
the desire he ignited in her. His strong fingers kneaded her
scalp and she couldn't contain a groan of pleasure. Enthralled
by his tender ministrations, she went limp, her arm falling to
her side. He smoothed his palm over her hair, dipping her
head beneath the water. She arched her back. He cursed
softly, and she opened her eyes to meet his heavy-lidded gaze.

His big hands spanned her waist as he lifted her onto his
lap, turning her to face him. Nudging her thighs apart, he had
her straddle him, the length of his erection pressed against her
womanhood. With one hand at her back, he watched her as he
brought the soap to her breasts. Lathering her chest and belly
with sensuous care, he massaged the creamy suds into her
breasts. Her breath hitched at the erotic sensations cascading through her body. She bit her lip before she embarrassed
herself by begging him to make love to her. Cupping the
water in his hand, he rinsed her off, then drew her to his chest.
He stroked his slick hands over her back down to her bottom.
She couldn't stand it any longer and rubbed shamelessly
against him, anything to rid herself of the deep gnawing ache
at the apex of her thighs.

"Christ, ye're goin' to drive me mad, love." He tangled his
hand in her hair and gently tipped her head back to claim her
mouth in a hot, all-consuming kiss. Bringing both hands to
her bottom, he rocked his erection against her slick opening,
his groan filling her mouth.

"Tell me, Evie, tell me ye want me as much as I want ye.
Tell me ye need me as much as I need ye."

She speared her fingers through his damp hair, dragging
his lips back to hers. "Yes, I want you. I need you," she said,
showing him how much with her kiss.

A loud crash reverberated through the bathing chamber,
the doors shuddering on their hinges. Lachlan drew his mouth
from hers. His expression hardened at the shouts of anger
coming from his room.

He slid her carefully from his arms then came swiftly to his feet. "Stay here," he ordered. As though aware his tone had been harsh, he brought his hand to her cheek before crossing to the other side of the pool. He bounded up the stone steps and grabbed a length of plaid from a hook on the wall. Wrapping it around his waist, he wrenched the door open.

Huddled beneath the water, Evangeline saw the royal guards trying to subdue a man before the door slammed behind Lachlan. She knew without seeing him who it was. Lord Erwn had come seeking retribution for his brother's death. The two men had been close and she was almost certain Erwn would challenge Lachlan. What if the sword Bana had crafted was only one of many, and on at least one, his attempt to create a magickal weapon had succeeded? A hundred different scenarios clamored for attention in her mind, each more deadly than the last. She swam to the opposite side and grabbed Lachlan's robe from the second hook. Wrapping it tightly around her, she rolled up the sleeves, glad for its length as it fell to her feet. In hopes that her magick had returned, she concentrated on the glass dome and waved her hand.

Nothing.

But Erwn didn't know she was without her magick. His fear of her had been readily apparent whenever they had crossed paths in the past. She'd use that to her advantage now. And as there was a possibility Erwn had managed to turn the royal guards against her husband, she had no intention of letting Lachlan face them alone.

She'd use their fear of her against them all.

Chapter 23

Lachlan studied the faces of the men who held Erwn for some sign they conspired against him. Nothing in their expressions caused him to doubt their loyalty—not yet.

"Bastard, you killed my brother!" Erwn spat out, fighting the men who restrained him.

Padding across the cold marble floor, Lachlan grabbed his sword and jerked his chin in Erwn's direction. "Release him."

"But, Your Highness . . ." the head guard began.

"I appreciate yer concern, but I'd rather deal with him now." And he wanted the opportunity to observe his guards' reactions.

Erwn shook off the men's hands. Smoothing out the creases in his dark robes with jerky movements, he raised his grief-stricken gaze to Lachlan's. "You couldn't wait for the challenge, could you? You had to lure him to the woods and ambush him."

Lachlan felt a measure of sympathy for Erwn. He'd lost his brother. Lachlan didn't want to think how he'd feel if something had happened to Aidan. But for all he knew, Erwn had been aware of his brother's plan to kill Evangeline. And if Lachlan found out he'd had even an inkling of what Bana meant to do, nothing would keep him from slaying the man there and then.

"I killed your brother while defending my wife. I would've preferred to fight him on the lists where all could bear witness to the outcome. But he'd lured Evangeline to the woods with the intention of killing her." His hand tightened on the hilt of his sword at the memory of his wife lying soaked with blood on the moss-covered ground. He vanquished the image and the horror that had accompanied it with an image of her in his arms only moments ago. Her beautiful flushed face and her warm lush curves filling his hands. If not for Erwn, he'd be inside her now.

The door to the bathing chambers opened, and Evangeline, in his white robe, stepped out.

"Bitch!" Erwn snarled and lunged in her direction.

Lachlan cursed, hurling himself between Erwn and his wife, who'd once again disobeyed him. He fisted his hand in Erwn's robes, shoving him into the circle of waiting guardsmen. Lachlan scowled at Evangeline, who stared Erwn down with a look of icy disdain. His bonny wife didn't fool him, he'd seen the fear in her eyes. Before he could order her back into the bathing chambers, Erwn managed to break free of his guards.

"Doona even think aboot it," Lachlan warned, slapping the flat of his blade against Erwn's chest.

"You would listen to her, your father's whore? You're a bigger fool than I thought, MacLeod. Even Arwan knew better than to keep the conniving, evil bitch in his bed for long. All she's ever wanted is to rule the Isles. She uses you as she once used your father."

Lachlan managed to hide his shock at Erwn's slanderous words, but not his fury. He grabbed Erwn by the throat and squeezed. "No' another word against my wife. I was there. Yer brother would've killed her if I hadn't been." He only released his hold when the man appeared ready to lose consciousness. Erwn stumbled away, gasping for air.

"If ye wish to challenge me over yer brother's death, do so. I welcome the opportunity to kill ye. Otherwise, ye have until nightfall to leave the Enchanted Isles. Consider yerself lucky I give ye a choice—I ken ye were part of the conspiracy to overthrow me. Take him out of my sight before I withdraw my offer," he ordered his guards. "Escort him from the Isles or keep him under guard until the challenge. On the morrow at dawn, Erwn."

"I'm leaving the Isles. But mark my words, one day you'll pay for what you did to my brother." He shot a scathing look at Evangeline, who'd taken a seat in the armchair beside the door to the bathing chambers, her delicate features pale and drawn. "Both of you will."

"Doona give me cause to change my mind, Erwn." If the man threatened Evangeline again, Lachlan vowed to see him dead before sunset. The only thing that stayed his hand now was the fact Erwn was distraught with grief and the knowledge he was the weaker of the two brothers and never would've acted on his own.

The guards hustled him out the door and Lachlan turned to his wife. Crossing to her side, he crouched before her. "If ye woulda done as I asked, ye never woulda had to listen to the vile lies Erwn spewed."

Her gaze averted from his, she twisted her hands in his robe. Lachlan slowly came to his feet, an uneasy feeling building inside him.

Sweet Christ, it can't be true.

A heavy sense of foreboding settled over him. "Tell me it isn't true. Tell me the bastard lied when he said ye'd been my father's who—ye'd been with my father." Simply saying the words caused his gorge to rise. An interminable silence stretched between them, straining the tension in his body to the breaking point. "I will have the truth, Evangeline!" he shouted at the woman who'd battered down his defenses and wormed her way into his heart.

She cleared her throat, her cheeks flushed. "He didn't lie."

His head spun at her admission, the realization she'd deceived him. She'd been manipulating him all along, using him. The heat of his fury hazed his vision. He caged her in, wrapping his hands so tight around the wooden armrests they cracked beneath the pressure of his fingers. "Did it amuse ye, Evangeline, to think of fuckin' the son as ye'd once fucked his father? Were ye goin' to compare our skills in the bedchamber?"

He ignored her shocked gasp, the hurt that shadowed her eyes at his crude remark. Fisting his hands in the edges of his robe, he dragged her to her feet. The plush fabric fell open, revealing a body so perfect it was no wonder she could use it as a weapon—bringing men to their knees, manipulating them to do her bidding.

He raked her with a disgusted look, keeping his gaze from her moisture-filled eyes. "If I'd kent ye were a whore and no' the innocent ye led me to believe, I would no' have waited to fuck ye." He shoved her away from him. Even though she'd used him, he still wanted her. The heavy weight between his legs throbbed and he knew he had to get out of there before he did something he'd regret.

He strode to the oak wardrobe and grabbed a tunic. Jerking it over his head, he belted his plaid. He sat on the edge of the bed and tugged on his doeskin boots, trying not to look at her. But no matter how hard he tried, his eyes sought her out. She looked small and vulnerable curled up in the big leather chair, her arms wrapped about her. He slammed down the urge to go to her, questioned his sanity that he was tempted to do so.

"I'm goin' to Lewes. I want ye gone from here when I return."

"If you would give me something to wear, I will leave now," she said with quiet dignity.

Lachlan cursed. He had her bloody magick. No matter that she'd deceived him, he couldn't send her from his chambers without clothing or the ability to defend herself. Even with Bana dead and Erwn banished from the Isles, he couldn't be sure someone else didn't wish her harm.

Christ, why the hell do I still care what happens to her?

"Ye'll remain here until ye recover." He rubbed the back of his neck to ease the tension there, then closed his eyes. He jerked his hand in her direction. At her startled gasp, he cracked one eye open.

"Bloody hell," he muttered upon seeing her naked body. He tried again, this time shutting out the image of her luminescent skin and womanly curves as he did so.

"Thank you," she murmured.

He cursed himself for the idiot that he was when he saw the gown he'd dressed her in. The silken fabric in the same shade as her eyes with its low draped neckline only served to heighten her allure.

"Where do ye think ye're goin'?" he growled when with familiar grace she walked to the door with her head held high.

"I'm leaving as you asked me to. I don't wish to damage your lily-white reputation with my soiled one."

"Doona try to turn this on me." He backed her against the door. "Ye admitted ye slept with my father, do ye deny it now?" Hope rose within him. He'd never wanted to be proven wrong so much as he did now.

"No."

"Tell me why."

Her breath, warm and sweet, caressed his cheek, drawing him to her, intoxicating him. He twisted his fingers in her silken mane and inhaled the scent of the soap he'd lathered in her long, luxurious tresses, over her full breasts and taut belly, her firmly rounded behind.

"Why should I? You have already condemned me."

"Yer actions condemn ye, no' me."

"Do they? I saved your life. I have only ever sought to protect you. Are those the actions you speak of?" She held his gaze. "I thought you were different from the others. You said you trusted me."

He removed his fingers from her hair and backed away, the urge to kiss the hurt from her eyes too strong. He needed answers. There was something she held back. He could see it in her expression, hear it in her voice. Yet she wanted him to trust her, accept her without telling him what she kept from him. He couldn't. Syrena was the one person he could depend on to tell him what he needed to know.

Sweeping her into his arms, he carried her to his bed, jerking the covers back before he laid her down. "I want ye to remain here until I return from Lewes. Ye're in danger without yer magick and 'tis my fault."

"Why do you go to Lewes?"

"To see Syrena. I need answers and I'm no' gettin' them from ye."

She averted her gaze from his and stared at the great oak outside his window, the branches scraping against the glass in a mournful cry. He waited, hoping it wouldn't be necessary for him to go, but she remained stubbornly reticent.

He turned and walked to the door. She stopped him just before he stepped from the room. "Syrena can't tell you what you need to hear. No one knows me like you do, Lachlan. I thought you cared about me, but if you did, you would already know the truth."

Closing the door quietly behind him, he strode through the corridor, ignoring the dull ache in his chest. By the time he reached his home on Lewis, he was about crazed with his need to speak to Syrena.

He met Gavin in the courtyard. His brother's red-haired friend surveyed him with a gimlet eye. "What's the matter with ye? Ye look like ye have a thundercloud hangin' over yer heed."

"I'm no' in the mood. Where's Syrena?"

"Where do ye think she is, ye big lummox?"

"Gavin," he snarled.

"Och, well, she'd be at Dunvegan."

Lachlan blew out a frustrated breath. Of course, she'd be at Rory's. Aidan wouldn't have allowed her and the bairns to travel yet.

"Unless ye're thinkin' of swimmin' across the Minch, ye'll have to wait until they return. The galley—"

Lachlan flashed to Rory's home on Skye. As he wrenched open the castle doors, Alex and Jamie barreled past him. His brother stormed after them without so much as a glance in his direction.

"Lachlan?" Aileanna frowned, coming from the grand hall with a plate in her hand. "What's wrong?"

"I need to speak with Syrena," he said, taking the stairs two at a time. "'Tis important."

"I can see that. She just got the babies to sleep, so be quiet about it."

Praying he met no one else, he strode down the long corridor to Syrena's room. He groaned when Rory hailed him outside her chambers.

"Lachlan, 'tis glad I am to see you." His cousin slung a companionable arm over his shoulder. "Come join me in the hall."

"Yer father-by-marriage is here, isna he?"

Rory dropped his arm from Lachlan's shoulder and grunted. "Aye, how did ye ken?"

"'Cause ye're always lookin' fer someone to deflect his attention from ye when he's aboot. Why do ye no' just ask yer wife to do it?"

"A lot of good—"

"MacLeod, where did ye get to?"Alasdair shouted from down below.

Lachlan ducked into Syrena's room before his cousin could stop him. Syrena sat in a chair with one foot rocking the cradle in front of her. Pressing a finger to her lips, she stood and leaned over to check on the sleeping bairns before tiptoeing across the room to him.

She reached up to kiss his cheek, her brow furrowing when she got a good look at him. "Something's wrong. What is it?"

"Evangeline."

She clutched his arm. "Is she all right?"

"Aye, but Bana tried to kill her."

"Come, we'll go to Ali's solar." Closing the door behind her, she said, "Now tell me what happened."

By the time they reached Aileanna's solar, Lachlan had filled Syrena in on the morning's events. She led him into the sun-filled room. "There's something more, isn't there?" She patted a spot beside her on the chaise.

"Aye. When Erwn found out about Bana's death, he blamed Evangeline. He accused her of bein' my father's who—mistress and manipulatin' me as she once had Arwan in her bid to take over the Enchanted Isles."

"You believed him, didn't you?"

"She admitted it, Syrena."

She sagged against the bolster and closed her eyes. When she opened them again, sorrow shimmered in her golden gaze. "She hated him, you know. I didn't realize how much until the day Arwan was murdered." Syrena plucked at the folds of her pink gown. "I wondered at the time if she'd been the one to kill him." Shaking her head as if the memory was too painful to bear, she rose from the settee and went to stand by the window. "It was obvious Arwan was enamored with Evangeline. He did little to conceal his lust for her even though he was wed. Morgana hated her, even before she found out she was Andora's daughter. She was jealous of Evangeline's beauty and the attention her husband paid to her."

Lachlan's hands balled into fists. Syrena, as though sensing his growing anger, looked over at him. "No, it's not what you think. Evangeline was sent by Rohan to protect me. She arrived at the palace a few weeks before my eighteenth birthday. My father knew what would happen if I didn't pass the test of my magick. If it wasn't for Evangeline, I wouldn't have."

Syrena cleared her throat, then went on. "I never questioned where she'd come from. She was the only friend I had and I was afraid I'd lose her if I did. But others did. Like Morgana, they were jealous of her powers and beauty. She kept herself apart from them, further garnering their distrust. I imagine they took their suspicions to Arwan and she had no choice but to give herself to him to remain with me. She sacrificed her innocence to protect me."

Lachlan's gut twisted at the thought of what Evangeline had withstood. What the hell had his uncle been thinking, sending her in to that pit of vipers? He didn't know how much longer he could sit and listen to what the Fae had put her through. Noting the pain in Syrena's eyes, he said, "Ye doona ken that fer sure."

"Yes. Yes, I do. Many of the men tried to gain her attention, but she ignored them. If they grew persistent, she didn't hesitate to put them in their place."

Lachlan could attest to that. She'd done it to him.

Shoulders bowed, Syrena returned to the settee to sit beside him. "I can't bear to think of what she suffered on my account. All she's ever done is protect me, and I didn't protect her from him."

"Ye didna ken. 'Tis no' yer fault."

"Nor is it hers, Lachlan."

He scrubbed his hands over his face. Sweet Christ, had she truly sacrificed her innocence to protect Syrena? Evangeline was right, the truth had been staring him in the face all along, but he'd let his jealousy and pride cloud his vision.

"I ken that. It wasna." His stomach roiled as he remembered what he'd said to her. What he'd called her. He left the settee and strode to the hearth, gripping the wooden mantel to keep from planting his fist in the wall. "Why could she no' have told me?"

"Did you give her a chance, or did you let your anger and male pride get the better of you?"

"Christ, I'm no better than my father. I doona ken how I can face her after what I said."

He didn't realize Syrena had come to stand beside him until he felt the warm pressure of her palm upon his back. "Trust me, you are nothing like Arwan."

She leaned against him, her tears dampening his tunic. He turned and folded her into his arms. "Oh, Lachlan, he was such a brutal man. It makes me ill to think what she suffered because of me."

He swallowed the bitter revulsion that clawed up his throat when he thought of what Arwan might have done to Evangeline. He kissed the top of Syrena's head and pulled away. "I should get back."

"Make her talk to you. Don't let her shut you out."

"Before I can do that, Syrena, I have to find a way to ask her forgiveness. And God's truth, I doona deserve it."

"She's given you her trust, and she does not do so easily. She cares deeply for you."

"If ye mean to make me feel worse than I already do, then ye're doin' a fair job of it."

"I'm sorry, that wasn't my intention." She hugged him. "And if you didn't care for her as much as you do, you wouldn't feel as bad as you do. I love you both and want the two of you to be happy. You need her as much as she needs you, Lachlan."

"Am I interuptin' somethin'?" His brother entered the room, his gray gaze intent upon his wife.

"Nay, I have to be gettin' home." It surprised Lachlan that he referred to the Fae realm as home, surprised him even more that he meant it.

His brother laid a hand on his arm as Lachlan went to leave. "Are ye all right, Lan?"

"Aye. Nay. I made a mess of it with Evie. I'm no' sure I can fix it this time."

"Yes, you can," Syrena said, coming to stand beside Aidan, who wrapped his arms around her. "And until you make this right, neither of you will be happy."

Lachlan didn't know if he was capable of being truly happy, although of late, he'd thought with Evangeline there was a chance he could at least be content. But Syrena was right, if anyone deserved happiness it was Evangeline. But before he went back to her, Lachlan needed to be sure he could put her past with his father behind him. If he couldn't, she would see the truth in his eyes and to remain together would do them more harm than good. He wouldn't be responsible for hurting her any more than he already had.

Chapter 24

The mournful melody of the branches swirling across the windowpane in Lachlan's chambers drew Evangeline deeper into despair. The image of Lachlan's face when he discovered the truth about her would remain with her for eternity. His scathing condemnation of her actions played over and over again in her mind. His revulsion mirrored her own.

Knowing she'd had no choice but to sacrifice her innocence to Arwan didn't make it any easier for her to live with it. She'd felt like the whore Lachlan accused her of being. She'd used her body to keep Arwan's suspicions of her at bay, to ensure her place by Syrena's side. Withstood his brutal seductions time and time again until he grew tired of her inability to please him and moved on to his next victim.

How foolish to think Lachlan could forgive her when she could not forgive herself.

She had nothing left. She'd lost the two things that mattered most to her—Lachlan and her magick.

Unable to withstand the thought of looking into his eyes and seeing only disgust, she slipped from his bed, determined to be long gone from the palace before he returned. With one last look around the room that held the essence of the man she thought to give her heart to, she stepped from his chambers, closing the door on the hopes and dreams she'd hadn't thought possible, hadn't known she had until Lachlan.

Two servants looked up from polishing the gilded balustrade as Evangeline walked past. Their contemptuous whispers followed after her and she stiffened her spine. Donning the familiar mask of haughty disdain, she held her head high. If only it was as easy to rebuild the walls around her heart as it was to pretend their vindictive barbs didn't meet their mark. With his companionship and tenderness, Lachlan had shattered her defenses, but she'd raise the shields again. She had to. It was the only way she knew to survive.

She ignored the pointed stares and derisive laughter as she made her way to the palace doors. The late afternoon sunshine offered no warmth; she knew she would never again set foot in the palace of the Enchanted Isles.

"Evangeline." Fallyn hailed her, tossing a command to the royal guards who milled about the stables before striding to her side "What are you doing? You should be resting."

"I'm leaving. I'm going back to Rohan's court."

Fallyn's intent gaze searched hers. "It will pass, Evangeline. I'm accompanying the royal guards to make certain Erwn is well away from here and is no longer a threat to you or Lachlan."

"The damage has already been done." Evangeline wrapped her arms around her waist, trying to contain her sorrow, the tears that burned at the back of her eyes.

"He cares about you. Give him some time and I'm certain he'll get past this."

With a hollow laugh, Evangeline said, "Broderick *loves* you. Do you think he could forgive you if he found out you'd slept with his father?"

Fallyn took hold of her arm as she went to walk past her. "Stop this. I've heard enough about Arwan to know you did what you had to do to protect Syrena. So you just get back in there and wait for Lachlan to come to his senses. And if he doesn't, my sisters and I will make certain he does."

Evangeline gave a grateful squeeze to Fallyn's hand, averting her gaze so her friend wouldn't see how deeply her support had affected her. "Thank you, but I can't remain here."

"You're too stubborn for your own good, Evangeline. If I can't get you to change your mind, at least let me transport you to Rohan's palace." At Evangeline's nod, Fallyn said, "Give me a moment, I'll tell the men to hold until my return."

As Fallyn strode to the waiting guards, Uscias and Aurora appeared in a burst of light. Uscias looked down at the little seer whose hand he held, then raised his gaze to Evangeline's. "Aurora has had a vision. Lachlan's in danger."

"No, he can't be. He's in the Mortal realm. No one . . ." Distracted by her concern for Lachlan, she hadn't noticed Aurora had come to her side until she felt her small hand slip into hers.

Evangeline tried to free her hand, but Aurora tightened her hold and in that dreaded voice of an old woman said, "The time has come. The prophecy will come to pass. You are the only one who can save him. Go to him now. He rides his steed at Uig beach."

Aurora released her hand. When she lifted her eyes to Evangeline's, they were blue and filled with pity. Evangeline cringed to think Aurora knew why he'd left her. But with Lachlan in danger, there was no time to dwell on her embarrassment.

"I don't know how to help him, Uscias, not without my—"

"Your magick will return," Aurora said with confidence.

Evangeline took a measure of comfort from the child's pronouncement, but if Lachlan was in danger now, she did not know how she could help him.

"We'd best go to him, Evangeline." Uscias motioned for Fallyn, who had been making her way back to them. "Can you watch Aurora for me while I transport Evangeline to the Mortal realm? I shan't be long."

"Of course. I've been informed Erwn has some last-minute arrangements he wishes to make before we can leave." She turned to Evangeline. "I'm glad you've come to your senses."

"Aurora had a vision that Lachlan's in danger." How could she explain to Uscias that the last person Lachlan would wish to see was her? But she had no choice, if there was even the slightest chance Aurora's vision was true, she had to go to him. Considering the validity of the child's prediction concerning Iain, Evangeline had no cause to doubt her. Evangeline would protect him as best she could. And until her magick returned as Aurora promised, at the very least she could show him how to use her powers to his greatest advantage. She'd just have to convince him he needed her help.

Coming through the standing stones of Callanish in the Mortal realm of Lewis, Uscias's brow furrowed. Scanning the hilltop they stood upon, he placed a hand on Evangeline's arm. "Did you feel it?"

Her emotions in turmoil at the thought of facing Lachlan again, she was certain a horde of ogres could come upon her and she wouldn't have been aware of them. She followed his gaze. "What do you think it was?"

"Magick. I felt its vibration, a leftover residue when I came through the stones."

"Perhaps it was Lachlan."

"Perhaps, but I don't think so. Stay alert, Evangeline."

"Of course I will. I may not have my magick but I'm far from inept."

Uscias's mustache twitched. "Good, now let us find him."

The wizard must have sensed her trepidation, as he placed a comforting hand on her arm. "Evangeline, you're as important to him as he is to you. Trust me in this, I know my pupil well, and together you will work through this."

"I wish I shared your confidence, but until I have my powers—"

"You know that is not what I referred to."

"I think we should—"

"Evangeline, look at me."

She drew in a shuddered breath then did as he asked.

"What's done is done. You must move beyond it. You have suffered enough. I wish Rohan had seen fit to take me into his confidence when he sent you to look out for Syrena. I would've found some way to protect you from Arwan had I but known."

She didn't like to think Uscias blamed himself for what had taken place. "It was Arwan who was responsible, no one else."

A gentle smile curved his lips. "I'm happy to hear you say so. Now perhaps you will remember that."

Before she could respond, he'd flashed them to a low-lying hill. The long white-tipped grasses swayed about her legs. In the distance, a great black steed pounded through the rolling surf, its rider as magnificent as the animal he rode.

"Go to him." Uscias prodded her back with a crooked finger. Drawing in a steadying breath, she picked her way down the rocky incline, bending over to remove her slippers before walking across the golden sand toward Lachlan.

Lachlan's heart thundered in his chest as loudly as his steed's hooves pummeled the surf. Evangeline stood alone in the sand, the ocean breeze whipping her long locks about her face, molding the silken fabric of her gown to her womanly curves.

As he drew closer, she held her hair from her face and his belly clenched at the vulnerability he saw there. Her beautiful eyes bore witness to her tears and he damned himself again for causing her pain. He jerked on Fin's reins, bringing him to a halt several feet from where she stood. He swung from the saddle. She stumbled as she backed away from him. He cursed under his breath. She'd mistaken his anger with himself—the rage that surely must be visible on his face—as if it were directed at her.

She held up her hand. "I know I'm the last person you wish to see, but—"

"Ye're wrong. Ye're the only person I wish to see."

He took advantage of her stunned disbelief to close the distance between them. "I'm sorry, Evie. I'm sorry fer every misbegotten word that came out of my fool mouth."

She turned away from him. Wrapping her arms around her narrow waist, she looked out to sea. "You have nothing to apologize for."

He spun her around to face him. "Look at me when ye say that. Ye look me in my eyes and tell me I didna hurt ye, shame ye with my words. Fer Chrissakes, Evie, ye doona deserve my anger."

She deserved compassion and understanding and instead he'd treated her with contempt.

She lowered her gaze from his and tried to pull away.

"Nay, I'm no' lettin' ye go until ye tell me what he did to ye."

"No!" Her eyes wide with horror, she fought against his hold. "Please, let me go," she begged, breathless from her frenzied struggle to break free of him.

"Nay, Evie. I ken 'twill be difficult, but 'tis the only way fer ye to get past it." He sat in the sand and tugged her onto his lap. Drawing up his knees, he cradled her against him. "I ken Rohan sent ye to look out fer Syrena, and as someone ye've tried to keep safe, I ken ye would do so at any cost. Even if it meant ye put yerself in harm's way. 'Tis why ye gave yerself to him, isna it?"

Lachlan rested his chin on top of her head, stroking her hair while he waited for her to tell him what she'd suffered at his father's hand. No matter how difficult it would be to hear, it was important for both of them to get it out in the open. He could barely hear her when she began her tale.

"Arwan came to my room one night to interrogate me as to who my parents were, how I'd come to be in the Isles and why. Looking back, I think even then he was aware of who I was. Rohan, for my protection, had kept my identity a secret, but I'm quite certain Arwan knew my mother well enough to see the resemblance. He was such a coldhearted, self-centered bastard, I doubt he even cared that my mother had been responsible for the Isle Faes' destruction. I didn't know that then, I wish I had as it gave him the upper hand. He exploited my weakness. If my answers were not to his liking, I was to be banished from the Isles, separated from Syrena. I would have failed both her and Rohan."

Evangeline lifted her eyes to his as if begging him to understand. "I couldn't let that happen. Other than Rohan, I had no one but Syrena. She'd befriended me and she'd suffered enough at Arwan's hand. I wasn't about to let her endure anymore. I knew . . . I knew he wanted me. I attempted to seduce him, distract him from his questions." The self-loathing in her hollow laugh was painful to hear. Lachlan glided his palm up and down her arm in an attempt to soothe her. "In my innocence I thought a kiss would satisfy him."

As if by rote, she related what she'd endured at Arwan's hand in a flat, empty tone. Arwan had got off easy; he deserved a slow and lingering death for what he'd done to her. Lachlan deserved the same, maybe more so since he knew her and should've realized the truth on his own.

Needing to look into her eyes when he begged her forgiveness, he lifted her from his lap and laid her gently in the sand. Careful not to crowd her body with his, he leaned over her, framing her face with his hands. "Ye didna deserve my condemnation, Evie, ye deserve my respect and admiration fer what ye have withstood. Fer being a woman who stands by her convictions and protects those she cares about without regard to her own suffering."

"Please, it is not necessary to flatter me. I don't hold your words against you. I understand where they came from."

"How the hell can ye understand when I didna?"

She gave a startled gasp. He closed his eyes, cursing his inability to keep his temper under control, then gentled his voice. "I was jealous, Evie. Angry another man had held ye, kissed ye, had been inside ye."

He hesitated, unsure he should tell her the rest, but he had no choice. There could be no secrets between them, not if they wanted their marriage to work, and he now knew that he did. He just hoped when all was said and done, so did she.

"I was disgusted that man had been my father. Nay, doona turn from me. I ken I look like him, Evie, and I admit to a certain amount of male pride. I didna like the thought ye'd used me as a replacement fer my father." He eased away from her and sat up. Taking her hand in his, he studied her slender fingers, unable to meet her gaze. "Ye're important to me. I've come to care fer ye, more than I wanted to. So the thought ye used me to gain control over the Isles didna sit well."

"No, that was never my intention."

He kissed her palm, then stretched out beside her, leaning on his elbow. "I ken that now. I shoulda kent it right away, but the thought of ye with anyone else but me, especially Arwan . . ."

She pressed her fingers to his lips then raised her gaze to his. "You are the only man I have ever wanted."

Her heartfelt declaration vanquished whatever doubts had remained inside him. The tension eased from his knotted muscles, replaced by a heady sense of well-being. He smiled, drawing her into his arms. "So is that why ye strung me from the rafters that day at Lewes when I kissed ye?" As soon as he asked the question, he cursed himself for being a fool and held her away from him, searching her face. "Sweet Christ, I scared ye, didna I? I look so much like my bloody father ye thought I was him, didna ye?"

"You don't, you know, not really." She touched his cheek. "Besides, it doesn't matter." A small smile played on her lips. "Once I found out you were the one upsetting Syrena, I would have done the same thing."

"Aye, it does," he said, unable to go along with her light-hearted attempt to dismiss the matter. "Do I scare ye when I touch ye, when I kiss ye? Does it remind ye of him?" The muscles in his chest constricted as he awaited her answer. Any chance they might have of a good marriage hinged on her aye or nay.

"Once, that first time in the caves. It was dark and . . . No, don't look at me like that. You are nothing like Arwan. You're gentle and kind. You make me feel safe and protected."

He expelled a relieved breath, then looking down into her beautiful face, drew his thumb over the bow of her sweet mouth. "Evie, just so ye ken, the last thing I want ye to feel when I kiss ye is safe and protected."

She frowned. "You don't? But I—"

"Nay, I doona. When I kiss ye," he brushed her lips with his, "I want ye to feel desired."

He tunneled his fingers through the thick tangle of her hair and slid his mouth slowly, back and forth, over hers. "I want ye to feel passion. I want ye hot, wet, and needy. As hungry fer me as I am fer ye."

She buried her face in his neck. His breath lodged in his throat. So soon after reliving her nightmare with Arwan, had he frightened her with his desire, a desire that had been obvious in his words, in his touch? He was about to pull away when her slender arms slid around his neck and he felt her lips move against his skin. She feathered soft kisses along his neck to his collarbone, to his chest. He sucked in a shuddered breath, forcing himself to remain still, loosening his grip on her hip. His fingers had tightened at the heady rush of lust that had all but consumed him at the evidence of her desire. The muscles in the arm he leaned upon quivered as he struggled not to give in to the urge to ravish her as her questing lips and the warmth of her breath heated his skin and inflamed his need to take her right then.

Her tongue swirled over his chest and he groaned a curse, his cock swelling painfully in his trews. "Ye're killin' me, Evie."

Her lips curved against his flesh and his chest tightened. He was determined that with his kiss, with his every touch, he would wipe away the last remnants of the nightmare she had endured at Arwan's hands. He eased back and brought his hand to her cheek, tilting her chin. Her cheeks were flushed and she raised her gaze to his. The trust and desire shining from the depths of her violet eyes destroyed what little control he had left. He bent his head and claimed her mouth in a deep, possessive kiss. *Mine.* Over and over the word hammered his senses, pulsating through his veins.

She whimpered into his mouth, twining the fingers of one hand in his hair while the other went to his waist, fisting in his plaid. He explored the moist warmth of her mouth with his tongue, enthralled by her sweetness, the drugging stroke of her tongue to his. The soft suction of her mouth sucking on his tongue, her hand kneading the tight muscles of his arse urging him closer, shattered his resolve to seduce her with slow, practiced finesse.

His body enveloped hers, the hard points of her nipples rubbing seductively against his chest. His tongue mimicked the rhythm of his cock thrusting against her belly and she raised her hips. Her body moved in time with his, matching him stroke for stroke.

Gliding his palm over her hip, he bunched her gown in his hand to bare her long, shapely leg. Her fingers found their way beneath his plaid and she smoothed her soft palms over his naked flesh, holding him firmly against her.

"Christ, Evie," he groaned, his voice a rough rasp. Rocking his cock against her belly, he murmured in the delicate shell of her ear, "I want to be inside ye, but if ye're no' ready, if ye need time, ye'd best tell me now."

"Yes," she said breathlessly, writhing beneath him.

He pulled back to look into her heavy-lidded gaze. "Did ye mean yes ye want me now, or yes stop now?"

A frustrated growl escaped from her throat. "For the love of Fae, I mean yes. Now, Lachlan. Right now."

"Ye're a verra demandin' woman." He laughed at the familiar look she shot him, as happy to hear her *aye* as to see her beautiful eyes were no longer haunted by the shadows of her past. They shimmered with a fiery desire. His Evie was back.

He trailed his lips along the column of her elegant neck, burying his face in the soft hollow there and inhaling her musky, floral scent. Rolling onto his back, he dragged her on top of him, his throbbing erection cradled in the moist heat of her folds.

"Sit up," he ordered gruffly.

She hesitated, then did as he asked, casting a surreptitious glance at the barren headland. "I don't know if we should . . ." she began, her legs straddling his hips. But whatever she meant to say was lost on a low moan when he rubbed his cock against her slick heat.

He knew this stretch of beach well. Confident they were safe from prying eyes, he drew her gown over her head and gazed hungrily at the ripe perfection of her body, content to drink in her beauty as the late afternoon sun slid low in the sky behind her, gilding her creamy skin in its luminescent light. A gentle breeze blew her long ebony locks across her flushed cheeks, carrying the scent of sea air with it. The water crashing against the distant rocks and the rustle of the tall grasses along the headland only served to heighten the magickal feeling of having this woman, his woman, in his arms.

Cupping the heavy weight of her breasts in his hands, he

drew his thumbs over her rose-tinted nipples and watched the play of emotion on her exquisite face. Eyes closed, she arched her back, pressing the globes more firmly into his hands, moaning as he took the peaked buds into his mouth, first one and then the other. Swirling his tongue over each perfect tip, he kneaded her breasts, reveling in her needy whimpers and the frantic manner in which she slid up and down his shaft.

"Please," she begged in a husky voice.

"I'm no' finished what . . . Sweet Christ." He groaned when she took hold of his cock and guided him into her wet sheath. Grabbing hold of her hips, his face buried in the soft bounty of her breasts, he thrust inside her, filling her welcoming heat.

He'd never seen anything more beautiful than Evangeline at that moment, riding him without restraint, with a fierce passion, her head thrown back, her breasts thrust forward. The sight of her giving herself to him as she did, taking pleasure in their lovemaking when she'd suffered so much at his father's hand, filled him with an aching tenderness.

But there was nothing gentle in the way she rode him, and he knew tenderness was not what she wanted. He gave himself over to his desire, to hers, and made love to her with a ferocity that matched her own, gratified when he could no longer contain his roar of fulfillment to hear Evangeline's cries of release join his.

Chapter 25

Evangeline's outraged shrieks did nothing to deter the handsome highlander, who dragged her into the frigid waters. With a hard twist of her hand, she managed to break free of his hold and made a mad dash for shore.

"Oh, no, ye doona." Lachlan laughed. Capturing her easily, he looped an arm around her waist and carried her beneath his arm into the icy turquoise depths. "Mind where ye're hittin'." He grunted just before he unceremoniously dunked her beneath a wave.

"Are you trying to drown me?" she sputtered as she resurfaced.

"Nay, 'tis the fastest way to rid us of all the sand we're wearin'. Now be still and let me help ye bathe." He stopped her protest with a demanding kiss. Sitting on the sandy bottom, he hauled her onto his lap. Her eyes widened at the evidence of his desire beneath her naked behind.

"Impressive considerin' how cold the water is." He grinned when she cast him an unamused look. No matter how much pleasure she'd taken from their tryst in the sand, she had no intention of doing so in the frigid waters.

"Doona worry, I want to reach Lewes before nightfall, and that willna happen if I make love to ye again. I plan on takin' my time when next I have ye beneath me, my bonny wife." He rose from the water with her in his arms. "And I doona plan on waitin' long fer that to happen. Without Bana and Erwn to contend with, I'm thinkin' we should have several days and nights of uninterrupted pleasure."

She caught her lip between her teeth, wishing she could withhold Aurora's prophecy from him.

He angled his head. "What is it?"

"Aurora. She's had a vision. She says you are in danger." All thought of the little seer's prophecy had vanished the moment Lachlan had told Evangeline she was the only person he wished to see.

Sharing the nightmare she'd endured with Arwan was the most difficult thing she'd ever done. She fiercely guarded her privacy, unwilling to let anyone close enough to see beneath the facade she'd erected. But she'd known instinctively if they were to make their marriage work, no matter how painful it would be, she could not hold back. She was surprised to find the exercise freeing, but knew it had more to do with Lachlan's reaction than anything else. He didn't condemn her, didn't turn away from her. He'd given her his support, his understanding. Both had gone a long way in ridding her of the shame she'd carried for all these years.

Looking at the man who was now her husband in every way, she was filled with an emotion so powerful it stripped away the last vestiges of her defenses. She loved him. Her heart swelled, filling the dark voids with a joyous light at the knowledge. Making her more determined than ever to let no one harm him or cause him pain.

He set her on her feet. Their naked bodies molded to one another. His gaze softened as it came to rest on her. "Evie, I need ye to promise me that from now on ye'll take no more risks with yer safety. Ye'll let me protect ye and whoever else may be in danger, including me."

"No. I'm not some helpless female. I . . ." She narrowed

her gaze on him when he used her magick to dress her in trews and a tunic like she'd worn in the Far North. "That is not amusing, Lachlan. And just so you know, Aurora says my magick will soon return to me."

He waggled his brows and dressed himself in the same manner.

She huffed out an exasperated breath. "You won't be so cocky once I have my magick back."

"Aye, I will." He placed two fingers between his lips and whistled shrilly. His black steed thundered across the sand toward them while Lachlan bent to retrieve her gown from where it lay half-buried in the sand along with his plaid and tunic. After he'd stuffed their belongings into a leather satchel, he settled Evangeline onto his steed, mounting with masterful grace behind her. She tightened her white-knuckled grip on the pommel, stifling a distressed yelp as the big beast took off at a gallop across the sand and bounded up the steep incline.

Lachlan chuckled, wrapping his arms around her. "Trust me, I'll no' let anythin' happen to ye."

"How far is Lewes from here?" she asked, praying it was not far.

"I ken a shortcut, 'twill no' take us long. We'll be there before nightfall and remain until mornin'."

"Have Syrena and the children returned from Dunvegan?" she asked in a manner which suggested she hoped they had.

"Nay."

Catching the rumble of amusement in his voice, she glanced over her shoulder. "Don't pretend you are not as relieved as I am that they have yet to return."

He nuzzled her neck, igniting a frisson of desire in her belly. "Nay, I'm verra pleased we'll have the keep to ourselves. That way when ye shout my name in pleasure, ye'll no' disturb the bairns."

"I didn't shout out your name," she muttered, her cheeks heating at the thought.

"Aye, ye did, and ye'll do so again this night."

She shook her head, wondering if all men were as arrogant and self-assured as her husband. It amazed her that he could get his swelled head through the doors of the palace. She was about to tell him so when she felt the increased tension in his arms.

"What's wrong?" she asked, searching the thick brush bordering the path they rode upon. What looked to be the burnt-out shell of a castle loomed at the edge of the woods just ahead of them.

She tipped her head back. A muscle jumped in the hard set of his jaw. His gaze fixated on the blackened remains of stone, the lines bracketing his full lips deepened. "Did you know the people who lived there?"

"Aye. Lamont."

Her pulse kicked up at the name. "The same Lamont who held you captive at Glastonbury?"

"The verra same." His expression shuttered.

"Tell me." He'd forced her to tell him about Arwan, and it had been helpful. She knew Lachlan had suffered much in the Mortal realm, and from his reaction she thought perhaps this place played some part in it.

He sighed when she pinned him with an unbending stare. "I can see I'll get no peace until I tell ye, but 'tis in the past, Evie. I—"

She covered the hand he pressed to her belly. "So was Arwan," she reminded him quietly.

He kissed the top of her head. "Lamont's sister Janet and I were lovers. We'd been together several months when she told me she was carryin' my bairn. I agreed to marry her and came here to ask her father fer her hand. The old crone who'd been my nursemaid was there. She kent what I was, she'd been the one to point out the mark of the Fae on my shoulder. On the day of my f—Alexander's death, Aidan sent her from Lewes with enough coin to buy her silence. We thought she'd gone to Edinburgh, but all that time she'd been nursemaid to the Lamonts, to Janet."

"Why did Aidan send her away?"

"She hated the Fae, encouraged Alexander's fear and hatred of me. She'd been with his family for years and he set great store in her opinion."

"Did she tell the Lamonts?"

He laughed. She heard the bitterness and pain in the harsh rasp and tightened her hold on his hand. "Oh, aye, she made sure they knew what I was, painting a vile picture of my evil tendencies. 'Twas little wonder the Lamonts, father and sons, beat me within an inch of my life. I was barely conscious when they tossed me onto my horse. Luckily Fin knew his way home. They sent a missive to Aidan demandin' he marry Janet in my stead and banish me from Lewes. If he didn't agree, they'd see that the bairn didn't survive and that all would ken what I was."

"Aidan didn't—"

"Aye, he did. He had no choice, Evie. He rode out the next mornin' to agree to their terms." He jerked his chin at the burnt-out shell. "This was all that remained when he arrived. Most thought I'd done it."

"You would never do anything so heinous. No one who knows you could believe such a thing."

He angled his head to look at her, holding her gaze. "Thank ye, but there were many who did, includin' my brother."

"So, ye've come back, have ye?" A stooped old woman dressed in a ragged black gown stepped from behind the crumbling wall.

Lachlan sucked in a shocked gasp. "How is it ye live? Ye were supposed to have died in the blaze."

She cackled, poking through the rubble with her long,

crooked staff before looking up at Lachlan. A hint of madness in her milky blue gaze. "Who do ye think nursed Lamont back to health so he could go after ye in London?"

Evangeline flexed her fingers with the urge to send a charged bolt at the woman who'd hurt him, surprised yet comforted to feel the faint glow in her belly. As though he sensed the direction of her thoughts, Lachlan laid a hand on her shoulder, giving it a restraining squeeze.

"He's back, ye ken, he and that Ursula woman. The one who birthed yer bairn. Looks just like ye he does. 'Tis a pity they stopped me before I could kill him. Fools, just like Janet. She'd no' take the potion to rid her of yer bairn, but I took care of it, didna I?" She shrieked with laughter, pushing her stringy white hair from her deeply lined face.

"'Twas ye who set the fire?"

She sneered. "Aye."

Taking advantage of Lachlan's stunned horror, Evangeline leapt from the horse before he could stop her. The old witch stumbled backward as Evangeline strode toward her, pulling on the faint wisps of her magick. "Never again will you torture a child with your vindictive lies," Evangeline said, shooting a weak bolt that took the old woman to her knees. The crone clutched her throat, her eyes widening in a silent scream.

Lachlan came up behind Evangeline, sword in hand. His horror had given way to a cold, hard fury. The sharp edges of his blade were obliterated in a fiery red glow. "Run, ye murderous witch, before I put my sword through yer black heart."

They stood side by side, watching as the old woman crawled through the charred rubble. Dragging herself to her feet, she hobbled toward the woods with one last terrified look in their direction. Evangeline waited until the old woman melded with the shadows to turn to Lachlan and wrap her arms around his waist. She laid her head on his chest, his heart thundering against her ear. He stood still, his hands hanging at his sides.

"I'm sorry, Lachlan. I'm so sorry for all you suffered because of that woman." A tear trickled down her cheek at the thought of the pain the spiteful witch had caused him, of all that he'd lost.

His arms came around her. "Doona cry, Evie, 'tis in the past."

She lifted her face from his chest. "That doesn't make it any less painful for you to hear."

"Havin' ye to stand with me does." He framed her face with his hands. Wiping her tears away with his thumbs, he kissed her forehead. "Come, let us be gone from here."

As they left the haunted grounds behind them, Evangeline could not help but ask, "Is there a chance she spoke the truth, Lachlan? Could Ursula have borne your child?"

"Aye. They didna only want my blood, they wanted my seed as well. Ursula hoped by getting herself with my child she'd gain my magick. They drugged me, Evie, chained me down so I couldna fight them."

She didn't know what to say. Mere words seemed pathetic in the face of what he'd withstood. Her throat ached from trying to contain her sorrow. She brought his hand to her lips and pressed a kiss to the faded scars that encircled his thick wrist. "I'm proud of you. You didn't allow what was done to you to make you bitter or cruel. It made you a man to look up to, to admire." She wanted to tell him it was one of the reasons she loved him, but didn't think he was ready to hear what was in her heart. The emotion was new to her, and she wasn't certain she was ready to open herself to rejection. She knew he cared for her and hoped someday he would feel as deeply for her as she did for him, but for now she'd keep it to herself.

"I'll remind ye of that the next time ye're beratin' me fer bein' a fool."

About to chide him at his attempt to deflect her praise, she remembered the little seer's prophesy. "Aurora said you were in danger. Do you think it's Lamont and Ursula she referred to?"

"Aye, it seems likely."

"What are we going to do?"

"Fer now we go to Dunvegan. I need to warn Aidan of the old crone's presence in the Hebrides and to tell him Lamont and Ursula are in the area."

She sighed. "Yes, I suppose we have no choice but to go to Rory and Aileanna's."

"Doona sound so disappointed, Evie, I'll find a way to muffle yer cries of pleasure."

"I don't understand how you can jest at—"

He cut her off with a breath-stealing kiss. "Aye, that should work." He grinned.

The angels were on his side, Morfessa thought as the half-blood king and his bitch rode past where he crouched in the woods. They'd given him another chance to rid the Fae realm of Andora's evil spawn.

He'd been beside himself with fury at Bana's ineptitude. The only thing that had calmed his rage was the hope he could coerce Erwn into doing his bidding. Waiting for a chance to get him on his own, Morfessa learned of the charges Erwn had brought against the queen. She was more like her mother than even Morfessa had thought. He'd overheard the woman warrior tell the palace guard they'd be escorting Erwn from the Isles as soon as Uscias had returned from transporting the she-devil to the Mortal realm.

Confident the highlander would kill her for having relations with his father, Morfessa had gone through the stones in hopes of witnessing her downfall. He'd reached the portal just before she and Uscias had come through. He'd been lucky to escape their notice, although he thought his old friend had sensed his magick.

His stomach roiled as he recalled their coupling on the beach. Sickened by the memory, he spat out his disgust on the scorched ground. In that moment he'd realized he could depend on no one but himself to rid the Fae realm of her evil. The old crone had been the answer to his prayers. When the highlander had been brought to the Enchanted Isles to recover, Morfessa had learned what had taken place at Glastonbury. All he had to do now was find this Ursula and Lamont and use their desire to free the dark lords to his advantage.

They were the perfect instrument to bring about the bitch's downfall. Soon his troubles would be over. He would be revered once more. Even better, if his plan worked out the way he intended, he would be held up as the hero of the Isles. Saving both the Mortal and Fae realm from the dark lords, an evil the villainous Evangeline would be accused of unleashing. Like mother, like daughter.

It would be a fitting end to the she-devil's spawn.

Chapter 26

The bairn's cry from within Dunvegan destroyed the fragile hold Lachlan had on his emotions, the gut-wrenching pain twisting his insides. An innocent child—his child—had been murdered because of who Lachlan was, the bairn's life snuffed out before it drew a single breath. And now, if the old crone spoke the truth, he had a son with a woman whose madness rivaled that of his old nursemaid.

"Lachlan?" Evangeline's hand slipped into his as she waited for him to enter his cousin's home. "Are you all right?"

"Aye." He attempted a reassuring smile.

"No, you are not." With a quick glance around the empty entry hall, she drew him back outside and closed the door quietly behind them.

He leaned against the cool gray stone for support, inhaling deeply of the rain-scented night air in an attempt to regain control over the barrage of feelings that threatened to bring him to his knees. Evangeline remained silent, as though she sensed how close he was to coming apart. He took comfort in the knowledge she'd stand by him no matter the cost. She knew him, understood the demons he battled as she'd battled her own.

She brought his hand to her cheek, pressing her soft lips

to his palm. Raising her gaze to his, she said, "We can't change the past nor can we take on the guilt for another's actions. You were not responsible for what happened to the Lamonts and your child. I won't allow you to take the blame for what that evil witch did."

"And will ye do the same, Evie? Will ye no longer bear the burden of guilt fer yer mother's actions?" he asked, drawing her into his arms.

"It's not the same," she muttered into his tunic.

"Aye, 'tis, and well ye ken it." He smoothed his hand over her long silky mane. "'Twill take time, but mayhap together we will find a way to put our pasts behind us."

She eased back to look him in the eye. "I promise you we will find Lamont and Ursula. If there is a child, and he is yours, he will not remain with them a moment longer than he has to." She took a deep breath then squared her shoulders as if setting out for battle. "We . . . we will take him back to live with us in the Enchanted Isles."

"Thank ye. I ken 'tis no' an easy offer fer ye to make." Her pained expression made it difficult to contain his laughter, and she narrowed her gaze on him. "I . . . I adore ye, my bonny wife." He'd almost said *love*, but held back. It was not an emotion he thought himself capable of, although, he admitted, if he felt it for anyone it would be Evie. Her quiet words of support were all he'd needed to regain his composure. She was right. Together they would find Ursula and Lamont, and God help them if they'd harmed his son.

Thunder rumbled over the Cuillans—the mountain range that dominated the skyline—and a clap of lightning illuminated the thick stand of pines ringing Dunvegan's courtyard. "The skies are aboot ready to open up. We should go inside," he suggested as two drops of rain splattered onto his forehead.

From within, footsteps as loud as the distant thunder followed by high-pitched squeals rattled the door of the keep.

"I quite like the rain," Evangeline said, snuggling against him as though she meant to remain there for the night.

"Doona worry, I'll protect ye from the bairns." Framing her face, he added, "And I'll make our excuses so we can retire early and then I'll make good on my promise to ye."

"What—"

The heavy oak door swung open and his cousin stuck his head out. "Mrs. Mac thought she saw ye. Get in here before ye're soaked to the skin," Rory said, motioning for them to come inside.

Placing his hands on his wife's shoulders, Lachlan had to firmly push her resistant frame through the door, smothering a laugh as he did so.

"If we woulda kent ye were comin', we'd have held dinner fer ye. Are ye hungry?" Rory gave his head a shake, then grinned. "What am I thinkin'? Ye're always hungry."

"Nay, doona go to any trouble on our account. Where is everyone?"

"'Tis no trouble. Mrs. Mac," his cousin bellowed.

"Rory, would you stop shouting, Syrena is trying to settle the babies. What do you need Mrs. Mac for? She's only now managed to get Alex and Jamie in their bath." Frowning at her husband as she came down the stairs, Aileanna turned her attention to Lachlan and Evangeline once she'd reached the bottom step. "I'm sorry, this place is a madhouse. Go on up to my solar. Aidan will welcome your company."

"Aye, he will. Alasdair's been talkin' his ear off fer the last hour."

Hands on her hips, Aileanna rounded on her husband. "Rory MacLeod, my father doesn't visit that often. The least you could do is be civil to him when he does."

"No' that often? He's here so much he might as well move in." Rory groaned when Aileanna's face crumpled and she appeared close to tears. Taking her into his arms, he said, "I'm sorry, *mo chridhe*. I promise, I'll try harder to get along with the . . . your da." *'Tis the bairn*, he mouthed over her head, gesturing for them to go up. "You're tired, Aileanna. Why doona ye get an early night?"

She sighed, leaning heavily against her husband. "I wish I could, but I have to get Olivia and Ava ready for bed."

"I'm sure Evangeline wouldna mind helpin' with the bairns." Rory cast a hopeful look in Lachlan's wife's direction.

Evangeline froze halfway up the stairs, shooting a perturbed look at Lachlan.

He shrugged and she scowled at him before turning to say, "Of course. Lachlan and I will be glad to help."

"Thank you," Aileanna said, allowing her husband to guide her up the stairs. "Olivia's room is beside the one Syrena occupies. I've put her and Ava together, but Mrs. Mac has them with her in the boys' room at the moment."

"I'll meet you in the solar once I see Aileanna settled, Lan."

"Oh, no, you don't." Evangeline grabbed Lachlan's arm when they reached the landing and he'd turned in the direction of Aileanna's solar.

"Now, Evie," he grinned, "ye ken I have much to discuss with my brother."

"Men." She lowered her voice and thumped her fingers on his chest. "You are very good at making babies, but when it comes to caring for them, you are nowhere to be found."

He wrapped his hand around her fingers. Bringing them to his lips, he nipped the tips. "Ye must admit the makin' of the bairns is the best part."

She freed her hand from his and turned on her heel with a disgusted sigh, muttering under her breath as she marched down the hall. Aye, Lachlan thought, noting the way the trews hugged his wife's bonny arse, his chat with his cousin and brother would be a brief one.

An hour after she'd left her husband on the landing, Evangeline entered the solar. Lachlan looked up from where he sat by the hearth and choked on his ale. "What?" she asked, unable to keep the sharp edge from her tone. Not only was she exhausted from wrestling the two-year-old hellions, she was a wet and bedraggled mess. Olivia and Ava had jumped into the bath after Jamie and Alex had run shrieking from the room at Evangeline's presence.

Rory's and Aidan's jaws dropped when she turned to greet them.

"Fer Chrissakes, Evie," Lachlan muttered, grabbing a length of plaid from the chair beside him. He strode toward her and wrapped the colorful red wool around her shoulders. "Yer tunic doesna leave much to the imagination."

She glanced down, the damp white fabric had molded to her breasts. "Oh," she murmured, her cheeks heating. Lachlan held out the chair beside him, but she shook her head, lowering herself to the floor to sit between his legs where she'd be assured of the fire's warmth. He combed his fingers through her hair, and she swallowed a moan of pleasure.

"Would ye like somethin' to drink, Evangeline?" Rory offered.

"No, thank you." She tipped her chin at the mug resting on Lachlan's thigh. "Lachlan will share his."

"Nay, he won't. No' after the last time," Lachlan said, giving her hair a gentle tug.

Syrena entered the solar, closing the door behind her with a drawn-out sigh. "They're finally asleep." Looking at Evangeline and Lachlan, she beamed like a proud mother. "I knew you'd work it out."

Lachlan's big hand curled around Evangeline's neck, his thumb caressing the skin at the base of her throat.

"Syrena, Lan has brought us some disturbin' news." Aidan held out his hand, urging his wife to sit. She took the chair beside him.

"What is it?"

"Lamont and Ursula are in the Hebrides." Lachlan's hand tightened almost imperceptibly around Evangeline's neck.

She laid her palm on his thigh. "The old crone said a child accompanies them. She claims the bairn is mine."

Syrena gasped, reaching for her husband's hand. "Oh, Lachlan, what are you going to do?"

Evangeline noticed her friend didn't question the validity of the claim. Syrena must have known the full extent of what Lachlan had suffered. It was not surprising. Lachlan had a strong connection with his sister-by-marriage. As children they'd communicated in their minds—Syrena from the Fae realm, Lachlan from the Mortal.

"I'm goin' to find them."

"'Twill no' be easy, there's too many places fer them to hide. And there will be those willin' to hide them," Aidan said. His eyes sharpened when his gaze shifted from his brother to Evangeline. She lowered hers, certain he would see her anger. She could not hide it, not after learning he'd been willing to banish Lachlan from Lewes and thought him capable of setting fire to the Lamonts' home, taking the lives of the woman he'd loved and his unborn child.

Aidan scrubbed his hands over his face then looked at her. "I imagine my brother has told ye what went on with the Lamonts and I can see ye're fashed with me, Evangeline. I admit I didna handle the situation well, but doona doubt my love fer my brother."

"Ye have nothin' to apologize fer, Aidan. I ken I was no' easy to deal with back then. My wife tends to be somewhat overprotective of me is all. It must be my bonny looks and charmin'—"

She interrupted him with a snort. Aidan's gray gaze warmed and he smiled.

"As to what ye said about Lamont and Ursula hidin', I'm thinkin' they'll no' have given up their beliefs and there will be talk soon enough of strange goin's on," Lachlan said.

Rory rubbed his mug, his brow furrowed. "Any goin's on in particular?"

"Have ye heard somethin'?" Lachlan asked.

"It may be nothin', but Alasdair was tellin' the lads a tall tale earlier."

"The one aboot the water horse?" Aidan asked.

"Aye, did he speak to you aboot it as well?"

Aidan nodded. "He managed to tell me a bit before Alex and Jamie dragged him out of here after their bath wantin' to hear more aboot it."

"Anytime ye'd like to share the story with me would be good," Lachlan said dryly.

Rory rolled his eyes. "There's been a sightin' of a monster in the loch. Several of the villagers have seen the beast and will no longer fish there. 'Tis said to look like a dragon or, as Aidan said, a water horse. Alasdair and some of his men took a boat out a few days past but saw nothin'."

"Is it near Armadale?"

"Aye, in Loch Ness, at the foot of Armadale."

Hearing where the monster had been sighted, Evangeline's heart thudded in her chest so hard and fast she felt faint. She pressed her fingers to her temples in an attempt to banish the loud buzzing in her head.

"Evangeline, what is it?" Syrena's voice seemed to come from a great distance.

Lachlan reached down, bringing her onto his lap, his arms tightening around her. "Tell me, Evie, what's wrong?"

Drawing comfort from his embrace, she raised her gaze to his. "Above Loch Ness lies another door to the underworld."

His worried gaze searched hers. "Are ye sure?"

"Yes." She nodded, swallowing the bile that rose in her throat. "It's the same door my mother opened to release the dark lords twenty-six years ago."

Chapter 27

The wind howled, rattling the window in their chambers, setting Evangeline's already frayed nerves on edge. She dug her fingers into the mattress, trying not to think of what she would face the next day.

Crouched at her feet, tugging off her doeskin boots, Lachlan watched her closely. "Ye're no' comin' to Armadale."

"Yes, I am. I will not let you face Ursula and Lamont on your own." The thought of being near the site of her mother's perfidy caused her stomach to lurch. Evangeline had vowed never to set foot near Loch Ness, fearing the evil her father had sworn dwelled within her, the evil she had sensed within herself the day she'd come through the realms, would gain a foothold there. But her fear for Lachlan won out over her fear for herself.

"We doona even ken if they are there. Besides, I'll no' be alone. Rory, Aidan, Fergus, and Alasdair will accompany me."

"You need me, I have—"

"Aye, I need ye safe." He came to his feet and drew her to hers, tugging the tunic from her trews. His fingers brushed her skin causing the muscles deep within her belly to clench. He felt her reaction, and a wicked grin curved his lips. He drew circles over her tingling flesh, grazing the underside of her breasts. His teasing touch chased away her fears, banished her dread of what they might face on the morrow. Her desire for him and the passion he aroused in her were all that mattered in that moment.

"Lift yer arms, Evie," he ordered in his deep seductive brogue.

A shiver of pleasure raced through her at his command. He drew the fine linen over her head, the cool air causing her nipples to tighten. Tossing her tunic on the bed, he leaned back to look at her breasts, heat flaring to life in his golden gaze. "I have another edict for ye to obey." He chuckled at the unamused look she shot him. "From now on, I forbid ye to use magick to disrobe. I find I enjoy performin' the task myself."

He cupped her breasts, caressing them, kneading them, and she decided this was one edict she'd gladly obey. Her nipples puckered in response to his expert attention and she couldn't contain a moan of pleasure. Tugging her into his arms, he stroked her back with his big hands, then slid them to her bottom, pressing his straining erection, thick and hard, against her belly. She smoothed her palms over his broad shoulders, down the sculpted muscles of his arms, luxuriating in the feel of his powerful embrace. She snuggled closer, aching to feel his naked flesh against hers.

"Perhaps I should help you disrobe, Your Highness." She smiled into his amused eyes, dipping her finger below the waistband of his trews, reveling in the feel of his muscles rippling in response to her touch.

"Ye ken, Evie, ye have the makin's of a perfect wife," he teased, but under the lightness of his tone she sensed something deeper, something she couldn't name but that made her think his feelings for her went beyond desire and companionship.

Her heart swelled at the thought and she barely managed to get the words past the emotions clogging her throat. "You'll have to help me." He was too tall for her to draw his tunic over his arms. She trailed her fingers over the golden hairs dusting his chest while he complied with her request.

Her nipples puckered as they brushed against his heated flesh, drawing a low, aroused growl from him. He threw his tunic onto the chest at the end of the bed then drew her back into his embrace. She stretched on the tips of her toes and wound her arms around his neck, bringing his mouth to hers. He cupped the back of her head, seducing her with the slow, sensuous slide of his lips over hers. He angled his head, taking the kiss deeper, torturing her with his tongue. She nipped it playfully, then soothed it with hers. His breathing roughened and the kiss grew hotter, wetter. His long, hard length rubbed against her and she moved her hips suggestively.

He groaned, breaking the kiss. "I need ye naked, now. Use yer magick," he demanded gruffly.

She hid a smile. "Didn't you just say I was not to use my magick to disrobe?" She pulled back, fighting to keep the amusement from her voice as she teased him. "I know how important it is that I obey you."

"Now ye decide to be the obedient wife? Don't torture me, love. I need to be inside ye, badly."

She bit her lip then shook her head, unable to contain a gratified laugh at his frustrated moan. Pleased for once to turn the tables on her teasing husband. He narrowed his gaze on her. Clamping his big hands on either side of her waist, he lifted her easily, bringing them eye to eye. She gasped, grabbing hold of his shoulders, her breasts jiggling at the movement. He growled low in his throat, raising his smoldering gaze to hers. Cupping her bottom with his hands, he lifted her higher, bringing her breasts level with his mouth. He flicked his tongue over her nipples, watching her as he did. She moaned, wrapping her legs around him.

"Ye taste so good," he murmured, licking first one breast then the other.

For the love of Fae, he was driving her mad. She clung to

him, arching her back, pressing her nipple to his lips in hopes he would draw it deep into his hot mouth. If he didn't soon, she'd have to relent and beg him to do so. He kneaded her bottom, a sinfully wicked smile creasing his handsome face as he slid her up and down his body.

"Doona torture us any longer, my bonny wife. I can feel ye. Ye're wet and hot, ye want me inside ye as much as I want to be." He wrapped his arm beneath her bottom, holding her in place while he brought his other hand between them. He cupped her mound, stroking her through her trews. She writhed against him, consumed by desire. Lifting her hand, she flicked her wrist, groaning when his fingers slid over her naked flesh.

"Now, there's a good, obedient wife," he rasped before he drew her nipple deep into his mouth.

"Please," she begged shamelessly, her nails digging into his shoulders.

He backed her against the paneled wall, lowering her until she could feel the head of his erection demanding entry. "And now I'll make you scream with pleasure," he growled just before he slanted his mouth over hers.

Wrapped in Lachlan's embrace, Evangeline lay sated by the warmth of the crackling fire. The steady rhythm of the rain pummeling the window and the sound of their breathing lulled her into a slumberous state.

"Good thing the thunder drowned out yer screams, or Rory and Aidan woulda come through the door with their swords drawn." Lachlan chuckled, nuzzling the hollow between her neck and shoulder.

"I did not scream." Overloud moans of pleasure and some not so quiet begging, perhaps, but screams, most definitely not.

"Aye, my bonny wife, ye did. And if I didna plan on gettin' an early start on the morrow, I'd make ye do so again."

Stifling a yawn, Evangeline snuggled against him. "What time do we leave?"

"Ye doona listen verra well. Ye're no' comin' with me."

She pulled back to look at him. "I will not remain here if there's even the slightest chance you'll encounter Lamont and Ursula. You no longer have my magick, Lachlan. You need me." A part of her wished she hadn't drawn attention to his lack of magick, afraid he would ask her to share her power with him. If he did, she'd have no choice but to refuse him. Uscias's warning had been clear—if she gave her blood to Lachlan again, she would lose her magick forever. And she could not bear to contemplate a life without her powers.

He searched her face. "Christ, Evie, I canna believe ye think I'd ask ye fer yer blood. Do ye truly believe I'm so selfish as to put my desires over yer well-being?"

"I didn't say that, I—"

"Ye didna have to. 'Tis written all over yer face," he muttered, clearly not happy with her.

Levering herself up on an elbow, she traced the hard set of his mouth with her finger. "No, I don't believe you would. But I also know how difficult it is for you to be without magick."

"In truth, it never bothered me before, at least I didna think it did. But after experiencin' yers, I admit I enjoyed the power that went along with it." He gave her a rueful grin then drew her finger into his mouth, nipping the tip. "I can understand how ye wouldna want to be without it."

He couldn't—not really. No one knew the void her magick had filled. "But you have me and my magick now. I will make certain no harm comes to you. I will protect—"

With a low growl, he rolled her onto her back and pinned her beneath him. "Do ye no' understand my need to protect ye is as great as yer need to protect me?"

"Yes, and that's why I must go with you to Armadale."

"Ye're no' makin' sense, Evie," he said with a frustrated shake of his head. And then, as though sensing her unwillingness to relent, he sighed. "Mayhap I should take ye with me. Ye could face yer fears once and fer all."

Her pleasure that he would allow her to accompany him without a fight was tempered by the anxiety swirling higher in her chest. The knowledge she would be but a stone's throw from the door to the underworld caused her to break out in a cold sweat, and she shivered. "Good, that's settled then." She struggled to keep the tremor from her voice, but Lachlan's gaze sharpened.

"Aye, 'tis. Ye'll remain here. Nay, doona argue with me. Once the danger has passed, I'll take ye to Loch Ness."

"But I—"

He smothered her protest in an openmouthed kiss that stole her breath away and any thought of arguing with him further.

Sitting in the grand hall at Dunvegan, Evangeline gritted her teeth to contain a frustrated scream. Jamie and Alex, shrieking with laughter, ran around the table where they'd gathered to break their fast, their barking dog chasing after them. Olivia and Ava repeatedly banged their spoons in a mind-jarring symphony, leaving dents on the already scarred wooden table. When Mrs. Mac entered the hall carrying Syrena's howling, red-faced infants, Evangeline no longer felt inclined to protect Lachlan, she wanted to strangle him. And if he hadn't already left for Armadale, she would have gladly done so.

Plop.

A clump of porridge landed on Evangeline's head. Glaring at Ava, who sat across from her giggling, Evangeline scooped the pile of mush from her hair. Olivia, not to be outdone by her cousin, shot a spoonful of oats at Evangeline's chest. Growling under her breath, Evangeline looked over at Syrena and Aileanna, expecting them to admonish the devious little demons on her behalf.

They didn't.

The two women sat staring into the bowls placed in front of them without so much as batting an eyelash. Wiping the porridge from her robes, Evangeline rose to her feet, concluding motherhood impaired a woman's ability to see and hear. Either that or they'd fallen asleep with their eyes open.

Well, she hadn't.

"Enough!" she said, lunging for Jamie and Alex as they raced by. Managing to grab hold of the backs of their tunics, she hauled them to the table and sat them firmly in the empty chairs beside their mother. With one set of twins taken care of, she marched over to Olivia and Ava and grabbed their spoons midair. "If you throw your food and bang your utensils, you don't eat!" The four children gaped at her.

Considering the squalling infants Mrs. Mac bounced on her hip in an attempt to quiet them, Evangeline knew they were too young to reason with and did the only thing she could think of. With a flick of her finger, she encased them in a soundproof bubble.

Blessed silence, she sighed.

"Evangeline!" Syrena and Aileanna stared at her in open-mouthed horror.

She frowned, surprised by their reaction. "What?"

"What do you mean, *what*? My babies are floating around the hall in a bubble!" Syrena looked ready to pull out her hair.

Angling her head, Evangeline narrowed her gaze on the babies bouncing off the wall. She didn't know what the problem was. They were no longer crying. Mrs. Mac, who stood on a chair, her arms flailing in an attempt to reach the children, was the only one in danger.

"Come down from there, Mrs. Mac. Don't worry about them, they're safe," Evangeline reassured the older woman.

"Aunt Evie, Aunt Evie." Alex and Jamie tugged on the sleeve of her robe. "Put us in a bubble," they demanded.

Knowing it would not be long before they returned to their boisterous ways, she shrugged and encapsulated first Alex then Jamie in the impenetrable membrane.

"Me . . . me!" Ava and Olivia pounded the table. Only too happy to comply with the little hellions' request, she flicked her wrist.

Returning to her place at the table, she sat down with a contented sigh and smiled at Aileanna and Syrena. She rolled her eyes at the two women. "You can stop with the evil looks. Your children are fine, and more importantly, they're *quiet*." Out of the corner of her eye, she caught sight of Jamie and Alex laughingly waving good-bye.

She shifted in her chair, and using her magick, shut the doors to the grand hall, then locked them before the boys could make their great escape. No one other than the immediate family, Mrs. Mac, and Fergus knew they had faeries in their midst, and it would not bode well for the MacLeods if their secret were to be discovered.

Arms crossed, Syrena kept an eye on the children. "You are not supposed to use your magick in the Mortal realm, Evangeline, unless you or one of the Fae is in danger."

"I was in danger of my head exploding, and since your father is well acquainted with the next generation of Mac-Leods, I'm certain he'd make an exception in this case."

Syrena rolled her eyes and Aileanna sat back, rubbing her distended belly. "I still can't believe our husbands left before we woke up."

Evangeline raised a brow. "Like Lachlan, I'm certain Rory and Aidan didn't wish to deal with our arguments." She was also certain anyone within earshot of Dunvegan had been well aware of Aileanna's and Syrena's displeasure at being left behind.

Before the children had rendered her insensible, Evangeline had been weighing her need to protect Lachlan against her desire to remain as far as she could from the door to the underworld. Considering what he might face, she knew she had no choice but to go after him. All she had to do was come up with a plan to deflect his anger when he discovered that she'd disobeyed him.

She studied Aileanna and Syrena. Now, if they were to agree to accompany her, or better yet suggest it, Lachlan would have no choice but to forgive her. Since Syrena, a woman trained in battle, and Aileanna, a woman raised in the future, had a problem with their husbands' narrow-minded tendencies, she knew exactly what to say to get them on board.

"I suppose we should be grateful they wish to protect us. Although, I must admit, it annoys me they think of us as helpless simpletons who have nothing better to do than raise children." Syrena bristled and Evangeline grimaced. Perhaps she should have given a little more thought to what she said. She cleared her throat and added, "They don't take into account our abilities and desire to protect our families. They're certain only a man has the strength and prowess to do so."

"You're right, Evangeline. My husband seems to forget I, too, am a warrior. I might be a little rusty on the battlefield, but I can certainly hold my own." With a determined nod, Syrena came to her feet. "I'm going to Armadale."

"So am I," said an equally determined Aileanna, although she had a difficult time rising from her chair. "If one of them is injured, at least I'll be on hand to see to their care."

"What about Iain?" Evangeline asked Aileanna.

"I do little more for him than manage his pain now. Mrs. Mac can do that as well as I can," she said, glancing over to where the older woman tracked the floating children with a steely eye. "I think it would be best if we make no mention to Iain of our plans. Rory is concerned his injuries have made him feel less than a man and has kept him in the dark about Ursula and Lamont's return."

"How will—" An insistent pounding on the hall's massive oak doors interrupted Evangeline.

Syrena nudged her. "The men are anxious to return to the hall. You'd best undo your spell."

Evangeline waved her hands, drawing the spheres toward her. Setting them in a row on the table, she waited until Syrena and Mrs. Mac were in place to grab hold of the babies. "Get ready," she said, her instruction followed by a series of loud pops. The film vanished, leaving the older children sitting disappointed and pouting on the table while Syrena and Mrs. Mac snagged the infants.

With the babies in her arms, Mrs. Mac headed for the door Evangeline had just unlocked. Four of the MacLeods' men-at-arms sauntered into the room.

Aileanna clapped a hand over Jamie's mouth when he appeared ready to tell the men about his adventure. "Jamie," she warned.

"I wasna goin' to say anythin'," he protested, sliding off the table.

Ava's scrunched-up face didn't bode well. Having witnessed previous temper tantrums, Evangeline thought it time for her to make her exit.

"Ava, we have no time for that. We must prepare for Armadale," Syrena said to her daughter, stopping Evangeline in her tracks.

She turned. "Prepare whom?"

"Why, the children, of course."

Evangeline groaned, earning a disapproving look from her friend.

As they left the hall, Evangeline looked down at her loose robes and decided she, too, would prepare for the journey.

Remembering the heated look in her husband's eyes when he'd dressed her in the form-fitting violet gown, she thought it might be just the distraction he needed when she greeted him upon their arrival at Armadale.

The midmorning sun burnt the last fingers of fog from the loch and Lachlan scanned the hills and shoreline of Loch Ness for some sign evil lurked there. But the picturesque setting did not easily give up its secrets. Their search of the lands and villages between Dunvegan and Armadale had proved as futile as it had long, adding an extra two days to the journey.

Lachlan brought his steed alongside his brother's. "I'm goin' to take the trail into the hills. I'll meet ye back at Armadale in a couple of hours."

"Fergus and I will join ye."

"While the three of ye do that, Rory and I will question my men and the tenants," Alasdair said, raising a silver brow at his son-by-marriage's pained groan. "Is somethin' the matter with ye, lad?"

"Nay." Rory scowled at Aidan before he headed off in the direction of the glistening white castle perched at the top of the rolling hill that led down to the loch.

"There's no sign of them," Lachlan finally conceded after combing the rocky shoreline and hills for several hours.

"Them, or the monster," Fergus muttered, sucking on the finger he'd scratched on a thorny bush. Fergus served more as a father figure than a man-at-arms to Rory and Iain, but his skills on the battlefield were second to none and Lachlan was glad to have him at his back.

"We might as well return to Armadale and see if Rory and Alasdair have learned anythin'," Lachlan said.

"Aye, Rory, we'll be needin' a reprieve aboot now," his brother said with a smirk.

Lachlan frowned at the high-pitched squeals emitting from behind the curtain wall as they drew closer to Armadale. "Is it just me, or does that sound like wee Jamie and Alex?"

"'Tis the demons all right," his brother said, looking none too pleased.

"If the lads are here, ye can be sure there mother is as well, and if her father and husband doona tan her arse fer comin' to Armadale in her condition, I'll be sorely tempted to do so," Fergus grumbled.

"Even if they left Dunvegan immediately after we did, they shouldna have arrived before us. No' cartin' along the bairns as they were." Aidan shifted on his horse to scowl at Lachlan. "'Tis yer wife's doin'. She must have transported the whole lot of them."

"It appears so," Lachlan said, jerking his chin to where Rory sprinted across the courtyard trying to grab hold of Ava and Olivia.

Upon seeing her father, Ava squealed and changed direction, stumbling toward them. Aidan caught her before she toppled over. Rory captured Olivia and swung her beneath his arm. Both men advanced on Lachlan.

"Do ye have no control over yer wife?" His brother's querulous question was muffled by Ava's gown as she attempted to climb to the top of his head.

"Aboot as much as ye have over yer daughter," Lachlan countered. Since Syrena, who like Lachlan could not transport herself, had obviously not been behind the family's arrival at Armadale, it made sense their censure would fall upon Evangeline. But it didn't mean Lachlan appreciated it or would allow her to take the brunt of the blame. "And just so we're straight on this, yer wives are as stubborn as mine. The only reason Evangeline would've brought them is because they demanded she do so." He imagined Syrena and Aileanna had to do some cajoling to get Evangeline to agree to bring the bairns.

His cousin and brother exchanged a look. "Aye, ye're probably right. 'Tis the transportin' of the bairns that concerned me is all," his brother said.

"Evie may no' be particularly fond of the wee ones, but she'd no' put them at risk."

"Uncle Lachlan!" Alex and Jamie raced to his side, panting. "Uncle Lachlan, can ye make Auntie Evie put us in a bubble again?"

"A *bubble*?" Lachlan frowned.

"Aye." They nodded. "She put us in bubbles and we floated way up high and all around the hall. We had a grand time."

"Ye musta been dreamin', Jamie, Evie would no'—"

"Nay, we were no' dreamin'. The babies were drivin' her mad with their cryin' and Ava and Olivia threw porridge at her."

With a clear picture of his wife amidst the chaos Jamie described, Lachlan laughed, then covered his amusement with a cough when he noted the furious expressions on Aidan's and Rory's faces.

"Lachlan!" his cousin and brother yelled after him as he sprinted across the courtyard. Forget Lamont and Ursula, he'd have to protect his wife from his family. When he entered Armadale, a manservant approached him. "Sir Lachlan?"

"Aye."

"This arrived fer ye aboot an hour ago." He handed him a sealed parchment.

Lachlan recognized the seal—it was Lamont's. He jerked his gaze to the man. "Did ye see who delivered it?" His fingers were unsteady as he tore open the missive.

"Nay, 'twas delivered to the kitchens."

Lachlan scanned the missive. *If you wish to see your son alive, meet me on the hill directly across from Armadale at sunset. Come alone or he dies.* "Thank ye." Keeping his expression devoid of the anger and fear simmering inside him, he dismissed the man.

Out of the corner of his eye, Lachlan spied his wife. She

cast a furtive look from left to right, then darted across the hall. Catching sight of him, she skidded to a halt. He surreptitiously brought his hand behind him. Folding the parchment between his fingers, he tucked it in the back of his trews.

She walked toward him, a stubborn jut to her chin, looking so beautiful it made his chest ache.

"I can explain," she began.

"I'm sure ye can. I'm just no' sure Rory and my brother will listen." He kept his tone light, wanting nothing more than to tell her about the missive. But he wouldn't endanger her, nor would he endanger his son.

Chapter 28

Evangeline paced in front of the fire in the well-appointed room Aileanna's aunt Fiona had placed her and Lachlan in, certain she'd worn a path in the oval rug. Lachlan had sent her up to their chambers hours ago with the whispered promise he would join her shortly. She refused to seek him out in case Syrena or Aileanna waylaid her with a request to help with their children.

Her head still ached from their riotous chatter at meal time. If not for Rory and Aidan's sour looks, she would have enacted the bubble spell as Jamie and Alex requested. Even Lachlan had supported the idea. Despite her displeasure he had yet to join her in their chambers, she smiled when she recalled how he'd come to her defense earlier in the day. No matter that he was not happy she'd gone against his wishes, he hadn't allowed his cousin or brother to say a word against her.

The dampness of the night air seeped through the stone walls and she suppressed a shiver, stoking the flames higher in the hearth with her magick. She glanced down at the delicate white nightshift she'd conjured, slightly embarrassed she'd chosen the barely there confection with the sole purpose of igniting her husband's desire. If he didn't come to her soon, she vowed to garb herself in a very plain, very thick nightdress.

Her fit of pique evaporated at the sound of heavy footfalls in the hallway outside their room. She chided herself at the unseemly excitement quivering low in her belly and lowered herself onto the chair by the fire. Not wishing to appear anxious for his return, she retrieved the book she'd attempted to read earlier from the table beside her. When he entered their chambers, she pretended to be engrossed in this literary pursuit. She suppressed a sigh; her reading material was upside down. She furtively righted the book, but she needn't have bothered with her pretense as Lachlan barely spared her a glance.

He crossed to the bed. His hair, damp and slicked back, brushed the collar of the tunic that clung to him like a second skin.

"Have you been out of doors?" It was obvious he had been, but his stony silence was disconcerting and she asked the first thing that came to her mind.

"Aye." His back to her, he muted his sword and placed it on the trunk at the foot of the bed.

Noting the jerky movements with which he removed his dirk from his boot, she returned the book to the table and came to her feet. "What is it?"

Head bowed, he released a ragged breath and her earlier disquiet came back. He slowly turned. The haunted look in his eyes stopped her cold.

"Tell me." She was surprised she could get the words past the stranglehold fear had on her throat. She walked toward him.

"'Tis my son, Evie. Ursula and Lamont have my son." His expression tortured, a lethal fury radiated from him.

"How can you be sure?"

He didn't answer her right away, wouldn't look at her as he strode past her to the hearth—gripping the mantel as though he meant to rip it from the wall. "Lachlan, please," she begged. Her legs went weak and she leaned against the bed for support.

"I was only a little older than the bairn when I sat for the portrait that hangs in the gallery at Lewes. He looks just like me." His mouth twisted with bitterness. "To this day I can recall the row Aidan had with Alexander over it. My brother refused to sit fer the portrait if I was no' included." He shook his head as if trying to rid himself of the memory.

She wanted to go to him, to offer him comfort, but his uncompromising stance warned her away. "I didn't think you, Aidan, and Rory intended to continue the search until morning."

"They were no' with me. I received a missive from Lamont tellin' me to meet them in the hills above the Loch—"

"You went alone . . . without telling me. How could you keep something like that from me?" She couldn't hold back her anger or her hurt. They were supposed to be in this together. How was she to protect him if he kept information such as this from her?

He whirled to face her, his eyes ablaze with fury. Shocked, she jerked back. "Because they threatened my son's life if I did." With a vehement curse, he sank into the chair she'd been sitting in.

At his obvious distress, she set aside her anger. He was suffering enough without her adding to it. "What happened?" she asked quietly.

He scrubbed his hands over his face. "I'd made it to the top of the cliff without bein' seen. I was hopin' to catch them unawares. A woman and child stood at the edge of the precipice. There was enough light that I could see it was Ursula and my . . . my son. I doona ken, but in my shock at seein' the lad, I must've made a sound. Ursula grabbed the bairn by his arm and held him over the Loch. She had a dagger in her hand."

A distressed cry escaped from her before she could contain it. She took a step toward him, but there was something in his eyes that held her back. It was more than just the horror of what he'd witnessed, it was as if he was somewhere else.

"Lachlan?"

He looked up at her, his gaze unfocused. He rubbed his hand along the side of his face. "The bairn was crying. All I could see was the terror on his wee face, and like a fool I ran toward them. Lamont jumped me and took me to the ground. The bastard had a blade to my throat before I knew what hit me."

Now more than ever she wished he had shared the contents of the missive with her. He shouldn't have gone to confront them on his own. She could only imagine how difficult it had been for him to face the two people who'd tortured him. To learn if it truly was his son they held. But now was not the time to dwell on the consequences of his actions. She could only be grateful he'd come back to her unharmed.

"Are they demanding coin for his return?"

He lifted his stricken gaze to hers. "Nay, they want . . . ye."

A wave of heat rushed over her and her vision dimmed. She grabbed hold of the bedpost before her legs gave way beneath her. Lowering herself to the bed, she shook her head. *No, this can't be happening.* "I won't do it! I can't!"

Without taking his eyes from her, he rose from the chair and took a step toward her. "Listen to me, Evie."

She sensed his determination, could see it in his eyes, in the firm set of his jaw. He actually meant for her to do this. To offer herself in exchange for his child, to put herself in the hands of two people who conspired to release the dark lords as her mother once had. "I won't do it. I can't believe you would ask it of me."

"Please, Evie, ye doona understand. They will kill him if ye doona."

His betrayal cut her to the quick and she held up her hands to keep him at bay. "Don't. Don't come near me." She hardened her heart at the look of anguish in his eyes.

"Evie, I promise ye, I'd never let them hurt ye."

"That's not a promise you can keep." Her body quaked and she wrapped her arms around herself. "You can't truly believe she would harm her own child. They were—"

A muscle jumped in his jaw. "Aye, I do. Ye didna see her. She'd kill her son as easily as Alexander woulda killed me if no' fer my brother." He turned away from her, but not before she witnessed the pain the long-ago memory caused him.

He stared into the flames. "She'd dressed him in nothing more than a nightshift. She didna care that she was nearly tearing his wee arm from its socket. You were no' there, you didna hear his cries nor see the fear on his face."

No matter her angry hurt at what he asked of her, she couldn't bear to think of what he had suffered, what he suffered now knowing the depravity of the ones who held his son. "How old were you when Alexander tried to kill you?"

"Eight."

"How did—"

"Nay!" He spun around to face her. "This is no' aboot me, this is aboot *my son*. Ye're the only one who can save him. Christ, Evie, ye're so bloody powerful they doona stand a chance against ye and yer magick. I canna believe ye can be so hard-hearted." His harsh breathing cut through the weighted silence in the room.

"Do you truly believe I don't want to help you? I would do everything in my power to protect you and your child, but I'm afraid. Afraid to be within ten feet of that door, afraid history will repeat itself, and . . ." She couldn't go on.

He sat down heavily in the chair, raking his hand through his hair. "I'm sorry. Forgive me. I should've taken yer fears into account. 'Twas no' fair of me to ask it of ye. But, Evie, ye must listen to me in this, ye're no' evil. Ye're no' yer mother."

"It's there, I've seen it. They'll use my powers to . . ." Her voice trailed off as an idea came to her. There was a way. She blinked back tears at the knowledge of what she'd sacrifice and stiffened her resolve. If she gave her magick to Lachlan they wouldn't be able to use it against her. She choked back a grief-stricken sob at the thought her power would be lost to her forever, reminding herself it was for the greater good.

Neither Lachlan nor his child deserved to suffer. And both Mortal and Fae needed to be protected from the likes of Ursula and Lamont. With or without her, they wouldn't give up on their quest to open the door to the underworld.

Her gaze went to her husband's bent head, the firelight playing in his golden hair. How she longed to comfort him. The images of their time together over the last weeks flashed before her. She found herself smiling at the memories.

At one time her magick had been the only constant in her life. The one thing she could depend upon, the one thing that brought her comfort, but that was no longer true. Nothing was more important to her than Lachlan, nothing had brought her more joy than he did. He filled the empty place inside her that her magick had never been able to reach. She could survive without her powers, but not without him.

He led the people she'd sworn to protect and now he would lead them with the benefit of her magick. He had much to learn. She was powerful not only because of her magick, but because of her knowledge. It would take time for her to teach Lachlan all he needed to know, but she wasn't worried—after all, theirs was an equal partnership. Together they were more than able to protect the Fae.

Elbows resting on his knees, Lachlan held his head in his hands. Christ, he'd been so worried about his son, so caught up in reliving his own nightmare he'd failed to realize he'd asked Evie to do the same. He couldn't think straight when he'd come into the room. It had been as though Ursula and Lamont had borne witness to his nightmares, reenacting the night Alexander tried to kill him.

The memories had assaulted him when he'd seen Ursula holding his son over the loch. For a moment he couldn't differentiate the past from the present. He'd felt Alexander's powerful hand crushing his, dragging him over the rain-slicked turf to the cliffs, his wet nightshift clinging to his stick-thin frame. The roar of the sea crashing against the rocks below had filled his head, the salty tang of the air his nostrils. He cursed, shoving the memories aside. Somehow he and Evie would find a way to get through this—one that kept her out of Lamont's and Ursula's hands.

He lifted his head, hoping by explaining what had come over him he could make amends.

She reached for his dagger.

In an instant he knew what she meant to do. "Nay," he bellowed, lunging for her.

She drew the blade across her creamy flesh and blood welled in the open wound, dripping on the delicate white lace of her chemise. He wrenched the blade from her trembling fingers and flung it to the trunk. "Why?" He shook her, horrified at what she'd done.

Preparing for the onslaught of hunger at the intoxicating sight of her blood, the desire for her magick, he held her away from him. There was no way in bloody hell he'd accept her sacrifice. The image of her lying bloodied on the forest floor had yet to fade, he didn't think it ever would. He'd vowed then never to leave her vulnerable again, and nothing, not even his son's rescue would allow him to do so. They would find another way.

"It's the only way I can help you, Lachlan. Without my powers they won't be able to use my magick to open the door. You can use it to save your son, to save both of . . . us." Her voice hitched on the last word.

He frowned, searching her face. "Ye canna think I wouldna save ye, Evie?"

She lowered her gaze from his and he cursed. Bracketing her face with his hands, he demanded, "Look at me." When she finally did as he asked, he said, "I would protect ye with my life, never doubt how important ye are to me. 'Tis why I willna take yer blood. Ye'll lose yer magick fer good this time, and I willna do that to ye."

A tender smile played on her lips as though his words had comforted her, as though how he felt about her was reflected in his eyes. Rising on the tips of her toes, she lifted her sweet mouth to his. "You must," she murmured, then pressed her lips to his.

Against his chest he felt the soft rise and fall of her breasts, and his gaze was drawn to the beads of crimson welling on the creamy swells. The hunger inside him intensified, but it was not for her blood; this time it was for her alone. He smoothed his palms over her back and brought her tight against him. Deepening the kiss, he groaned when she eased away from him.

"Take my blood now." Threading her fingers through his hair, she brought his mouth to her breast.

"We have until midnight to come up with a plan, Evie. Ye doona have to do this." His words were muffled in the plush pillow of her curves—her fragrance warm and intoxicating.

"Please, I need you to do this for me. I can't risk having even a small amount of magick left in my blood."

He searched her face and saw her desperation, her fear. Christ, what was he supposed to do? Would she really be safer if she didn't have her magick? "Evie, I canna do it, love. We have time, we'll think of somethin'."

She gave a fierce shake of her head. "No, this is the only way."

He forced himself to comply with her wishes, no matter how much it pained him to do so, humbled she was willing to give up her magick to help him save his son. Once they vanquished their enemy and retrieved the child, he would make it up to her. Her blood no longer enthralled him, but she did. He wanted to bury himself inside the warmth of her tight sheath and rid himself of the fear he could lose her.

He laid her on the bed, following her down. She moved

sinuously beneath him, as if she could not get close enough, her need as great as his. He didn't want to deny them both the comfort they'd find in making love, nor did he wish to weaken her. "Mayhap we should wait until we return. Wait until this is over."

"I don't want to wait. We might not . . ." She caught her bottom lip between her teeth and turned her head on the pillow, averting her gaze from his, but not before he'd seen the moisture gather in her eyes.

"Nay. I'll allow no one to harm ye, my bonny wife, no' ever," he said, stringing kisses along the delicate line of her jaw. Determined to take away her fear and show her with his touch, with his body, how much she meant to him.

Chapter 29

Evangeline waited until Lachlan's back was turned to drag herself from the bed. She didn't want him to see how weak she was. She could barely lift her arms or her boneless legs. It was worse than the last time he'd drained her of her blood. Instinctively she knew Uscias had been right, her magick would not return.

Determined not to wallow in sorrow at the loss, she sought out her husband, now dressed in trews and tunic, his foot propped on the chair as he concealed his dagger in his boot, his head bent over his task. The firelight cast him in an ethereal glow as if to remind her his safety was all that mattered. Her sacrifice had been worthwhile. Lachlan would be well protected, and Lamont and Ursula would be unable to use her to open the door to the underworld.

Inching her way along the edge of the bed, she wrapped her fingers around the thick oak post and heaved herself up. Her legs gave way and she uttered a startled cry, crumpling in a heap on the floor.

With a vicious curse, Lachlan strode to her side. Helping her to her feet, he sat her on the bed. He cupped her cheek and studied her face. "I wish we had time fer ye to regain some of your strength, but we doona."

He flicked his wrist and clothed her in trews and a tunic, reminding her once more of what she'd lost. But it was nothing in comparison to what her life would be like if she lost Lachlan. Before she had a chance to thank him, he'd replaced her outfit with robes, very heavy and thick robes. She appreciated their warmth but not their weight and was about to tell him so when he took her mouth in a breath-stealing kiss. She sensed in the tenderness with which he held her that he apologized for taking her magick.

He eased away from her, resting his forehead against hers. "When we get back to the Isles, ye're goin' to remain in yer bed fer a month."

"Alone?" She smiled. Her body still hummed from the pleasure he'd given her earlier. She'd been desperate for his touch, the reassurance she found in his strength. Her mind had been in turmoil and her fears had gotten the better of her. She'd been surprised that despite losing her magick, she'd gained more than comfort from his all-consuming passion. He'd managed to banish her fears. She trusted him more than she trusted anyone else.

"Nay, ye'll never be alone again, Evie."

"And neither will you." They had each other now.

He reached for his sword. She laid her hand over his to stop him. "I think it best if you leave your sword here. We can't risk Ursula or Lamont getting hold of it."

He raised a brow. "I'll no' let that happen." Rubbing his fingers along the hilt, he relented. "Aye, ye're right. Of late my blade's been displayin' its colors like it did fer Syrena. I doona mind, but 'tis no' helpful when ye're tryin' to catch someone unawares at night."

Angling his head, he traced her lips with the pad of his thumb. "I've seen ye smile when it does. Why is that?"

"The sword amplifies your emotions. Only recently has it shown any sign . . ." Her voice trailed off. She didn't want to remind him of the reason he'd shut down his feelings.

He seemed to consider her answer. "I see," he said. Wrapping one hand around the jeweled hilt, he drew her to him with the other. He lightly brushed his lips over hers, then devoured her mouth in a soul-searing kiss. She was breathless by the time he released her.

Holding his sword up for her inspection, he said, "What does this mean?"

She ran her finger over the blade's golden glow. "It means you're happy."

"Nay, if it truly reflects my emotions, 'twould no' be happiness but love. I love ye, Evie. If anythin' should happen, I need ye to ken just how verra much I do."

Her heart swelled along with her temper. "What do you mean whatever happens? You have more power in your little finger than all the Fae put together."

He laughed. "Ye're right, I do."

"And do you not think a better time to tell me you loved me might have been when you were making love to me?"

"Nay, if ye remember, my mouth had more important things to take care of."

His mouth had indeed been busy. She blushed at the erotic memories.

He grinned down at her, caressing her heated cheek. "Besides, if I told ye then, ye might have thought I was referrin' to yer body or the act itself. It's what's in here," he touched her head, "and in here," he touched her chest, "that makes me love ye as I do."

Blinking back tears, she framed his face with her hands. "I love you, Lachlan MacLeod, more than I can say, more than you'll ever know."

A sliver of moonlight slanted through the window and their eyes met and held. It was time. "Let's get this over with so ye can tell me all the reasons ye love me. I'm sure there are many, and we doona have the time fer it now."

Lachlan laughed at the irritated expression on his wife's face, surprised he could be amused when he considered what they were about to face. But the knowledge that Evangeline had imbued him with her magick, her love and trust, lightened his spirits and made him believe together they could conquer anything. Holding firm to the thought, he transported them to the hills over Loch Ness a ways from where they were to meet Lamont and Ursula.

"Put me down," she demanded in an urgent whisper.

He hesitated. It would be best if Ursula and Lamont didn't suspect her weakness, but he had a difficult time getting past the pallor of her face and the tremors he felt quaking her limbs.

"Christ, Evie," he yelped when she pinched his arm.

Releasing an exasperated sigh, she said, "I needed to gain your attention. Besides, it wasn't that hard."

"Words are always a good choice," he grumbled, setting her carefully on her feet.

"I tried, but you ignored me," she said, scanning the silver birch that circled them on the high braes. Steadying herself with a palm pressed to his chest, she looked up at him. "Remember, you're not to worry about me. As soon as you retrieve your son, take him to Armadale and then come back for me."

"'Tis my decision to make, no' yers. If I can get ye away at the same time as the bairn, I will. Nay," he said when she opened her mouth to protest, "the less time ye spend in their hands, the better." He had no intention of leaving her, but he wasn't about to argue with her now.

Guided by the light of the full moon, they slowly made their way up the steep incline. At the sound of her labored breathing, he knew he had no choice but to change the plan. He transported them to the meeting place.

She nudged him with a perturbed look upon her face. "We were supposed to sneak up on them," she said in a rusty whisper.

He kissed her furrowed brow. Noting the chill of her skin

and increased pallor, he knew he'd made the right decision. "Doona worry aboot it." The hair on the back of his neck stood on end and he heeded the warning, reaching for the sword he'd replaced Nuie with.

"Ah, ah, ah, no weapons," Lamont commanded.

At Evangeline's pained gasp, Lachlan jerked his attention behind her. Lamont, his face concealed by a black leather mask, held the tip of his blade to her back. Fury hazed Lachlan's vision and he fought to regain control before he did something he'd regret. His son would pay the price if he did. Even though he recognized that, it was difficult for him to release the sword. He forced himself to loosen his hold on the hilt, then flung it into the trees ringing the clearing.

"Move away from her," Lamont ordered.

"Take yer sword from her back and I'll think aboot it."

Ursula stepped from the shadows with his son. Lachlan's skin crawled at the sight of a woman most would think beautiful with her voluptuous curves and long, dark hair. But after being on the receiving end of her madness, all he saw was the maniacal gleam in her light-colored eyes and the cruel twist of her mouth.

"Do as he says, Lachlan," Evangeline said, holding his gaze as though she thought to reassure him she would be all right. She had to be.

Reluctantly, he did as she asked, squeezing her shoulder before he set her away from him. Her hands were balled into fists at her sides, her teeth clenched as she struggled to remain upright. The muscles knotted painfully in his belly as he fought the urge to grab Lamont's blade and ram it in the man's black heart.

Lamont motioned him away, then removed a chain from beneath his cape, flicking the iron links at Lachlan with a spiteful laugh. "Look familiar?" he jeered before wrapping the long length around Evangeline's neck.

Only the warning shake of Evangeline's head kept Lachlan

from lunging at the man. Slanting a look in his son's direction, she silently reminded him to hold his temper and keep to the plan. Aye, he would, but before the night was out, he'd wrap the cursed chains around the bastard's neck.

"I've done as ye asked. Give me my son."

"Ursula, did ye hear him? He wants his son."

Lachlan was so intent on Evie, he hadn't noticed Ursula had moved closer to the edge of the cliff. She shook the child's hands from her gown, ignoring his terrified whimpers. Lachlan's heart thudded in his chest and he took a step in their direction. She held his gaze, then, with a vindictive smile, grabbed hold of the bairn's arms.

"Nay," he shouted, racing toward her. But it was too late. She threw his son over the edge.

His pulse pounded in his head as he fought against his panic. He sprinted to the edge of the cliff. Turning back to Evie with the intention of helping her before he went after his son, he lifted his hand, hoping to get a clear shot at Lamont, but he was using Evie as a shield. Lachlan couldn't risk it. He wasn't even sure he would be able to conjure a bolt as Evie did.

With one last tortured look in her direction, he dove from the cliff into the dark murky waters far beneath him. The weight of his clothes dragged him deeper and deeper beneath the icy depths. He held his breath, his lungs threatening to explode as he fought his way toward the watery light above him. Breaking through the surface, he gasped for air and shook the water from his hair, shoving it from his face as he tried to get his bearings.

Moonbeams danced on the inky mirror of the loch lighting his way. Treading water, he twisted and turned, searching for his son. He scanned the shore at the point where Ursula had thrown the child off the cliff, steeling himself against the thought he'd see his son's broken body lying amongst the rocks. He thanked God when he found no sign of him, but that small sense of relief did little to assuage his panic. The loch had yet to release the child.

If not for Evangeline's magick, the frigid waters would've stolen his strength. At the thought of her, his heart lurched. He had no choice but to shut out the image of her pale face, her elegant neck wrapped in chains, and his need to go to her.

The waters around him churned, the waves rocking his body. A gust of hot air rushed past him and he slowly turned—coming face-to-face with the monster of the loch. With a strangled gasp, he kicked his feet, moving his arms in an attempt to get away, then abruptly ceased his frantic movements. He had to find his son and get to Evangeline; he couldn't allow the creature to chase him from the loch.

"I doona want to hurt ye, so be a good beastie and go away," he said, flicking water at the long-necked creature with its piercing yellow eyes. The monster held his gaze, then dove beneath the water. Its slick black-leathered hide disappeared in the murky depths.

Lachlan blew out a relieved breath and set out across the loch. He'd made it but a few feet when the creature reappeared several yards from him with a white bundle in its mouth. His limbs weakened with relief. It was his son. The gentle way in which the monster handled the child alleviated some of Lachlan's fears. Not wishing to startle the creature, he cut through the water with slow, careful strokes. Craning its reptilian neck, the monster deposited Lachlan's son on a rocky outcropping. Then, with a nod of its ancient head, its body undulated beneath a wave.

Shaking off his disbelief at what had transpired, Lachlan swam to the water's edge. Grabbing hold of the granite ledge, he dragged himself over the slime-coated rocks to make his way to his son. The child whimpered, knuckling his eyes as he sat shivering in his white nightshift.

Tentatively, Lachlan reached out to touch the bairn's damp curls. "Ye're safe now, laddie. No one will hurt ye ever again."

His chest was so tight the words came out in a harsh rasp. The backs of his eyes burned and he rubbed them, straining for control. He inhaled deeply, then crouched by the little boy, searching for some sign of injury. Relieved the child appeared to be unharmed, he quickly dressed him in warm nightclothes and conjured a length of plaid. Once Lachlan had garbed himself in dry clothing, he wrapped his son in the thick wool and lifted him into his arms. The child released a shuddered breath then burrowed into the hollow of Lachlan's neck.

A dull ache filled his chest and he tightened his hold on the bairn. He had a son and he was safe. But Evangeline wasn't. No matter what she'd demanded of him, Lachlan wouldn't leave her a second longer in their hands than he had to. He transported to the clearing where he'd last seen her.

Chapter 30

The splash of Lachlan hitting the water echoed in Evangeline's head. She calmed the anxious churning in her belly with the knowledge he had her magick. Straining to hear some sign he'd rescued his son, she was unaware Ursula approached until she felt the woman's malevolent gaze upon her.

"How does it feel to matter so little to your husband that he'd sacrifice you for his child? His child with another woman."

After witnessing what Ursula had done to the terrified little boy, Evangeline would have sacrificed herself without Lachlan having to ask.

"Answer me!" she screeched.

Evangeline's anger at what the woman had done to Lachlan and his son was stealing what little strength she had left. She refused to let the spiteful witch goad her and kept her mouth firmly shut.

Ursula lunged, jerking the chain from Lamont's hand. She maliciously twisted the cold metal, cutting into Evangeline's abraded flesh, stealing her breath. Gasping for air, Evangeline fell to her knees, frantically curling her fingers around the chain to loosen its strangling hold.

Lamont cursed then yanked the chain from Ursula. He

slackened the tension on Evangeline's throat. She sagged against a boulder. "She'll be no good to us if she's dead," he said. Fisting his hand in Evangeline's robes, he forced her to rise.

"Move," he ordered once she'd managed to stagger to her feet.

"She's Fae. I can't kill her. Although if you ask me, she looks half-dead. I find it difficult to believe she's as powerful as he said she was." With a contemptuous snort, Ursula pushed her from behind.

Evangeline wondered who Ursula referred to, but the effort to remain upright took all of her concentration.

"Ye ken well enough the iron steals their power." Lamont shoved Evangeline down a steep path.

"Then remove it or she'll be of no use to us," Ursula demanded from behind them.

"Nay, we canna risk it."

Evangeline tripped over a rock and once more fell to her knees. With no give from the taut links, her head whipped back and she swallowed an agonized cry. Ursula was not far from the truth when she said she looked half-dead: it was how she began to feel. She tried not to dwell on what delayed Lachlan, to let her fears take hold of her. Instead, she searched for a way to escape from Ursula and Lamont before they reached the door.

Digging furtively through the dew-dampened grass, she found a fist-sized rock with a sharp edge and pried it loose. Lamont bent over to haul her to her feet. She slammed the rock into the side of his head. He stumbled. She wrenched the chain from his hand. Gathering what little strength she had left, she whipped the length of iron at his legs. He howled, but before she could topple him to the ground, Ursula hurled herself at her with an enraged cry. Evangeline's breath left her on a whoosh, but she managed to throw herself in Lamont's direction. She caught him off balance and he fell, rolling down the hill. Ursula rammed her forearm into the back of Evangeline's head, planting her face in the bracken.

"You'll pay for that," Ursula spat out, hauling Evangeline up by her hair. Ursula's hot, sickly-sweet breath caused Evangeline's stomach to lurch. Through the haze of her pain, she recognized the scent—laudanum.

Lamont struggled to remain upright, cursing the damp earth as he slid back down the path. He motioned to Ursula. "Bring the bitch to me."

Ursula snorted, shoving Evangeline toward him. "Fool, you've made him angry now."

Before Evangeline could react, Lamont backhanded her with his gloved hand. Her teeth slammed together and her mouth filled with the metallic taste of blood. She drew back and spat it at his masked face. He raised his hand, his eyes glittering with rage. A robed form slipped from the shadows. Long white fingers encircled Lamont's wrist, and he uttered a pained cry.

Evangeline stared in stunned disbelief at her rescuer. Morfessa.

Relief further weakened her legs and she weaved unsteadily on her feet. Morfessa hated her, but she knew he'd do everything in his power to stop Ursula and Lamont from releasing the dark lords.

"You're wasting time. Get her to the door."

Evangeline gasped. No. She must have misunderstood him.

Lamont threw off Morfessa's hand and grabbed Evangeline by the arm, dragging her the rest of the way down the path. She jerked her gaze to where Morfessa stood, his face cloaked in shadows. "No." She struggled against Lamont's hold. "You don't understand. They're trying to open the door. Stop them!" she cried.

Lamont dragged her to a ledge protruding from the sheer rock face, the inky black waters of the loch lapping at the rocks far below them. She tried to pry his fingers from her arm. He kicked her legs out from under her, bringing her to her knees. A wave of nausea washed over her and she covered her mouth.

Ursula took a cautious step onto the precipice. "I don't like . . . perhaps I can stand over there," she said, pointing a trembling finger back to the path. A gust of wind buffeted the ledge and Ursula released a panicked cry, clinging to the vines that covered the granite walls.

"Stay where ye are," Lamont growled at Ursula. Unwinding the chain from Evangeline's neck, he pressed a dagger to her throat. "Doona try anythin'," he warned, flinging the length of iron over the ledge. Several strangled breaths later she heard the accompanying splash.

Lamont tore the vines from the wall, and then it was there, Evangeline's worst nightmare—the door to the underworld. She arched her back in horror. Her knees scraped across the loose pieces of sharp shale as she tried to escape. She could feel the blood trickling from the wounds. She had to get away from them.

As though Morfessa read her thoughts, knew she meant to hurl herself into the watery depths beneath them, he flashed to stand behind her. Dragging her to her feet, he wrapped his fingers in a bone-crushing grip around her wrist. "Now they will have no choice but to believe in your evil," he said as he forced her hand to the door. She fought him, but in her weakened state her effort proved futile. He slammed her palm onto the raised pentagram etched in the middle of the stone door.

"Don't do this. Don't let the Fae suffer because of your hatred for me," she begged, twisting her hand, trying to break free of his hold.

"They won't, but you will," he promised next to her ear. "Keep her hand there," he ordered Lamont before he disappeared in an explosion of light.

Lamont's knuckles dug into her back. "Where the hell did he go?"

"It doesn't matter, we no longer need him."

In Evangeline's mind, the pieces clicked into place. He had gone to retrieve the blue stone. Each of the wizards held a quarter of the magickal rock. In the wrong hands, in the hands of evil, the stone was the key to the underworld; in the hands of the pure of heart, it was the lock. Twenty-six years ago her mother had stolen Morfessa's. For his plan to succeed, he would have to steal Uscias's. She knew now what he meant to do. He would win his way back into Rohan's good graces by saving the day, using Evangeline as a means to an end.

She squeezed her eyes closed. She wouldn't cry. She'd always known he'd hated her, but never had she thought he'd go this far to seek his revenge. Her stomach roiled. She clamped her mouth shut to keep from expelling the bitter revulsion that rose up inside her.

The door heated beneath her. Lamont no longer held her in place, but she couldn't move. It felt as though the fabric of her robes were fusing to the stone. She tried to pull away, her gaze landing on Lamont and Ursula, who held worn pieces of yellowed parchment between them. The last of her hopes disappeared. She'd clung to the belief they wouldn't remember the words Jarius used to call upon the dark lords, but they didn't need to remember them. Somehow they'd managed to rip the pages from the *Grimoire of Honorius*—the book of dark magick—before Syrena had destroyed it.

Their voices joined together, the cursed ancient words rising in a powerful hum. The door vibrated beneath her and she fought the urge to seek out what little was left of her magick. Afraid of what she would find, what it would do. A hairline crack formed at the upper edge of the rock. A sulfuric smell leeched from the stone. No matter how miniscule the magick inside her was, the stone was using it. She had to fight against it in the only way she knew how.

Centering herself, she calmed her breathing, trying to ignore the noxious fumes and the heated vibration beneath her fingers. Deep inside her, she searched for the subtle glow of her magick, the white light. There was nothing. The voice she'd heard on the day she'd come through the realms seeped through her conscience, and she jerked in horror. Tempted to give up, she heard Lachlan's voice in her head, telling her she was not evil, assuring her of her goodness. Holding on to his love, fighting past her fears, she was able to hear it for what it was. It was not the voice of evil, it was her voice, her own fear talking.

The knowledge filled her with the strength to fight. Inch by excruciating inch, she peeled her body from the door, feeling as though her flesh tore away as she did. She couldn't contain her anguished cries.

"Come to me, Evie."

Afraid she was delirious from the pain, she slowly opened her eyes. She choked back a relieved sob when she saw Lachlan standing on the path, big and powerful and holding out his hand to her. Free from the door's hold, she took a shaky step toward him.

"No!" Ursula cried and threw herself at him.

A loud crack rent the air. The rock shuddered, then a deep fissure appeared at the top of the door, running down its length to cross the center of the ledge inches from where she stood. The thin layers at the edge crumbled, giving way, taking Lamont with it. Evangeline jumped back, clinging to the vines to keep from falling.

"Help me," Lamont cried, hanging from the rock by the tips of his fingers. Lachlan shoved Ursula away from him and took a step toward Evangeline.

"Don't. Don't come any closer," she warned. "It will use your magick."

Behind the door she could hear them. Deep guttural voices raised in excitement at the thought they were about to escape their prison. Tendrils of black smoke seeped from the cracks, winding their way around Ursula, who crawled toward Lamont. Choking on the fumes, Ursula batted at the inky haze. Evangeline covered her mouth and nose, motioning for Lachlan to do the same. The stench of evil was suffocating as the garbled voices grew louder.

"Lachlan, get Uscias. We need the blue stone."

"Nay, I willna leave ye." His attention shifted from her to something that moved to the right of him. "Nay, laddie, stay there."

"Lachlan," Evangeline groaned. "Take him to Armadale."

"Help us," Ursula cried. Through the thick mist, Lamont and Ursula were no longer visible.

Lachlan blew out a disgusted breath and took a step in the direction of Ursula's cries. Before he'd ventured more than two steps, their high-pitched shrieks cut through the haze. A loud splash followed by another. There was a shout, then a terror-filled scream. "Colin!"

"Ursula! Oh, God, what are ye? No. . . no, get away from me." Someone thrashed wildly in the waters below them. Evangeline tried to block out the sound of Lamont's hysterical crying, and then the night grew eerily quiet.

In a clap of light, Uscias appeared behind Lachlan—followed in quick succession by Fallyn, Shayla, Rohan, Gabriel, and Broderick. The bright flashes illuminated the ledge and Evangeline gasped in horror. "Lachlan!" His son had crawled halfway across the granite shelf, the black smoke writhing around his tiny frame.

Lachlan cursed. Tension hardening his chiseled features, he stepped onto the ledge. The rock groaned beneath his weight.

"No, don't move. Lachlan, hold out your arms and concentrate on him. Picture him coming to you," she said. He did as she advised, and his son appeared safely in his arms. She leaned against the wall, her shoulders sagging with relief.

"Evangeline, catch," Fallyn said and threw her the blue stone.

The rock pulsated and glowed in Evangeline's hand. Her long-held fears rose up to taunt her and she wanted to throw it back. Any of the others would be a better choice. She lifted her gaze and met Lachlan's; her breath hitched at the look of love in his eyes. "Ye can do it, Evie." His confident smile calmed the panicked gallop of her heart.

She nodded, then inched along the ledge, the shale crumbling beneath her curled toes. Clinging to the vine, she swung to face the door. Holding her breath, she pressed the stone in the center of the pentagram. Pain-filled cries split the air, then receded, and the cracks resealed. The crumbling ledge rebuilt itself. Slowly she drew her hand from the door, folding her trembling fingers over the stone. The thick verdant vines crawled across the rock to once more conceal the door.

As the tension flowed from her, a loud cheer broke out from behind Lachlan and she looked up to see Uscias, the three kings, Fallyn, and Shayla beaming at her. She shook her head but couldn't keep the smile from her face. Lachlan reached for her and drew her into his arms. He held her as if he never meant to let her go, and she was filled with an overwhelming sense of well-being.

"'Tis over now," he said and kissed her.

A small hand worked its way between their lips, forcing them apart. With an arm wrapped possessively around his father's neck, the child attempted to push her away. She took a step back and he snuggled into Lachlan's embrace.

"Or just beginning," she muttered, scowling at her husband when he laughed.

Chapter 31

Despite the aggrieved look his wife shot at him, Lachlan couldn't keep the smile from his face. Evangeline and his son were safe and in his arms. Lamont and Ursula would never threaten them, or anyone else, again. But more importantly, Evangeline had proof she was not evil. Soon the Fae would see her as he did—a woman of great strength and courage. He couldn't love anyone more than he loved her.

Along with Uscias, Rohan, and their friends, they transported to Armadale. At the door to the keep, Evangeline eased from his arms. "All of you be quiet. We don't want to wake up the chil—anyone."

His wife had obviously not noticed that Armadale was ablaze with lights. Humoring her, Lachlan crept into the house. Rory and Aidan, their dark hair standing on end, wearing only their plaids, scowled at him, as did Aileanna and Syrena, who stood beside their husbands in their night robes.

"Where have you . . ." Syrena began, then looked from Lachlan's son to his wife. She gasped. "Evangeline, what happened to you?"

"Lachlan, take her to her room, I'll—"

"No, I'm fine," Evangeline said to Aileanna while she batted Syrena's probing fingers away.

He drew back to look at her. "Christ, Evie, why did ye no' say somethin'?" With the moon as their only source of light, the true extent of her injuries had been concealed from him— bruises on her face, weeping sores on her abraded neck.

She touched her throat and winced. "It will heal."

"Aye, with plenty of rest 'twill. Come, ye're goin' to bed." His tone was harsh as he struggled to contain his rage at what Lamont had done to her. If the monster of the loch hadn't made a meal of him—as Lachlan assumed it had from their screams—Lachlan would've squeezed the breath out of him with his bare hands.

She brought her palm to his cheek, calming his fury with a soft smile. "No, I need to know what happened with Morfessa."

Before he could question her about her father, Alasdair came down the stairs, followed by Aileanna's aunt Fiona. "What's goin' on here?" the older man asked, scrubbing his face.

Syrena angled her head to look at the crowd at Lachlan's back. "Father? . . . Uscias, Fallyn, what in the name of Fae has happened?"

His brother and Rory exchanged a commiserating glance. "It looks like we're no' goin' back to our beds anytime soon. Who wants ale?" Rory asked, leading everyone to the grand hall.

Knowing Evangeline had no intention of going to their chambers, upon entering the hall Lachlan conjured a bed beside the hearth and built up the fire. They all turned to look at him. He shrugged. "She needs her rest." Closing his eyes, he flicked his fingers to dress her in nightwear.

At the shocked gasps that exploded around him, he opened his eyes.

"Lachlan," Evangeline muttered, standing in a sheer chemise, her face flushed.

"Sorry," he said, and instead of envisioning her in nightwear he'd like to see her in, he dressed her in robes similar to Syrena's and Aileanna's.

The women crowded onto the bed with Evangeline, who succumbed ungraciously to Aileanna's ministrations. Despite the women's attempts to cajole Lachlan's son to join them, he steadfastly clung to Lachlan.

"Except for the blue eyes, he looks like ye did as a bairn," Aidan said. Pulling up a chair beside Lachlan, he stroked the baby's hand. His son wrapped his fingers around Aidan's. Holding Lachlan's gaze, Aidan said, "Ye'll make a grand father."

"Thank ye. I had a good teacher. Ye've been like a father to me. I doona think I realized that until now." It was the truth. His brother had always been there for him, protecting him from Alexander, stepping into the role of a parent when he'd been little more than a boy himself.

"I'm no' that old," Aidan said gruffly.

"At least this nephew seems to like ye," Rory observed wryly, tousling the bairn's baby-fine curls.

"Now that Evangeline's injuries have been seen to, it's time for someone to tell us what took place this night," Syrena said.

At the sight of the white linens wrapped around Evangeline's neck, Lachlan waited for his anger to subside before relaying his version of the events. In a strained voice, Evangeline took up where he left off and told what had happened with Lamont and Ursula. His gaze shot to hers when he learned the part Morfessa had played. He handed his sleeping son to his brother and went to her side. "Morfessa was the reason Lamont and Ursula kent aboot ye and the door?"

He wrapped an arm around her. Leaning against him, she nodded.

"He wasna there when I arrived. Where—"

"He came back to the Isles for the blue stone. Since Andora had stolen his all those years ago, he needed mine," Uscias interrupted, sheepishly rubbing the back of his head. "I'm afraid he took me by surprise."

Absently gliding his palm up and down Evangeline's thigh, Lachlan asked, "Do ye ken where he is now?"

Uscias sighed. "Aurora alerted Riana, Shayla, and Fallyn to what happened. Shayla and Fallyn went to both Broderick and Gabriel to retrieve the blue stones from their wizards. Riana went after Morfessa and has yet to return. Until she does, we have no idea as to his whereabouts." Uscias came to his feet. "Now that you're both safe and Evangeline has taken care of the dark lords, I think it's best if I return to the Enchanted Isles."

"Thank ye, Uscias. Evangeline and I will be home on the morrow."

His mentor nudged him aside to get to Evangeline. He kissed her cheek. "You did well, my dear. The Fae owe you a debt and I'll be certain they are made aware of it."

Her cheeks flushed. "It's not necessary. I—"

"Aye, 'tis," Lachlan said firmly.

Rohan rose from his chair by the fire. "Lachlan and Uscias are right, Evangeline. You have withstood the Faes' contempt for far too long. I'm afraid I have much to answer for where Morfessa is concerned. I should have had some inkling to the lengths he would go to harm you. Please accept my apologies."

Evangeline looked heartily embarrassed by all the attention. "You have nothing to apologize for, Your Highness. Without your friendship and support . . ." She trailed off, averting her gaze.

Rohan leaned over and kissed the top of her head. "I have always thought of you as a daughter, Evangeline. I hope you will allow me to continue to do so." She nodded, biting her lip. Seeing the shimmer of moisture in her eyes, Lachlan gave her knee a reassuring squeeze.

"Take good care of her, nephew," his uncle said gruffly.

"I will."

"Syrena." Rohan leaned across Evangeline to kiss his daughter's cheek. "You're long overdue for a visit to the Fae realm. My subjects are anxious to meet my grandchildren. We'll discuss it further when I come to my granddaughters' christening."

Aidan cursed under his breath and Rory snorted into his ale.

Rohan arched a brow. "What was that, MacLeod?"

"Nothin'," Aidan muttered.

"I should be off as well," Gabriel said after Uscias and Rohan had departed. "Evangeline, you have the gratitude of me and my subjects. Take care of yourself."

Lachlan followed his friend from the hall. "How goes it with yer wife?"

Gabriel grinned knowingly. "Feeling guilty, are you?"

"Mayhap a wee bit," Lachlan admitted with a grimace.

"Don't. I had a love match once. I didn't expect nor want another."

"Ye doona think it's possible, given time, ye—"

"No." He clapped Lachlan on the shoulder. "But I'm happy you have found it with Evangeline. And rest assured, I'll be keeping an eye out for Morfessa."

"Ye doona think Riana will find him?"

"I have my doubts. I didn't want to mention it in front of Uscias; he feels bad enough. But we need to retrieve the stone before it falls into the wrong hands."

"Do ye think he'd go to Dimtri?"

"Since Morgana and Erwn are there, I wouldn't be surprised if that's where he ends up. And Dimtri is the last person we want to have access to the stone. I have eyes and ears in his court, so we'll find out soon enough. Hopefully before it's too late."

Shayla, Fallyn, and Broderick joined them. "We'll be taking our leave now," Broderick said, nudging Fallyn. "Are you not going to tell him?"

She rolled her eyes. "Now is not the time."

"Time fer what?"

Broderick grinned and wrapped an arm around Fallyn's shoulders. "Fallyn has agreed to become my betrothed."

"Ye're leavin' the Isles?" Lachlan's voice cracked.

Fallyn snorted. "Don't get too excited. I won't be leaving anytime soon."

"Where are you going?" Evangeline asked, coming to stand beside him.

"What are ye doin' up?" He looked down at her. The dusky shadows beneath her eyes and her colorless lips caused his belly to clench. He knew what he had to do, and the sooner he did so, the better.

"I'm going to bed. Syrena and Aileanna fell asleep and they're snoring."

He frowned. "Where's the bairn?"

She looked up at him with a grimace. "He's . . . asleep. I suppose I should have brought him with me."

Lachlan grinned, tucking her beneath his arm. "Nay. I'll take care of him."

She patted his chest and leaned against him. "Good. Now what was that you were saying, Fallyn?"

"Broderick and I have agreed to a trial betrothal."

Angling his head to look at Fallyn, Broderick frowned. "I don't recall using the word *trial*."

Shayla rolled her eyes and Gabriel waggled his brows. Tiptoeing backward, they both raised a hand in silent farewell and quickly made their escape.

"Aye, ye should just get it over with and marry now," Lachlan advised.

Evangeline leaned back and arched a brow.

He shrugged. "It worked fer us, didna it?"

She smiled up at him. "Yes, it did."

"Is someone gettin' married?" Alasdair asked, coming up behind them.

"Alasdair, no meddlin'," Fiona said. Aileanna's aunt came to stand beside Lachlan. She held his sleeping son in her arms. "I thought I'd put the wee one in with Alex and Jamie. There's an extra cot in the lads' room. He'll no' be able to climb out, so ye doona have to worry aboot him."

Lachlan suppressed a smile at his wife's relieved expression. Aye, he thought, it might take some time for Evangeline to adjust to having the bairn around. "Thank ye, Fiona." He stroked his son's cheek with the backs of his knuckles before she took him upstairs.

"Go to bed, Evangeline. You're dead on your feet. I'll see you when you come home," Fallyn said, giving her a hug.

"Mayhap ye should go home with Broderick. Spend some . . ."

Both women scowled at Lachlan. "All right, good night, then," he conceded.

With his wife in his arms, Lachlan nudged the door to their chambers open. He frowned at the empty space where their bed had been.

"Ah, Lachlan, where's our bed?"

"I doona ken." He flicked his fingers.

"No!" She reached for his hand, then winced at the series of loud thuds coming from down below.

"Lachlan!" Aidan bellowed.

Lachlan grimaced. "I stole the bed out from under them, didna I?"

She nodded, her violet eyes brimming with amusement. She compressed her lips and her shoulders shook. Then unable to contain her mirth any longer, she began to laugh.

Lachlan grinned at the sight of his wife helpless with laughter. "I'm glad ye think 'tis so amusin'." He laid her on the bed.

"I shall have to give you some lessons before you hurt someone." She wiped her eyes.

He nudged her over and crawled in beside her, removing his clothing with a flick of his wrist.

"Now *that*, you do very well." She smiled. Turning into him, she trailed the tips of her fingers over his chest.

"Aye, I do." He waved his hand and removed her shift, folding her into his arms.

She released a contented sigh and snuggled into his embrace.

Leaning back, he cupped her chin. "Are ye truly all right, Evie? They didna hurt ye too badly?"

"Don't worry about me. I'll heal."

He gently touched her swollen cheek. "But no' as quickly without yer magick."

She pressed her fingers to his lips. "I'm tired and sore, nothing more."

He knew she was in pain. He could see it in the way she held herself. Hear it in the husky rasp of her voice. As when she'd joined him in the entryway, he knew what he had to do. The only reason she suffered was because of her willingness to sacrifice her magick to save his son. A magick that now pulsated in his veins with an addictive power. Less than a week ago, he'd reveled in that strength, the knowledge no one could have him at his mercy nor taunt him for his lack of magick. It didn't matter anymore. All that mattered to him was his wife's well-being.

His sword, his own strength and abilities had served him well in the past and would do so again. It didn't make a difference to Evangeline that he was a half-blood, and hers was the only opinion he cared about. He decided he had the best of both worlds. His love of the highlands flowed through his veins while his beautiful and magickal wife held his heart.

Certain she would try to stop him if she saw what he did, he held her tight to his chest and conjured a dagger behind her back. The blade glinted in the firelight and he gritted his teeth, fighting off the memories of Lamont coming at him with a burning dagger. Holding the tip of the blade to his wrist, he tightened his grip on the handle to keep his hand from shaking. Sweat beaded on his forehead. He wiped it away, reminding himself why he did what he did. He closed his eyes and drew the cold steel across his flesh.

He shut out the images of Ursula's torture and rid himself of the dagger. Carefully, he rolled Evangeline to her back.

"What are . . ." Catching sight of his wrist, her eyes widened. "No, I won't, I—"

"Shh. Take your blood, Evie," he said, holding his arm above her pale lips.

She shook her head, her lips compressed.

"Please, let me do this. I need to do this fer ye." And he needed to do it for himself. To prove he'd put the past and Glastonbury behind him.

She searched his face, then tentatively touched the tip of her tongue to the wound. "Take it." At the gentle suction of her mouth on his wrist, his cock swelled. "More." He rocked against her, allowing his desire for her to take hold.

His worries had been for naught. His fear the action would drag him down into the dark tortured depths where he'd lived for so long, were wiped away. Their love for one another was too powerful for the nightmares to intrude upon.

She lifted his arm and drew a circle in the air, bandaging his wrist.

He frowned. "Are ye sure ye have taken enough?"

"Yes. Thank you," she murmured, rubbing her cheek in his palm.

"Nay, I doona think ye did." He levered himself up on his elbow and flicked his finger at the hearth. When the flame shot to life, he looked down at her, awaiting her explanation.

"I thought we could share." When he went to object, she framed his face with her hands. "Your love has brought me more happiness than my magick ever did. I know what it cost you to do what you just did, and I love you even more for doing so. I have enough power, Lachlan." Her lips twitched. "Besides, this way we truly are equal partners."

His heart overflowing with love for her, he smiled at the

teasing light in her eyes. "I would do anythin' fer ye. I adore ye, Evie MacLeod."

"So, does that mean you agree to sharing the responsibilities of running the Isles and—"

"Oh, aye, and sharin' in the care of the bairn." He laughed at her grimace. "I'm teasin' ye. Doona worry, we'll work it out, Evie. But now, instead of talkin', I thought I'd show ye how much I love ye."

"Well," she nudged him onto his back, "since we're equal partners, perhaps I should show you first."

Chapter 32

Syrena nudged Evangeline, who looked up from her conversation with Aileanna. "What . . ." Her voice trailed off. Lachlan walked into the grand hall carrying a cake ablaze with candles. Aileanna had not only brought her healing skills with her when she'd come from the future, but her customs as well. So Evangeline was well acquainted with this particular celebration. Her eyes filled, knowing what her husband did for her. He walked toward the dais where she sat, a small crowd of their family and friends following behind him, singing: "Happy birthday to ye. Happy birthday, dear Evie, happy birthday to ye."

"Oh." She waved a hand in front of her heated cheeks. Her throat constricted at the tender smile creasing her husband's handsome face. Trying to contain her tears, she bit her trembling lip and blinked her eyes. But to no avail—the tears rolled unchecked down her cheeks.

Lachlan came to her side and placed the white iced cake in front of her, directing the others as to where the array of brightly wrapped packages should go.

"'Twas no' meant to make ye sad, Evie," he said. Framing her face with his hands, he wiped away her tears with his thumbs.

"I'm not sad . . . I'm . . . I'm happy," she choked out on a sob.

His gaze softened. He crouched beside her, taking her hand in his. "I hope ye doona mind sharin' my day of birth. 'Tis the day we met, and I thought it only fittin' since my life held little meanin' or happiness before ye."

"Thanks," Aidan commented dryly, grunting when Syrena elbowed him.

Evangeline's heart overflowed with love for Lachlan, but she was embarrassed by all the attention and didn't know what to say. She blurted out, "I don't have a present for you."

His lips twitched then he curved his big hand around her neck, bringing her ear to his mouth. In erotic detail, he told her exactly what he wished her to gift him with. What he wanted her to do to him and what he in turn would do to her later that night. Under his heated gaze, she fanned herself, squirming in the chair.

"Uncle Lachlan, the candles," Alex said.

"Aye, the candles." Lachlan didn't rise from his crouched position and she had a fairly good idea why. Considering the aroused state his words had left her in, she thought it served him right. "Evie, ye need to make a wish, then blow out the candles," he instructed her.

Lifting her eyes from the flickering flames, she turned to him and shook her head. "I don't need to make a wish. I have everything I'll ever need or want. I have you," letting her gaze light on those gathered around the table, she added, "and all of you."

Jamie drowned out the womens' sniffles with a loud "good." With Alex's help, he set about blowing out the candles. Ava and Olivia, who'd crawled onto their mother's laps, banged on the table demanding their turn.

Out of the corner of her eye, Evangeline saw Lachlan's son Kamden standing off from the others. She felt a pang of sympathy for the child and waved him over. Evangeline wasn't surprised when he shook his head. The little boy had yet to warm up to her. She thought perhaps he was jealous she stole the attention of the father he adored. But Lachlan seemed to think it had more to do with her coloring being similar to Ursula's.

After the cake had been eaten and she'd opened her presents, one for every birthday that had gone uncelebrated, she sat back to enjoy the relative quiet of the hall. The children had gone to play out of doors, supervised by their doting grandfathers and Fiona. Half listening to Aileanna and Syrena's conversations, she noted the hand signals that Gabriel and Lachlan sent to each other. She snorted at their futile attempt to keep their silent exchange from the women's notice. Lachlan leaned over and kissed her cheek. "I'm goin' to join the others fer an ale by the hearth," he said as the men rose as one, their chairs scraping loudly across the stone floor.

Evangeline fisted her hand in his tunic to hold him in place. "What do you mean to discuss that you don't wish us to know?"

"Yes, Broderick, do tell," Fallyn said, then added, "And before you answer, you may wish to consider the word *trial*."

"And you," Evangeline narrowed her gaze on her husband, "may wish to consider the words *equal partnership*."

When Syrena and Aileanna opened their mouths to speak, Lachlan released a loud, put-upon sigh. "'Tis but a rumor that has yet to be substantiated."

Evangeline crossed her arms over her chest. "Tell us."

"Gabriel received word that Dimtri sent out search parties after Morfessa in hopes of retrieving the blue stone."

"His attempts will prove as futile as ours," Evangeline said with a measure of frustration. Not only was it imperative that they be the ones to retrieve the stone, Evangeline wanted to find Morfessa, to hear him admit he'd been wrong about her. The Fae had gone a long way in making amends for their past treatment of her, but she needed a simple acknowledgment, an apology from Morfessa for what he'd perpetrated against her, to let go of the past completely.

"My men seem to think Dimtri has acquired knowledge we do not have," Gabriel said.

"Where do they believe him to be?" Evangeline asked.

Gabriel held her gaze. "The future."

"The future? But how . . . why?" She looked to Uscias for the answer.

"As to how, the blue stone is reputed to have powers beyond our comprehension. It is not difficult to conceive of the standing stones being used as a portal to another dimension. It has happened before." From his tight-lipped expression, it appeared Uscias had said more than he intended to. Evangeline was going to question him further, but he continued, "Aileanna is just one example of Fae magick's ability to cross time. I only speculate as to why. For all that the act he committed against you was evil, Evangeline, his motivation, though twisted, was not. I believe he seeks a way to make amends."

Lachlan stood behind her, the comforting weight of his big hands resting on her shoulders. "How does taking the stone to the future accomplish that?" she asked, finding it difficult to hear Uscias's defense of Morfessa.

Uscias sighed. "I suppose it's something you should've been told. We now believe your mother found a way to the future. If I'm not mistaken, it is why Morfessa would go there."

Lachlan, kneading the tension from her shoulders, said, "So Morfessa believes if he returns both stones, he will regain my uncle's esteem?"

"As I said, I can only speculate as to his reasons. But yes, I imagine that is what he hopes."

"Is . . ." Evangeline took a deep breath before continuing, "is my mother alive?"

"No," Aurora said.

Evangeline looked up, startled to see Aurora standing beside Lachlan. She thought she'd gone out to play with the other children. "How can you know that for certain?"

Aurora's gaze flicked to Uscias, and he gave an almost imperceptible shake of his head. "I can only tell you what I know to be true."

Evangeline sought her husband's gaze. "Do you have a plan?"

"I wouldna call it a plan as such, there's too much we doona ken. But one thing is certain, someone must go to the future and find him before Dimtri does."

Everyone spoke at once, arguing who should lead the quest. Lachlan's fingers tightened on Evangeline's shoulders when she claimed the right as her own. "Nay, 'twill no' be ye."

"It must be Iain who goes." Stunned into silence by Aurora's pronouncement, everyone gaped at the little seer.

"Ye canna mean my brother," Rory said.

Aurora nodded.

Evangeline understood Rory's disbelief. Iain was the last person she'd choose for the mission. Perhaps, before the loss of his wife and his injuries, she would have considered him. But he was no longer the man he'd once been. The man who'd once thirsted for adventure could not even be cajoled to leave Dunvegan. Bitter and angry, he kept his distance from them all. Evangeline had gone before the Seelie Council to ask that Aurora be allowed to heal him—a talent only the little seer held. Permission had been granted but Iain had refused the offer. Rory thought his brother refused in a misguided attempt to punish himself for his wife's death.

A part of Evangeline—the part of her that felt guilty for Iain's suffering—wished he would take up the challenge, afraid if he went on as he did, the Iain she remembered would no longer exist.

Fallyn and her sisters proceeded to tell the three kings how they thought the mission should proceed. Lachlan bit back a frustrated oath and held up his hand. "The Seelie Council convenes on the morrow. We'll—"

"I shall be attending," Evangeline said.

"As will I," Fallyn added with a look that dared Broderick to deny her.

"That ale is soundin' mighty good aboot now," Rory said, escaping from the dais with Aidan.

Before Lachlan could follow them, Evangeline took hold of his hand. "We will be discussing this when we get home."

"Aye, we will." He leaned in and added on a heated whisper, "But no' until ye've given me my day of birth gift." Tipping her chin, he kissed any thought of protest from her head.

With the women's talk centered on the latest development, Evangeline hadn't noticed Aurora kneeling beside her chair until she felt the light pressure of the child's hand on her belly. The little girl bent her head as though she listened to something inside Evangeline. At the child's giggle, Evangeline asked, "What's so funny?"

"Your baby."

"My what?" The question exploded from her lips, drawing the attention of the men on the other side of the hall.

Aurora tilted her head, a glimmer of amusement in her blue eyes. "Your baby. He's playing inside you."

"I'm having a . . . *baby*?" she croaked.

Syrena, Aileanna, Fallyn, and Fallyn's sisters loudly expressed their delight. Evangeline shushed them, having a difficult time believing the news. "Aurora, are you . . ." Her voice trailed off when the little girl lifted her swirling eyes. *No*, Evangeline groaned inwardly.

"The child within you is destined for greatness. Both Mortal and Fae will look to him to lead on the day of reckoning. But beware, even now evil seeks to destroy him. His enemy is close at hand. Guard him well."

Evangeline stifled a shocked gasp behind her hand. Syrena rushed to her side. Taking the chair next to her, she reached for Evangeline's hand and squeezed. "Don't worry. No one will harm your child. We won't let them."

"Syrena's right, Evangeline, your son will have all of us looking out for him. No one who seeks to harm him will get near him," Fallyn promised.

As the other women added their support, Aurora lifted her gaze and Evangeline started. There was a maturity in the little girl's bright blue eyes she hadn't noticed before. Although, if she thought about it, over the last months there'd been other changes. Aurora had become more serious about her studies, not given to bouts of mischievousness or playing with the other children.

"I have been sent to protect your son. His destiny is intertwined with mine. I shall guard him with my life." Coming from any other child, the promise would be nothing more than a sweet gesture, but Evangeline knew instinctively that one day Aurora would prove to be her son's closest ally.

"Thank you, all of you. I just wish I knew from whom we protected him," Evangeline said.

"Aurora, dear, why don't you go outside to play?" Syrena suggested.

Once the child had left the dais, Syrena said, "No one knows as well as we do, Evangeline, that Aurora's prophecies can be misinterpreted."

"I would say the gist of that one was pretty clear," Evangeline said dryly.

"I'm just saying now is not the time to dwell on it. Enjoy your good news. You are happy about the baby, aren't you?"

Evangeline couldn't help but notice that Fallyn and Aileanna were having a difficult time containing their laughter. She supposed she couldn't blame them. After all, she had never done a very good job of hiding her intolerance of whiny children, especially Ava and Olivia. But she had no need to worry where her child was concerned. He would be perfect in comparison to the little hoydens.

Syrena nudged her. "Here comes the father-to-be. Will you tell him of Aurora's vision?"

"Yes," Evangeline said. Watching her husband stride across the hall, she wondered what his reaction would be to the news. "Not now, but later this eve."

"Why don't you let Kamden spend the night? Aileanna and Rory are staying, so he'll have all his cousins to play with."

"You don't mind?"

"Not at all."

Concern furrowed Lachlan's brow as he came toward her. "What's wrong, Evie?"

"Nothing, nothing at all." She reached for his hand. "Aurora has just given me the most wonderful news. I now have a birthday present for you. We're having a baby. You're going to be a father . . . again."

Lachlan laughed so hard, Evangeline was tempted to hit him. "What's so amusing? I thought you'd be overjoyed with the news."

"I am. I've never been happier. But ye, on the other hand, look as though ye're aboot to be ill." He drew her from her chair and into his arms.

She leaned back, her hand resting protectively on her flat belly. "I'm delighted." And she realized beneath her apprehension she truly was happy to be carrying Lachlan's baby. A child that was part of them both—a child conceived in love, an extension of their love for one another.

He nuzzled her cheek. "Mayhap we should go home and I'll show ye how happy I am."

Enveloped in her husband's embrace, knowing her friends would protect her son as fiercely as she did, her fear eased and her confidence returned.

As they said their good-byes, Evangeline decided the more women who stood with her to protect her son, the better.

"Lachlan," she said as they stepped through the standing stones, "I think it's time for Fallyn and her sisters to open their school for women warriors."

Lachlan stumbled into the Fae realm. "That's no' goin' to happen. Fallyn and Broderick will soon wed and she'll be openin' her school in his kingdom."

"Hmm, that's true," Evangeline said as they flashed to the palace. Lachlan held the gilded doors open for her. "But, you know, I think I shall speak to Riana and Shayla. Perhaps they would like to open a school in *our* kingdom."

Following her up the stairs, she heard him mutter something about God granting him the patience to deal with his expectant wife. Walking down the corridor to their chambers, he said, "I think 'tis time we had ourselves a wee chat."

No, Evangeline thought, shutting the door to their chambers with a smile. She would be giving him the day-of-birth gift he'd requested earlier, and then they'd have their wee chat. In her experience, her husband was much more malleable after making love.

About the Author

Debbie Mazzuca thinks she has the best job in the world. She spends her days cavorting through the wilds of seventeenth-century Scotland with her sexy highland heroes and her equally fabulous heroines. Back in the twenty-first century you can find her living in Ottawa, Ontario, with her very own hero, one of their three wonderful children, and a yappy Yorkie. You can visit Debbie on the web at www.debbiemazzuca.com.